Other Books by the Author:

Disfigured, a Gothic Romance,
Book One in the Disfigured Series

About-Face,
Book Two in the Disfigured Series

Spirit of Revenge,
Book Three in the Disfigured Series

ABOUT-FACE

Book II in the Disfigured Series

By

Wendy Coles-Littlepage

'I had married a man I thought to be good, and found he was a scoundrel. Then I married a man I thought to be bad, and found he was good.'

Wendy Coles-Littlepage, 'Disfigured'

happy birthday ?
Edna !

Wendy Coles-Littlepage

Cover design by Sharon Robertson

For my mother, Mary Frances Coles. She always had faith in me.

ACKNOWLEDGEMENTS

First of all I want to give a huge THANK YOU to all the wonderful people I have connected with who loved my first book, 'Disfigured, a Gothic Romance'. I have made some great friends in the Phantom Universe since the publication of that book two years ago. Lisa, Stephanie, Kayla and Carlene – *merci beaucoup*! A special thanks to Sharon Robertson, Awesome Photoshop Wizard, who designed the cover art for this book, and to Lisa Gomez, Erik Expert, for reviewing my manuscript and offering her wisdom.

I also want to thank my dear friends who read and helped me to edit my manuscript – never an easy task. Many thanks for their forbearing and patience to Lisa Gomez, Janan Boehme, Susan Pineschi and of course my husband, Robert.

My husband Robert deserves an extra thank you for his support and encouragement throughout my writing of this book. We make a good team!

This book is a sequel, or continuation if you will, of my first novel, 'Disfigured'. Therefore it would be remiss of me not to acknowledge Gerard Butler, whose sensitive portrayal of the Phantom led to my writing it in the first place. It is his Erik that I write about here.

Note: all quotes at the beginning of each chapter are from "Disfigured, A Gothic Romance".

Prologue

Early spring, 1873

Reader, I am sure you must be familiar with this: in fairy tales and in your own imagination, if you could have what you most desire in the entire world, everything would fall into place and you would live happily ever after. I am certain this must be a commonly shared dream. I cannot be the only one guilty of such shortsightedness. You think and dream of how happy you will be once you have obtained your heart's desire, but seldom do you dwell on the days and years that follow. I freely admit, I rather hoped and dreamed that I'd have a 'happily ever after', but I never examined the idea very closely. The day-to-day details had escaped me somehow. But those details are the very things that make up a marriage, as I ought to have known.

Although I was married once before (of that, more later), I suppose I could not even imagine what my life would be like with such a man as I had just espoused. How could I? Not only had he never been married before, he wasn't even *tame*. He was dangerous, terrifying, and wounded inside, his soul irrevocably damaged. And I know that does not sound like the attributes one looks for in a husband, but he was wonderful nevertheless. And to tell the truth, I *could* not have made any other choice. For me, there was no choice. It must be this man or none at all.

In the very early days of our association, when I was his cook, I succumbed to the dark mystery surrounding Erik. Or more truthfully, the mystery that he drew around himself like a shadowy cape. Even the places I met with him then were other-worldly; his flair for the dramatic added to my fascination with him. *Vraiment*, he was always vexed and annoyed with me about one thing or another in those days, but I could not seem to stop myself from burrowing into his private life. He always appeared to be *more* than just a man – swirling about in his black cape and black leather gloves, with his endless uses of the motifs of Death, even his cold, icy expression – rather than being repulsed or frightened by all this, I had been helpless to resist it.

But it was not the Phantom, that supernatural being he worked tirelessly to create, who called to me and drew me toward him; it was the *man*, Erik, who hid himself behind that larger-than-life persona. Instead of some mythic figure, I saw a lonely, desperate soul in need of care and affection. Like me.

Eventually, when he was sure of the sincerity of my love and my willingness to spend the rest of my life with him, taking him just as he was, in some ways Erik was transformed. It did not happen overnight, but it did happen. Once, I had to walk on eggshells to avoid the bite of his sharp tongue, and I never knew when some stray comment might provoke a scornful response. And I must admit my share in that: I was always forcing my way into his life, violating every order and rule he laid down. I wanted him to trust me and yet I always pushed him too far. I could not help myself, but that was a poor excuse. There was a wealth of affection deep inside him, just waiting to have someone to lavish it upon.

It isn't as if I was unhappy in my marriage to Erik; far from it. It's just that being married to the former Phantom of the Opera, aka the Opera Ghost, aka the Angel of Music, brought with it many challenges. And believe me, I am not talking about challenges like learning he dislikes roast chicken and you love it. I willingly married a wanted criminal, a murderer twice over, a kidnapper, a genius, and a self-proclaimed misanthrope. Erik was all these things, and more. When I accepted his rather unorthodox proposal of marriage, I instantly became complicit in every criminal action in his colorful past. Once we were bound together, I became a criminal as well.

But rather like his face, his good side was very good indeed. Not to mention he was a perfect specimen of manhood.

But sometimes, I must confess, sometimes…he taxed me to my limits and beyond. Bear with me, and you shall see for yourself.

CHAPTER ONE

"I wished that he would look at me as tenderly as when I knew he was thinking of her."

"Christine...Christine. How could you...? No...no..."

My husband's sleep-thickened voice subsided into incoherent muttering, his arms thrashing restlessly as though trying to ward off an unseen enemy. Jolted awake by the nightmare that tormented him, I lay in the dark feeling his body jerk and tremble next to mine. It hurt to hear that name on Erik's dreaming lips again, but it was hardly surprising under the circumstances.

I wondered if I ought to wake him. I had often done so, when evil memories of the past came back to haunt his dreams. I had long since learned, from painful experience, to be careful how I woke him. If he were touched while in the throes of a nightmare, he often would strike out in his sleep. Sometimes just saying his name a few times would pull him out of whatever vision of the past tormented his dreams. If it was particularly bad, I would carefully place my hand on his chest and make gentle circles, soothing and comforting him until he drifted off to sleep again.

Erik would not always remember his dreams upon awakening, but sometimes he did. In the early days of our marriage, several dark nights were made even darker by the confessions he made after one of those disturbing dreams. Each time, I tried to give him some measure of absolution for his sins. All these events were, after all, in the past and could not be changed. The dreams that tormented Erik were borne of anguish, violence and guilt, but over time they had tapered off. Although I wished such dreams did not occur, at least Erik's punishing nightmares told me that he had a conscience.

Scrubbing my hands over my eyes, I gazed up into the dark silk of the canopy bed. What time was it? We did not keep a chiming clock in the bedroom, for the sound disturbed Erik's sleep. Feeling thoroughly alert and restless now, I carefully lifted the blankets away and slipped out of the bed, my bare feet soundless on the thick Aubusson carpet. Quietly lighting a candle, I peered at the clock on the mantel by the candle's flickering light. It was nearly half past two in the morning. Blowing out the candle, I crossed to one of the windows that overlooked my beloved *potager*.

8

Our private rooms were at the back of the *château*. Beyond the neat boxwood hedge that bordered the *potager,* a thick forest of chestnut and oak ran up a hill, giving us the impression of sleeping in a tree house. It was a view that I never tired of seeing, having been a city-dweller all my life. Hugging myself, for the room was chilly, I stared out into the night. Nothing could be seen from the windows except the darker masses of the trees, and far above them, the sparkling points of stars. No answers waited for me in that deep, dark night, only questions. And a name from the past.

Christine. After almost three years of marriage, there was that name again, back to haunt Erik's dreams. Sighing, I returned to the warm bed, careful not to disturb my sleeping spouse. As I arranged myself beside him, I could see his shadowy outline as he lay on his back, quieter now, with only the occasional unintelligible sound escaping his lips. His breathing was gradually slowing to normal; the nightmare passing. Slowly I extended my hand, rested it on his chest, and soothed him with light circular motions over his warm skin. He made a little sound of satisfaction and sighed softly in his sleep, murmuring: "Kitten," before falling into peaceful silence.

He had been, I was certain, reliving in nightmare the fateful moment from his past when Christine, the girl he loved to the point of obsession, had exposed his disfigured face to an entire theatre of people. He would never admit as much, but I knew it was a betrayal he had never quite recovered from.

I really could not blame Erik for dreaming of Christine Daaé, now the Comtesse deChagny. It was not only that he once loved her with all the hopeless desperation of a madman; but after all this time without any contact whatsoever, this very afternoon she had appeared with shocking suddenness, uninvited, unexpected and unwelcome, on the doorstep of our home.

Why had she come? How did she find us? I knew in my heart that it was not only Erik's sleep she had disturbed, but the very fabric of our lives. And unfortunately, I was not mistaken.

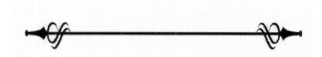

The day that would end so fatefully began like any other. I experienced no premonitions, no sudden sensation of someone stepping on my grave. Perhaps I had been lulled into a false sense of security, our lives having gone fairly smoothly up until now. We had lived in our *château* deep in the French countryside for a little over two years, and in that time Erik, with the help of our uninvited but essential man-of-all-work, Robert, reclaimed the neglected vines and planted new ones, rebuilt the wine-making structures, and this year we looked forward to our first harvest of grapes.

We had furnished the house, planted a garden, repaired the derelict stable nearby, had a baby, and settled quietly into our simple life. No one knew who the Bessettes really were; they knew only that M. Erik Bessette was badly disfigured in a fire as a child, and preferred therefore to remain away from prying eyes. None of our few neighbors or people from the village had the remotest inkling that M. Bessette was anything but a *vigneron*. His true identity was by necessity a closely guarded secret.

Even after all this time, I still felt the incongruity of *Erik*...Erik, the misanthropic, dark-souled creature I had first met...choosing to live on this beautiful estate. With Robert's help, he had searched for some time to find a home for us, and this was the place he eventually purchased. It had been all his own doing, and I wondered many times since first seeing it what he had been thinking, or dreaming of.

It was quite isolated, *bien sûr*, and that would have been crucial to him. He would always carry within him an aversion to strangers, and to being stared at. But there must have been more...Erik could master anything he put his prodigious mind to, but I never dreamed he would decide to become a *vigneron*. I knew he loved being outside, in the sun, he loved the rows of neatly tended vines, the field of sunflowers, even the *potager* behind our house. He loved to ride and no man could look better on horseback. It was clear that this active life suited him tremendously. I never asked him, but I always suspected that he was living a life that had haunted his dreams. It had been his darkest, deepest secret perhaps: Erik wanted a home and a family, even though he did not truly believe he deserved such things.

Erik drew around us as our employees a very motley group indeed — all of them men who had been in the war, men who were missing an arm or a leg, an eye, or fingers; parts of themselves lost to the superior firepower or the bayonets of the Prussians. They all had the young-old faces of wartime veterans, but still were a cheerful lot. Whenever I saw them at work it seemed to me that we lived among a band of merry pirates, and the captain was my husband, Erik. But at the moment, said captain was quite out of temper.

Stalking into my sitting room, he flung himself into a chair near the window, growling, "That idiot! He is going to drive me to violence!"

Needless to say, I did not allow this demonstration of ferocity to intimidate me in the slightest. *Après tout*, since I had always made a habit of standing up to Erik's fierce temper, it wouldn't do to stop now. Silently I handed him a small white cup filled with an inky black liquid – the Arabian-style coffee he loved. I had long ago learned that Erik disliked tea and could not understand why anyone would drink it willingly. Sweetened dishwater, he liked to call it, to my chagrin.

I knew who he was railing against, of course. It was the same person he always railed against: Robert, without whom we would never have escaped Paris alive. I could relate, however; Robert considered himself in charge of the vineyard and the grapes, and it tried my spouse sorely to acknowledge that someone knew more than he did about anything.

Erik snatched the tiny cup from my hand and tossed the hot, thick liquid down his throat in one swallow. I immediately poured him another.

"What now?" I asked, looking at him sympathetically as I handed him the cup.

Erik turned to me, his colour rising. "Sylvie, *Bon Dieu*, you know I have poured a small fortune into this place, and now, *now*, that old idiot has ordered a shipment of aged oak casks from Provence! You cannot believe how expensive they are!" He slammed the little cup down on the tea table, and I was rather surprised it did not shatter. "He didn't bother to tell me about it until it was done." He paused to run his hand over his long fine hair, in a familiar gesture of frustration I had seen him make many times. "They will be delivered next week," he added.

"Oh dear," I murmured. "No doubt Robert has a perfectly good reason for wanting those particular casks." I was certain in fact; we knew next to nothing about winemaking when we came here, but Robert knew everything, and often said so. He had grown up on a winemaking estate; his father had been an employee there.

"*Oui, bien sûr,*" Erik began, determined to argue the point, "but…"

We were interrupted from our discussion by a light rapping on the door, and one of Celestine's housemaids, Berthé, entered, a calling card in her hand. Berthé was young, barely out of her teens, with a plain, round face and a ready smile, although rather shy. She seldom would make eye contact with Erik, for I think she found his appearance disconcerting, but he was invariably kind toward her. She came every morning from a nearby farm to work under Celestine's command. I liked her very much. Now she looked

11

from one to the other of us apologetically, not certain which of us should receive the visiting card.

"We have a visitor? How odd," I said, surprised. Living deep in the countryside and mostly keeping to ourselves for safety's sake, it was unusual for us to receive an uninvited caller. Even now, as Erik reached out to take up the calling card, no premonition or feeling of foreboding came over me. And yet it should have, for a terrible upheaval of our lives was now imminent.

"Well, who is it, Berthé?" He asked nonchalantly, glancing at the name on the little card. He studied it blankly for a moment, and then all the color drained from his face. When he raised his eyes to mine, he looked almost frightened, as though he had seen a ghost. I felt my breath catch in response.

"Sylvie," he whispered hoarsely, "I do not understand this. What...." He stood abruptly and paced in a tight circle, eyes flashing.

"What is it? What is the matter?" I asked anxiously. All sorts of horrible scenarios were running through my mind. In answer to my question, Erik handed me the calling card. I stared at it as blankly as he had at first, and then recognition dawned. Our eyes met, mine wide with shock.

"You...you didn't know...you were not expecting her to call on us?"

"Of course not!" He snapped. "Do not be absurd, Sylvie. We have not spoken or communicated with each other since...since that last night. It's been almost three years!" Placing the card carefully on the side table, I rose and came to Erik, resting my hand on his arm.

"I believe you, my love. It is just...so strange! Why is she here? What are we to do?" Erik placed his own hand over mine. He emitted a frustrated growl.

"We must welcome her, I suppose. It is the civilized thing to do, is it not?" He turned back to the housemaid. "Where is she now, Berthé?"

"She is waiting in the foyer, sir," Berthé answered nervously. She had followed our exchange closely and now watched us with wide eyes full of interest.

"Bring her here to my sitting room, please, Berthé," I said, trying to sound calm though I was anything but. "And see about bringing tea to us."

Erik watched the door close behind her, and stood staring at it bemusedly. "Tea," he muttered, "Woman's universal solution to all dilemmas. I wonder if it will resolve this one."

Erik

Nothing in Erik's extraordinary and often violent past had prepared him to be a husband or a father – god help him, he did not know how to be a lover or even a friend to the wonderful woman he married. His greatest fear was that he might actually do harm to her, for his former life had consisted primarily of dark loneliness interspersed with rage and violence. But he was not without resources and certainly not without the tenacious will to succeed. And he had never wanted anything more. He had seized upon the chance to be happy like a drowning man grasps a life preserver. He had no idea what it would be like to be happy, but he longed to find out.

He would rather die than admit the truth to her, but in fact when he decided he would take the love Sylvie freely and willingly offered him, he did not actually feel passionate love for her in return. He cared for her, trusted her, needed her, but he had only recently been desperately, madly in love with another, and that experience ended so very badly. He did not believe he could ever love someone else, and was not certain he ought to try. What he wanted, though, what he had always wanted, was someone who loved him, and needed him. He wanted to know what it was like to make love to a woman who really wanted him, who did not fear him. Or indeed, just to have the experience of making love to a willing woman.

And what had happened? Erik should not have been surprised – not where Sylvie was concerned. By the time he finally fell into an exhausted sleep on their wedding night, he discovered he was well and truly in love with his new wife. He thought he knew all there was to know about Sylvie, but that night proved him very wrong indeed. And he discovered there was a great deal to be said for warm, bountiful curves, free of all the layers of skirts and fabric women seemed to think they needed.

Erik was the first to admit he knew absolutely nothing about marriage, or even how to be with a woman, but thanks to the loving, patient tutelage of Sylvie, Celestine and even on occasion Dr. Philippe Gaudet he had begun to turn himself into the head of a household. Unbelievably, considering what his life had been like before, he was learning how to be a responsible man, a good husband (at least his wife assured him this was the

13

case) and a father to his little daughter. It was tremendously difficult, but he was getting better at it all the time. When he lapsed, which he sometimes did, Sylvie responded with kindness and understanding. The occasional lapse was inevitable, he supposed, while he learned how to govern his temper, his dark moods, and his controlling tendencies.

Erik had reacted with full-scale panic when Sylvie, with child for the first time, informed him of their expectations. It would surely end in disaster.

There was not only the horrible dread that somehow his disfigurement was hereditary and could be passed on to his own offspring; but there was also the secret fear Erik harbored that he might turn out to be as terrible a parent as his own had been. The example of parental awfulness they set never left him – the agony of being rejected, unloved and unwanted by the very people who should have protected and cared for him stayed with him always. It lived like a disease in every fiber of his being. Sylvie had no idea what this felt like, for she had come from a loving family.

Erik did not know what sort of father he would be, but he did his best to conceal his desperate fears and anxiety from Sylvie. Her deepest desire was to become a mother, and he would never think of denying her something so important to her happiness, but he himself had never given children any thought at all. He really did not care for the creatures. Most of the time during her confinement, he simply tried not to think about the prospect of fatherhood except in the most cerebral sense. Erik's primary concern was the nightmare possibility that the *enfant* might bear his disfigurement. His other fear was that something would go wrong when Sylvie had the baby – didn't that sort of thing happen sometimes? Beyond that, he was sure it would be best for all concerned if he stayed out of the way, enjoyed his child from a safe distance, and avoided becoming emotionally involved.

At least, that was his intention up until the moment when the midwife approached him with a nervous smile and carefully placed an incredibly tiny, weightless, squirming bundle in his arms. He had been somewhat reassured when the doctor and midwife both looked pleased with the results of Sylvie's efforts. Holding his breath, he pushed the folds of a soft wrap aside, and looked for the first time into the face of his newborn daughter, Marie Celestine. At first, he only registered the important fact that her face was normal.

Wet and red-faced, she scowled up at him formidably, one little fist waving aimlessly, her eyes not quite focused. Clearly, she was quite resentful over her abrupt change of residence, and not sure what to make of her new surroundings. Erik stared into her cloudy blue eyes and thought that he had

14

never seen any creature as beautiful, as perfect, as Marie in her first minutes out of her mother's womb. And she was perfect, from the wispy tuft of golden hair on top of her head to her tiny wrinkled toes. Not a scar, not a freckle, nothing to mar her lovely, baby-soft skin; to the consternation of the midwife Erik insisted on immediately unwrapping her from the blanket so he could make absolutely sure. She was perfect, perfect!

In a heartbeat, from one breath to the next, everything in Erik's world changed. It was the first time in his life he had ever held a baby. It astonished him how tiny and light she was. His strong hands, hands that once made short work of strangling a man to death simply because Erik did not like him, now gently cradled the delicate spark of life that he himself had helped to create. He felt his heart tear open in his chest, felt the order of the universe rearrange itself. A sob rose in his throat but he fought it down; he would not cry in front of the midwife – but oh, how he wished for his daughter's sake that he had been a better man!

Erik had never imagined himself capable of such love as this – it was terrifying, because the object of his love was so small and fragile, so helpless. And this tiny creature was suddenly as necessary to him as his next breath. It was exhilarating, because it showed him how much more love he was capable of. When the midwife reached out to take his daughter from him to return her to her waiting mother, Erik had not wanted to release her. He barely restrained himself from snarling at the poor woman. Instead, making a real effort, he carefully wrapped Marie in the warm blanket again and carried her to his wife's bedside, sat beside her and gently placed the baby in her waiting arms.

He'd stayed with Sylvie every minute of her labor and the birth, refusing to wait in another room in spite of the doctor and the midwife's insistence that his presence was not necessary. *En fait*, he had made them both very nervous despite the fact that he was wearing his mask. But he could not bear to leave Sylvie. He'd smoothed her hair off her face, given her water and slivers of ice, and cringed inwardly every time her body was wracked with the pains of labor. Now he gazed into Sylvie's exhausted blue eyes and discovered he was speechless with wonder and amazement. She saw the tracks of tears on his cheeks and smiled at him with great tenderness.

"See, what did I tell you?" She had said, her voice scratchy. "She is *parfait*!" She was still his Sylvie, always determined to be in the right of an argument. He could not imagine loving her more than he did at that moment. And he learned something quite vitally important about himself: he was indeed capable of rising to this momentous occasion.

But recently their old friend Dr. Philippe Gaudet, while visiting on his annual week's holiday from St. Giles Hospital in Paris, had confirmed Sylvie was with child again, perhaps two months along. And Erik was worried about her. She sailed through her first time with only the usual amount of morning sickness, blooming like a rose, and made short work of delivering Marie. The midwife said Sylvie possessed a perfect build for giving birth, and Erik had to agree — her figure was bountiful and curved in all the right places.

But this time something was different; every day was a struggle for her. She was ill a great deal, had no appetite and could not keep food down when she did eat. She lost weight when she should be gaining, her face was pale and there were shadows under her eyes. Dr. Gaudet, before returning to Paris when his holiday visit ended, had strongly advised they not wait to bring their local doctor to attend to her. She would end up confined to bed, he was certain.

And now this: the audacity of *Christine* of all people arriving at their home after almost three years of no contact, being shown to the room where Sylvie usually took afternoon tea with Celestine. Sylvie was going to come face to face with the girl she once considered a rival for his affection. A flare of resentment coursed through Erik at the thought of putting Sylvie through this ordeal when she was already unwell, and so fragile. But there seemed no way to avoid it.

Guilt washed over him, for he knew the pain caused by this unexpected and unwelcome visit was all his own creation, his own fault. There was ultimately no one to blame but himself, and he was well aware of it. But in addition to his resentment, Erik was aware of a burgeoning sense of shame; he never expected to see Christine again, and he never wished to see her, after his unforgivable behavior that last night. He had done terrible things to her and because of her, and these things haunted his dreams. And now she was here, in his home.

Erik could not comprehend Christine's purpose in coming here after the horror that lay between them like a smoking ruin. Adding to his guilt was how her presence here made him feel. He damned himself to Hell a thousand times for the uncontrollable way his heartbeat drummed in his chest, the way his blood coursed in his veins, and for the unholy mixture of anxiety and eagerness he felt knowing he was about to see her again, the girl he had once considered the love of his life.

CHAPTER TWO

"And now you have seen me. I hope you are satisfied."

My sitting room was my favorite room in the *château*. It was a small, inviting place, with a fireplace against the wall, facing a long row of French doors on the opposite side. The walls were papered in apricot silk, the furniture feminine but comfortable. All the art was personal to me, and there were always fresh flowers. My small apartment in Paris had been decorated with hand-me-downs, so I was pleased to find that with unlimited funds at my disposal, I actually had good taste.

Outside the doors bloomed a garden of beautiful, fragrant roses, peonies and iris. I spent all my life prior to coming here in Paris, and never had there been space or time for a garden. I loved to look out on this one, my very own. Beyond the informal garden, one's eyes were drawn to the view of vine-covered fields sweeping down to the river, a tiny slice of which glittered in the distance. I found it enchanting.

Now there was a stranger in my sitting room, a girl I had never met. The girl I had felt nothing for except horrible jealousy. I confess I felt a little guilty about my unkind attitude toward her in those days. I had been so envious of her because the man I loved, loved *her* and not me, and that jealousy had clouded my mind. I used to compare myself to Christine, and always came up wanting somehow. She was taller than me, prettier than me, and she could sing like an angel. I used to torture myself with these useless comparisons.

Erik and I departed my sitting room precipitously, for neither of us was quite prepared to suddenly come face to face with our unexpected guest. We quickly slipped into Erik's nearby music room. It felt a little like we were hiding, I suppose. But we both needed to gather our wits, him especially.

We stared blankly at each other for several seconds, neither one of us sure what to say. Erik's expression was unreadable, guarded.

"It would be impolite to keep the Comtesse waiting very long," I murmured finally. That brought a flash of amusement into his eyes.

"Oh, of course not. Never mind that she is apparently paying us an uninvited social call, and is therefore committing the first social sin." He said sardonically. "Come, we may as well get this over."

As we prepared to leave the quiet music room, I turned to Erik questioningly. "Will you wear your mask?" I knew it was stored away somewhere upstairs, in our bedroom.

"No!" He said defiantly. "She knows what I look like." And with that, he stalked toward the sitting room, radiating discomfort.

The door to the room was closed. We approached it slowly, reluctantly, as though there might be a dangerous creature lurking inside rather than an innocent young woman.

"What has brought her here, I wonder?" I murmured, thinking out loud. I felt a growing sense of vexation toward the girl on the other side of the door, for Erik's sake. Seeing the Comtesse deChagny again would be much more difficult for Erik than for me. No good could come of it, of that I was certain; it would only serve to dredge up all the painful memories he had spent the past years trying to forget. It is odd, in hindsight, that it never occurred to me to feel threatened by her presence here. My concern was all for my spouse.

"She will tell us herself, I expect," Erik replied. "For myself, I would very much like to know how she found us. There are only two or three people who possess that information."

This was a question I felt confident I could answer. "From Meg, I should think," I said matter-of-factly. "Meg has been here twice to visit her mother, and we know Meg and Christine are still friends. Celestine has told me they correspond often."

"Oh yes, *bien sûr*." Erik fell silent, and when I glanced up at him I was startled to see how hesitant he looked. Suddenly his warm hand grasped mine, holding it tightly. He took a deep breath. "I am sorry, Sylvie. Sorry to put you through this." Bless him, he was trying to comfort *me*.

Thus emboldened, I turned the knob with my free hand and opened the door.

A tall, slender young woman with a thick mass of pinned up dark hair stood in front of the empty fireplace grate. Her profile was averted as she studied a set of small framed drawings propped on the mantel: sketches of Marie, Celestine and myself that Erik had done in colored pencil as a birthday gift for me.

The Comtesse deChagny was elegantly attired in a rich magenta visiting gown of the latest *mode*, and a matching feathered hat was perched jauntily atop her thick hair. Everything about her spoke of *richesse* and good taste.

She turned toward us upon hearing the door open, and her big brown eyes flew instantly to Erik's face. Her gloved hands clenched together and her eyes widened slightly as she stared at him. She made a sudden audible intake of breath, almost a gasp. Her reactions were not lost on Erik. He made a small snort of derision, and his eyes turned hard.

"Have you forgotten what I look like, Christine?" He asked, his voice soft but menacing. "Is it worse than you remember?"

The Comtesse deChagny's face bloomed with color. "I...I..." She stuttered, and no more words came out.

I frowned. This was not a good start. It was time to take matters into my own hands. Gently pulling my hand from Erik's iron grip, I came forward into the room and dropped a formal curtsey, as befitted her elevated station.

"Welcome, my lady," I said, and was pleased that my voice sounded relatively normal. Out of the corner of my eye I stole a quick glance at my husband, holding my breath, willing him not to be rude.

Erik was staring at the Comtesse intently, his face inscrutable. But when I touched his arm, I could feel that he was trembling slightly. Finally he spoke, still in that soft, almost menacing voice.

"Allow me to introduce you to my wife, Sylvie, my lady." The way he said it, it sounded like a threat. I thought I detected a subtle emphasis when he said 'wife'.

"Please," the Comtesse said hesitantly, fixing me with a wide-eyed gaze, "do call me Christine." Her voice was low and pleasing. "I have heard much about you from my friend Meg. Also I hope...that is, if Madame Giry is here, I should love to see her as well. It has been a long time. " As she spoke her eyes went again to Erik's face searchingly.

Before I could reply Erik spoke, his voice no longer soft. "And I should like to know why, after all this time, you are apparently paying us a social call. You and I did not exactly part on the best of terms." Christine acknowledged the truth of this with a sheepish little smile. Her eyes dropped, and I noticed that her fingers pleated the fine material of her skirts nervously.

"I...I am visiting friends who reside in Bordeaux, and as the distance is not great, I decided to take their carriage out today to see if I could find you. I have not seen Madame Giry in so long, and I wanted to see how...how you all are." Her eyes darted to Erik and then away again, like a nervous bird. She seemed to have difficulty meeting his eyes. I could not help but wonder why she was putting herself through this ordeal, for clearly she was deeply discomfited.

"We are well, as you see." Erik responded to her curtly, his mouth firming into a thin line the way it always did when he was vexed with something, or someone.

I frowned at him in consternation. As awkward as this meeting was for all of us, there must be a reason for it, and being polite might make it easier to discern.

"I will ring for tea, my...er, Christine, and send for Madame Giry. I'm sure she will be very pleased to see you."

Erik did not take the hint. He was in no mood to behave politely. Bowing stiffly, he said, "You will forgive me, but I do not take tea." Without another word, he turned on his heel and left the room, his back rigid. An uncomfortable silence ensued as we both stared at the closed door.

"He really doesn't drink tea," I murmured apologetically. "He prefers Turkish coffee, which no one else in the house can bear because it is so strong."

The Comtesse looked distressed. "He cannot stand to be in the same room with me," she lamented, her eyes glittering with unshed tears. It was a reaction I had not expected. She must have cared for him more than I realized. I touched her arm gently, and guided her to a comfortable seat on a nearby *settee*.

"He will be back, once he realizes he has left me alone with you." I said matter-of-factly, going to the bell pull and tugging it. "He is acting this way because he is afraid your coming here is going to cause me pain, not because he does not want to see you. You must understand that Erik is a man with many regrets, and most of them concern you and me."

Christine shot me a bewildered glance. "But...I have never seen you before today. How could you possibly have been..." she stopped, frowning at me curiously with those damp, doe-like brown eyes. She had, I realized, absolutely no idea of the small part I played in their long ago drama.

"I am sorry; I suppose I thought perhaps at some point Celestine might have written something about it to you, but I can see that is not the case."

The Comtesse shook her head. "No, Madame Giry and I have not kept up a regular correspondence such as the one I have with Meg." She continued to examine me with frank curiosity in her eyes.

Carefully I smoothed my skirts and settled back on the *settee*. As I did so I gave silent thanks for having assumed a becoming day gown in my favorite shade of blue, though it was nothing compared to the elegant and expensive gown and *au courant* little jacket that she wore.

"Well, I can explain a little to you, if you like," I said, wondering where to begin. It was a rather difficult tale to put into words. "It is not only what happened to you, and the theatre, that my husband regrets. He…he is afraid your visit will bring back bad memories of things that happened to me as well. You see, I knew Erik before the fire at the Opera House and all the events leading up to it, because I was his cook."

"*Quoi?*" Christine exclaimed in surprise. "His *cook?* But I had no idea…" I smiled ruefully, understanding her confusion. I long ago overcame my feeling that because I was a mere cook, Erik might find me beneath him. But it did sound rather odd, even to *me*, who had lived it.

"I suppose there would be no reason for you to know about me," I explained. "Erik was the most secretive person I've ever met. I do not doubt he even forbade Celestine to speak of him to anyone. But I saw him nearly every day for months, and during that time we became friends of a sort. It wasn't easy, but I persisted…why, he even cared for me when I fell ill." I had, in fact, stubbornly wormed my way into his life, but I was not about to tell *her* that.

"What you do not know is that my life was placed in danger as a direct result of his actions that…that horrible night of the fire," I continued. "I was kidnapped and almost killed because of him. Fortunately he found me before any actual harm came to me, but he has never forgiven himself for that terrible night. His actions affected so many. He has tried, over the years, to make amends as much as possible." I glanced at her quickly. "I don't know if you are aware, my lady (I confess I found it all but impossible to call her by her name), but he set up a trust to help those theatre employees who were unable to find other work and were out on the streets after the fire. I believe the trust still supports some of them."

Christine's eyes grew wider and wider, and her mouth rounded in an 'oh' of astonishment.

"But…it sounds as if…you *know!*" She stammered in confusion. "You mean to say you know what happened that night?" I looked at her in some surprise. Did she really think that Erik would not have told me of his actions that night? *En fait*, he had confessed everything to me that very night.

"Yes, I know what happened – what Erik did." I said calmly. Christine seemed at a loss. Clearly she wanted to ask more questions, but at that moment Berthé came in, pushing a tea service on a little cart. I was happy to see her; whatever Erik may say, a cup of tea is soothing balm indeed. Christine subsided into the *settee*, looking slightly dazed. Once the tea cart had been wheeled near us I sent Berthé to find Celestine and have her come to the parlor at once. What a shock this would be for her! I regretted I could not warn her beforehand.

We did not often have guests, since Erik was, *après tout*, still a wanted man, a fugitive from justice, for the crimes he committed. Only three people knew his real identity: me, Celestine, and the lovely young woman sitting next to me on the *settee*. Celestine had loved Christine like a daughter. At one time, she would have preferred Christine to choose Erik over the man who was now her husband. I did not blame her for that; I always knew that Erik's wants and needs came first with her. I was fairly sure they still did.

While we waited for Celestine, I found myself studying my guest thoughtfully. I had seen her only once, from a distance, when she was performing on stage. She had been perhaps eighteen or nineteen then, an innocent young girl who still wore her hair down. She must now be twenty-one or thereabouts, with a more womanly figure and an air of grace about her. It was difficult for me to remember how horribly jealous I had been of her then. It made my cheeks burn just thinking about it.

Meeting my eyes, Christine smiled tentatively. "I am happy to learn that he had a friend such as you in those days," she said softly. "I never knew his name was Erik; I wonder why he never told me. During all the time he was giving me voice lessons, he never divulged anything personal to me at all." Her voice sounded wistful.

"Nor to anyone, not even Celestine," I said. "By creating such a larger-than-life persona to hide behind, he was protecting himself."

"But he told *you*. He trusted you." There was an odd note of petulance in her voice. She turned her face to the mantel again, seeming to wish to change the subject.

"Is that a sketch of your…your child, Sylvie?" She asked after a moment.

"*Oui*. Marie was just over a year old when Erik drew that sketch of her for my birthday last year. "I expect you will meet the subject in person soon, for he cannot resist showing her off."

At that moment there was a brief knock on the door and Celestine entered, the quizzical look on her face changing first to a perfectly blank expression, and then brightening with joy as recognition dawned.

Christine rose and the two women hastened toward each other, meeting in a warm embrace. There were tears and incoherent murmurs from both women; I reflected to myself that Celestine had been a surrogate mother to the orphaned Christine. I knew this was the first time they had seen each other face to face since just before Christine left Paris for the north of France and marriage to the Vicomte de Chagny. Celestine once confided to me that Raoul, the Vicomte, viewed her with mixed feelings because of her loyalty to Erik and the fact that she actually lived in his household now, and so had declined to allow his wife to invite Celestine for a visit. I felt his stance was unfair, because if it had not been for Celestine, worse things might have happened.

I retreated tactfully to sit behind the tea tray and pour, allowing the two women a few minutes to enjoy their unexpected reunion. Soon Celestine and Christine were sitting side by side, holding hands and catching up with each other. Meg's name came up frequently.

Celestine turned briefly to me during a lull in their conversation, and allowed a worried expression to cross her alabaster features.

"Does he know?" She mouthed, out of sight of the young woman sitting on the other side of her. I nodded, hoping I looked reassuring.

A plate of sliced lemon cake and fresh fruit rested on the table, and Celestine glanced at me again with a little frown of concern, as she was wont to do lately.

"Aren't you going to have any cake, *ma chère*?" She asked quietly. I sighed with resignation. It seemed as if Celestine was forever monitoring my appetite. I knew she did so out of concern, but the fact was that sweet tea was one of the few things that still tasted good to me. I drank many cups a day, liberally sweetened with demerara sugar. It was acceptable because it did not make me sick. I had even been forced to give up my morning *café au lait*, for the milky coffee made me nauseous.

I found the scent of the cake revolting, but said only, "*Non*, thank you. I am not hungry."

"But…" I held up my hand in a stopping gesture.

"Please, Celestine, do not fuss over me so. I promise I will have some digestive biscuits later."

At that moment the door abruptly opened. Erik stood there; I had been expecting him for some time. I was glad for the distraction, for though she meant well, sometimes Celestine's fussing got on my nerves. I smiled up at him, trying to appear quite at my ease, and was not surprised to see that he carried Marie balanced on one hip. Pausing in the doorway in that unconsciously dramatic way he had, Erik's eyes met mine and he gazed intently at me for a moment, as though trying to read my mind. It should have been easy; all other thoughts were temporarily pushed aside while I succumbed to admiration of his handsomeness.

His cool blue eyes swept over the two women seated together on the *settee*, his expression enigmatic. I was relieved to see that he seemed to have regained some measure of control over his feelings. Marie was looking particularly angelic, with a white bow in her wispy golden hair. At just over two years old, Marie was turning into an unabashedly feminine little girl, fond of dolls and hair ribbons that matched her pretty frocks. She looked a little shy at the moment, one hand gripping her father's shirt in a small fist and peeking at the strange lady on the *settee* from the shelter of his neck. I thought she looked adorable.

Once both women's faces were turned expectantly toward Erik, he said with exaggerated politeness, "Permit me to present our daughter Marie to you, my lady."

Celestine looked as proud as if Marie had been her own child, and Christine smiled at the little girl with genuine warmth. Erik set her gently on to her feet and tousled her hair. Celestine held out her arms coaxingly and Marie toddled over to her, studying the stranger carefully as she did so.

Marie proceeded to ask innocently, "Who are you?"

Before either of us could think of an appropriate response to this awkward question, Christine herself spoke. "What a charming little girl you are! I am very pleased to make your acquaintance." Utterly undone by this courteous remark, Marie promptly burrowed into Celestine's bodice, peering out shyly.

Several minutes of stilted and uncomfortable conversation dragged by. Erik's expression was stony, his lips drawn into a thin line. He was, I felt certain, working to keep his emotions in check. He spoke not at all, leaving it to me to keep some form of conversation going. We discussed the journey from Paris, the weather, and Meg, and now awkward silence threatened.

I was absolutely certain that the Comtesse deChagny would not have come all this way to pay us a social call. She must wish to speak to Erik about something in particular. I could not imagine what it might be, but I knew I must contrive to give Erik and Christine a moment or two of relative privacy. Although the younger woman was outwardly composed, once or twice I caught sight of her twisting her gloved hands together in her lap, and her cheeks seemed to bloom with color as though she were embarrassed by something. I suspected she must feel discomfited to be in Erik's presence again after what had transpired between them before. Something must have driven her to make this dramatic appearance, but what?

My inspiration lay just outside the doors. I rose and shook out my skirts in what I hoped was a casual manner, and then called to Celestine to bring Marie outside to admire a bright pink rose with exuberant blooms as large as a baby's head outside on the terrace.

"You will excuse us for just a moment, won't you, Christine?" I asked. "I want to show Celestine one of my roses." She assented so quickly,

I was certain I had been correct. Thankfully, Celestine instantly comprehended my intention and came willingly and without a backward glance.

I had successfully contrived to give Christine time to speak privately to Erik, but what I did not know was that Erik had something to say to her, as well.

Erik

The moment the others had slipped out to the terrace, leaving one of the tall French doors standing open, Christine turned almost eagerly toward him. Her face was slightly flushed, her eyes wide and liquid.

"Tell me, are you still composing music?" She asked, surprising him with the question. Her voice sounded the same as he remembered, low and melodic. That voice had captivated him to his very soul.

Feeling flustered and in disorder had made him angry at first, but he was in control of himself now. He was able to answer her question with tolerable calm. Sitting here talking with Christine – it was unimaginable, and yet it was happening.

"*Oui, certainement.* I have never stopped composing. Some of my music has been published, but I compose under an assumed name. It has not," he added wryly, "met with great approval as yet." He looked at her alertly. "You have not sung in public for some time I understand; I hope you have not given it up entirely. You had a beautiful voice, and a great deal of potential." As he spoke he could not help but remember his selfish attempt to keep that voice all to himself. What a fool he had been!

Christine shook her head and gazed down into her lap, where her gloved fingers were entwined tightly. "I stopped performing soon after my marriage. My...my husband disliked for me to perform in public, you see. I still practice though; I return often to the vocal lessons you gave me, when you were my Angel." Her voice had lowered to almost a whisper.

Erik felt a bolt of shock course through him at her use of that name. He had not heard it, or used it, in a long time. The Angel of Music, she called him back then. And he had not lived up to the name, unless it was as a dark angel.

Christine looked up into his face. "I can see that you are happy." She said matter-of-factly, her expressive eyes filled with a tender regard. "You have all that you wanted."

"Yes," Erik answered simply.

"I'm glad. I truly am. I knew you were married of course. I...I've thought about you often, hoping you had found...found contentment."

Erik looked away from her, feeling inordinately confused, a state he disliked intensely. Was she telling him that she still cared in some way? Damn her, if she had any regard for him...then why...but it was of no matter now.

His pale blue eyes travelled toward his wife's form as she bent to sniff a large pink rose on the terrace. He watched as she gently pulled the blossom down by the stem so that Marie could smell the fragrance too.

Just the sight of Sylvie steadied him. Momentarily distracted, he watched her intently, looking for any sign of fatigue or distress, but she appeared perfectly well at the moment. He tried to avoid looking back at Christine, because seeing her again affected him in so many ways his emotions were a confused turmoil inside. A part of him had been half-afraid of what seeing her would do to him, but finally he dragged his eyes back to her lovely oval face.

He thought she looked different; she had grown into her tall, slender figure, and with her cascades of dark hair pinned up to reveal her swan-like neck, had a regal air about her. Her marriage and the passage of a little time had transformed her from the sweet, pretty, innocent girl he remembered into a real beauty. Erik had always seen that potential in her. He knew he would never stop loving her, would never forget the feel of her warm palm on his disfigured face or how she had given him the first kiss of his entire life, but he found now that those feelings and memories were no longer accompanied by despair or the searing pain of loss. It was a great relief to him.

"I have been more than content, my lady." He said, and decided to be honest with her, which he had never really been before. "I would have to say that no other woman could possibly have given me what Sylvie has. She knows that I require quite a lot of managing and a firm hand. She understands me. Her pet theory is that I am only half-tame," he added sardonically. It was more than a theory, he reflected silently to himself.

Christine blinked, surprised at his frankness. But she found that she did understand. He required a woman with some experience, a strong personality to match his own. Characteristics Christine in all her innocent youth had lacked. And in a way, she still lacked. Looking away from him, she glanced around the room, taking in the terrace and the little group outside.

27

"I have to admit, I never imagined you in such peaceful surroundings. It seems...incongruous somehow."

Erik gave her a mocking smile. "You thought I lived alone in a cold dark cave because I liked it? *Non, non.* I always wanted to be able to feel the sun on my face, as others could do." He said softly. "I needed someone who could love me as I am." To this poignant comment Christine made no response. She looked, he thought, suddenly uncomfortable.

Erik fixed his eyes on the floral pattern of the carpet at his feet. If he was going to be honest with her at last, he might as well go all the way. He felt color rise in his face as he spoke. "I never expected to see you again, Christine," he murmured. "But now that you are here, there is something I..." he shook his head, wondering how to proceed. He felt awkward, and he *hated* feeling awkward. Rising, he went to the mantel and stood with his back to her, one hand gently fingering the edge of the frame containing his sketch of Sylvie.

In a low voice, still turned away from her, he said, "I hope you know I would never have hurt you, no matter what. I...I wanted to marry you. I would not have...I would never have dishonored you. I know you thought the worst of me then, and for good reason." Shame at his wicked deeds left a bitter taste in his mouth, but he was glad to have this unexpected chance to apologize. "You trusted me, and...I failed you. I will always regret that."

His eyes strayed to the doorway again, where the others were now slowly moving back inside. As she entered the room, holding Marie in her arms, Sylvie's eyes went to his inquiringly. He gave her a brief reassuring nod, and turned back to Christine.

He saw that she was blushing, and he realized he had embarrassed her. Unable to meet his eyes, she was staring intently at the floor. She spoke very softly, for his ears only.

"It is alright, you know. All that is in the past."

A few minutes later, Christine glanced at the clock on the mantel and declared she must depart, or her friends' carriage would have to make part of the return journey after dark. She and Celestine embraced warmly once more, and after thanking Sylvie for her hospitality, the Comtesse deChagny took her leave. Her last parting glance was for Erik, her eyes filled with warm affection.

Erik realized as the door closed behind her with a last swish of velvet that he felt only relief that she was gone. It could have been worse, but he would rather have spared Sylvie this visit in its entirety.

Erik became aware that Celestine was observing him closely. Out of Sylvie's field of view, his old friend was gazing at him earnestly, her wide eyes telegraphing her concern. She of all people knew how this visit might affect him, perhaps even more than Sylvie did. Erik gave her a nod and a rueful smile, which seemed to reassure her.

Erik reflected wryly that there was a time when Celestine's concern would have been more than justified, but that time had passed. Before his marriage, if he had come face to face with Christine it would have driven him mad if he could not have her – in fact, it had done just that. Even though seeing her today stirred up a maelstrom of complex emotions and bitter memories inside him, the desperate longing for her was, thankfully, gone. Some of the empty places inside him were now filled. He had come to understand that he and Sylvie were perfectly suited to one another, whereas he and Christine together would have been disaster.

He cringed inwardly when he even tried to imagine what it would have been like to take her to bed; he a reclusive, misanthropic, sexually inexperienced thirty-something virgin and she a very young, timid, innocent, awkward virgin. In spite of the passion that raged in his breast and the urgent desire to wed and bed her that maddened him so in those dark days, he knew now that a coupling between them would have ended in a weltering nightmare of humiliation and ignorance. Whereas Sylvie....

Erik supposed his intense fixation on Christine Daaé was a natural outcome of his isolation and loneliness at the time. He had not seen it coming, was not even certain himself when his fondness for her and pleasure in giving her voice lessons grew into something else. He wasn't sure if he could even call it love – he had thought he needed her; that somehow she completed him, and without her, his music would fail him. From the first time he ever saw her, a sad-eyed, bony young girl with her hair in plaits, he had felt that somehow they were kindred spirits. She was but a child, only recently orphaned, brought to live in a strange place, frightened and lonely.

The first time he saw her, she was in the chapel of the Opera building, crying. Erik heard her sobbing, and peered at her through one of his secret openings in the wall. No one understood loneliness as he did, and so he spoke softly to her, though she could not see him. In a faltering voice, she had asked,

"Are...are you an Angel?" There was an angel painting on the wall of the chapel, so perhaps she thought the voice was emanating from it. Erik could not now recall what his answer had been, but ever after, she called him her Angel of Music. He would visit her now and then, and speak to her, and listen to her small, childish problems, and it was a comfort to them both. He gave her advice and guidance. Erik was a man, and Christine a child, but he was so isolated and alone, so far removed from the world, he never saw this as odd or strange. She was isolated, too. She had no friends but himself until Meg, Madame Giry's daughter, grew old enough to be a playmate to her.

Throughout those years Christine of course heard the stories about the Opera Ghost, or Phantom who haunted the Opéra Populaire, but she never associated that mysterious being with her Angel, nor did she ever speak of him to anyone. Erik took care that she never saw him, and eventually he came to realize that to her he must actually be an angel, or a ghost. It was disconcerting, especially when he began giving her voice lessons in secret in the chapel. Seldom did anyone go to the chapel, since most of the denizens of the opera house were anything but religious, so it was a private place. He would have liked to show himself to her, for it would have been helpful since much of his lessons were about breathing exercises, but something held him back. Would she be disappointed to find he was but a man after all? Would she be frightened of his mask?

She must have been about seventeen when one evening Erik looked at her as she waited for him in the chapel and was suddenly struck by how beautiful she had become. Christine was beautiful and sweet and devoted to him. Her voice was almost perfect; for some time he had been harboring a secret scheme for her to sing the music he would write just for her. With the proper precautions taken, they might even tour together, as she had done with her father long ago. She would become famous, *sans doute*, and through her, he would take his proper place in the world. In hindsight, Erik knew this to have been a fantasy, but at the time it took root strongly in him.

Suddenly, he saw Christine differently, as a young woman, and one who seemed to know and understand him. Without meaning to do so, Erik tumbled headlong into love with her. But he knew nothing about love; he was essentially a feral creature who lived in darkness. He simply thought if he wanted her, he should have her. She must be his. There must be some way he could persuade her to love him in return. It had all been so pointless, so horrible.

In the end he lost everything he had worked so hard to create because of his terrible possessiveness – his home, Christine, the opera building he had loved, and he was contemplating throwing himself into the dark canal water and putting a final end to his misery, for how could he go on without Christine?

And that was when Sylvie found him. Sylvie, who he had sent away in tears, and ordered to stay away from him forever, had braved the fire and the smoke to find him. He had been standing near the end of the stone causeway that ran from his secret door across the waters of the underground canal, staring down into the dark, still water, when he heard rapid footsteps approaching from the other direction.

Acting on impulse, not conscious thought, he had quickly moved to the stone wall nearby and pressed himself against it. In the next moment, Sylvie flew out from the labyrinthine pathway he had constructed and came to an abrupt halt, panting breathlessly. She did not see him standing only a few feet behind her. All her attention was focused on his secret door across the causeway. She heard the noise emanating from there, saw the glow of light, and suddenly whispered, "oh no, oh no…" in an anguished voice. She gathered up her skirts and he realized that she was about to dash over there and pound on his door. They would both be discovered if that happened. He could not let her be captured with him. It would be yet another disaster to be laid at his door.

Without even thinking, he took the two steps forward that brought him close to her, and just as she made to bolt away, he wrapped his arms around her, one hand over her mouth, the other across her body. He pulled her back against him, and felt the terror that ran through her. She was helpless and afraid. He whispered in her ear, and felt her body go limp. She turned in his grasp and looked up into his eyes with a searching expression he did not understand. He was glad to see Sylvie one last time, but he was annoyed as well; how could he throw himself into the canal with her standing by?

He was just about at the end of his rope, and he tried to make her go away and leave him, but she would not relent, stubborn shrew that she was. He had to do whatever was necessary to protect her; he gave in and went with her, leading her back up the stairs and into the smoke-filled night air. And because of that, because she was such a stubborn little harridan, he was here, on this *château*, living a life he would never have dreamed could be possible.

Erik paused on his way outside to check on how the sunflower seed sowing was proceeding to observe as his wife made her way up the staircase, holding Marie's hand and helping while the little girl's short legs climbed laboriously along beside her. Marie exhibited an alarming tendency to precociousness, and always wanted to see if she could do something by herself.

…Whereas Sylvie seemed to have been created exactly to his own specifications of what a perfect woman should be. Physically she was what the English so aptly called a 'pocket Venus' – petite, with a lushly-curving hourglass figure, bountiful breasts, a small waist his hands could span, widening out again into the voluptuous curve of her hips. Erik never really appreciated women's breasts until he married Sylvie, but he had made up for lost time. Her small stature and delicate bone structure made him want to protect her, as well as making her a perfect fit for him in bed. Her long, wavy hair was a dark blonde shade with streaks of gold that caught the light, her eyes big and blue. She wasn't beautiful, exactly; her face was a little rounder than was considered desirable in a woman, her lips were fuller as well, and there was that stubborn chin, but she was more than pretty. To Erik, she was simply the most desirable, irresistible creature in the world.

He supposed that his fascination with her must partly stem from the fact that she made no secret that she found him irresistibly desirable, too. She had been completely devoted to him almost from the first, in spite of his determined efforts to keep her away. Erik could not fathom why, but he was eternally grateful for that devotion. From the very first days of their marriage she was able to make Erik feel almost like a normal man, and when they were alone together there were times when he would forget altogether about the disfigured side of his face. His ghastly appearance bothered her not in the slightest. To Sylvie, it was just his face, and she loved it the same way she loved all the rest of him: passionately, eagerly, hungrily. Once she even said to him, in the heat of lovemaking, "You are so delicious, I could eat you with a spoon." She even loved the way he smelled.

The object of his musings had by now reached the top of the staircase with Marie and they turned and disappeared in the direction of the nursery; it was time for Marie's afternoon nap. Erik gave himself a shake and put the distracting thoughts of his delightful wife aside. There was work to be done and he did not think it would be a good idea to pounce on her demanding his husbandly rights, with Christine having just departed. Sylvie might think that it was the other woman who inspired his amorous thoughts, rather than herself. He would wait until tonight, when they went to bed for the evening.

Although I confess I was afire with curiosity about what was said between Erik and Christine during their brief *tête-à-tête*, I did not broach the subject until we had retired to the privacy of our bedroom. A maid had built a small fire in the fireplace to chase the early springtime chill from the room, and I stood before it, brushing out my hair, and waiting for Erik to help me with the buttons on the back of my gown. This one had a long row of tiny pearl buttons that ran down the back from the high neck to just below the waist. Once again I gave silent thanks that I was wearing it today of all days, for the gown suited me very well in spite of my lost weight.

Erik had spoken very little during our evening meal, which we always took with Celestine, and we all made an effort to talk about anything but our unexpected visitor. She and I had, in fact, found a few moments between tucking Marie into her crib for the night and *diner*, but we could do no more than puzzle over Christine's purpose in coming. Erik, I could tell, was troubled indeed, and by the worried glances he kept shooting in my direction, he was also concerned about how the visit had affected me. Poor man! I knew, *bien sûr*, that it was much worse for him than for me.

Behind me the bedroom door opened, and Erik came to stand behind me, his warm hand brushing tendrils of hair from my neck. Silently, he began working carefully at the long row of tiny buttons. Corsets were gradually falling out of favor, but I had always hated corsets even when they were *de rigueur* and refused to wear them. It would have been difficult indeed to have done the kind of work I did while wearing a corset, and I was not wearing one now. Instead, I preferred wearing a lacy silk camisole or a chemise under my gowns. Erik seemed to like it as well.

Deciding that it was time to introduce the subject we had been dancing around all evening, I murmured thoughtfully, "What a strange day this has been. I cannot but wonder at the nerve it must have taken for her to come here today. Why do you suppose she did it, Erik? Did she say anything to you when Celestine and I contrived to leave you both alone this afternoon?"

I tried to twist my head to look at him but he held me in place, continuing down my back until all the buttons were undone. Gently he helped me slide my arms from the long lace sleeves and pushed the gown down over my hips, his warm hands gently caressing the curves of my hips through the thin silk of my camisole.

Self-consciously aware of my lost weight, I wriggled, blushing a little.

"I am not sure why she came today, Kitten," Erik replied, his voice troubled. "But I don't imagine she would have come here unless she had a reason. It isn't clear to me, though. She said very little, *en fait*." Erik always used his pet name for me when we were alone – he told me once that it was because I so often reminded him of an angry, spitting kitten who thought

33

herself much bigger and fiercer than she really was. While he was speaking he pulled me tenderly against him, back to front, and wrapped his arms around me.

"Perhaps it was just as she said," he continued, murmuring into my hair. "She happened to be nearby and took it upon herself to come and see what had become of us." He paused thoughtfully. "She did say she could see that I was happy."

I went perfectly still, absorbing his words. "She did?" Erik's arms tightened their hold on me, and he pressed a soft kiss to the side of my neck.

"It would be hard to miss, considering that I am indescribably happy. I love you and Marie *petite* so much, Kitten." The sudden roughness in his voice gave him away; I could tell he was worrying about me again. This would never do. It would ruin the mood I was hoping to create. I pulled at his encircling arms until he loosened them, and turned in the circle of his embrace (somewhat encumbered by the gown puddled on the floor at my feet). I looked up and into those pale eyes. There was a frown of worry notched between them. Erik stroked the hair back from my face carefully, tenderly, as though I were made of glass.

"I'm sorry," he whispered contritely. "I'm sorry about today."

Fortunately, I knew just how to improve his mood. Men are so easy to manage. I reached up and began unknotting and unwinding his cravat, then I pulled it away and let it drop to the floor. I decided I must order Erik some of the new *mode* of cravat that did not wind about the neck.

"I know," I answered softly. "I know you are. But this was not your fault, my love. I think…" I paused, going to work on the buttons of his white shirt. "I think we should endeavor to put it out of our minds."

He made no attempt to stop my effort to undress him, but instead said musingly, "Seeing Christine again today, I had to ask myself in hindsight, if I ever truly loved *her*. I remember thinking that the main reason deChagny wanted her was because of her *singing*." He paused to watch me undo the last button and pull his shirt open, exposing one of my favorite sights in the entire world.

"So I have to ask myself, did I love Christine for herself, or because of her voice? I will probably never really know the answer."

By this time I had opened the shirt far enough to slip my hands inside to feel the warm smoothness of his skin, and was rewarded by the soft sound of his indrawn breath. It was quite obvious that there was now only one thing on his mind, and it was not his former love. He smiled and pulled me against him.

34

"*You* cannot sing a note, but I know that I love you," he said playfully. "Of course, you do have other very appealing qualities."

I placed a kiss on his chest. "How happy I am to hear it," I said.

Erik had been an enthusiastic but inexperienced lover on our wedding night, but he had definitely improved his abilities in that area quite rapidly. Not that I really had anything to compare it with, since my former spouse was inebriated for much of the year of our marriage. As soon as Erik and I began our married life together, it became obvious to me that I was probably almost as inexperienced as he. Therefore, he clearly hadn't learned anything about it from *me*; I suspected the source of his knowledge of the bedroom arts originated from several odd-looking books he kept in a locked drawer of his desk. It mattered not in the least to me; what mattered was...well, *you* know, Reader.

Hours later, I lay quietly in the dark next to my slumbering spouse, while his nightmares gradually subsided into peaceful sleep once more. I could only hope the shock of seeing Christine again after such a long time would not trigger more bad dreams for him; it had taken so long for him to get over them. But now my own sleep eluded me. It does always seem that in the middle of a dark night, all one's worries magnify and become impossible to vanquish.

Lying on my back, my hand strayed to my stomach, as it often did of late, smoothing it gently, soothing the *enfant* within. Was it to be *fils*, or *fille*? I had a name picked out for each sex, just in case. If it was a boy (my secret wish), he would be called Stèphane after my dear old friend, Father Barbier from St. Giles Hospital, and if a girl, she would be Noëlle. But since I already had Marie, I did rather hope for a boy, so that Erik might have a son.

It was becoming increasingly difficult for me to conceal from Erik and Celestine, the two people who knew me better than anyone, my own concern over this pregnancy. But *en vérité*, I was *very* worried. Clearly something was wrong; I had not felt this tired and drained with my first baby, and certainly never experienced so much sickness and discomfort. I had, in fact, been in the bloom of health throughout.

Of course I knew I needed nourishment, for the baby as well as me, but it was so difficult to keep anything down. I never felt hungry, and everything except tea made me quite nauseous. My fingers threaded and kneaded the thin folds of my nightgown. Oh, if anything should go wrong, I did not think I could bear it. I so wanted to give Erik another child to love, and to love him.

Children loved their parents unconditionally, and unconditional love was the gift Marie gave to her father. To her his face was just his face, the face of her adored *papa*. Marie was still too young to really notice how different Erik's face was from other faces, but it held no horror for her, she had no sense that because of his disfigurement he must be a bad man, or an object of fear. And she never would. When she eventually asked why his face looked the way it did (as I was sure she would one day), we would simply tell her what we told everyone: that he was badly burned as a child.

I thought perhaps it would be a good idea to write to Father Barbier and ask him to say some prayers for the health of the baby. I was not, sad to say, particularly religious myself, and being married to a complete barbarian had made me even less so, but it could not hurt. I had a feeling I would need a bit of divine intervention. Sighing, I curled myself delicately around Erik to absorb his hot-blooded warmth, and willed sleep to come to me. Eventually it did.

CHAPTER THREE

"You might find yourself under arrest."

A lmost a full week passed before the blow fell. Just enough time to lull us into a false sense of security. Just enough time needed to reach here from Paris.

It was a lovely afternoon, rather too warm for early spring, but perfect for sprouting the sunflower seeds that had been planted in the lower fields. I loved deep summer here, and this year there would be even more sunflowers filling the fields, their wide yellow faces following the sun. The sight of them in full bloom never failed to remind me of the very first time I ever beheld the *château*. It had been deep summer then, too.

I'd had a restful nap with Marie, so I decided to make the walk down to the river to where Erik was working with a small crew of men. Watching him working outside was one of my favorite pastimes, I must admit. I put on a sun hat and my stout walking boots and started out. It seemed to me that I was beginning to feel marginally better of late, a hopeful sign. I had even enjoyed my lunch today – delicate baked custard the cook had prepared from my own recipe, liberally dotted with fresh raspberries from our patch in the *potager*.

I made my way along a dirt cart path between rows of grape vines, their young leaves bright chartreuse and opaque in the sunlight. Soon I reached the flatter fields nearer the river; here were the furrows where sunflower seeds had just been planted, the moist brown dirt still bare. The shoots would appear soon, little green leaves with the seed husk still clinging to them, and I eagerly awaited their appearance. Ahead of me now I could see my destination: a cluster of stone buildings that housed the wine-making facilities, storage for farm implements, and of course where the wine was stored while it aged quietly in the cool dark. At Robert's behest, we had purchased a quantity of grapes from other vineyards so that we might make something now. This was the wine, a white variety, that slept quietly in the oak casks.

Here, in a neat little upstairs apartment, lived Robert. We would have been happy to have him live in the *château* with us, but he insisted he must remain close to his vines, close to the wine sleeping in oak casks in the dark. There was no point in arguing with him, as we knew from long experience. He usually took his breakfast and supper in the kitchen.

Below the group of buildings the path became more of a road, leading to the river and our small private dock. Most of our supplies arrived via the river, and eventually cases of wine would be shipped out from there as well. As I passed the largest of the old stone buildings, the musty, grapy smell of wine-making assailed my nostrils. I liked the smell of fermenting grapes; although heretofore unknown to me, I found it was a rich and comforting smell. The restored vines were primarily white varieties, although Erik was experimenting with a light red variety that was showing promise. Most of the grapes grown in our area were white. Robert, of course, was aghast at the idea that Erik wished to try something different, and he only very grudgingly went along with the plan. He was convinced it would turn out to be undrinkable, and I strenuously prayed that he would be proved wrong.

Catching sight of *mon mari*, I paused for a moment to give myself time to admire him. I loved to watch Erik do anything; he was so graceful and sure in his movements. It was something I'd noticed about him from the first – and admired. At the moment he was standing on the floor of a long wagon in his rolled up shirtsleeves, having discarded his jacket and waistcoat to work. His shoulder length hair was gathered at the back of his neck and tied with a bit of leather cord, making him look delightfully like a pirate. René, one of our younger workers and a firm favorite with me, was handing oak wine casks up to him from the delivery they had just received on the dock.

These must be the oak casks Robert had ordered and that Erik had been complaining about last week. Erik was taking them from René and loading them in the wagon, his forearms flexing with muscle, his sweat-dampened linen shirt clinging to his chest and back. He looked so magnificent my breath caught in my throat. Christine's loss was my gain, but it wasn't something I ever took for granted.

As I have mentioned earlier, Erik had taken to the outdoor life from the first. He loved working side by side with the men; a small, carefully chosen band of workers who seemed not to mind that he looked so strange and disfigured. He paid them well, and their working conditions were excellent, and that was all that concerned them. René, who functioned as a foreman of sorts, had only one eye, and wore a black eye patch with jaunty flair. He walked with a pronounced limp. They were all wounds received during the War of 1870. In spite of these afflictions he was as handsome as Adonis, and he knew it too.

In the early days of our acquaintance, Erik's skin was pale from many years living below ground, where the sun never penetrated. But since coming to live here in the Perigord, he was healthily tanned and his soft brown hair was streaked with blond. Erik himself was not sure how old he was, but I guessed that he must be thirty-eight or thirty-nine. He was as vigorous and trim as when I first met him.

Just then René glanced over and caught sight of me, and a white-toothed grin split his swarthy features. I felt myself blushing, embarrassed at being caught out gawking at my husband like a love-struck girl. René spoke to Erik, gesturing toward me as he did so. I had just enough time and wits about me to continue my progress down the road before he straightened up in the wagon and, wiping his damp forehead with his sleeve, turned to look for me.

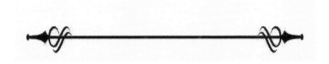

Erik

He vaulted from the wagon and came to meet Sylvie, his eyes making a careful assessment of everything about her. He was pleased to see that the walk had put some color in her pale cheeks. A warm glow took root inside him as he saw how happy she was to see him; her eyes shining and a smile on her lips as she walked toward him on the rutted path, untying the ribbons of her straw sun hat as she did so. She seemed to be feeling a little better these last few days, but he decided she ought not to attempt the long uphill walk back to the *château*. She was, after all, the center of his universe, his own personal sun, and therefore nothing must ever happen to her.

The first time Erik ever set eyes on his future wife, he was lurking far above her on a catwalk while she stood on the stage of the opera house below. She had been brought there on a pretense by Madame Giry so that Erik might have a look at her before he agreed to an arrangement with her to prepare his meals. She had been unaware of his presence, giving him ample time to study her. Erik was good at reading people quickly, assessing them, understanding their weaknesses and strengths. He used the information he gleaned to ruthlessly further his own ends, and to determine where a threat to his safety and privacy might come from.

The young woman standing on the stage below him was clearly no threat. She was a comely-enough wench, he supposed, with dark gold hair knotted rather severely at her nape and a petite yet voluptuous figure. He did not, however, find her attractive. He had already formed a decided preference for another type of girl altogether: someone tall, slim and willowy, dark-haired and beautiful. Madame Bessette would do very well as his cook, however, providing she followed his rules. She appeared to be a docile, subservient little thing, so he had no worries on that account.

The second time he met with Sylvie Bessette, she was lurking in wait for *him*. Driven by her insatiable curiosity, she forced a meeting with him after he had explicitly forbade any face-to-face contact between them. It was the first of many times that she willfully violated his rules. She was, he soon discovered, anything but docile.

In those days Erik knew himself to be a seething mix of misdirected resentment, self-hatred and anger, and the only time he ever felt even remotely tranquil was when he was composing music. At those times, all else was forgotten. So upon finding his new cook waiting to ambush him when he came to pick up his dinner, he lashed out at her with all the fury at his disposal, and that was quite a lot. He would never forget how she looked then – irritated, angry, and intimidated by him but trying not to show it, lifting her rounded chin and glaring at up him while saucily telling him off.

"I wonder, Monsieur, at your finding anyone willing to work for you if you threaten to murder them whenever you chance to meet." She had said, hands on hips, staring him down. Erik found himself staring blankly at her, bereft of speech. How dare she speak to him that way? How dare she challenge him so boldly? With shock he realized something very strange about her: she was not afraid of him.

Erik had been livid with his cook for her bold invasion of his privacy, and furious with himself for feeling a reluctant, fleeting enjoyment of their brief exchange. And even, were he to admit it, a little admiration for her audacity and fearlessness in the face of his obvious displeasure. He took his fury out later on Madame Giry, strongly impressing upon her that he never wished to see Madame Bessette again. He could not afford the weakness of even a reluctant enjoyment of her company; it was too risky, too dangerous, and no annoying female, no matter how well she cooked, was going to infiltrate his defenses. Sylvie had responded with a charming note of apology, and yet somehow Erik knew without a doubt that she meant not a word of it.

He saw no more of Madame Bessette for several weeks, and forgot all about her except those times when he was sitting alone in the cold by the underground lake, eating what she had made for him. He appreciated her then; she was a gifted cook, and every forkful of delicious food he ate seemed to warm his very soul. He came to realize that he would tolerate a great deal of annoyance from her rather than part with her cooking. In his lonely, miserable, love-starved existence, picking up the daily tray she left for him brought a moment of pleasant anticipation, a brief respite from everlasting darkness and cold. She was a pest, a harridan to be avoided at all costs, but worth every franc he paid her and then some.

Then came the night when everything changed. Erik arrived as usual to pick up his dinner only to discover a small form huddled on the floor in a mass of skirts; it was Madame Bessette, and she was hurt, dazed, and helpless. Somehow she had tripped and fallen, hitting her head and dropping his dinner on the floor in the process. He took in what had happened at a glance, but when he looked back to her face again her big blue eyes were staring into his, and they were unmistakably filled with fear. Her entire body was rigid with it. *Now* she was afraid of him.

All at once Erik felt like a cad for his previous enraged behavior. He wondered what Madame Giry had told her about him. Something terrifying, no doubt. She must think him a monster now. He wanted to help her, and he did not want her to fear him any longer. He knew how to pull a thin temporary veneer of civilization over his essentially feral nature, how to soften his hard edges in order to seem safe, not dangerous. He did this often when speaking to Christine, tutoring her and giving her voice lessons. Erik did so now, so that he might put Madame Bessette somewhat at ease while he tended to her.

Before they parted ways that night, Erik had made sure she did not have concussion, gathered up the spilled dishes for her, escorted her back to her waiting hansom, learned she was unmarried, and to his everlasting disbelief, found himself telling her his name. He was never quite sure how that happened. He suspected her of bewitching him. Erik, for once in his life, was in grave danger of making a friend.

Somehow or other, seeing Sylvie every evening, if only for a few moments, came to mean more to him than mere sustenance. Idiot that he was, he still did not find her attractive, and he certainly could not imagine that she might feel that way about him, but he came to need her company in ways he did not understand in the slightest. She was kind, inquisitive, relentless in her efforts to worm her way into his life, and god help him, he let her, in spite of himself. Her food may have warmed his soul, but her company seemed to warm his cold dark heart like a rock in the sun.

If only Sylvie had told him how she felt about him then. There was no point in going over it all now, but if he had known, perhaps he would not have been so determined to win the love of a girl who did not understand him, when he could have had Sylvie, who accepted him as he was, and loved him not in spite of his hideous visage, but because of it. *Bien*, he told himself, and he wanted to believe, things could have been otherwise, but who knew?

Only when his crazed and tortured mind had created a disaster of unimaginable proportions, when he had become a cold-blooded murderer who thought that he could kill a man one moment and force a girl to love him the next, only when he was being hunted like an animal and his life was worthless, had Sylvie finally spoken up and confessed her feelings for him. She only did so because she thought she would never see him again, and could not bear keeping her secret under such dire circumstances. She believed, ridiculous creature, that somehow because she was only his cook her love would mean less to him. To Erik, the real question was how on earth she could find anything in him worth loving.

But Erik had taken Sylvie and her gift of love, married her, bedded her and never looked back. He owed her his life, his soul, his happiness, his daughter, his very world. He loved her like he had never loved anyone before in his entire life — he knew that if someone should try to harm her he would kill him without a second thought, in spite of his promise to Sylvie never to kill again. Did she know how much power she had over him? Once, she had saved his life, but now she *was* his life.

"Kitten," he murmured softly as they met on the road, pitching his voice too low for the workers to overhear his pet name for her. "You look well, love. The walk has put some healthy color in your cheeks. I think you ought to ride back, however."

"I will if you like," she murmured, looking adorably self-conscious in front of the men. "But I do not want to take you away from your work. I only wanted to...to..." and she blushed a little. They both knew she had walked that way on purpose because she wanted to see him. It would not have been the first time. She had a way about her, did his Sylvie, of making him feel...well, like a handsome, desirable male creature. The novelty of this had never yet worn thin.

Erik laughed good-naturedly, his eyes gleaming with amusement. He decided to reward her, so he took her by the arm, leaned in close, and kissed her softly on the cheek, finishing with a little nuzzle. Straightening again, he was delighted to see her blue eyes looking slightly dazed. Erik stepped back, took her arm quite properly and led her down to the river. Glancing toward the workers, he saw that they quickly wiped grins from their faces and began being busy. He was certain, however, that they had been paying close attention to the brief exchange.

"René," he called. "See that the rest of the casks are loaded and taken to the barn. I am going for Danté". Danté was Erik's horse, a big black. Pausing as he passed by one of the old stone structures, he spared a moment to admire the great press within. Although Erik had always enjoyed wine, he had never imagined himself actually making it. The process, he had to admit, was complex and fascinating. And, he must grudgingly admit, he had learned a great deal from Robert.

Danté looked fearsome, but he was actually very well-mannered and gentle for his size. Erik took Marie for rides on him, nestled in front of Erik in the saddle. Now Erik helped Sylvie to mount and walked beside her, leading Danté. She preferred to ride astride, like a man.

"Thank you, Danté," She murmured, leaning forward a little to give the gallant horse a pat on his gleaming neck. "I was beginning to feel a little tired." She smiled down at Erik as they walked. "I'm looking forward to a cup of tea when we get to the *château*."

He knew that sweet tea seemed to be the only thing that could settle her, and it was better than nothing, but he wished that she could take some proper nourishment. Staring at the ground, watching Danté's big hooves strike the soft earth, Erik frowned. This pregnancy was a nightmare to him. Why could it not be like her first? He could think of only one reason, and sometimes the dark terror that seized him was almost unbearable. There were times when he simply could not allow Sylvie to look into his eyes. She had always possessed the knack of seeing into his soul.

Erik led Danté back slowly, in no particular hurry, just enjoying his time alone with Sylvie, talking softly to each other and admiring the neat rows of vines. The fresh green leaves seemed to be the epitome of spring. At the end of one long row they passed, Robert could be seen gesticulating with one hand while delivering a lecture to one of the workers. In his other he wielded a pair of pruning shears, looking for all the world as if he were about to take off the worker's ear. Erik shook his head in bemusement.

"I cannot convince him to take a rest now and again, the old fool. He's not as young as he thinks he is." How Erik could have found himself actually fond of Robert, who had never liked him, he had no idea. But it was so. Perhaps it was due to the fact that Robert was so devoted to Sylvie. Sylvie half-turned to contemplate Robert from her perch on the horse. She smiled and shook her head.

"He would not know what to do with himself if he were to slow down, Erik. He has always worked, and he loves wine-making. These vines are like his children. Sometimes it seems to me that he has grown younger rather than older since we came here. Have you noticed that he never complains about his arthritis any longer?"

"That is because he has so many other things to complain about now," Erik said derisively, earning a little chuckle from his wife. "By the way, did I tell you I've had another letter from Poligny in Australia?"

"What...another one? What does he want this time?" Sylvie asked, glancing down at him from her perch atop the horse. Erik laughed.

"Oh, the usual. His new theatre is apparently not making enough profit. He wants more advice."

"Hmmm. Advice for which he does not intend to pay, I gather," she said.

"Oh, yes, I know, but I don't mind..." Erik suddenly ceased talking and came to an abrupt stop, stopping the horse as well. He drew a gasp of air, and yet it felt as though his lungs were empty. Sylvie turned her head inquiringly, and then looked in the direction he was staring.

"What..." she began, but said no more.

Soldiers. Many soldiers – at least twenty. They were fanned out all along the edge of the vineyard, standing still, alertly watching their slow approach. Danté s ears pricked forward and he whickered uneasily. Each and every one of the soldiers had a rifle with attached bayonet trained on Erik. Glancing sharply around him, Erik saw more soldiers gathered near the château.

"Oh no," Sylvie whispered, her voice shaking with fear. "Help me down." She said urgently.

Moving in a trancelike way, not taking his eyes off the soldiers ranged before them, Erik automatically reached up and took her by the waist. Resting her hands on his shoulders, Sylvie slipped from the horse to stand next to him, but instead of releasing him she wrapped one arm around his waist while her other hand came to rest on his chest. He could feel her trembling, and he knew that under her hand his heart was pounding hard. Was it all to end now? Was this to be their last day together? Holding the reins in one hand, Erik put his free arm around his wife's shoulders, pulling her against his side, as though he might hold her there forever. She glanced quickly at his face. He looked down into her horrified eyes, and he knew she felt it too: they might only have minutes left.

"No," she whispered again, her voice breaking on a small sob.

There was a long, taut silence, broken only the distant drone of Robert's voice as he continued his lecture on how to care for the vines when they first began shooting in the spring, completely unaware of the drama taking place at the edge of the vineyard. Erik and Sylvie stood silently, gripping each other, hearts hammering, and the soldiers were like blue and red statues standing in a semi-circle around them. To Erik, it seemed to go on for a lifetime. If only this were another nightmare, one that he might wake up from as he had all the others.

In the few seconds before anyone moved, Erik's thoughts flew wildly by like leaves in a storm, images chasing each other: the cherubic face of his daughter, Celestine in the garden harvesting peas for dinner, the taste of new wine, the smooth cool feel of the piano keys when he ran his fingers over them, his wife's lush body beneath his, the feel of the sun on his face. And finally, whirling tighter and tighter like a whirlpool, his thoughts narrowed down to one face, one person. Christine.

She had betrayed him yet again. Once was apparently not enough for her – this time she had found a way to destroy all that was dear to him. What would happen to Sylvie, Marie, and the unborn babe now that all was discovered? He was a wanted criminal, and they were going to drag him back to Paris to be tried and hanged. Who would take care of his family? Erik felt tears of fear, panic and anger welling in his eyes – he could not bear it. He had loved that girl with every fiber of his being, and she had to know that. Why, why had Christine done such a thing?

CHAPTER FOUR

"I cannot see that you have a choice."

I stared in wide-eyed horror at the semi-circle of soldiers surrounding us. I was suffused with that helpless sense of being trapped in a nightmare, but this was *real*. My mouth went dry as dust. When I tried to speak, no sound came out. And then, in the heavy silence, I saw a man I had not noticed at first disengage himself from the rest and step forward. His dark civilian attire separated him at once from the distinct blue and red uniforms of the infantrymen he had been standing behind. As I watched him approach us a peculiar sense of unreality settled over me; how could this be happening? And why? Why *now?*

Helpless horror gave way to a wave of furious despair, for I could think of only one answer. *En vérité*, ever since Christine's visit the previous week, I was aware of a growing unease; a sense of foreboding. The depth of her betrayal was beyond measuring. I was sorry, now, that I had been so kind to her. But why? Why had she done this? And even after Erik had tried to make amends.

The man stopped a few yards away from us. I saw that he was rather short, although there was something about his bearing that telegraphed authority. His rather officious dark suit and ostentatious gold watch chain reminded me of our old family *notaire*, M. Blanc. The stranger wore an incongruously friendly expression on a ruddy face bristling with thick side whiskers that met long sideburns on either side of his face. His eyebrows were almost as thick as his sideburns, looking like furry caterpillars. Pronounced crinkles at the corners of his eyes indicated a propensity to smile readily, although he was certainly not smiling now.

He did not spare a glance for me, but instead gazed avidly at my husband. It was difficult to read his expression, but he did not appear to be angry or repulsed. After a moment, he slowly rotated in place, looking around him curiously while the tense silence spun out. Finally, he spoke.

Looking back to Erik, he murmured, so quietly he might have been talking to himself, *"Alors,* this is where you have been these past few years. No wonder we were never able to find you – we were obviously looking in all the wrong places. Hiding in plain sight, I believe it is called." Abruptly he transferred his gaze to me; he studied me intently, not in an insolent way, but rather as if he were fitting together the pieces of a puzzle. I knew he did not fail to notice the way I clung to Erik, or the way his arm was wrapped protectively around my shoulder. His eyes took in everything as though he were trying to file it away for future reference.

"A wife and small daughter, I understand," he said in a rather conversational tone. "And a wine-making business – not exactly what we would have expected from what we knew of you, Phantom."

I felt Erik tense against me, his body growing rigid with rising temper. His breathing came fast and shallow. I raised the hand that rested on his torso up to his chest and rubbed him soothingly with the flat of my hand. He glanced quickly down at me, and a wordless communication passed between us. He made a valiant effort to control himself, and drew a long breath before looking up again.

"You are here to arrest me, presumably." He said, his voice cold and controlled.

"That remains to be seen, *Monsieur le Phantom*, or as you apparently are now called, Monsieur Bessette. It is a distinct possibility, although…." The officious little man paused and glanced back toward the semi-circle of soldiers. Turning back to Erik, he made a little gesture with one hand, the meaning of which was perfectly clear: he did not wish to speak too freely before the soldiers.

Erik's eyes narrowed. "What…"

"Not out here, my good fellow. We have much to discuss, so let us do so indoors, where we can make ourselves comfortable; perhaps somewhere private. Oh, *mille pardons*, I have not yet introduced myself; allow me." He stepped forward and bowed formally, quite as if he were being introduced to someone at a ball. I gaped at him in astonishment. How cavalier he was!

"I am M. Frédéric Moreau, of the Ministry of Defense. I cannot tell you how very pleased I am to finally make your acquaintance, Monsieur."

"Forgive me if I do not return the sentiment," Erik replied icily. Releasing me, he tightened his grip on Danté's reins. Gesturing toward the *château*, he said "after you," in a voice loaded with sarcastic politeness.

With a surprising lack of concern, M. Moreau nodded easily and, turning, began to walk up the drive. The ring of soldiers parted, and we walked up between them to the gravel drive that led to the *château*. Danté was nervous, no doubt sensing the thick tension in the air, but Erik murmured soothingly to him and he allowed himself to be led along. Behind us the soldiers closed ranks and followed, silent except for the metallic clinking of their weapons and the crunch of their booted feet on the gravel.

Walking beside Erik, I could not help but turn my head to glance behind. I wished I had not; for the sense of being drawn into a waking nightmare intensified. Although the men presented an impassive *façade* to us, none of them was as calm as they appeared. I wondered if it was the fact that they had finally succeeded in trapping the Phantom or the shock of beholding him that was the cause of their obvious disquiet. Several of the soldiers returned my gaze with a mixture of curiosity and active dislike. Quickly I turned back, just as we reached the steps to our door.

How strange this was! All the while we had lived here, I always felt safe and secure, as though the house and the land protected us, shielding us from the dangers of the outside. Now my entire world was upside down, and I could not bear to think of anything beyond this moment, this moment that my beloved husband was still beside me. For I was certain he would not be there for much longer.

Erik stopped to tie Danté to a rail, and I saw that his hands were shaking ever so slightly. It meant, I knew, how hard he was fighting for control. Celestine appeared in the doorway, looking pale and frightened. Yet another uniformed soldier was standing just inside the door, next to her.

"Celestine!" I gasped, "where is Marie?" I could not bear for her to see all these strange soldiers, and perhaps her *papa* being led away in restraints. She would be terrified.

Celestine put an arm around my shoulders in a motherly gesture, turning as she did so to glare fiercely at the soldier by the door. He promptly fell back a pace. "She is still in the nursery. I looked in on her only a few moments ago." Relief washed over me. We went inside, Erik following, looking grim and pale.

M. Moreau was already there. Once we entered the foyer, he stepped back and spoke in a low voice to the group of soldiers on the steps. I could not hear what he said but they melted away and did not enter the house. Only the man already inside remained there, silent and watchful.

Mr. Moreau turned to us, rubbing his hands together briskly. "There is, perhaps, a sitting room or a *salon* where we might talk privately?" He asked. To Celestine he said, "I wish to speak to M. and Mme Bessette in private, if you please, Madame Giry."

Her eyes widened in surprise that he knew her name. But of course, it was no surprise to me. He would have learned it from Christine. After exchanging a worried glance with Erik, she bowed slightly and withdrew.

"We do have a *salon*," I said, amazed that my voice sounded normal. "Will you come this way?" I led the way there, with the silent soldier following behind, gripping his rifle firmly. I did not take M. Moreau to my sitting room, but rather to a more impersonal one we reserved for the occasional visitor. Now and then a neighbor from one of the surrounding estates might come by to discuss some business or other, or one of the ladies from the village pay me a social call. This was our receiving room at those times. It was a comfortable room, but it lacked a beautiful view, being instead focused on a wide inviting fireplace with *settees* and cushioned chairs ranged around it.

Automatically I rang the bell and ordered tea and *café* for our unwelcome guest. In hindsight this seems an absurd thing to do, but such habits are hard to break. To say that I was not really myself at that moment would be an understatement; my mind had somehow blocked out anything beyond what was happening this moment. The future was too terrifying to contemplate.

Our guest, meanwhile, made himself at home. After a cursory glance at his surroundings, he seated himself in the best armchair and gestured for us to sit on the nearby *settee*, for all the world as if we were the guests and he perfectly at home. My temper flared, but I knew I must keep myself in check. I felt a scream trying to work its way up my throat, and I had to keep my lips closed to seal it in. My hand found Erik's, and he gripped it tightly, almost painfully.

M. Moreau studied us for a moment, his eyes straying to our clasped hands, and he frowned ponderously, drawing his heavy grey brows together. It was Erik who broke the silence. The raw pain in his voice made me wince.

"It was Christine." He stated flatly. "Why did she do it? I meant her no harm. I have not seen her for almost three years." His eyes, full of the betrayal he felt, went to the man sitting across from us. "How could she do this to me, to my family? Why?"

M. Moreau cleared his throat, and had the grace to look somewhat discomfited. "*Oui,*" he admitted, "It was she, but it was not out of any sense of malice toward you." He took a moment to adjust his position, as though settling in for a long talk. "You see, in spite of everything else happening in France, the police have never ceased to search for you. Madame Giry disappeared a few months after you did, although her daughter remained at school in Paris. We suspected that the two of you had been friends, so we kept an eye on the daughter. There were letters that began going back and forth, and eventually it was discovered that they were coming from here. All that remained was to have a visual confirmation that where Madame Giry was, you were also. Once conditions in Paris settled down at the conclusion of the War, we returned our attentions to the crimes committed at the Opéra Populaire."

"We therefore approached the Vicomte deChagny and his young wife, and asked if she would be willing to come here on some pretense or other, and identify you. She was reluctant to do so at first, for fear some harm might come to you because of it, but we assured her that was not the case. Her husband was able to convince her it was the right thing to do. She appears to be a rather compliant young woman."

Erik looked skeptically at him. "You told her no harm would come to me? Surely she did not believe you."

"Her husband, the Vicomte, persuaded her that she must do her duty as a French citizen."

"I'm sure he did," muttered Erik under his breath. "I am sorry I did not kill him when I had the chance. And so once again, Christine has betrayed me. Once was not enough, apparently." He said bitterly.

"Do not blame her overmuch; she was only told that the French government wished to be made aware of your whereabouts in order to keep a watch on you." M. Moreau said, his voice unexpectedly gentle.

I leaned forward, fixing him with a sharp stare. "But you *are* here to arrest my husband, are you not?" I asked him angrily. "You lied to Christine, and she believed you."

At that interesting moment, the door opened and the rattle of cups and saucers announced the entrance of Berthé, pushing the tea cart. We fell silent as one. Her eyes were huge and frightened as she brought the tea cart to rest near us.

"That will be all, Berthé," I murmured.

Erik started to speak, but M. Moreau shook his head, holding us silent as he watched the frightened housemaid until she had closed the *salon* door. Then he spoke.

"As I said, arrest is a possibility, *certainement*. But I have come to offer you an… alternative."

Erik made a derisive noise. "An alternative…to hanging. You are offering me a choice? What would that be exactly; a firing squad?"

Instead of answering what was obviously a rhetorical question, M. Moreau gazed at him piercingly. "Let me ask you a question before I answer yours. Tell me this, if you will…and be frank with me I beg. The night that you set the Opera building on fire, there was a full house. I comprehend that it was for a distraction so that you might abscond with Mlle. Daaé. But I would like to know, would you have been at all concerned had all those people perished in the fire and destruction of the building?"

Well, Reader, let me assure you that neither Erik nor I were expecting such a question. I knew the answer, for I had once heard it from Erik himself, but what would he say now? I turned my head to look at him, waiting for his response. It pierced my heart to see the despair in his eyes.

He looked the way a cornered stag might, facing a pack of hungry wolves. I gave his hand a surreptitious squeeze. For some odd, inexplicable reason, I thought he should tell the truth, and apparently, he did also.

Erik faced M. Moreau squarely, looked into his eyes, and said, "No. Not in the least. As a matter of fact, I rather hoped at least those two idiot managers would succumb, but they escaped as well." He glared fiercely at the man sitting across from us. "What do you want me to say?" He demanded angrily. "I am telling you the truth, as far as it goes. That is the creature that I was then, that is what I had become. Someone who didn't care about any life other than my own, and perhaps…perhaps one or two others." He glanced obliquely at me then, and gave a little quirk of a smile. At any other time, that look and smile would have stopped my heart.

M. Moreau did not seem unduly surprised or shocked. He nodded placidly. "*Oui,* what you were then. You were identified as the Phantom of the Opera. But who are you now, M. Bessette? Who have you become now?" He glanced around him. "I must admit I did not expect to find you in such…civilized circumstances."

"Ah. You thought I might find another underground cave to live in, did you? But whoever I am now, I can tell you that I am no longer the man I was…I am no Angel, but nor am I the Phantom. I am…"Erik paused for a moment, as if searching for the right words.

"A husband and a father." I said firmly, finishing his sentence for him.

M. Moreau nodded sagely. "Indeed, I believe that is so. The Comtesse deChagny told me the same thing: that against all odds, you seemed to have made a good life for yourself here. You were happy now, she said."

The words fell like stones into a pool, creating ripples. If we seemed so happy, if Erik was happy, why had she…but there was no use speculating. She was still that malleable creature she had been before. Erik sat silent, his pale blue eyes turning icy. Only Celestine and I could truly comprehend the depth of this betrayal and how much it hurt him. It may not have been healthy, it may not have been right, but he had truly loved Christine, and she had to know that.

M. Moreau adjusted his position slightly. "You are happy here, and you have a wife and child, and a number of employees who depend upon you. You would not, I am sure, wish to part with all that, or leave your family alone in the world, which is precisely what would happen were you to be brought to trial. You are, *après tout,* guilty of the murder of three men, in spite of how you may have…"

51

I gave an involuntary start, exclaiming, "What do you mean *three?*" I knew that the deaths of Joseph Buquet and the baritone singer Piangi would be laid at Erik's feet, but I was certain there were no others. Erik would have told me if there were.

It was Erik who answered my question. In a flat voice he said, "M. Moreau refers to Chief Inspector Gaston, I believe."

"What? *No!*" Suddenly I was on my feet, glaring down into M. Moreau's irritatingly complacent face. "That is *not* true, Monsieur! That was a duel, a fair fight. I should know; I was there."

Erik put his hand on my arm and tried to pull me back down. "It is no use, my little Firebrand. He will not believe you. I am sure the bastard's servants destroyed any evidence of our duel, and made sure also that the room where he held you was never discovered."

I sat reluctantly, bristling with indignation. Erik was right, of course. Why would anyone believe us now?

"Besides which," Erik continued matter-of-factly, "I was in such high spirits after killing him that I left my mask behind." He glanced at me, looking almost cheerful. "Do you remember?"

I turned to him, frowning. "Yes, I remember that very well, *et aussi*, I remember where you left it. And I *told* you that you ought not to have left your mask there, because we would need it later, which we did…"

"Shrew."

"Stubborn, irritating *braggart!*"

And suddenly we were both laughing, laughing until tears flowed from our eyes, and I was hugging him so hard, and I could not stop the flow of tears. It was the sound of M. Moreau clearing his throat loudly that brought us back, and when I turned to look at him, wiping my eyes on a corner of my skirt, he was watching us with a perplexed expression on his face.

"You will tell me, please, what you are talking about. What is this about a duel, and Mme. Bessette being held? I would like to know more about this. I am intrigued."

Erik and I exchanged glances. "Shall I…"

"No, I will." He turned back to face M. Moreau. "I am sure you know that the Chief Inspector of the *Sûreté*, Victor Gaston, was in charge of the investigations at the Opera House. He was quite good at his job, but he was also a sadistic, cruel *bastard* who took pleasure in torture and torment. I do not regret killing him and I only wish I could do it again. He discovered that Sylvie, who was my cook at the time, and I had…feelings for each other, and he did not scruple to use that against me. He wanted to capture the

Phantom at any cost, and to him she was but a tool, bait to set his trap." His face darkened as he spoke, the evil memories returning to haunt him. I could almost hear his teeth grinding together.

"Go on, if you please," murmured M. Moreau. I was somewhat surprised that he was willing to hear our side of the story.

Erik was staring into space, remembering those terrible days and nights. "He...he kidnapped Sylvie out of her apartment, he hit her..."he paused and drew a long, shaking breath. M. Moreau sent a quick frown of dismay toward me before looking back at Erik. "He carried her back to his private rooms, and locked her in a secret chamber known only to his trusted servants. I saw it; it was a dark, bare cellar with no light. She was there for over a week, and scarcely anything given to her to eat except scraps. He would appear every so often and threaten her with...*Mon Dieu*, vile things. During that time, Gaston told me through letters he left for me, he planned to cut off one of her fingers and leave it for me to find, unless I turned myself in to him. If I missed his deadline, he would then torture and...kill her. Slowly."

An awful silence fell, and for a moment we were both lost in those dark memories. A shadow seemed to creep across the warm spring day. My imprisonment in the cellar had been the worst, most terrifying time of my life. I had made a concerted effort to forget, but now I took up the tale, because I could see that Erik was becoming too upset to continue. There had been certain events in that cellar I could never tell him, for he would not have handled it well.

"Actually, Gaston took a great deal of pleasure in telling *me* what his plans for me were, as well." I explained wryly. "But thankfully, before... I lost my finger, Erik came. He'd been searching for me for days. He found where Gaston lived and broke in. They fought, and Gaston slashed Erik's arm, he still has a scar from that." I could not repress a shudder, remembering the bright red blood that soaked through the sleeve of his shirt. "But Erik beat him fairly, and killed him; there was no choice. We escaped out the balcony window and later, we managed to escape Paris." I made no mention of the fact that we hid in and were protected by St. Giles Hospital like two orphans of the storm. No one need know about that. I finished my story and looked pointedly at M. Moreau.

"*C'est la vérité*, Monsieur, whether you believe us or not." I felt my chin go up as I gazed challengingly at him.

M. Moreau looked thoughtful. "Hmmm. I am, as a matter of fact, rather inclined to believe you in regards to the late but unlamented Chief Inspector Gaston. I never met the man, but there have been rumors for years about his…unorthodox…methods. Since his demise, the Préfecture of Police in Paris has taken the *Sûreté* under its control. More oversight was called for." He glanced at us and went on briskly, "Nonetheless, it is your word against that of the police that he was killed in a fair fight. You are wanted for three murders and I cannot change that fact. Nor would it matter. Even one murder is too many."

There was a brief silence. The tea cart sat forgotten, the tea growing cold. Erik spoke at last. "You are right, *bien sûr*. What is this choice you say you have for me? Am I to choose between hanging and firing squad?"

A little sound of distress escaped me at those harsh words, and he rested his hand on my knee in a staying gesture.

"*Non*, my good man, *non*. I will explain," M. Moreau glanced at the door, as if checking to see that it was still closed. Turning back to Erik, he leaned forward, resting his hands on his knees. "We have a fairly extensive *dossier* on you, Phantom. I have studied it at length, and your abilities appear to go far beyond the ordinary. In certain areas, you are quite gifted. I believe the Ministry of Defense might be able to make use of those…gifts."

Something in his voice made the hairs on my neck stand up. He was not referring to Erik's musical talent or use of firework ingredients, I was certain. The other thing he excelled at, I knew, was….

"Go on," said Erik, sounding wary, as well he might.

"*Certainement. Prèsidente* Thiers has just been forced to resign, and there is great turmoil in the Republic. We have learned through our sources of a secret movement of the Monarchists to return a king to the throne of France. I need not tell you how disastrous such an event would be."

If M. Moreau expected a dramatic reaction to this pronouncement, he was fated to be disappointed. Erik looked blankly at him. "Who is this Thiers?" He asked.

"The President! The President of France; at least, he was until quite recently." M. Moreau explained, his furry eyebrows shooting up in shock. "Do you mean you do not know of him? He has been president since the Republic was formed after the War." He stared at Erik in consternation.

Erik, unmoved, gave a little snort of derision. "I have paid exactly the same amount of attention to politics here as I did when I lived in Paris…which is none whatsoever."

"*Je vois*. Well, in spite of your ignorance of French politics, a serious crisis is approaching. Henri, Count of Chambord, and heir to the Bourbon throne, is in Paris at this very moment attempting to restore the Monarchy and have himself crowned as Henry the Fifth. There are those who are in favor of a return to the old ways, but the Ministries feel otherwise. We wish to maintain the Republic and strengthen it, if we can. If we do not succeed, we will never reclaim what has been lost to us – Germany will always be stronger than France."

While M. Moreau was speaking, I gazed at him, perplexed. Why was he telling us all this? What had it to do with us? Erik must have felt the same, for he asked impatiently,

"What has any of this to do with me?"

M. Moreau held up a staying hand. "Just this: today you are Monsieur Bessette, but once you were the Phantom. I want you to be that man again, for a short time. *Alors*, there is a person, an unofficial diplomat if you will, who has been acting as a spy for the Count of Chambord, and before that, we have good reason to believe he was in the service of the Prussians. He knows too much. We suspect he is the man behind several violent incidents in Paris. We cannot return to such evil times as before, after the War. Before he does any further damage, we want him to be…eliminated. And in such a way that the Ministry is not implicated." M. Moreau looked at Erik, and his rather kindly face grew stern.

"This is your choice. You can return with us to Paris and perform this task for the Ministry, and if you are successful, I promise you will receive a full pardon, personally signed by President MacMahon. You would no longer be a wanted man. But if you refuse, then you will still return with us to Paris, to stand trial and face the consequences of your actions."

Erik stared at M. Moreau, a deep frown creasing his forehead. "You…you want me to assassinate this man for you? Is that what you are asking me to do?"

I, too, was staring at M. Moreau in wide-eyed horror. "But why Erik?" I demanded. "Why must *he* do this thing?"

M. Moreau replied, "Because he has nothing to lose – or everything. All our other operatives are known, but he is not. If he is successful, he gains his freedom and the knowledge that he has done his government a great service. And he possesses all the skills necessary, Madame." Oh yes, he did indeed, in abundance. Erik stood up abruptly and began to pace the room like a caged wolf.

My hands were clenched together, and I realized I was rubbing my fingers over my wedding ring, a large heart-shaped ruby. It was something I did unknowingly when I was worried about something.

"But this is untenable, Monsieur!" I cried. "If Erik is brought to justice and stands trial, he will hang, *sans doute*. And to avoid that fate, you wish him to kill again?"

Erik ceased pacing and stood near the cold hearth, watching Moreau. His expression was bleak, as bleak as I had ever seen it. "This is why you told Christine no harm would come to me. You knew it wasn't really a choice."

"You agree then? You will do it?" M. Moreau asked eagerly.

"*Oui*. It's the devil's own bargain, and if it were only me to consider, I would rather hang. I promised my wife I would never harm anyone again." Erik stopped and looked down at me, his expression soft and sad. "But it isn't just me now. I have a wife and child, as you say. And there is another on the way."

Moreau had the grace to appear nonplussed at this news. "Ah, I see; I did not know...most unfortunate timing I fear, but there is nothing for it. We have only a brief window of time before we are overtaken by events." He turned to Erik. "I give you an hour to make ready, and then we must depart for Paris."

"An hour?" I gasped. "That is not enough time!" I felt tears burning at the corners of my eyes. I confess, Reader, I was beyond horror-struck over this cruel turn of events. Dread and fear and the sensation of being caught up in a nightmare made me feel almost lightheaded; I was not certain I could stand.

I do not believe it had yet sunk in that my husband was being summoned to Paris to murder someone, someone he did not even know. Did this man have a wife, children? Erik might be buying our own freedom at someone else's ultimate expense. And in an hour, he would leave and might possibly never return.

CHAPTER FIVE

"Et alors, I made my choice."

Erik

The irony of his situation was not lost on him; being forced to make a choice against his will; both of them evil beyond reckoning. Christine must have felt this way when he almost killed her helpless *fiancé* before her eyes: caught in a trap. But there was no time to wallow in self-pity. He was certain that when Moreau said an hour, he meant it. Erik was consumed with cold fury. It was a shame he could not kill Moreau instead. He would have done so gladly, were it not for all the infantry lurking outside.

Sylvie looked ill; she was drained of color and fighting back tears. She was holding onto her composure by a thread. Within an hour he must leave her. Love and hate roiled inside him, because of the two women in his life, the two women he loved.

He extended his hand down to her, and said, "Come." He had not meant it to sound stern, but it came out that way. He found he was avoiding her eyes; it would not do for her to see what was in them at this moment. It was pure, unadulterated hatred. Any lingering affection he still felt for Christine had turned to hate. He would never, ever forgive or forget.

His hand closed gently but firmly over Sylvie's icy fingers and she rose obediently but unsteadily. He spoke to Moreau, his voice hard. "I am going upstairs to change my attire, and say goodbye to my daughter. You need not fear I will try to escape."

"You could not escape in any case, Monsieur *le Fantome*," Moreau replied serenely. "Your house is surrounded."

Erik rounded on him with a ferocious snarl that caused the other man to step back. "Do not call me that ever again!" And he stalked from the room, pulling Sylvie along with him.

There was no time, no time! He felt the seconds slipping away. There was so much to say, with no time to say it. In their bedroom, he pulled a valise out of a closet, and began to strip off his vineyard work clothes. As though she were sleepwalking, Sylvie went to his armoire and brought him a clean white shirt. She stood before him, her blue eyes wide and terrified. Erik could not stop himself from gathering her against him, holding her tightly and pressing his face to her hair.

"*Mon Dieu*! I cannot bear this." He whispered, more to himself than to her. He was afraid, so afraid, he might never see her again.

"Erik," Sylvie sobbed, her face buried against his chest, "Erik, I'm frightened." His heart twisted when he heard those three words; it was the first time since they met that he ever heard her admit to being frightened. She was the bravest woman he had ever known.

"I know, I know, my darling girl. But I will come back to you, I swear it. Whatever it takes, I will do it. Help me to pack, and try not to worry. It will be all right." He heard her sniffle a little, and she pulled back and looked up into his face.

"Do you promise?" She asked tremulously.

He cupped her face in his hands and pressed a hard kiss on her mouth. "I promise," he said. He gave her a piercing look. "Do not forget, *ma belle*, what I promised you once before. And if I cannot keep every promise, do not forget our vows."

He changed hastily into proper attire and between them they packed his valise with a few essentials. He was anxious to go to the nursery, but stopped suddenly, struck by a thought.

"Where is my mask? I will have need of it I expect."

"Oh. Oh, *bien sûr*. Where is it, I wonder? Go and say goodbye to Marie, and I will look for it." As she spoke, Sylvie nudged him gently toward the door. She had pulled herself together. Sylvie had always been competent in a crisis.

The nursery was just down the corridor from their room. He could hear Marie before he entered. Even at two years of age, she had taken such an interest in Erik's grand piano that he bought her, at ridiculous expense, a little toy piano of her own. It was shaped like his, in miniature, and though the sound of the keys was rather light and tinny, it could be tuned and she loved to sit and pretend to play it. Only, it did sound to him as though she were putting notes together rather than just making noise. Had he been that precocious when he was her age? He could not remember, but undoubtedly he had.

When he entered the room, a nursemaid who was sitting nearby rose, collected an empty hot chocolate cup and, with a look of compassion that told its own tale, left the room. News traveled fast among the servants; no doubt they all knew what was happening this day.

"*Papa!*" Marie cried happily, a big smile splitting her face. With her soft blond hair, big blue eyes and little, pearly teeth, she looked like an angel, a real one. Erik was certain Sylvie must have looked exactly the same at Marie's age.

Erik went to her and knelt on the floor by her small chair. She immediately linked her chubby arms around his neck. She smelled wonderful, sweet and chocolaty. He held her carefully, mindful of how small and delicate she was. His small daughter's love and trust was an endless source of joy to him, and he could not imagine life without her now. How strange that his entire life revolved around these two beings: his wife and his child. Sometimes Erik still found himself marveling at how his life had changed so much. But now, now, he was about to exchange heaven for a return to Hell.

"*Ma petite, papa* has to go away for a while. But I will be back soon," he whispered. His throat was tight, and he fought back tears. "A…a business trip," he added. He became aware of Sylvie standing in the doorway, but she did not enter, allowing him this moment with Marie.

Marie sat back and frowned, looking weirdly like her mother did when out of sorts. "How long, *Papa*?" She asked imperiously.

"I am not sure – perhaps just a week or two."

"*Papa* bring me a present?"

Erik laughed in spite of himself, and hugged her again. "*Oui, Petite*. I will bring you a present." She was the best thing he had ever created; no piece of music could compare. "I love you, little cabbage. Keep practicing your piano while I am away." He fluffed her hair, and then he rose and left the nursery.

Sylvie was dabbing at her eyes with a sleeve of her gown. She never seemed to have a handkerchief. In the hallway, outside the nursery door, she silently handed him his mask. It was an old one, of white leather, a copy of the one which had been rescued from his cavern by Meg, Celestine's daughter. That particular mask had been left to decorate the body of Victor Gaston.

Erik seldom wore a mask these days unless in the company of what he considered outsiders. He still had a tendency toward misanthropy; it would probably always be a part of him. Hard to break the habits of a lifetime. Wordlessly, Erik took the white mask and fitted it into place on the right side of his face, the disfigured side. Sylvie stared at him.

"How strange to see you wearing that again," she murmured.

"Let us go down; our hour is almost up. I don't want them coming up here looking for me." He realized he sounded brusque, but he could not help it. To leave was impossible, and yet there was no choice. He looked down at Sylvie.

"I can't say anything, because there is too much and no time. But it is here." He took her hand and pressed her palm against his heart.

"I love you," she murmured, while his heart beat against her palm. "I will come back to you."

When we came back downstairs, we found M. Moreau waiting in the foyer, hat in hand. He had been checking the time with his gold pocket watch; now he slipped the watch into his waistcoat pocket. Celestine was standing nearby, her face pale. She appeared to have been crying. Erik went to her, and put his hand on her arm. They gazed wordlessly at each other for a moment, and Erik bent to murmur something quietly in her ear. She nodded her affirmation. They had been friends for a long time, and I knew that Celestine regarded him almost as a brother.

"Are you ready, Monsieur?" Moreau asked. "I have had the men bring my carriage around, and I wish you to ride with me. They will bring your horse along, for you will have need of it later."

Erik eyed him narrowly, but said nothing. He turned instead to me, and in an instant his expression changed from chilly to warm, but his eyes could not conceal his anguish. In spite of M. Moreau's watchful presence, I reached for him and we embraced as if it were the last time. "Come back to me," I whispered.

"I will." Slowly he pulled away, leaving my empty arms still extended, still trying to hold him. But as they were about to walk out the door, I was startled to find M. Moreau standing close to me, a troubled expression on his face.

"Monsieur?" I asked, puzzled.

In reply, he said softly, "*Je regrette, Madame. Je regrette.*"

Because his face seemed oddly sympathetic, and his regret sincere, I asked, my voice breaking a little, "Please, please will you send word to me?" I could not bear to hear nothing of them once they were gone.

"*Certainement,* Madame. You will hear from me when we reach Paris." And with this I must be satisfied. M. Moreau made a little bow to me and clapped his hat on.

Then they were climbing into the carriage, while soldiers on horseback positioned themselves all around it, in front, beside and behind.

They were taking no chances on losing their catch. I saw the door close on the form of my husband, and then he was looking out the window at me. He blew me a kiss and then they were rolling down the gravel drive accompanied by the jingling sound of harnesses and crunch of hooves, raising a little cloud of dust behind them. My vision was blurry, and I became aware of Celestine beside me, her arm around my shoulder.

When all was quiet again, and the last mounted soldier had disappeared, I slipped away from the comfort of Celestine's arm and wiped my eyes on my sleeve. I have never enjoyed receiving anyone's pity, and at this moment there was much to be done. I turned to the young footman who ran errands and went for our mail and newspapers in the village. He had been standing near us all the while, looking frightened.

"Go down to the winery and get René. Tell him I need him here at once. *Aller!*" As soon as he had scampered off down the path, I turned to Celestine.

"Celestine, I need you to gather all the servants together and tell them…tell them there has been some misunderstanding but that M. Bessette was called away to Paris. Make them promise to say nothing of this to anyone of our acquaintance. I want no word of this to spread to the village." Celestine had been our head of housekeeping since we first came to the *château*, and all our staff had been hand-picked by her, with great care.

She nodded her understanding, and turned to go back into the house. "*Bien sûr*, my dear. I will see to it. But what about Robert? Will you speak with him, or shall I?"

Robert! I had forgotten him; he would still be among his vines, *sans doute*, and would have no knowledge of what just transpired.

"I will go myself and find him," I said firmly.

I was glad to have a few minutes alone. So much had happened so quickly, my head was in a whirl. I could only allow myself to think of the matters that were directly before me; to think further ahead was impossible. However, my solitary walk toward the vineyard was soon interrupted by René, approaching me in haste. The footman must have told him something of what had occurred.

I had summoned René to me because I thought of him as Erik's second-in-command, and he was well-respected by the men. I intended to put him in charge of all the winery operations, and of the men as well.

Quickly I explained what I needed him to do. His tall, lean, piratical form towered over me, but his face was kind and sympathetic. I trusted René, in spite of the fact that he looked like a young highwayman, and I knew he was devoted to Erik. Now he looked at me askance with his one good eye.

"What of Robert?" He asked, raising an eyebrow quizzically.

"I am looking for him now. He will not mind you being in charge, if that is what you mean. He prefers to tend the vines. And besides, you know that the men do not really respect him."

A knowing grin split René's handsome face. He gave me a salute, saying, "Do not worry about the winery work, Madame. We will all do what must be done. *Et alors*, I have just seen Robert down at the end of that row, where there is a small bench."

Relieved to have one worry at least off my shoulders, I walked in the direction he indicated, and soon observed Robert sitting on the bench drinking from a canteen of water. We had placed several of these wooden benches about the vineyard specifically for him.

Seeing me approaching, Robert stood awkwardly and touched his old plaid cap by way of greeting, as he had always done.

"Do resume your seat, Robert," I said quickly, sinking down onto the bench beside him. I stared out across the neat rows, watching the play of sunlight on the fresh green leaves. Robert said nothing; only waited for me to speak. My throat was oddly constricted, and I had to clear it before speaking.

"Robert, have you heard what happened today? Did you see...the soldiers?" I asked him at last.

Robert looked at me quickly, frowning. His rather bleary eyes looked wary. "*Non*, Madame. I have been out among my vines. Why were there soldiers here?"

"They came to...to arrest M. Bessette. They are taking him back to Paris." I never knew if Robert was aware of Erik's true identity, and we never spoke of it. Robert came with us when we fled Paris, I was certain, because he was mistrustful of Erik and wished to look after me himself.

"Madame!" He exclaimed, looking shaken. "I thought the police had given up looking for the Master, what with chasing after all them Prussians!" (Robert had taken to calling Erik 'master' shortly after we came here. Erik secretly enjoyed the title, telling me once it made him feel quite feudal).

"You...you knew already Erik's true identity, Robert?" I asked in a faltering voice, while thinking to myself that I had vastly underrated him.

"*Oui*, Madame, I have known for, oh, a long time. The Master himself told me, even before we came here."

"I see. He…he never told me that." I frowned. All this time, the taciturn Robert knew our secret. Shaking my head, I returned to the unpleasant present. Turning to him again, I blurted out,

"But that is not all, Robert! It is worse than just that. Oh, Robert, they want him to kill someone for them, or he will hang! That is why they came for him today. If he does this wicked deed, they will pardon him. He agreed; he said he would do it. He is doing this for my sake, I know." A wrenching sob tore from my throat, and then I was weeping, covering my face with my hands. After a moment I felt Robert hesitantly put his arm around my shoulder and I found I was leaning against him, and there in that safe haven, smelling of fresh grass and tobacco, I cried until I could cry no more. I realized that this was why I came looking for him myself. Robert, for all his annoying ways, had always been all for me.

"Who is it they want killed, Madame?" He asked matter-of-factly when my tears came to a stop, as though assassinations were discussed on a daily basis.

Wiping my wet eyes on a corner of my skirt, I replied, "Some Monarchist, I did not hear the name. And apparently he is suspected of being a spy for the Pr…Germans."

"Good riddance then, Madame. Don't you be worrying yourself when you ought to be resting. The Master can look after himself. He'll be back before you know it," was his pronouncement. Standing, he adjusted his cap. "Must get back to work now." And he limped off down the row. Watching him go, I had to admit I did feel strangely comforted.

There was nothing more to be done, so I rose and turned back to the *château*. I followed the same path Erik and I had used this morning, only this morning! Now he was gone, Danté was gone, and there was only me trudging up the path. It seemed that everything had changed in a heartbeat. He said he would come back, he promised me. But at what cost? What the cost to his soul, and to ourselves, this return to evil?

I felt weary beyond belief. Once inside, I mounted the stairs and went to the bedroom. Slowly I removed my boots and my day gown, and crawled into the bed. Curling toward Erik's side of the bed, I sought for his scent on the pillow. Finding it, I closed my eyes and went to sleep.

CHAPTER SIX

"I will hunt him down like the dog that he is and kill him for you."

Erik

Erik had never felt so helpless. It was the one thing he had fought against always. The need to be in control of his surroundings had been the driving force of his life. It was at the root of so many of his choices, for good or ill. He refused to contemplate why this was so, for introspection was not one of his strong points. But down to his bones he knew it was because of his parents, and how much at their mercy he had been as a child. But they showed no mercy to him, only repulsion, and it had shaped him, in some strange warped way.

As the miles rolled by carrying Erik further and further from all that mattered to him, a part of him that he had worked so hard to suppress began to surface. The misanthropy so much ingrained in him welled up again unbidden, and with it hatred and anger such as he had not felt since those evil days at the Opera House. He sensed it simmering just below the surface like a cauldron, and it seemed to him that he would erupt any moment and howl like a wild beast. Oh yes, he would happily kill whoever this unfortunate 'diplomat' happened to be, and if possible, the complacent middle-aged man sitting across from him in the carriage. It was a pity there were soldiers riding on either side of the carriage, next to the windows. How quickly that buried side of him had reappeared.

Moreau was watching him closely and Erik had the uncomfortable feeling that the older man understood exactly what was happening inside him. They had been traveling for perhaps an hour, with no word spoken between them in that time. Erik did not trust himself to speak, so great was his pain at this sudden and unexpected leave-taking.

"We will stop for the night in Limoges," Moreau said suddenly, inspecting the gold watch he extracted from his waistcoat pocket. Erik almost jumped at the sound of his voice, and then cursed his jangled nerves. "We will be ready for food and rest by then, *sans doute.*" Moreau added. Erik shot him a baleful look; did he expect him to be grateful for the consideration?

"It is not necessary for you to wear your mask here in the carriage with me if you prefer not, M. Bessette." He added unexpectedly. Erik made note of the fact that Moreau had obeyed his order not to refer to him as

'Phantom'. He realized that he never wanted to hear that word again. He was so solid now, so rooted to a place and a life; it seemed absurd to think he had ever wanted to be thought of as a ghost, or a phantom. Such things had no substance.

Gazing indifferently out the window, Erik removed the white mask and set it on the seat beside him. After a pause, his companion spoke again.

"I would have expected you to be surprised that I showed no...er, concern upon seeing your face for the first time," he said conversationally. "It appears that in the past the sight of your face has caused quite a stir."

Erik made an irritated noise in his throat. Was this Moreau an imbecile? "I assumed that Christine gave you a detailed description of my appearance." He answered sardonically. He looked pointedly across at Moreau. "Was that not part of her task? Identifying me?" No one else, in fact, could have done so with any great accuracy.

Moreau shifted his position on the seat, and for a moment said nothing.

"We have a long day's journey ahead of us, young man. I would like you to tell me please of your life."

Erik stared at his companion in astonishment. "What do you care of my life, damn you, as long as I do what you ask of me?" He demanded irascibly.

"Strangely enough, I find I do care. It is not mere curiosity, I assure you. I have learned more than I expected since embarking on this journey to find you." He made a gesture of invitation with his hand. "Begin at the beginning, if you please."

Erik felt a tortured laugh escape him. Did Moreau realize what he was asking? "Why don't you tell me your life story?" He asked, his voice harsh. Moreau merely chuckled.

"You surely do not want to hear the dull life story of a government employee, my good sir." He answered.

"How dull could it be?" Erik asked softly. "You are a man who orders assassinations, are you not?"

"*Touché*, sir! *Mais non*, I assure you this is the first time such a thing has happened in all my years in the Ministry. The time and the circumstances make it necessary, but it is not necessarily palatable."

Erik made a derisive sound. "Indeed? It is I doing your dirty work, not you." He frowned, gazing down at his boots. After a pause he continued bleakly, "The last time I killed a man, it was because I was possessed of a madness I could not control. I was...consumed by jealousy, and angry at the world. All those other people, they were not even real to me. There was no need to kill old Piangi, he was perfectly harmless, and I regret it, to this day. And now you ask me to kill again...I am sick of killing, Monsieur."

"You may not believe me, but I do understand how you feel." Moreau said gently. "However, there is a difference in this case. This man is not harmless; he has caused damage already, and will cause more. As a spy for the Prussians he was responsible for untold French lives lost. He hides in a shadowy world of false diplomacy, but I know for a fact he is for sale to the highest bidder. This is justice, I tell you." As he spoke, his voice became harder, a flash appeared in his grey eyes, and his thick eyebrows drew together until they formed a solid line.

"Calm down, Moreau. As you yourself said, I am well-equipped to do your dirty work. *Très bien*; sit back and I will tell you a bedtime story, such as you have never heard before." Erik smiled at him, a particularly feral smile, showing his large white teeth. Moreau had asked for it, after all. Let Erik's bloodcurdling life story be the punishment for rendering him helpless in this way. Once, years ago, he told his life story to Sylvie at her request, but that time, he omitted a number of things: things that to this day she did not know, though she might guess. He knew he could tell Sylvie much, but not what miseries and cruelties he had suffered in his younger days. She could not bear to hear of those things.

Now he omitted nothing. He considered his true life story to be a form of torture he was inflicting on his captor. He talked softly for a long time while the miles rolled by, and Moreau listened raptly to him, his wide affable face growing paler as he listened. Twice they paused to change horses and take refreshment, but Erik did not finish until they were on the outskirts of the city of Limoges.

He ended at long last with a brief account of Christine's visit to them, and in the profound silence that followed, drank some water from a canteen that had been provided for them at the last stop. His throat was parched from so much talking. He was not one for lengthy conversations or idle chatter; so much time alone had made him taciturn by habit. He took a moment to fit his mask into place again.

Moreau dug a handkerchief from his coat pocket and wiped his forehead with it. "You...you should write a book of your life, young man," he said after a moment. "Never have I heard such a tale. I must admit..." he paused, staring at Erik with what might have been apprehension in his eyes, "I had no idea you were so deadly in your past. But your wife...she is not afraid of you?"

66

Erik allowed himself a slightly bitter smile. "She used to be, when she was my cook, but she loved me anyway. Now, she has me wrapped around her little finger." He fixed Moreau with a cold stare, all traces of amusement gone. "Sylvie gave me this life, the life you have seen today, and I owe her everything. I am only doing this deed for you because of her, and Marie. I meant it when I said I would rather hang."

"Well, I believe I will have nightmares tonight, *sans doute*." Moreau shook his head, as though trying to clear it of unpleasant pictures. Erik had spared him nothing. This man had ruined his life; Erik was more than happy to give him a sleepless night or two in return. He looked out the carriage window to see where they were. A soldier riding alongside fixed him with a fascinated stare, eyes wide, and then looked away. Erik let the curtain drop.

"We will be staying at a military outpost tonight; it is on the other side of the city. Tomorrow, I will tell you more about your task." Moreau patted his rather rotund stomach and added, "It will be not a moment too soon, for I am hungry."

Glancing across at Erik, he said musingly, "That was interesting, what you told me about Chief-Inspector Gaston. I am glad that you told me all that, for as I said earlier, we have heard rumors of his organization going too far at times. Too much autonomy is not always a good thing. But we never realized he could be capable of such evil deeds."

Erik could tell from Moreau's voice that he believed him, and was gratified. He said, "Sylvie told me that he would come down to the room where he held her prisoner and tell her stories of the things he had done." He paused. "They were bad things, and he was proud of them. I am no angel, I admit, but he…he continually threatened her with…threatened her physically, but never made good on his threats." Erik grimaced at the evil memory. His only regret about Gaston was that the killing was so quick. He was sorry there had not been time to make Gaston suffer, as he had made Sylvie suffer for days.

Moreau nodded sagely. "I have heard from reliable sources, after his…er, demise, that he did not, in fact, care for women." He said delicately.

Erik stared at him, startled. "Oh," was all he could say. That thought had never occurred to him, for why should it? "So that is why he never actually…"

"*Oui,* I believe that to be the case," Moreau replied. Holding up one finger, he went on, "Talking of him made me remember something else: it was rather odd, but after his death there was never an official inquest held. His staff and the men under him at *La Sûreté* gave him a rather hasty private burial, with no public funeral at all. Most unusual circumstances for someone of Gaston's position." He shrugged. "But those were unusual times. The war threw everything into upheaval."

"All that bastard deserved was to be dumped in the Seine and eaten by the fish." Erik replied sourly.

It took three days to reach Paris, a journey that seemed endless. As they travelled, Moreau explained that many things had changed in the city since Erik left it three years before. The war that France ought never to have engaged in and that she lost, had made the people angry and unforgiving. Their hatred of the Germans, as their old enemy was now called, grew and grew. All the talk was of revenge – *Esprit de Revanche*, as Moreau termed it.

"There is much anger and resentment over the loss of Alsace and Lorraine, and calls for another war to reclaim them," he explained. "The political climate is dangerous, and this is not the time to fight yet another battle amongst ourselves over a new Monarchy."

Erik slanted him a sardonic look. "Moreau, I lived for ten years in a cavern below the Opera building. I took no interest in what went on in the world above, and I still do not. I doubt if I would notice any difference to the city now." He crossed one leg over the other, trying to find a comfortable position in the carriage. He had grown heartily tired of it, and would have preferred to ride Danté. Danté was being well-cared for on the journey, he had made certain of that.

"Tell me what I need to know. We will be there soon."

I am not possessed of a great deal of patience, Reader, and that first night without Erik was, in its own way, one of the worst in my life. I felt bereft, and the house seemed so empty. There was only I and Celestine, and little Marie. It was a comfort to spend an hour or two with Marie before her bedtime, for she, innocent as she was, knew only that her *papa* had been called away on business, and would soon return with a present for her.

Night fell, and it grew chill out, as it often does here in spring thanks to our proximity to the river. Celestine and I huddled in the sitting room with the curtains drawn, and a fire in the grate. I had no appetite, and to her dismay refused everything except some soup. How could I eat, knowing I might never see my husband again? And somehow it was even worse to think that if – when - I did see him again, he would be a murderer, buying his freedom with the life of another thanks to this unholy agreement.

Bringing me a small glass of sherry, Celestine sat nearby and watched me worriedly. "*Ma Chère*, how are you feeling?"

"I am fine, Celestine," I murmured wearily, accepting the sherry and taking a small, fortifying sip. "I always knew there was a chance something like this might happen. But I thought we were safe here. I was always afraid, in the back of my mind, that Erik would be found somehow and captured…that was bad enough, but this…this evil choice that has been forced on him…I never imagined such a thing could happen to us." I had told Celestine everything by now, and she was as horrified as I was.

"That Monsieur Moreau, I did not think he was the sort of man to do such a thing," she said, frowning. "He seemed rather kind, at least when he spoke to me."

"It would appear that to a government man like himself the restoration of a king to the throne of France must be avoided at all costs, even if the cost is cold-blooded murder," I replied, realizing that I sounded jaded.

Rising, I went to the fire and gave it a little stir with the poker. I gazed at Erik's sketches on the mantel, remembering when the one of me was done. I had been captured by his pencil while standing in the *potager*, holding a shallow basket of berries. I was wearing a white pinafore apron and looked for all the world like a milk maid. It possessed a pastoral quality I always liked.

"The thing is, Celestine, I know it is wrong of me but I wanted only to keep him here with me, safe and happy. I have always known he did those bad things, and why, but he isn't that man any longer. He is a good man, but…" I paused, and looked at her bleakly. "But he *was* guilty, and I did everything I could to protect him. I still want that."

She smiled ruefully. "We both wanted that, as you know very well. There was always something about him that made us want to save him if we could." I could not help but smile a little in my turn, for it was true indeed. I had always known there was a good man underneath it all, and Erik had proved me right.

Sighing, I said, "I feel so helpless now. I can do nothing to help him, and I am trapped here, worried and afraid. And I feel…I feel a little angry at him also, because *vraiment*, this is entirely his fault."

"Not entirely his fault," Celestine said tartly. "I am very sorry for Christine's part in this."

"It was wrong of her, but M. Moreau told us that he and her husband both lied to her about their intentions." Wandering back to the *settee*, I plumped a pillow restlessly. "She thought they only wanted confirmation of where Erik was."

Celestine shook her head. "That absolves her up to a point, I suppose. But I would much rather she had refused to cooperate with them."

I shot her a wry look. "So do I, Celestine. So do I."

CHAPTER SEVEN

"If anyone needed comfort more than Erik, that person would be difficult to find."

Erik

He approached the heavy wrought iron gates of St. Giles Hospital on foot and leading Danté. After a meal in a small, out-of-the-way inn, Moreau had given Erik the necessary instructions as well as some money and allowed him to slip quietly away into the night. There was no question of his trying to bolt, for that would mean abandoning his wife and child, and Moreau knew he would never do that. He asked him no questions, offered no further assistance; seeming to comprehend that Erik could take care of himself. He merely told Erik quite complacently where to find him once the deed was done. Moreau would have been surprised to find Erik taking shelter from the night in a secret Leper Hospital.[1]

Residing in St. Giles Hospital was Dr. Philippe Gaudet, a trusted friend and the closest thing to a father Erik had ever known. He did require shelter, of course, but more than that, Dr. Gaudet could shelter his soul. The number of people he trusted could be counted on the fingers of one hand, and the good doctor was one such person. Although he was loath to admit it, even to himself, he was in dire need of comfort, and the company of a trusted friend. A master manipulator himself, he now felt like a puppet, with some government stuffed-shirt pulling his strings.

Erik found he was looking forward to seeing Philippe again, even though he had visited them only a short time before. To sit in Philippe's cluttered room by a fire, drinking a glass of wine, was to feel safe, secure, and in the company of one of the kindest men in Paris.

As he expected, the tall black gates were barred for the night, but he did not anticipate that would present a problem. As he vaulted over the wall near the gates, he wondered idly who the hospital had hired to replace Robert. Hopefully they were able to find someone with a more pleasant disposition, he thought wryly. Robert worked for the hospital until he

---

[1] St. Giles Hospital for Lepers is featured in 'Disfigured, a Gothic Romance', the first book in this series. Sylvie Bessette prepares meals for the patients at the hospital and the location plays an important part in the story.

elected to accompany Erik and Sylvie when they escaped Paris. Thanks to Robert, it had been a very uncomfortable trip, under a load of scratchy hay in an old wagon. Robert had served the hospital faithfully, in spite of his taciturn nature – he was the one who locked the gates after dark, and opened them again in the morning.

Erik was soon leading his tired horse inside the grounds. Erik had made the trip to Paris in a carriage, but Danté had walked all the way. With economic but efficient movements, he replaced the bar and locked the gates again. The hospital building itself sat far back from the road, as though guarding its secrets from the outside world. Once inside, he made directly for the stables at the back of the old building, where he could attend to Danté. There was no hesitation or uncertainty in Erik's personality; once he made up his mind on a course of action nothing could or would stand in his way. It was how he had always been, and he was not going to change now.

Once Danté was comfortably ensconced in a stall, munching some hay and free of the saddle, Erik glided silently across the open space to the back entrance of the hospital. This door opened directly into the refectory, where Sylvie had always brought her meal deliveries to the patients inside. If he remembered correctly, this door was never locked, and when he tried it, found nothing had changed. This was all to the good; he did not wish to announce his arrival to anyone other than Philippe.

Slipping inside and closing the door quietly, he paused for a moment to listen. Silence enveloped him. The few remaining nuns and patients would be in their rooms by now, but Dr. Gaudet was usually to be found in his office at this hour, writing letters or poring over medical books on his specialty, leprosy.

The old hospital smelled exactly the same as he remembered: like ancient stone, lemon furniture wax, and old books. Without consciously intending to do so, Erik found himself crossing the refectory and entering the darkened chapel. Here he had been married, on what was the best day of his life up to that point. He remembered the vivid colors of the tall stained glass windows, invisible now in the dark of night. He had not been back here in all this time, but everything seemed the same, as though time stood still in this place. It wasn't true of course; Erik knew that Dr. Gaudet had lost two of his eldest leprosy patients to *la grippe* during this last hard winter.

Erik glanced down at his left hand, at the wide gold band he wore. It contained one small perfect ruby set flush in the band, a match to the ruby in the ring he presented to Sylvie on their wedding day. He rubbed the fingers of his other hand over the band, remembering with a little *frisson* of amusement her stubborn insistence that he wear a wedding ring. She wanted

72

to make sure everyone knew he belonged to her. Erik gave a little sound of amusement at the thought; who else on earth would want him? He was secretly pleased, however. It was such a wonderful feeling, being wanted.

Erik gave himself a mental shake and brought his thoughts back to the matter at hand. Retreating from the chapel, he made his way across the large entry foyer, toward the hallway where Dr. Gaudet's office was located. The foyer contained a wide fireplace, where a few glowing embers softly lit the way. As he had hoped and rather expected, Erik saw a light under the office door. He knocked on it gently. This would be interesting. It was only a little over two weeks since they had last seen each other at the *château*. Erik knew Philippe would be shocked at his sudden, unexpected appearance here. There had been no notice, no letter in advance.

Erik smiled to himself when he heard a little mumbling from inside the room, as Philippe muttered to himself about who it could be. Then the door opened and Dr. Gaudet stared quite blankly at him for several seconds. He was wearing a plaid dressing robe, and the light from his office reflected off his mostly balding head.

"My dear boy," he murmured once he had recovered from his shock of seeing Erik outside his office door. "What on earth brings you to Paris, and here?" They embraced in the French way, kissing each other's cheeks, and Dr. Gaudet wrung his hand most enthusiastically, but his eyes were worried.

Erik glanced around cautiously. "May we go up to your private rooms, Philippe?" He asked quietly. "I can explain there. I am sorry for this sudden visit, but I could not contact you beforehand."

Soon they were seated before a small fire in Dr. Gaudet's sitting room on the third floor, and he had poured Erik a generous glass of wine. The room was exactly as he remembered – the scattered papers could even be the same ones.

He looked at Erik seriously. "What is it, *mon fils*? Why are you here? It isn't anything to do with Sylvie, I hope."

Erik frowned. He ought to have anticipated the older man would jump to such a conclusion. He reassured Philippe at once. "No, no she is fine, and at home." He hesitated briefly before speaking again, fixing his friend with an earnest gaze.

"I am in trouble, Philippe, serious trouble," he said in a low voice. "I had to come to Paris, I had no choice. I need to stay here at the hospital for a short time, where no one can find me. And I would rather that the patients not be aware of it. Believe me when I tell you that my life depends on it, Philippe."

"I do not understand, my boy. Are you in danger?" The older man asked in a troubled voice.

You could say that," he replied wryly. Erik took a deep, comforting swallow of burgundy wine and set the glass down carefully. Glancing at his companion, he asked slowly, "How much do you know of my life, Philippe?"

Dr. Gaudet's brows shot up. He said, sounding perplexed, "Only what you and Sylvie have told me; that you were her cousin from Rouen. Why do you ask?"

Erik did not know what to say for a dumbfounded moment. Studying his friend's blank expression, thoughts flashed rapidly through his mind. He recollected how Philippe had accepted him from the beginning, how he had appeared to believe everything he and Sylvie had told him before, even though some things were obviously not true. Could he really be such an innocent? Perhaps he was, living in isolation here, quietly tending to his flock of sick priests and missionaries, and studying leprosy. Ever since Erik had provided him with the funds he needed to travel to Norway and meet Dr. Hansen, Philippe seemed to think Erik walked on water.

Erik suddenly realized he could not tell Philippe the truth about himself. If Philippe didn't know who Erik really was, he could not tell him after all this time. Though he hated to admit it, he did not want this good man to know what he had once been. He would have to improvise.

"You surely recall, Philippe, that night we came here seeking shelter…when you stitched up the wound in my arm?" Taking another restoring sip of wine, he smiled gently at Dr. Gaudet. If the good doctor could have seen him earlier that night…what a fight! In truth, Erik knew he was not particularly proficient with sword, but he had surpassed himself that night; there had been no choice.

"But of course! Someone attacked Sylvie and you came to her defense."

"Y-yes, exactly so. But I do not know if you understood that I killed the man, Philippe. It was a fair fight, but as it happened, he was…a member of *La Sûreté*. That is why we fled to you that night." It was an abridged version of the truth, for the entire truth of that night would have boggled the poor doctor's mind.

Philippe's brow puckered as he listened. He removed his spectacles and polished them on the hem of his dressing gown, and replaced them carefully. Erik could almost see the wheels turning in his head. Then he looked at Erik again, and his eyes widened.

"Not…it was not…wait, let me think. I recall reading in *Le Monde* of the murder of the chief-inspector. It was quite sensational, as I recall. Gas something…Gaston, I believe his name was. You are not telling me it was he?" Philippe asked incredulously. At Erik's silent nod, he continued, "I had no idea. At the time, I assumed some ruffian set upon Sylvie. But…but why should *he* have attacked her? I do not understand."

"Because he was a wicked sadist, who thought himself above the law," Erik explained grimly. "But I…I also am a law unto myself. Unfortunately, the Paris police did not see things my way. You say the papers called it murder, but I assure you, Philippe, it was a fair fight. That bastard – pardon – would have killed Sylvie had I not intervened when I did."

"I do believe you, in fact I seem to recall Father Barbier saying something about her having been in danger, but I had forgotten it." Philippe took a bracing sip of his own wine and glanced curiously at Erik. "I also seem to recall that you wore a sword with a skull on it. Hmmm."

Erik found himself grinning at the older man. "You have a good memory, Philippe," he said, feeling unaccountably cheerful. "I still have that sword." Then his face grew serious again. "I am not carrying it now, as you see. The rest of the story is quickly told. It is a sordid tale, I fear." Quickly Erik told Dr. Gaudet about Monsieur Moreau of the Ministry of Defense, the unholy choice he had offered Erik, and why he was here in Paris again. Philippe was understandably distressed, especially when he was told of the task Erik must perform.

"I know, Philippe, and I would not do it if it weren't for Sylvie and Marie, and the *enfant* to come." He gazed earnestly at his friend. "It means a full pardon. No more hiding; we can be free."

Dr. Gaudet shook his head. "But at such a cost. *Mon Dieu*! How can they ask such a thing of you? And why do they think you would accept such an evil bargain?"

Erik smiled grimly. "As Moreau himself said, I have everything to lose, but also everything to gain. I can't let them hang me now, Philippe. I…I want to see my little Marie grow up, and Sylvie needs me, she isn't well, as you know. I am afraid for her." He stared bleakly into the fire. "I have often wished I had been a better man, but never more so than now."

Erik could tell Philippe did not understand that last remark, but he did understand Erik's dilemma and rose to the occasion as Erik knew he would.

"*Bien*, the hospital is at your service as long as you need it, of course. But there is another matter I wished to discuss with you, and your arrival here at this time, though unexpected, is most fortuitous." As he spoke he rose and went to a cluttered table, covered with the usual flotsam of books and papers. Philippe's private apartment was always as messy as his clinic was neat. Sorting through the papers, he retrieved a pamphlet and handed it to Erik.

"Look at this, *mon fils*. This fellow is here in Paris now. He has just presented a lecture to my association – *de Médicins Catholiques*. I attended, and it was most edifying."

Erik studied the pamphlet for a moment, and his eyebrow went up. "Dr. Edward Arlington. He is an American?"

"*Oui*, and a well-known Civil War surgeon; at least, well known in America. His specialty is in what is called Plastic Operations. He has a clinic somewhere in New York. His lecture was about the techniques he has been developing there in facial reconstruction." While Dr. Gaudet was speaking, Erik opened the pamphlet and found himself staring at several grisly photographs.

"Ugh," he said, grimacing.

Philippe smiled indulgently. "Those are a few of his before-and-after photographs. Those men are his patients – men who were badly injured in their war. Look at this one..." he pointed to a particularly hideous photograph, in which the man was missing most of one side of his face, including his nose.

"I would rather not," Erik replied, but he looked anyway. The 'after' photograph revealed a marked improvement in the man's appearance. Scar tissue was apparent even in that grainy photograph, but there was at least the semblance of a nose.

"No one has been doing anything like this here, have they? There must be many men in France who received such injuries during our own war," he added thoughtfully.

"*Non*, no one. That is why *de Médicins Catholiques* invited him to speak. But listen, my boy..." Philippe looked bright-eyed and excited. "I approached Dr. Arlington after his lecture and...I spoke to him about you. About your face."

Erik stared blankly at Philippe. "You did? But why?"

Dr. Gaudet waved one hand as though swatting at a fly. "Because he might be able to help you, *naturellement*. And indeed he has expressed interest in seeing you, but of course I did not realize you would come to Paris like this. But now you are here, I can arrange for there to be a meeting between you." He sat back, looking pleased, and poured himself a bit more wine.

Erik was momentarily stunned. He looked again at the photographs, seeing the improved faces shown there in a new light. "I wonder..."

"It cannot hurt to at least meet with Dr. Arlington. He can do nothing for our patients here, *naturellement*, but your case is different. It is his specialty," said Philippe.

"How are the patients, by the way? How is Stèphane? Sylvie writes to him; I am sorry I cannot see him, for her sake." Erik was glad to change the subject, for his thoughts were spinning around. He had never held any hope that his face could be made less revolting; but what if it could? He was dubious, but also curious to know the answer.

Dr. Gaudet shook his head, momentarily despondent. "He is not very strong – the winter was hard on him. I can see that he is failing, but sadly, that is the course they all follow," he shrugged. "I fear this will be his last summer. He will be missed. I know I should not have favorites but I confess Stèphane was always my favorite of the patients. I loved listening to him read from the bible, but alas, he cannot do so now. His voice is no longer strong enough. He seldom comes downstairs now." Shaking his head, he drained the last of his wine and stood up. Glancing at the clock, he said, "Well, enough of that; it is making me melancholy. Let us get a bed made up for you. Would you like the room you had when you were here before?"

As Dr. Gaudet was preparing to go to his well-deserved evening's rest, Erik stopped him in the doorway of his own bedchamber with a hand on his arm and said, "I will meet with your Dr. Arlington, Philippe, if you will make the arrangements. But remember, I need secrecy for now." And so the die was cast. As Philippe himself had said, what harm would there be in merely meeting the man?

In the early afternoon of the following day, Erik went on a reconnoitering trip in the hospital's ancient closed brougham. He wished to have a look at his target's current abode without being observed himself. It was located in a part of Paris he was not familiar with. The carriage driver employed by the Hospital was yet another young Frenchman wounded in the war, but his wooden leg did not detract from his ability to drive the two old nags.

Erik was able to observe the city from the seclusion of the carriage. Some parts of Paris were familiar to him, though not all, and it was odd indeed to find himself back here again. But it was shocking to see how much had changed, and was still changing. Moreau had spoke to him about the political climate, but he never mentioned that large sections of Paris were being torn down and carted away.

On the Ile de la Cité, where St. Giles Hospital was located, he saw that entire neighborhoods were being demolished to make way for wider roads and modern buildings. Fortunately the Hospital appeared to be safe, being in a lightly inhabited area, and no doubt under the protection of the church. Not only on the Ile de la Cité, but in other *arrondissements* as well, similar projects were underway. Erik was not certain that he approved; perhaps he was beginning to sympathize with those who wished to restore a monarchy. It was just like this new government bureaucracy, he thought sourly, to spend so much money on unnecessary building projects. He had never been a lover of change. Trapdoors, perhaps, but not this wholesale change. It was unsettling, for what should have been familiar was now strange. The entire city seemed to be in a constant state of change.

Erik was searching for an address in the 1ˢᵗ *Arrondissement*, an area where much new construction had already taken place. It was home to rows of large, new apartment buildings set back from wide, tree-lined streets. Diplomats and men of industry alike apparently found this a highly desirable address, and his intended victim was one of them. As distasteful as his mission was to him, he was determined to carry it out as soon as possible and be gone from this place. He focused, therefore, on what steps must be taken to ensure a successful result.

But then the brougham rattled across the Pont Royal Bridge, so familiar to him from before, and he was instantly assailed by memories. Abruptly he called to the driver and directed him to take them on a detour. He was gripped by a strong desire to see the street Sylvie used to live on, the apartment above her kitchen where she had sheltered him, and where she told him she loved him for the first time. The Rue de la Marché, so called because a street market had been held there for many years. He remembered the plane tree outside her balcony, how easy it was for him to climb it and enter her apartment at will. He remembered her teaching him how to cut vegetables without taking off the end of his finger. He did not see himself as a sentimental man, but he thought perhaps that familiar balcony would make Sylvie seem closer somehow. He wondered who lived there now. Were they still using Sylvie's precious cook stove? He could not recall the name, only that she hated having to leave it behind.

When the brougham, moving sedately along Blvd. Haussmann, approached the Rue de la Marché, Sylvie's old street, Erik realized it was a terrible mistake to come here. Nothing was left of the narrow, tree-lined street, where the old buildings had leaned against each other as if for support. There was nothing here except fuming piles of old brick and cobblestone. The street was blocked off and carts were hauling away rubble; all that remained of his wife's old neighborhood. Even the stately trees were gone. He felt his throat constrict, and he ordered the driver to continue on their way. He would never tell Sylvie about this, he decided, as he wiped his damp eyes with his sleeve.

The diplomat's apartment proved to be in an ideal position for his purpose. It occupied the entire top floor of the two-story building, and each window had its little white iron balcony. It would be a simple matter to lower himself down from the roof by rope to reach one of those balcony windows. It was unlikely that the windows would be kept locked. He need only to observe the habits of the apartment's occupant for a night or two before making his move.

Satisfied, Erik ordered the driver to return to the hospital. He relaxed back on the old, crackling, sprung leather seats and allowed his mind to drift. He wondered what was in store for him this evening. In response to Dr. Gaudet's message, Dr. Arlington had invited them to dine with him in his hotel room. Apparently his daughter was accompanying him on this trip, for the polite invitation had come from her.

Pulling out the pamphlet Dr. Gaudet had given him last night, he perused it thoughtfully. He had not had much time to think about anything but the unpleasant task ahead of him, but he admitted to himself that he was intrigued. He wanted to know more.

There was one immediate problem, however. Erik had not forgotten that when Sylvie first introduced him to Dr. Gaudet, they told him a hastily concocted lie: that his face sustained its hideous injuries in a kitchen accident when he was a child. And clearly, Dr. Gaudet believed the tale. Later, after settling into the *château*, they told everyone they met that Erik had been burned in a fire. But neither tale was true, and Erik was certain that Dr. Arlington would take one glance at him and know that. He had, after all, spent much time trying to help men who had been burned or shot in America's recent War Between the States. One might fool Dr. Gaudet, but never this man.

79

Almost a full week went by before the message I had been impatiently waiting for arrived. I wasn't sleeping well for worrying about Erik and what might be happening in Paris. I was in the kitchen downstairs doing what I always do when I am worried about something: cooking. Today I was making chicken soup. It was, for the moment anyway, one of the few things I could contemplate eating without becoming ill. Mathilde, our official cook, a plump, handsome, merry lady in her mid-forties, was baking *madeleines*. Another little sweet that I could eat, dipped into a cup of tea.

I knew that it would take some time for any word to come back to me, but it was frustrating nonetheless. I had just fished the cooked carcass of a chicken from the stockpot and was about to shred the white meat with two forks when suddenly René loomed up in the kitchen door. From his self-satisfied expression, I knew he was the bearer of good news. My eyes went at once to what he held in his hand: a cream-colored envelope garnished with an important-looking seal. My breath caught. Hastily I wiped my hands on my apron.

"Madame," René said cheerfully, "I have just returned from the village and this was waiting for you at the *Bureau de Poste*. I thought you would wish to see it at once." He handed it to me with a flourish, blew a kiss to Mathilde, who blushed, stole a *madeleine* from the platter and took himself off. Turning the envelope over, I saw at once that it was from the Ministry of Defense. M. Moreau had been as good as his word.

Turning to our cook, I spoke hurriedly. "I am sorry, Mathilde, I will return in a few moments but would you please watch the soup so that it does not boil? *Merci.*" Mathilde nodded understandingly, still pink-cheeked from the effect of our local thief of hearts. I untied my apron and hung it on a peg, and went upstairs to the bedroom, where I had a little *secretaire*. Here, in the privacy of the bedroom, I opened the envelope with trembling hands and spread it open on the desk.

M. Moreau had penned the missive with his own hand, rather than entrusting it to a secretary. His handwriting was small and neat, but the signature at the bottom of the single page was an untidy scrawl.

"My dear Madame Bessette,

As promised, I am writing to assure you we arrived safely back in Paris yesterday evening. I told your husband there was much unrest in the city but I do not think he believed me. However, upon arrival we found the government buildings surrounded by protesters. I was never able to determine what they were protesting but I have no doubt it was something about revanche. We proceeded to a quieter part of the city and after having a meal, M. Bessette went on his way. He was perfectly well when we parted and requested me to send you his love. I expect him to complete his task within the week and then he shall be returned to you. You see, I have no doubts of his success and so I predict a happy outcome.

I must say it has been a very interesting experience getting to know your husband, and I believe our association will be a successful one.

Votre serviteur,
Frédéric Moreau

Hmmm! I was certain I could not view their association in such a positive light. How casually did M. Moreau refer to Erik completing his task, as if it were some kind of game, and not a man's life! Frowning, I folded up the letter, replaced it in its envelope, and locked it in a drawer of my *secretaire*. It would have been no trouble for M. Moreau to allow Erik to write his own message to me, but since he had not done so, I must infer that he and Erik had already parted ways by the time he penned this note.

I rose and wandered to the window, wondering what was happening in Paris, so far away. Had Erik been sent out on this dangerous, wicked mission alone and with nothing? Where would he go? I prayed this was not the case, but M. Moreau had not been very forthcoming in his note. It would be so easy for Erik to be recognized and caught if he were wandering the streets alone, with no place to hide. It was regrettable that Erik had lost track of his old friend the Persian, or he might seek a safe haven with him. Opening a window, I leaned over and looked out on the garden below. Even up here on the second floor, the scent of sweet peas in bloom drifted in to the room. I decided to go and pick some to put in the nursery for Marie. They reminded me of her, so sweet and innocent.

As I closed the window and turned to go, I stopped in my tracks, while a sudden sense of security washed away the worry, replacing it with calm. I knew without a doubt where Erik was at this very moment. He was safe, at least for now; he had found a sanctuary in the city, even as we had done together those years ago. I wondered why I hadn't thought of it before. Passing out of the bedroom and down the stairs, I felt as if an angel had just brushed me with its wings.

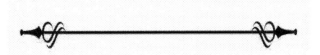

Erik

Erik was relieved that Dr. Gaudet chose to hire a hansom to carry them to their destination that evening. To have arrived at Le Grande Hotel in the hospital's rattletrap old brougham would have been embarrassing indeed. He made a mental note that when all this was over, he would buy Dr. Gaudet a newer carriage…and horses to pull it that were not on their last legs.

The Le Grande was grand indeed, having been constructed at the same time as the Opèra Garnier, and was in fact located not far from that ruined edifice. Erik had never been inside the hotel but he was certainly aware of it. It had been hard to miss. The interior was decorated in the same golden, glowing baroque style as the Opera building. Ornate, elegant, almost *de trop*, with crystal chandeliers and parquet floors, it was considered one of the preeminent hotels in Paris. It was the sort of hotel where one was expected to wear evening attire, and Erik had brought none with him. He wondered how he was going to get through the enormous, brilliantly lit lobby and upstairs to Dr. Arlington's room without his mask and inappropriate attire garnering unwanted attention.

After a brief muttered discussion with Philippe, Erik instructed the hansom driver to find a quieter side entrance, and they soon found themselves on their way upstairs without being observed. Apparently, it was not unusual for those not wishing to attract undue attention to use a side entrance to the hotel. Nevertheless, Erik was relieved when they arrived at

Dr. Arlington's suite of rooms on the third floor without encountering anyone other than a harried chambermaid carrying a stack of white toweling.

Standing outside the door of the suite, Philippe paused for a moment and peered uncertainly at Erik. "I do hope, my boy, that some good will come of this meeting. I know you would wish to…to look more normal if you could." He was looking a little doubtful. "When I spoke to him after his lecture, Dr. Arlington seemed to be a kind man." Erik held back a smile. Was Philippe worried the American might hurt his feelings?

Clapping him on the arm, Erik said, "It is alright, Philippe, you need not worry about me. We will see what comes of this. At any rate, I can do nothing until my other business is finished." Decisively, Erik knocked on the door.

It was opened almost instantly, while his hand was still raised to the door. Silhouetted in the doorway of an elegant sitting room stood a tall, breathtakingly beautiful girl. Erik was momentarily speechless, for he had been expecting a man to open the door, not this stunning creature. Her black, waving hair was styled half up, half down atop a high, white forehead, and black tendrils streamed halfway down her back. Her eyes were also black and thickly lashed; her lips rosy against pale skin. All this profligate beauty was set off by a gown that to Erik's eyes seemed like a cloud of white lace, with lavender roses flowing down the skirts and a matching lavender ribbon in her hair. The low, square neckline of the gown revealed the tops of small breasts that were lifted unnaturally high by her corset. It was his first glimpse of Edythe Arlington, and he thought her astonishingly lovely.

But with his innate ability to read people, he recognized something unsettling in her sparkling eyes: experience and sophistication, and complete confidence in her ability to captivate. She knew herself to be beautiful, and how to take full advantage of it. He realized with a *frisson* of unpleasant shock that she reminded him of a girl he once knew in Persia – she was known then as the little Sultana. She had been very beautiful as well, and as bloodthirsty as a Turk, with a passion for blood sport. Erik took the unwelcome reminder as a warning.

After offering Dr. Gaudet a cursory glance and polite nod, she fixed her striking dark eyes on Erik's face with an almost unnervingly bold gaze. It almost appeared to him that she was seeing someone she already knew.

Stepping back from the doorway, Miss Arlington bowed them into the suite with a smile. "We are so glad that you could join us this evening," she said in a low voice. "Do come in and meet my father. He has been looking forward to this all afternoon." It was the first time Erik had ever heard an American accent, and he thought it sounded flat and strange, but the voice itself was pleasant. Her French was faultless. Then Dr. Gaudet bowed politely and smiled, looking past her, and Erik became aware of the other occupant of the suite.

Coming forward to shake hands, Dr. Edward Arlington appeared slightly shy and diffident. He was tall and thin, and must have been in his mid-fifties although his slight stoop and the gold spectacles perched on his thin nose made him appear older. His hair was rust colored, and he had a matching rust colored goatee which did not flatter his long narrow face. Dr. Arlington studied Erik with shy interest, his gray eyes fixed on the white mask as though trying to see beneath it.

Dr. Gaudet performed introductions, and while the two physicians were exchanging polite greetings and pleasantries, Erik was aware of Edythe Arlington's intent gaze on him. Boldly, she swept her eyes over him from head to foot and back again. Opening a lace fan hanging from one wrist, she held it to her face and her dark eyes smiled flirtatiously at him over it.

Even Erik, who had never been flirted with in his entire life, knew what that look meant, but he could not understand why she was doing it. He finally attributed it to the fact that she was a brash American. He was not susceptible to flattery, nor did he enjoy being stared at; he stared back at her with a stony expression. It was a cool look that had intimidated many in his past, but apparently Edythe would not be one of those. He doubted she would be quite so flirtatious if she knew what was behind the mask he wore.

After being introduced to Dr. Arlington and his bold daughter, Erik and the doctor shook hands in the American fashion. Once these formalities were attended to, Edythe invited them to sit, indicating an elegantly appointed dining table placed in the center of the room. A white damask tablecloth set off gleaming silver candlesticks and a low arrangement of flowers. Acting as her father's hostess, Miss Arlington offered them wine.

Philippe, seated next to Erik at the table, said earnestly, "It was very kind of you to make the time to meet with us, Dr. Arlington."

"It is no trouble, I assure you, Sir," replied the surgeon in his soft, shy voice. His eyes shot to Erik and then back to Dr Gaudet. "I was most interested in your friend's case, and besides, this is my daughter's first trip to France. We plan to spend a few weeks here before we go back to New York."

"What of your clinic?" Philippe asked. "Can they manage without you?"

Dr. Arlington explained for Erik's benefit, "I have established a clinic in New York for men who were wounded in our War Between the States. I have left a very competent surgeon in charge there, Dr. Gurdon

Buck; he and I worked together during the war." He looked again at Erik as though he could not help himself. "My specialty, as well as Dr. Buck's, as I am sure Dr. Gaudet here has told you, is facial reconstruction."

There was a pause in the conversation at that moment, while hotel staff entered the suite pushing several trolley carts filled with silver domed covers. At Miss Arlington's gesture, they proceeded to serve the first course, little *quenelles* of some sort of delicate fish in a creamy sauce. Erik observed that the Le Grande produced what Sylvie called *'haute cuisine'*. It would be delicious, but there would not be enough of it.

"You and your daughter speak French very well," Erik noted as the conversation continued.

"Thank you…I do find that actually being here has improved my grasp of the language even more," the doctor answered with a smile. "My late wife's family hails from Provence, and she spoke French quite fluently." He nodded toward his daughter with a look of pride. "Edythe learned from her mother, but I took French while studying medicine at Columbia University in New York."

So Edythe Arlington was part French, mused Erik. That explained a great deal.

"My association would be very interested in your giving a teaching course at the Catholic Hospital here in the future, if you would be willing," Dr. Gaudet said hopefully to Dr. Arlington. The conversation turned to this subject and Erik remained silent.

They had finished the salad course and were contentedly sipping a lightly *pétillant* white wine from the Alsace, when Dr. Arlington returned to the subject that had claimed his attention.

"I am curious about your mask, Mr. Bessette," he said interestedly. "Where did you have it made? It is leather I believe."

"I made it myself, several years ago. You are correct, it is leather. It was one of a number of different masks I made for myself." Erik replied, wondering why the surgeon was asking about his mask.

Dr. Arlington studied it thoughtfully. "Do you find it comfortable, Sir? I would think it could be quite warm, and perhaps not good for your skin."

Erik heard an echo inside his head; a little flash of *déjà vu*. Where had he heard that before? It came to him in a moment: Sylvie had said much the same thing to him once, while they were having dinner together in the cavern. He smiled, more to himself than to the others.

"It is not uncomfortable, but *oui*, it can become warm. But I do not wear it when alone, and I never wear it at home."

"You are wearing it for our sakes, then," the doctor murmured in his quiet voice. Edythe said nothing, but she was following the conversation closely.

"At the clinic we have been experimenting with some new materials, cellulose for example, that are lighter in weight and have a more natural skin color. If you should ever come to New York, I could show you, and perhaps make something better for you to wear."

"How would you do that?" Dr. Gaudet asked curiously.

"Simply by making a plaster impression of the normal side of Mr. Bessette's face, and then creating a mirror image of it in the material we are developing." Dr. Arlington explained. Erik was intrigued; he would have preferred to have something more natural looking, but had never found any material that would be malleable enough and yet hold its shape.

Studying Erik's white mask again, Dr. Arlington added, "This technique will result in a much more natural appearance, for it will be exact."

"I shall consider it," Erik said. And he meant it.

They finished dessert, a delicious *Poires Hélène*, and the hotel staff removed the trolleys and left them alone. Dr. Arlington went to a sideboard and poured cognac for the men, and lit a cigar for himself. Neither Erik nor Philippe smoked and so declined the offer of a cigar. Miss Arlington sipped delicately from a little glass of something sweet, her dark eyes watchful. A contented silence descended and the after-dinner mood turned mellow, but it was soon dispelled by Dr. Arlington's next words.

"I wonder if you would permit me to examine your face, Mr. Bessette. We can do so in the privacy of my bedroom."

Although Erik was expecting this, he still felt himself tense. He wasn't sure why; at home his workers and the household servants saw his face every day. But this felt different; it was as if he was balancing on the brink of something momentous. He gave Dr. Arlington a stiff nod, and heard Philippe, seated next to him, give a barely audible sigh of relief.

As he followed the American into the bedroom, he heard Miss Arlington offering Philippe another cognac before the door closed.

Erik was relieved to be alone with Dr. Arlington for this examination; he could tell him the truth about his face without Philippe discovering he had been told a lie. Dr. Arlington moved about the luxuriously appointed room, turning up gaslights and lighting extra candles. Then he opened a leather case and removed a magnifying glass from it. He approached Erik until they were standing face to face.

"There is something I should tell you, Doctor," Erik said slowly. "The circumstances when I first met Dr. Gaudet were somewhat unusual. I

86

was in hiding at the time, and Sylvie, now my wife, told him that I was her cousin visiting from the north. We told him my face was burned by boiling water falling on it, but that isn't true. He doesn't know; I never wanted him to know we lied to him. He has been very kind to me. But the truth is, I was born with this disfigurement." As he spoke, he reached up and removed the white mask.

"*Regardez*," he muttered. He did not expect Dr. Arlington to flinch or be shocked; having seen the photographs in his pamphlet, Erik was certain he had seen far worse. But it still felt strange to reveal his face to this stranger.

"Dr. Gaudet appears to have led a somewhat...sheltered life, I gather. He spends most of his time at his hospital," Dr. Arlington said unconcernedly. He was studying Erik's face avidly, peering through his magnifying glass and moving it up and down slowly. "Hmmm," he murmured. "May I?"

Fixing his gaze on Erik's right eye, he reached up and touched the skin very carefully. Erik's right eye was the most hideous of his deformities – the skin was livid and puckered and the lower eye socket looked as though it were falling away, like flesh rotting off a corpse. He *hated* it.

All at once the bedroom door opened, and Edythe Arlington strode into the room with a swish of white skirts, trailing the scent of honeysuckle. She closed the door behind her and said briskly, "I want to see, too!" As though looking at Erik's face was a rare treat.

"Edythe..." Dr. Arlington began to remonstrate with her, but disregarding her father, she approached Erik and looked intently at his face. She was almost of a height to him, he noticed. He thought her rude beyond belief. A flush of anger crossed his face, and he felt his expression harden. She noticed, and smiled teasingly at him.

"This does not look like a burn scar," she said matter-of-factly. Erik was surprised at her calm; he supposed she would be horrified at the sight of his face, as others had been in the past. Even Sylvie had been horrified the first time, although she did her best to conceal it from him.

Dr. Arlington explained, almost apologetically. "My daughter always assists me in my photographic endeavors. She is quite an accomplished photographer," he said proudly. So that explained it; Miss Arlington had already looked upon many repugnant sights, probably some much worse than his own. Interesting, these American women.

Turning to his daughter, Dr. Arlington explained, "It is some sort of birth defect or disfigurement that occurred in the womb, my dear."

Miss Arlington again subjected Erik to one of her thorough glances, and then she asked pertly, "Tell me, Mr. Bessette, does that scarring occur anywhere else on your...person?"

"Edythe!" There was definitely a note of reprimand in the surgeon's voice now. He frowned at his forward daughter, his mouth turning down in disapproval.

She looked all innocence back. "I was only asking out of professional curiosity!"

Frustrated and angry and perhaps a little shocked, Erik said sternly, "We have left Philippe alone too long. I am returning to him now." He glanced at Dr. Arlington. "He and I should probably be going at any rate; it is getting late and Philippe is not as young as he used to be."

"Of course," Dr. Arlington acquiesced at once. His daughter pouted prettily but accompanied them back to the sitting room.

They were donning their outer garments and preparing to depart when suddenly Miss Arlington uttered an incoherent exclamation of surprise. The men stopped and looked at her inquiringly. Her eyes were riveted on Erik's left hand as he was straightening the collar of his tailcoat.

"You are wearing a wedding ring!" She exclaimed, sounding vexed. "You are married!" For some reason, she made it sound like an accusation. All three men stared at her in some confusion.

Erik finished shrugging into his coat and adjusted his cravat. Meeting her almost angry gaze, he said, "Yes, I am married. What of it?" With a flash of irritation, he wondered if she was implying that he was so ugly no woman would want him.

She appeared discomfited, and a slight flush of color warmed her pale face. "I thought you would have mentioned it during dinner, is all," she said, frowning.

Philippe and Erik exchanged perplexed glances with each other. "The subject did not arise," Erik replied shortly. What was the matter with the girl? He turned to Dr. Arlington and they shook hands again in the American way. "It was an interesting evening, Doctor," he murmured.

"I hope we will have the chance to meet again while we are in France, Mr. Bessette," Dr. Arlington replied, walking to the door with them. "I am paying a visit to Dr. Gaudet's hospital in a few days, and then we will be traveling." He turned to Erik earnestly. "I would like the opportunity to talk to you about my clinic, and what we might be able to do for you...for your face."

"I know!" Miss Arlington suddenly exclaimed. Her cheeks were still becomingly flushed and she was smiling again. "Father, why do we not stop and visit the Bessettes on our way back from Nice?" She glanced slyly at Erik, adding, "I should dearly love to see where Mr. Bessette lives, and meet his wife."

"My dear, it would be much too far out of our way," her father said, looking rather hopeful at the suggestion nevertheless. Erik felt suddenly out of his depth, and he disliked that feeling. He felt a sense of unease at having Miss Arlington come to their home, but he wasn't sure why. At the same time he would like a chance to talk more with her father. Perhaps just a brief visit would not be amiss. Assuming, of course, that all went smoothly with his mission. If it did not, the Arlingtons would be visiting him in prison.

"I have some…business I must attend to soon," he murmured, exchanging a quick glance with Philippe. "I do not know exactly how long I will be in Paris before I start home again. I will send word to you here or with Philippe at the hospital. Philippe knows where we live and can direct you." With that the Arlingtons would have to be content for now.

As they took their leave, Edythe Arlington impulsively stepped forward into the corridor and offered him her hand in a gesture that clearly invited him to raise it to his lips. Erik did not want to kiss her hand. He had the annoying sense that she was manipulating him. That he had manipulated many people in the past did not make it any more acceptable. Her dancing eyes were daring him.

"You never answered my question, Sir," she murmured in a low, throaty voice. Erik felt himself color slightly. What nerve this girl possessed! Slowly he took her pale hand in his, and she smiled in anticipation. Her smile was returned with a scowl.

"That really is none of your business," he said curtly. Bowing formally over her hand, he released it, turned and walked away with Philippe. Behind him, he heard a sharp hiss of indrawn breath.

Back in their hired hansom, Erik loosened his cravat and breathed a sigh of relief. He would be very glad to get back to the quiet seclusion of the hospital.

"Dr. Arlington's daughter is *la jolie fille*," Dr. Gaudet ventured after a moment. This made Erik smirk a little. Philippe did have an eye for a pretty girl.

"*Oui*, she is quite striking, but she will lead her father on a merry dance until they return home," he replied. "She is far too forward."

Dr. Gaudet chuckled, but then his countenance sobered. "You know, I was enjoying the evening so much, I completely forgot why you are here, and what you must do. I wish there was some other way for you to earn your pardon. This is so…so barbaric."

Erik murmured something noncommittal. There was so much about his own barbaric past that Philippe did not know, and would never know. Philippe led such a sheltered life, even the ravages of the war had passed him by.

Much later that night, long after the good doctor had retired to his bed, Erik sat quietly on the bench of an old upright piano in the hospital's chapel. Unsurprisingly, sleep was eluding him, and he felt claustrophobic in the narrow confines of his upstairs bedroom. Because he did not wish the remaining patients to know he was here, he could only come downstairs at night, when they were all asleep. He felt like a vampire, skulking around after dark and hiding from the day.

Idly, he lifted the lid of the old piano and stroked his fingers across the worn ivory keys, being careful not to make any sound. During the time he was hiding from the Paris police in Sylvie's apartment, he would come here with her every day and after the midday meal had been consumed, he played for the patients and their caregivers on this ancient, pathetically poor excuse for a piano. It was kept in tune, which was really all one could say in its favor. He thought wistfully of his black lacquer grand piano in the *château*, and abruptly closed the lid and stood up.

Erik didn't believe in God, or Mohammed as the Persians and Turks he had once lived among called God. He had not come down to the chapel to pray. He was here because he missed his wife, and in some way felt closer to her in this room where they had exchanged their vows. He, who had always gone his own way and never needed anyone, wished more than anything that he could talk to her, ask her for advice on what he ought to do.

Wild ideas ran through his mind: he could flee the city tonight, before Moreau or anyone knew he was gone. He would have time to get home, collect Sylvie and Marie (and Robert and Celestine?) and disappear as they had done once before, hiding out and then finding another secluded place to start again. He would not have to kill anyone, not have to break his promise to Sylvie never to kill again. And Philippe…he knew that Philippe would never look at him the same way if he did this thing. And somewhat to his own bemusement, this mattered to him.

Years ago, in the darker days of his life, he was a paid assassin, among other things. He was young and hard; killing a stranger never gave him pause. He wondered why it was so different now. But he knew why, *bien sûr*. When Sylvie rescued him, she saved more than his life, she had saved his soul. She told him once that she believed in his redemption, and more or less single-handedly set about making it happen.

90

After tomorrow night, he would return to Philippe, to Sylvie and Marie a tarnished soul, if he returned at all. For there was no guarantee he would not be apprehended in the attempt. And in his heart, he wondered, could he live with himself after this? He had embraced life, thought himself free at last from blood and death; who would have expected it to be thrust upon him again like this?

Erik bent his head for a moment, feeling utterly overwhelmed, and then he straightened, squared his shoulders and strode from the chapel. It was the last time he would ever set foot in that beautiful room.

CHAPTER EIGHT

"I would have killed him before he could draw another breath."

Erik

In an elegant, wood paneled library a fire burned low in the grate, and an ornate marble and gilt ormolu clock on the mantel ticked softly toward midnight. On a small inlaid side table, a glass of claret glowed scarlet in a circle of soft lamp light. Books lined the walls, but the lone occupant of the room had not read any of them, for he was only renting this apartment for a short time. His tastes ran more to political intrigues than to literature, anyway. At the moment, he dozed, head slumped, in a plump chair near the fire, with the claret bottle in easy reach. The papers he was examining lay on the floor, having dropped from his lax fingers.

All that could be heard was the ticking clock and the soft whisper of coals settling in the grate. Then came into this hushed quiet a small sound, and a breath of night air soft as a sigh. And suddenly a figure was standing in the shadows, just inside the open window. The man in the chair slept on, unaware. The stranger reached behind him and silently drew the window closed again. The hinges made no noise, for they had been oiled. He was tall, broad, dressed in dark clothes and with a hat pulled low over his face. He was as silent as the grave, as stealthy as a ghost. His eyes darted around the small room, taking in every detail at a glance. He was alone with his intended victim, as expected.

Could one see the face hidden beneath the hat, its expression would be grim, set, and determined. It was the merciless face of an experienced assassin. One hand moved stealthily to a coil of thin rope at his side, and detached it. The man held it in both hands, testing the loop and the knot at one end. It had been a long time since he used rope this way, and he was out of practice. This would not, however, be a difficult killing, for his victim still slumbered.

The reclining figure in the chair never moved; apparently quite heedless of the danger only a few feet behind him. The assassin drifted stealthily toward the chair, and the circle of rope floated up as he held it out before him. It would be quick and quiet, with no struggle, since his target was sleeping soundly. He must do what he came for and get out, before a servant should appear.

And then the assassin froze. Time seemed to stand still. For there happened to be a framed mirror hanging above the mantel, and in the mirror the killer saw himself, his face shadowed by the hat, his arms outstretched, the rope grasped in them. He saw in the mirror's reflection the occupant of the chair as well. His sleep was indeed profound, and of the most permanent sort, because he was already quite dead. A large knife protruded from his chest, and the entire front of his body was wet with dark blood.

Erik was so startled by this unexpected sight that he stood frozen in place for several seconds. Then he straightened and, with hands that shook slightly, coiled up the thin rope and reattached it at his side with deliberate movements. The discovery of the murdered man had temporarily unnerved him. He drew a long breath and let it out slowly, pulling himself together, and his eyes darted again around the quiet room.

He was alone for a certainty. The *bona fide* assassin had done the deed and escaped by some other route. Was there a servant lying dead somewhere within? It seemed strange that no one had yet come to attend the fire. Erik did not care how long his would-be victim had been dead, or who killed him, or if there were other victims in the apartment. *Dieu merci!* Erik was not the man to be shocked by violence, and it was relief that made his hands shake, or so he told himself sternly. He was only thankful his own hands were clean.

Clearly the fellow had other enemies, and the reason for their visit was soon ascertained; a safe in the wall stood open, and it appeared the diplomat had been looking through papers when he met his unpleasant end. A document of some sort was lying on the floor near his lax hand. After taking the precaution of locking the door of the library, Erik approached the open safe. He saw at a glance that it had been efficiently rifled; whether the attacker found what he was looking for could not be known.

Quickly he gathered up what was on the floor and inside the safe and glanced through the various letters and documents. There were one or two German postmarks among them. Interestingly, there was some money in the safe which had not been touched. He took the money and put it in his pocket, in case he should need more than Moreau had given him, and stuffed the papers inside his shirt. Taking the money would also make it appear the diplomat had been killed by a common thief. Lastly, he stooped to pick up the document the murdered man had dropped. There was a smear or two of dried blood on the paper. Moreau might find a plum hidden among the papers, Erik did not know and really did not care. But if it served to soften Moreau, he would do it. All he wanted was to get his hands on that pardon, signed by someone or other; he could not recall the name. Finally, he picked up the claret bottle, held it to his lips, and took a fortifying swallow. It was delicious.

In two steps he was at the window again, and then outside on the narrow parapet, breathing in the cool night air. He stood quite still, his heart beating in hard strokes, his thoughts whirling. This had to be the most amazing piece of luck to come his way since meeting Sylvie. The Ministry of Defense had decreed that this man must die, and now he was dead. Erik would tell Moreau the deed was accomplished, and no one would be the wiser. He would be free, and he would not return to Sylvie with blood on his hands. He was lightheaded with relief, and the knowledge that their ordeal was almost over.

Perhaps it was his overwhelming sense of relief that caused him to be just a little careless. He was eager to find Moreau and get the promised pardon, so he decided to use the rope to drop down to the street below rather than haul himself up to the roof again. This proved to be a grave error on his part.

Securing the rope to a balustrade, after only a cursory glance at the street below, he lowered himself over the side and went down hand-over-hand. The rope ended about eight feet from the sidewalk, and as he was hanging there preparing to drop to the ground, he was startled by a shout. This was followed almost instantly by a shrill whistle.

He had been spotted by a *gendarme*. Erik uttered a series of really foul oaths directed at himself for his unusual carelessness. Dropping to the ground, he took off instantly at a run in the opposite direction. A policeman was pelting after him, blowing his whistle.

Erik realized the desperateness of his plight the instant he heard the whistle: to be caught at this moment would be utter disaster. Even if he were to turn on the *gendarme* and disable him, the whistle was attracting too much notice. If he were caught, the officer would think him a common thief, but they would find the papers and money on his person, *sans doute*. That would lead inevitably to the discovery of the dead man above. Erik would be accused of yet another murder and it would be the end of all. Moreau had told him in no uncertain terms that should he be captured while carrying out his task, the Ministry would deny all knowledge of him. He was alone in this.

His dire predicament gave wings to his feet, but he could not run all the way back to the Hospital or even to Moreau's house. By now he was not certain of his location, or in which direction he was running. He had no knowledge of this part of Paris. Suddenly he found himself running into a wide boulevard filled with considerable traffic. He could hear the *gendarme's* feet pounding along behind him, and he began to feel real panic. His lungs were laboring and he knew he could not keep up this pace much longer, and indeed, the traffic and pedestrians made it impossible. The whistle blew again, closer now, and Erik was aghast at the thought that some pedestrian might try to intercept him. His hat had flown off in his wild flight and he felt utterly exposed. And then, quite abruptly, Erik's luck changed.

It was not a moment too soon. He had already considered leaping on to the back of a passing carriage, but cast that idea aside at once because they moved too slowly. He was dodging agilely through a steady stream of traffic when the most peculiar carriage he had ever seen appeared, chugging along the boulevard belching steam and sounding a loud horn. People were parting on either side of it, pointing and staring. Some were laughing. Erik had never seen anything like it – a carriage barreling along, without any horses to pull it.

It was an open carriage of sorts, with curtains flapping at the windows, and carrying a few passengers who were apparently brave enough to ride on it. Whatever it was, Erik did not care. What mattered was that the thing was moving rapidly along the street, at a much faster pace than any horse-drawn carriage could possibly manage.

As the odd contraption passed him, he saw painted in gold script on its dark green metal side, "*L'obéissant*": the Obedient. The determined *gendarme* was gaining on him, so with the talent for quick thinking that characterized him, he lunged for the thin metal rung at the back of the moving carriage and hauled himself up. Clinging there, suddenly feeling unaccountably hot, he looked back and saw the policeman standing in the street gasping for breath and staring at him. Erik gave him a jaunty salute.

It was soon apparent why he felt so hot – a man in a sort of conductor's uniform was feeding short pieces of wood into a cylindrical black stove at the back of the carriage – directly in front of him. But no matter; he was moving and at excellent speed. The man feeding wood closed the little door on the stove, made an adjustment to a valve, and looked at Erik impassively.

"That will be 20 *centimes*, Monsieur, *s'il vous plaît*," he said loudly, to be heard over the rattle of metal wheels on the pavement. Feeling as though he were in the midst of an odd dream, Erik fished about in his trouser pocket and was fortunate to locate a bit of change, which he handed over. In return, he was given a ticket and waved toward a wooden bench directly in front of the conductor.

After he had caught his breath, he ventured to ask, "What is this thing?"

"It is a steam car, the very latest invention," replied the apparent conductor with a touch of pride. They were whizzing along at what seemed to Erik a dangerously rapid pace, but the driver in the front of the steam car was unconcerned, and the other passengers appeared to be enjoying the ride.

The conductor studied Erik interestedly, his eyes lingering on the white mask covering one side of his face. Erik began to feel uncomfortable. Was he about to be recognized? Unexpectedly, the conductor began chuckling merrily. Erik stared at him, nonplussed.

"That is an excellent costume, Monsieur," he said wiping his eyes gleefully. "You have been to a *bal masque*, I gather. It took me a moment to recognize your costume."

Feeling the answer was inevitable, Erik asked slowly, "Who do you think I am supposed to be?"

"Why, the Phantom of the Opera, *bien sûr!*" The conductor looked quite pleased with himself. Erik found he was beginning to enjoy this bizarre experience.

"Yes, you are quite correct; I am the Phantom of the Opera. The costume is not exact, however. I believe there was meant to be a cape also." How he was looking forward to telling Sylvie about the steam car and this conversation.

"Where do you wish to be let off, Monsieur? We arrive at our turn-around point soon."

Erik glanced about, realizing the steam car was gradually slowing down. He recognized the Blvd. des Capucines, and knew himself to be back in familiar territory.

"Along here will be fine," he replied. In another moment, he was standing on the sidewalk watching *L'obéissant* rattle off down the boulevard, belching steam. He shook his head wonderingly; Paris certainly had changed.

The Blvd. des Capucines was a wide, busy thoroughfare, and Erik knew he could not linger here. Just a short distance away lurked the blackened hulk of the burned out Opera House, behind a high fence. He turned and walked quickly in the opposite direction, until he came to a quiet side street. He slipped into it with relief, for he needed a few minutes to think of his next move.

96

Soon invisible in the shadows that swallowed him once he was away from the gaslit boulevard, Erik leaned against a wall and pondered his situation. Earlier in the evening he had been dropped off by the hospital's brougham in an area not far from the apartment building housing the unfortunate diplomat. But it had long since returned to the hospital for the night. It had been his plan to go straight to Moreau's house to tell him the job was done, and turn over all the stolen papers. At that point, he could reasonably expect Moreau to help him get back to St. Giles. Now he was not sure what to do. It was most unfortunate that he had been seen by the police, for of a certainty the body would have been discovered by now and a hue and cry raised.

Moreau lived on a quiet, genteel street near the Cimetière de Montmartre, a long way from here. Could he hail a hansom to take him there? It was not that late, and he was in possession of all that stolen money. He decided this was the best course. Making his way cautiously back to the main street, Erik had just made up his mind to flag down the first hansom he saw, when the sound of a rapidly approaching uproar caught his attention. He drew a sharp breath, pressing himself against the side of the building. A large group of men were running down the street, throwing rocks and shouting unintelligible things. Erik heard the word "*Allemagne*" several times as they passed, followed by the sound of glass shattering. The rioters were pursued by a group of *gendarmes* and militia, trying unsuccessfully to quell the riot.

He had but a few seconds to draw back into the shadows and beat a hasty retreat. More cursing appeared to be in order. Erik found himself wishing for a magic carpet that would carry him away from this mad city and back home, where he belonged. Here, there appeared to be no safe place. Paris was boiling over with fury against Germany and Erik did not want to get caught up in that. He was exhausted, and he needed to rest.

Suddenly he raised his head and glanced about alertly. There was a place, perhaps, where he might find sanctuary and rest, and it was not far from here. For the moment, the streets were too dangerous for him. Quickly he turned and continued rapidly down the darkened side street, and then on to another, smaller and narrower street. He hurried down it, studying the windows along the right side. Most of the windows had some sort of notice pasted on them, but it was too dark for him to make out the print. Although he did not know it at the time, they were tear-down notices; this entire street, long unused, was slated to be demolished soon.

His sharp eyes found what they were looking for; a small splash of red in the corner of one particular casement window. Would it still be unlocked? He tried the handle, pushed, and there was an earsplitting screech of protest as the window, long closed, opened reluctantly for him. He remembered that he always kept the window oiled to make it easier for Sylvie to open it when she came here to deliver his meals. Erik doubted any one had touched this window since the night he and Sylvie fell through it on their desperate escape from the opera house. Now he slipped cautiously through the opening and landed on the dusty floor of an empty room. It had a marble floor and inset marble shelves, and was completely empty.

Looking across the room at the shelves along the wall, he saw in his mind's eye a covered tray resting there next to a glowing oil lamp. But there was nothing but dust, the dust of years. Fighting against a wave of melancholy that threatened to engulf him, Erik quickly pulled the window shut and crossed the room, where he knew a gaping doorway and an old stone stair were concealed behind a tapestry.

The tapestry was one of many items he purloined over the years from the Opéra Populaire's vast stock of props. He had hung it there to disguise the opening when he knew Sylvie was going to begin bringing him a daily meal. But of course, one of her first actions upon coming here was to peer behind it. The tapestry was still there, rotting slowly in place.

As he crossed the floor, he paused for a moment at the exact spot he and Sylvie had met face to face for the first time, and the memory drew a slight smile from his tense face. He pulled the tapestry aside and went down the stairs into stygian blackness. His feet remembered the way, and he could still see well enough in the dark.

Erik felt reasonably certain that his old home, the cavern far below the opera house, would be almost as he left it. It had been searched and rifled by the police, but he knew that by the orders of the late unlamented Chief-Inspector Gaston it was cordoned off. After that, of course, the entire property had been fenced off at the request of the Vicomte. Some disarray was to be expected, but it ought otherwise to be as he had left it. There was a bed, a place to lie down and sleep in safety, and Erik needed that desperately.

As he was walking across the long stone causeway over an underground waterway, approaching his old door, Erik pondered the bizarre circumstance of his being here once more. It was a place he never thought to see again, nor did he want to. What memories waiting to be stirred up! He drew to a stop outside the closed door leading to his old storeroom. He had painted it long years ago to exactly mimic the brick surrounding it. The disguised door was one of many tricks and traps he had relied on to safeguard his privacy. But that had not stopped Sylvie. She had fussed at the

98

false door until she found the hidden catch that opened it. He pressed the little catch himself and it still worked; the door rotated open slowly and he passed inside, into the storeroom. The door rotated closed behind him silently.

Here was more darkness, and the smell of damp and disuse. Crossing the small room, he found what he was hoping to find: a small pottery oil lamp resting on a little table. Some oil still remained in the lamp. In the drawer below the tabletop were matches, and when he tried one found they were still good. Turning up fresh wicking, he lit the lamp and looked about him in the soft glow. There were still some packing crates holding candles, parchment and other supplies, but the crate that had held all his Russian Imperial Tokay was empty. He sighed regretfully and then went on.

Entering the cavern by brushing aside a hanging, he stepped carefully over broken glass – the remains of a mirror he had smashed upon leaving here for what he thought would be the last time. He could still remember the overwhelming sense of despair he had felt at that moment; how close he came to taking his own life.

Bringing the matchbox with him, Erik moved slowly around the main living space of the cavern, stepping carefully over debris, and lighting candles that had not burned in almost three years. Then he walked down to the edge of the underground lake and stood looking around him. The quiet, still water held a watery green glow. Everything was familiar, everything was as he had made it, but he saw it all with new eyes. He had lived here for ten years, but it was not his home any longer. There were no words to describe how desolate and alone he felt.

Here, in this extraordinary place, terrible things had happened…no, that wasn't right; Erik corrected himself quickly. Here, he had done terrible deeds. But there were a few good memories lurking among the bad. And all those memories featured the woman who was now his wife. Sylvie once told him that when she saw his home for the first time, she thought it was like something out of the Arabian Nights, exotic and theatrical. Now he just thought it was strange.

He saw that his gondola boat had sunk in the shallow lake. The silver skull on the prow of the boat was sticking eerily out of the water. Someone must have used it to come here, because the last time he had seen the boat, Christine and Raoul were leaving in it. The floors were littered with debris from careless searchers, and there were the piles of broken mirror here and there.

Otherwise, the place was the same – there was the ruin of the little model he had painstakingly built of the beautiful theatre stage above, and then deliberately destroyed. There stood the organ where he sat playing and composing all those lonely years. He stopped next to the beautiful dark wood instrument and with the flat of his hand wiped a layer of dust from its surface. Stealing that organ and the pipes and getting them down here to the cavern had been an incredibly difficult task, but he managed to do it.

Beyond the instrument were the stone steps leading up to his bedroom. Up those steps was an alcove hidden by a drapery…the memory of what might still lurk behind that drapery chilled his very blood. Unwillingly he walked slowly up the stone steps and forced himself to pull aside the hanging to see what was behind. He held his breath, but the little alcove was empty. He released his pent breath with a sigh of relief. He did not think he would be able to sleep at all knowing that the automaton of Christine was still standing there. He wondered what had become of it, and then his face split in an enormous yawn. He felt dead on his feet. He passed into what once functioned as a bedroom for him.

It was really just a hollowed out section of the cavern, but the bed was still there. It was a large gilt swan that had started life as a boat prop above, for a long-ago musical performance about Cleopatra. Quickly he pulled out the bedding and took it to the main open space and shook it, sending dust flying. Replacing the bedding, he sat nearby and tugged off his boots with a groan. He wasn't accustomed to running on pavement and cobblestones and his feet hurt. He paused when his eyes rested on an object sitting on a nearby table. It was his old monkey music box, which he had made long ago, in Persia. Originally it was made as an amusement for the little Sultana, but she had not liked it. Odd, he had forgotten all about it. He picked it up and wound it, wondering if it still played. It did.

Erik listened to the sad little tune until it came to an end, and wiped his wet eyes. He had forgotten how sad that song was. It brought back with it the memory of all the loneliness of his years here, under the opera house. And sharper still was the memory of the last time he listened to that particular tune. Thank god he didn't have to live like that anymore, or feel that dire loneliness. Setting the music box down, Erik pushed all the memories aside, fell into bed, pulled a blanket over his fully-clothed body, and fell into an exhausted sleep within a few minutes.

Hours later, he woke up in the dark and in confusion, momentarily forgetting where he was. He put an arm out, murmuring, "Kitten". When his hand encountered only emptiness, he came fully awake and then he remembered. He lay in the dark listening; all he could hear was silence, broken by the occasional drip of water. Another thing he had forgotten: the profound silence of this deep place.

It was a disconcerting feeling, lying here alone and knowing that far above him, instead of a great, many-leveled building as busy with activity as a stirred anthill, there was utter desolation. Above was a blackened hulk, bereft of life, and it had happened by his own hand. He was now the only living creature in the entire barren place. It felt like a great weight pressing down on the cavern, and the ruin of the opera house looming far above him seemed malevolent somehow. Erik knew that he could die here, and no one would ever know, or find him.

It was cold, it was dark, it was empty; an empty tomb waiting for a body. Suddenly he hated this place, all of it, and if he did not get out at once he would scream. He had lived in this cavern for ten years; it was no wonder he went mad.

He tore off the blanket, pulled himself out of the bed, and quickly lit some candles so he could see. Then he opened the *armoire* standing against the stone wall. It was really just a large wardrobe packing case, which he had repurposed to hold his clothing. He was almost astonished to find most of his things still hanging inside, clean and dust free. Hastily Erik pulled out a few pieces of clothing – trousers, clean white shirt, waistcoat and a tailcoat. His clothes were of good quality, ordered to his specifications from a tailor in London. He liked to dress well, and he knew that the elegant clothing set off his tall frame to good advantage. It had been part of his veneer of civilization.

He changed as quickly as possible, dogged by an urgent need to be gone from this forsaken place. Then he tugged on his boots, found a cape in the *armoire* and threw it on over his clothes. He was about to leave the bedroom when he remembered the stolen papers; hurrying back to the pile of clothing on the floor, he dug through them and collected all the papers from the diplomat's safe and shoved them into a deep inside pocket of the cape. The money he stored safely in his trouser pocket. He would have need of it soon enough.

He spotted one of his dark wigs on a table in the cavern, and donned it after giving it a good shake. He needed to change his appearance as much as possible. The policeman who had chased him last night would be unlikely to recognize the dark haired gentleman who climbed out of the casement window onto the street a few minutes later. Erik now looked exactly like the man Sylvie had seen for the first time; it was as if no time had passed at all. Tall, dark and dangerous looking, cape swirling dramatically around him, it was a good thing Edythe Arlington could not see him now.

Dawn had arrived, and the sun would soon burn off an early morning mist when Erik thumped the brass doorknocker of Frédéric Moreau's staid and proper two-story brick house. He was hungry, tired of skulking about Paris, and felt as if he could kill for a *café espresso*. He had taken a long, circuitous route to get here, once in a hansom, once by clinging to the back of a large barouche, but most of the time on foot. When the door was finally opened by a sleepy-looking footman, he had to practically force his way in, so reluctant was the footman to admit him.

But when he was standing in a neat but nondescript foyer waiting for Moreau to be roused, Erik found himself confronted by his own reflection in a large mirror. He had to admit he was an intimidating figure. He gazed back at himself with an arrested expression; it was a vision from the past: the clothes, the hair and mask, even the cape. He realized how much he had changed in the last three years. He was still contemplating this when the foyer door opened and Moreau shuffled in, yawning. He was wearing a robe over a long white nightshirt, and his gray hair was sticking out in tufts.

Erik turned from the mirror and felt a reluctant smile tug at his mouth; something about Moreau's disheveled morning appearance reminded him of Philippe. But Moreau did not smile back at him; in fact, his blank and wary expression indicated he did not recognize Erik at all. With an exasperated gesture, Erik pulled off his mask and the dark wig.

"It is me, Moreau," he said, and then replaced both mask and wig. "It is a disguise so I won't be recognized. I am here for my pardon."

M. Moreau recovered himself at those words. "Forgive me, M. Bessette; I did not recognize you dressed like that." Glancing around hastily, he took Erik's arm and pulled him along through the door. "Come, we will go to my study, M. Bessette," he said, all traces of sleepiness gone from his countenance.

Moreau's study was also his private office; in addition to the usual shelves of books and a comfortable chair or two, the room was dominated by a large roll-top desk. Closing the door behind them, he motioned Erik to a small table. Enigmatically, he said, "I was not expecting you this early."

Erik looked at him alertly, and then realized the obvious. Moreau was in the Ministry of Defense, after all. "You have already heard the news," he said flatly.

Moreau nodded. *"Oui, c'est vrai.* Late last night, a message was delivered to me here." He studied Erik for a moment. "You were quite quick and efficient." He added with a discomfited expression.

Erik said brusquely, "the sooner done, the better in my opinion. I wish to go home to my wife." He pulled off the cape as he spoke, tossed it carelessly over a chair, and extracted the bundle of papers from the inner pocket. These he placed on the table in front of Moreau. The sight of them caused Moreau's thick brows to shoot up.

"I brought these for you; his safe was open when I arrived, so I helped myself to some of the contents." While Moreau was staring at the little pile of documents with a gleam in his eye, Erik added, "What chance of getting something to eat and some coffee, Moreau? I have not eaten since yesterday afternoon."

Moreau tore his eyes away from the papers with reluctance. "Of course, my good fellow! You shall have *petit déjeuner* at once." He shook his head, and his heavy eyebrows drew together. "I am in need of refreshment myself." He pressed a button on the wall and Erik heard a distant buzzing sound. Glancing up at Erik, he added, "It was clever of you to drug the servants, M. Bessette. They were hired with the apartment, and perfectly harmless." Erik managed to school his features into impassivity while Moreau was speaking so as not to betray his surprise. He shrugged casually, saying nothing.

So that explained why no servants had come to the library to check the fire. Erik gave silent thanks that their lives were spared by the real killer.

Fortunately Moreau was anxious to examine the stolen papers. He stood by the table and began turning them over, picking each one up and studying it with great interest, until he came to the one with a smudge of dried blood on it. He shuddered delicately and seemed reluctant to touch the paper.

"You wanted the man dead and now he is dead. No point in being squeamish about it now." Erik said ruthlessly. Moreau had the decency to look at little chagrined, but still did not pick up the bloody document.

When the pot of hot coffee arrived, the aroma was so enticing Erik felt almost lightheaded. Moreau poured a generous splash of brandy into his own cup, but Erik refused it. He was too hungry for brandy.

After a delicious breakfast and more coffee, Moreau went to the roll-top desk, unlocked it with a skeleton key hanging from his fob, and lifted the lid. Searching about inside the desk, he removed a large, stiff envelope, and presented it to Erik with a formal bow.

"Your pardon, Monsieur, as I promised. It is signed by President MacMahon himself, and can never be revoked." As Erik took the large envelope in his hands, Moreau smiled at the no doubt blank look on his face. "You are now a free man." He added, as if concerned Erik did not fully comprehend its significance.

Perhaps thirty minutes later, Erik was alone inside a closed carriage belonging to Moreau, on his way back to St. Giles Hospital. He was almost dumb with disbelief, and found himself pulling out the pardon and staring at it as though to reassure himself it was real. It was real; he was free. All his crimes were forgiven. Moreau had no reason to doubt that Erik completed his task, and as Erik had hoped, he was so interested in the papers from the man's safe that he did not think to question Erik closely about how the assassination was carried out. Erik's relief at not having to fulfill that devil's bargain was indescribable. All he wanted now was to saddle Danté and start for home.

Pulling off the dark wig, which carried a pervasive odor of dust, he tossed it aside on the leather seat and looked out the window to see where they were. Since they had a few miles to go yet, he leaned back and contemplated the ramifications of his conversation with Moreau. He wanted so much to dislike the man, but there was something inherently jolly about him that made it difficult. And Erik's instincts told him that this officious government worker liked him, even though he had not expected to do so. Moreau had clapped him on the shoulder, inquired if he needed money, and then shocked Erik tremendously by asking if he would consider working for the Ministry again sometime in a more official capacity.

"Nothing like this particular assignment, I assure you," he added hastily upon observing Erik's darkening countenance. "But we could use someone like you for certain, shall we say, unorthodox assignments. And the Ministry would pay you well. Think it over, M. Bessette. Do not be surprised if you hear from me again in the future."

Dangerous times called for dangerous men, he had added cheerfully as they parted at the door. In the carriage, mulling over this odd conversation, Erik smiled to himself wryly. This coming from someone who spent all his time sitting at a desk, dreaming up dangerous and deadly assignments for others to carry out.

"I used to be dangerous," Erik mused to himself wonderingly, "but am I still?" He would have carried out the assassination without a moment's doubt or hesitation, but in his heart he was thankful indeed that he had been spared that killing. He had done enough killing in his lifetime.

By the time he arrived back at St. Giles Hospital morning was well advanced, and he knew the patients would be at their light breakfast. He slipped silently around the massive red stone building and into a small side door, and thence into Dr. Gaudet's clinic. Philippe was not there, so Erik paced around the room, feeling too agitated to sit down.

Presently the clinic door opened and Philippe entered in that absent-minded way he had, wiping a bit of butter from the front of his waistcoat. Then he looked up and saw Erik standing there. His eyes widened, and a look of intense relief crossed his face. He quickly closed the door behind him. Something about the light in Erik's eyes must have alerted him; he came forward almost eagerly.

"You...you have your pardon, my boy?" He asked hesitatingly.

Without speaking, Erik held up the precious envelope and watched a multitude of emotions flicker across the older man's face. And then he allowed his own face to break into a smile, a genuine, happy smile.

"It is all good news. It is alright, Philippe! He was already dead, Philippe...he was dead when I got there. Someone stuck a knife in him and saved me the trouble." And then he laughed, and it was a laugh of pure joy.

"*Dieu Merci!*" Philippe exclaimed in amazement, clasping his hands together. "This diplomat fellow must have had other enemies then." He sank into his chair, relief palpable on his wide face.

"If it is true he was a spy for the Prussians, I would not be surprised. But Philippe, Moreau thinks I did it, and I let him think so."

"I am thankful it has all worked out for the best," Philippe said. "I was worried when I saw that you had not returned last night."

"I know; I am sorry it took so long to get back here. I had to dodge at least one riot!" Erik shook his head ruefully. "I have the pardon, but Paris is too hot for me now. I intend to get my things and leave this morning."

Philippe smiled understandingly. "Of course, you wish to get home and tell Sylvie the good news. But write me once you are there, *mon fils*, and let me know how she gets on. I am worried about her."

Erik let his hand rest for a moment on Dr. Gaudet's arm. "So am I. I will write you soon, Philippe. *Au revoir* for now."

Two hours later, Danté was crossing the bridge at Petit-Pont and heading south, out of the city. Erik's departure was slightly delayed owing to his sudden recollection that he'd promised Marie a present. Dr. Gaudet had hastened out to a toy shop and returned with a small doll, a gift that Erik was certain his daughter would adore. Erik would not have had a clue what to buy for a small child, and probably would have ended up bringing her home a bag of sweets.

He intended to follow the same route homeward that Moreau's carriage had taken to bring them to Paris, with a few small detours. Danté, unused to the noise and bustle of city streets, was nervous and frightened. Erik thought it best to stay on the lesser roads. It would take at least three days, possibly four, before he would see the lights of home. Home and the prospect of seeing Sylvie and Marie again, of holding them and sharing his good news, drew him homeward like a bee to its hive. Soon, he thought hopefully, these past few days would be but an unpleasant memory.

It was his third day of travel; His progress had been slowed by his strong desire to skirt around Limoges rather than ride through the middle of the city.

Erik awoke from an uncomfortable and troubled sleep with a start. He had bedded down for the night just beyond the border of a thicket of trees and brambles, well away from the road. He sat bolt upright in the chill night air, sweat beading on his forehead, heart pounding. He'd been having a nightmare, something awful; there was blood and someone screaming. A woman, screaming in terror. He dragged a sleeve across his brow, scrubbed at his face with his hands and tried to pull himself together. In the complete silence of the night he could hear only Danté nearby, blowing at the ground beneath his big hooves.

Try as he might, Erik could not shake the awful feeling that something was wrong at home – something wrong with Sylvie. It was a fear that had nagged at him for some time, but now it was full-blown. Feeling panicky, he threw back the thin blanket and stood.

"I have to get home," he muttered aloud. "What time is it?" He peered up at the dark sky; was there a faint lightness just at the horizon? Dew was thick on the grass where he had laid. He reckoned it must be between four and five in the morning. He would sleep no more, and was determined to start for home at the earliest moment. Once again giving thanks to his ability to see so well in the dark, he went to Danté, put some oats in the nosebag and placed it over the horse's head.

"Eat, my lad," he murmured, stroking the great black neck. Danté obliged him. While Danté munched his oats Erik staggered down the hill to the cold stream flowing there and stretched out by it, put his head over the water and splashed liberally, finishing with a deep drink. The cold water was refreshing and blew away the last of the cobwebs in his head. Quickly and efficiently he gathered up his meager bedding, threw the saddle on Danté and tied the bundle to the back of it. After removing the nosebag, he led the horse down to the creek and urged him to drink.

"Go on, boy. We have a long road ahead." Seeming to understand, the horse drank the cold water noisily, and then shook his head, sending droplets flying. Erik pulled him around, tightened the straps, and mounted. He urged Danté into a trot, and then a gallop, not bothering to avoid the road. No one would be on it at this hour, and it was dangerous to pass through the grass along the side in the dark. The horse could put his hoof into a rabbit hole.

Once during their journey Erik reached inside his shirt and felt for the parchment envelope hidden therein, warm from his skin, containing the freedom he had bought in that unholy agreement. *Sacré*! If something had happened to Sylvie while he was away, if she lost the baby...*no*, he could not think such things. Not when he was bringing her such good news. No more hiding, no more fear of arrest. She would be so happy.

They kept up that punishing pace for hours, sometimes slowing to a trot, sometimes galloping like a horse messenger in the war. Dawn grew up around them, and they could see much better. Though part of him wanted to ride away from the road out of long habit, Erik reminded himself that if anyone stopped him, he could prove he was no longer a criminal. He knew they would not reach Sarlat or anywhere near it in one day; it was too far and it would kill Danté.

Tonight, rather than camping along the side of the road, he would stop at an inn he knew of, one that he and Sylvie had stayed at when they were fleeing Paris, in fact. If anyone looked askance at his mask, he would tell them it concealed a war wound. Such things were never questioned, for there were many such sights in France since the war.

When he was not worrying about Sylvie and anxiously counting the miles still to go, his thoughts returned often to the zealous but kindly Dr. Arlington and his flirtatious and beautiful daughter. Before leaving the hospital Erik had given Philippe permission to write a letter for Dr. Arlington, assuring him he would be welcome to visit if they were to pass that way. They were a strange pair, he thought; seeming opposites. Where the father was soft-spoken and shy, yet passionate about his work, the daughter was brash and forward, everything one heard about the Americans.

Edythe Arlington was beautiful, there was no doubt; hers was the dark, slender beauty Erik had once admired above all others, but there was something about her, something strange lurking in her black eyes. She possessed confidence in her looks, her appeal; it was clear she was no inexperienced girl. The way she had looked at Erik – so blatantly, he had been aware all the while of her intense regard, and wondered at the meaning of it. It seemed almost to be...sexual in nature. This was perplexing, considering his appearance. He hoped Sylvie would not mind his extending the invitation to them considering she was not feeling her best. Since the Arlingtons were traveling, the visit would likely be of short duration, if it happened at all.

Erik had to admit he was attracted to the idea of a new mask, something that looked more natural. It would make it so much easier to appear in public when the occasion demanded, and perhaps he would not need to live in such seclusion any longer. Though she never complained, he sometimes regretted their forced isolation on the *château* for Sylvie's sake if not his own, for she seldom had the opportunity to go places and socialize. Even in Paris her life had been restricted due to her circumstances; it seemed a shame that someone as sweet and lovely as Sylvie should live forever in such forced isolation. A better mask could make a difference and it seemed to him worth investigating further. But was it worth travelling all the way to America to find out?

By the time he reached the coaching inn that night, he and Danté were both exhausted and hungry. The horse had a noble soul, and would try his best to do whatever Erik asked of him. Before retiring to his own well-deserved bed, Erik came to Danté's stall and offered him an apple. He was reassured to see that the horse was well-fed, brushed and comfortable.

"Rest for tonight, my lad," he told the horse, watching him crunch the apple with his big teeth. "Tomorrow will be more of the same I fear." He ran his fingers gently down the horse's velvety nose. "I need to get home by dark tomorrow, but it will mean a long day for us both." Danté shook his head, throwing his mane around in protest.

"What, don't you want to be home in your own stable?" He laughed. "I will bring you a few apples for the road, I promise."

CHAPTER NINE

"All my torments have been of a different kind."

Almost two weeks had passed since Erik was taken away, and for the most part I was coping fairly well. I managed to maintain a cheerful demeanor with little Marie, but I drove poor Mathilde to distraction by interrupting her in the kitchen all the time. I found it helped a great deal to be doing something with my hands, even if all I was doing was peeling potatoes or making a little treat for Marie.

René and Robert were an enormous help if one overlooked their squabbling with each other. If one of them happened to corner me outside, it was to rail against the other one. I decided that the winery and vineyard operations could do very well without me.

Not unsurprisingly, I found nights to be the most difficult; when I would retire to my lonely bedroom. Even a cheerful blaze in the hearth did nothing to chase away the chill I felt in that empty room. When I was feeling particularly lonely and bereft, I would open the *armoire* containing Erik's clothing and press one of his shirts to my face, inhaling the lingering scent of him that I found there.

By the light of day, I kept up a good *façade*, but alone in the dark, I was haunted by the fear that he would never return. Alone in the dark, one's mind cannot be stopped from thinking of all the evil things that one has managed to put aside during the day. I wished for some word to come to me from Paris so that I might know what was happening, but none came.

This particular afternoon at least, Celestine and I had something to occupy us for a time, and distractions, however temporary, were much needed. Once a week she received a bundle of the latest Paris newspapers from Meg, so that we could keep abreast of what was happening in the world and especially, to follow the latest fashion trends. Meg's packet had arrived today, and Celestine and I prepared to settle in to read them over a glass of sherry in my sitting room. It was a weekly ritual that we both anticipated with pleasure. That afternoon a summer storm blew in, bringing rain with it, giving us the added comfort of a fire in the grate.

"My goodness! Look at the bustle and train on this visiting gown!" She exclaimed, pointing to a fashion plate and laughing. "I cannot imagine how one can be expected to sit down in such a thing."

"We can be thankful that we do not reside in Paris, Celestine," I replied, glancing at the fashion plate while sipping my sherry. "That does not look flattering if you ask me. Why must they stick out so far in the back?" I could never abide bustles or corsets. Instead of a bustle, my gowns were made with a gathering of extra fabric at the rear, arranged so that it would fall in becoming drapes. It was rather old-fashioned, to be sure, but I could at least sit down comfortably. None of my gowns needed to be let out yet to accommodate a corresponding increase in size. This was a concern, for Dr. Olivier, the village physician, was always telling me I needed to gain weight. I could not seem to do so. Thinking of this, I forced myself to nibble at a small sweet slice of cake.

Celestine handed me the fashion segment and turned her attention to the rest of *Le Monde*. She clucked her tongue in disapproval. "I could not agree with you more about not living in Paris, *ma chère*. There is so much discontent there, I would not feel safe. Every week we read of more rioting and violence. It is almost as bad as when the Prussians were attacking us! I am glad that Meg is safely in school."

I smiled reminiscently, thinking of those exciting yet frightening days, and one particular *Noël* when the blockade was still in place. How I ever managed to acquire those oysters…

"But Celestine, do you remember…" I began, but a sharp gasp from her made me pause and look at her inquiringly.

"Oh!" She exclaimed, and her already pale face went paler.

"What is it?" I asked in concern, setting aside my fashion page.

Recovering herself, she shook her head. "It is nothing, just another riot. I thought at first it was…near Meg's school, but I see now I was mistaken." She folded up the newspaper and rose to toss it on the fire. It was a section I had not read yet.

I am not stupid, Reader, and I knew at once she was trying to conceal something from me. I moved with alacrity to pull the newspaper from her fingers before it reached the fire.

"Let me see," I said firmly.

Celestine gazed at me warily. "Very well, but I think…you ought to sit down."

I knew then that it was something about Erik. Abject terror gripped me. Was he already dead? Captured? I returned to my chair and sat, feeling breathless. Then I opened the newspaper to the front page and scanned it, forcing my brain to function so that I might actually comprehend what I was reading.

111

After a moment my eyes focused on a short article on the front page, describing the night-time stabbing of a minor diplomat in his second floor apartment. Robbery was apparently the motive, for money and papers were missing from his safe. The servants had all been drugged. A man in dark clothing was seen leaving the dead man's apartment by means of a rope from the balcony. The police were unable to apprehend him, and he made his escape. No sign of the murderer had yet been found, but the police were searching the city. The diplomat, who had ties to the Count of Chambord, was stabbed once in the heart and died instantly.

I remembered that name – it was the Count of Chambord, according to M. Moreau, who believed himself next in line to the Throne, should France return to a Monarchy. This was undoubtedly the same man that Moreau wished to eliminate.

I went to the fire, crunched the newspaper into a wad and threw it into the flames. The thin paper crisped up and turned quickly to black ash. As I turned back to her, Celestine sprang from her chair and caught me just as I was about to sag to the floor. For a moment, everything had gone black, and all I could see were little dancing points of light. When I came to myself, I was propped rather lopsidedly on the *settee* with her beside me, patting my hand. I sat up slowly.

"I did not faint," I said distinctly. "I never faint."

"*Mais non*, of course not, my dear. It was just the shock," she murmured. She poured me another little *soupçon* of sherry and handed it to me. "Here, drink this."

I was sick of sherry. Setting the delicate glass down, I turned to look into her distressed blue eyes. "He did that, Celestine. I know he did. Erik…fulfilled Moreau's assignment for him, and that means…he will return to me." Her eyes were as bleak as my voice. I turned my gaze to the fire. The full horror of what I had just read came home to me, and I felt tears leaking from the corners of my eyes. I pressed my hand to my eyes, as if I could wipe away the dreadful images haunting my mind. Now the deed was done, and nothing would ever be the same. Shakily, I rose and smoothed my skirts.

"I…I think I will go upstairs and lie down. I do not think I will want any supper tonight." In truth, I felt sick.

"But Sylvie…" I deliberately closed the door on her protest. How could Celestine possibly expect me to have an appetite tonight?

Feeling drained and nauseous, I pulled myself up the staircase and turned toward the bath chamber. I took a long bath with rose oil added to the water, staying in the bath until the water grew too cool. After slipping into my dressing gown I went to sit by the bedroom window, brushing my hair. It was still light outside, and I could see the dark hedges boxing in my *potager*, and a row of raspberry canes flushing with the fresh chartreuse of spring. Sitting quietly, I thought of Erik.

I loved my husband deeply, but never his deeds of violence, manipulation and trickery. He was a rogue who lived by his wits and followed no rules. He had done much to redeem his character since those dark days, and he was a happier man because of it. Nevertheless, I knew the rogue still lay close to the surface.

But who was the man returning to me? A murderer; a cold-blooded killer who had stabbed a stranger in the heart. Unpleasant images flitted through my mind, though I tried to cast them off.

Eventually I went to bed. After my bath Celestine had caused a tray to be brought to me with some soup and bread, but I refused it. There was a twisting, sick feeling inside me and I could not bear the thought of food.

I fell asleep eventually, though the horrors of my imagination dogged me even in sleep. Reading about the murder of the diplomat had upset me more than I realized. The fact that he was stabbed to death hardly meshed with what I knew of Erik's preferred method of killing someone.

I knew he was forced into this vile act against his will, and would never have consented to it if it were not for Marie and me. He had been caught in a trap, but it was a trap of his own making.

When I finally drifted off I was plagued by disturbing dreams, and woke several times to find myself staring up into the dark folds of the canopy bed, the sheets twisted around my legs. The dreams dissolved like mist whenever I woke, but I sensed rather than knew they were violent, frightening nightmares.

Awake again a little after the bedroom clock chimed two, I drank thirstily from the water bottle next to the bed, for my throat was desperately parched. Something was amiss; I felt peculiar, hot and cold, and as the minutes passed I began to feel painful cramping down low in my belly. Fear curled like mist around the bed, and I stroked my fingers over my stomach, murmuring softly to the little one, trying to sooth him. I told him how much I loved him, my little Stèphane. My other arm went automatically to the other side of the bed, seeking comfort where none existed. My hand found only emptiness.

I wondered if I ought to get up and go to Celestine, and tell her something was wrong. But what could she do? I decided to try and sleep again – perhaps if I could only sleep, and stay quiet, all would be well. But the pain grew worse, not occasional now but constant.

Suddenly my eyes flew open in the darkness. I gasped with fear. There was something hovering above my head! It was a horrible little demon, only a little larger than a baby, with black horns sprouting from his forehead, red wings flapping on his back, red eyes and an evil grin splitting his face. He flew about over me, cackling, and began poking me with something sharp, a stick of some sort. I screamed in terror, and swatted desperately at the creature with my hands, trying to keep him away from my stomach. He flew high above me, red wings buzzing like a hornet, into the canopy of the bed, before suddenly swooping down again, stabbing into my stomach. Blood rushed out, and the pain was unbearable. I screamed and screamed…

And then I was awake. Gasping, I looked wildly around, but the room was dark; there was no evil demon, nothing flying over my head. All was silent. But the pain was still there, and the sheets felt horribly warm and wet. The cramping in my lower region was excruciating. A wrenching sob tore from my throat, for I knew, I knew my baby was gone.

Summoning what little energy was left in me, I called out to Celestine, once, twice, three times. If I could just get to the door and open it; I struggled out of bed only to fall to the floor in a heap of blankets and my nightgown, dark and wet with blood. I lay on the floor, crying, and felt my heart break.

I don't recall very much about the rest of that night, or the next day. I do remember Celestine finding me on the floor. Somehow she must have heard me calling out to her. She knew instantly what was wrong, and as from a great distance I heard her waking up servants and giving orders. Celestine seldom raised her voice, but it seemed to me that she was shouting things – for a warm bath to be drawn, for someone to send the footman to the village to bring back the doctor *maintenant*, for someone to help her get me up off the floor. I was in a haze of pain, and it was not all physical. I wanted it all to go away. It was too much, just too much.

Various things happened to me but I did not really participate in any of them. I remember being helped from the bath into a clean nightgown. I

114

will never forget the sight of the bathwater, tinged rose-pink from my blood. After that I found myself being put to bed in Celestine's own room. The footman had to carry me for I could not walk.

At some point Dr. Olivier was there in the room, hovering over me, doing things to me, and talking, but I paid no attention to anything he said; it might as well have been another language. I felt only numbness inside; it was as if everything was happening to some other person. I turned my face to the wall until the doctor left. Celestine listened to him and asked questions, and I heard quite clearly when she said to him, in a voice I was not meant to hear,

"I have been afraid for some time this might happen."

I was made to drink something dissolved in water which tasted bitter. And then I slept.

Erik

Erik arrived home late the next afternoon, after a long, punishing day's journey. He was hot, sweaty, thirsty and saddle-sore, and in dire need of a bath. He was desperately anxious to see Sylvie and Marie, but first took a moment to find someone to take Danté to the stable and care for him. The horse had developed a slight limp during the last few miles.

Erik had not forgotten the nightmare from two nights ago; it had haunted his thoughts ever since. He frowned as he approached the *château*; there was a small cabriolet with the top up standing in the gravel drive near the front door which he did not recognize. Perhaps Sylvie had a visitor for tea, he thought, feeling irritated that he would not find her alone.

He ran up the steps, pulling off his riding gloves as he did so, and entered the house. It was wonderful to be here; he had to admit to himself that once or twice, he was not sure if he would ever see home again. Marching across the foyer in ground-eating strides, he glanced around for Celestine or a passing housemaid who could tell him where Sylvie was. He was so anxious to see her, hold her, to see that she was well, he could almost taste it. He started for the stairs, but came to a halt almost at once, one hand gripping the banister.

Two people were descending the stairs, engrossed in a low conversation. One was Celestine, the other a thin, soberly dressed man carrying a medical valise. Studying the man more carefully, Erik was dismayed to realize he was the village physician, the same physician who attended Sylvie when she was carrying Marie. A frown notched between his eyes when he saw the grave expressions they both wore. Remembering that Philippe had suggested calling the doctor in when he was here last, Erik tried to reassure himself it was only that.

"Celestine," he called peremptorily. "I am home. How is Sylvie? Where is she?"

Celestine's head swiveled toward him and her face blanched. Her mouth rounded in a silent 'oh', but she said nothing. Erik saw her shoot a quick look of alarm at the doctor, and his heart plummeted to his feet. Terrible thoughts whirled through his head, and he felt almost wild with fear. He moved swiftly to meet her on the stair, but before he could say anything more, the doctor spoke.

"Your wife is resting, M. Bessette," he said in a low, compassionate voice. "But I am sorry to tell you that she suffered a miscarriage." Seeing Erik's blank expression, he amended, "She has lost the baby."

Erik looked from the doctor to Celestine and back again. His insides turned to ice. Staring intensely at the doctor, whose name he remembered was Olivier, he asked the most important question.

"How is she, Dr. Olivier?"

Dr. Olivier hesitated briefly before replying. "If you will come upstairs with me, I will take you to her. I am glad you arrived while I am still here, for I need to speak with you about her condition before you see her."

Erik clenched his hands into fists and bit his tongue to avoid saying what he was about to say, which was to threaten the doctor with instant death if he did not answer his question. But Celestine, who knew him well, took his arm gently.

"Sylvie is not going to die, Erik. Go with Dr. Olivier *maintenant.*" Erik studied her face for a moment, and read the truth in her candid blue eyes. He nodded, noticing that Celestine looked exhausted, her long hair hanging in a plait over her shoulder as though she had not had time to put it up. There was a wet stain on the front of her gown. Dr. Olivier watched them, prudently remaining silent.

"Go on," Celestine encouraged him. So he did.

At the top of the stairs Erik stopped and looked around him, feeling suddenly overwhelmed. Down that hall was the nursery, and Marie. He touched his coat pocket briefly, feeling the outline of the dainty little English doll he had brought her from Paris. Their bedroom, his and Sylvie's, lay in the opposite direction. He could not be in both places at the same time.

"Where is my wife?" He bit out through clenched teeth.

"She is lying down in Madame Giry's room," the doctor explained.

"Why is she there? Why isn't she in our room?"

"Your wife lost a great deal of blood, Monsieur," Dr. Olivier replied cautiously. "It happened two nights ago, in your bedroom."

Erik listened to the doctor with an arrested expression. Two nights ago. The night he had camped along the creek and the nightmare woke him with the sound of a woman screaming.

"I need to see her. Now." He growled fiercely.

The doctor's expression was kind. He was unfazed by Erik's growls, having been the physician who had delivered Marie. Now he merely looked weary. Erik realized he always looked that way.

"*Bien sûr*. We can go to her now. But I must tell you..." Dr. Olivier paused as though searching for the right words. "It happens sometimes that when a woman has lost a baby, she may go through a period of sadness and be withdrawn. It usually passes with time. You must be patient with her, M. Bessette."

Erik frowned. "What caused her to lose the baby, do you know? I...I had to leave her and go to Paris. She was worried about me..." he trailed off, feeling guilty.

Dr. Olivier shrugged. "We do not always know what causes these things to happen. Sometimes it is nothing at all, and sometimes it happens because the *enfant* is not developing properly. It is not uncommon, you know." As he spoke, they walked slowly down the corridor and stopped outside the door to Celestine's small suite of rooms.

"Madame Bessette is sleeping now. I have examined her today and she is doing as well as can be expected in these cases. I gave her something to help her sleep as rest promotes healing." Dr. Olivier began walking briskly toward the staircase.

"I will return tomorrow," he called over his shoulder. "I have left all the necessary instructions with your estimable housekeeper. I must take leave of you now; I am needed in the village." And then he was gone.

Erik entered Celestine's small sitting room, the doctor instantly forgotten. The door to the sleeping chamber was closed and he stopped in front of it, running his hand through his hair. He tried to sort through his feelings; he had never been very good at understanding himself, not really. A few minutes ago he was on fire to see his wife, and now he found it was hard to open the door.

117

He was thinking about what Dr. Olivier had said about the baby not developing properly. If the babe had something wrong with it...he felt chilled to the bone. All his fears about this child carrying his disfigurement came home to him, and he realized the strongest feeling he had at this moment was relief. He could not have borne it had he cursed an innocent child with that.

Sylvie would not feel that way, he knew. He must not let her see his true feelings about her loss. Perhaps when he told her his good news, it would bring her some measure of cheer. Brightening a little at that thought, Erik quietly opened the door and went in.

The room was darkened, the curtains drawn across the window blocking out the late afternoon sun. It took a moment for his eyes to grow accustomed to the gloom. He had never been in Celestine's bedroom before; it was a small room, without a fireplace, and the four-poster carved wood bed was pushed against the wall. Huddled in the bed was a small, fragile-looking shape, and his heart turned over at the sight.

Sylvie lay curled on her side in a fetal position, with the blankets pulled over her, so that all he could see of her was her tumbled hair. One hand extended across the bed, palm up, fingers lightly curled. She was so still, and until he saw her draw breath, he felt insane fear she was dead. She was deeply asleep, a healing sleep the doctor had said. Staring at her still form, a memory came to him unbidden, a memory long-forgotten.

It seemed another lifetime ago, in those days when Sylvie was nothing to him but his cook. She pestered and annoyed him beyond belief, poking and prying into his life, with a curiosity which culminated in Erik finding her in his cavern, an unimaginable invasion of his privacy. As punishment, he had deliberately set about terrifying her into believing he was about to kill her. In fact, he would never have harmed a hair on her head, but he wished to frighten her that night. He felt the punishment was just, or at least he thought so until the next evening, when Sylvie failed to appear with his dinner at the appointed hour.

Guilt and anger warred within him, until he finally went fuming to Madame Giry and forced her to tell him where Sylvie lived. He never allowed himself to feel guilt for anything, and he didn't like it. Angrily he pulled a wide-brimmed hat over the right side of his face, donned his cape and went out into the shadowed streets to seek out his cook.

On the way to her apartment, he thought of all the things he would say to her when he got there. How dare the little virago not come with his dinner, and not send any word? Had he frightened her that much? But when he arrived at the door of her apartment, some of his anger drained away. He found himself staring at darkened windows. A painted sign with her name was on the door, so this was obviously her kitchen, where she prepared the meals for the hospital she worked for, as well as for him. Looking quickly about him, he satisfied himself that he was alone there, so Erik knocked on the door and rang the bell imperiously.

"Sylvie!" He called brusquely. "Sylvie, open this door!" His demand was met only by silence.

Beginning to feel uneasy, he stepped back and gazed up at the balcony overhead. Sylvie's private rooms were upstairs, Madame Giry had explained. Could she be hiding up there, trying to avoid him? Damn her…this would not do. Who did she think she was?

Fortunately, a large plane tree was situated close to the balcony, with one thick branch overhanging it. Erik gathered himself and leaped up, catching the lowest branch with both hands. He hung for a moment, and then swung himself up and into the tree. In another few seconds, he had landed silently on the balcony itself. If Sylvie thought she could hide from him, she would soon know better.

The tall French doors were not locked, so he opened one, pushed the lace panel aside, and stepped into Sylvie's *salon*. He called to her again, but there was no answer. Listening for a moment, he could hear only silence. The rooms were dark; the gaslights had not been turned up. There was no fire in the grate. It was as if she had never set foot here today. Erik padded silently across the room and turned up the lights.

He glanced quickly into the two other rooms – a small *garde-manger* and the bedroom, with a bath chamber opening from it. Both rooms were empty. Erik felt a prickle of, not fear exactly, but a sixth sense that something was very wrong. He frowned, feeling the last of his anger give way to guilt; why had he treated her so cavalierly last night? Why could he not have been more of a gentleman? *Dieu*! What a question.

Shaking his head in frustration, Erik crossed the room and stepped onto a small landing. A narrow staircase, its walls lined with a few old framed prints, led down into the kitchen area below. Turning up the lights as he went, he hurried down the stairs.

The kitchen was in darkness, and he could just make out counters, shelves, and a large black cooking stove. His booted feet found flagstone beneath them. He turned up the lights, and the first thing he saw was his cook. He swore, feelingly and in Arabic, which he had always found to be an excellent language for swearing.

She was lying in a heap on the cold stone floor, skirts puddled around her, as though she had been struck down. One cheek was resting directly against the stone. She was still, so still, for a horrible moment Erik thought she must be dead. But then he saw, as he approached her, that her small body was wracked with chills; she was shivering violently. But *Dieu Merci*, she lived!

He turned her over gently so that she was on her back. Her eyes were closed, and her lids looked blue and bruised. When he touched her face, it flamed with heat, though her body shook with chills. Without doubt she was very ill.

Erik glanced around him desperately, wondering what to do. It was the first time in his life he was called upon to help someone in need, and he did not know what must be done. Should he summon Madame Giry, or a doctor? *Mais non*; that would take time, and Sylvie must be moved, made warm; she could not remain here on the floor all that time.

He gathered her up in his arms and began carrying her up the stairs. She was small, but not exactly light. Her heavy trailing skirts threatened to trip him. Why did women insist on wearing such impractical garments?

About half way up the stairs, Sylvie woke from her swoon and became aware of him. Her eyes opened. One of her arms crept around his neck and with her other hand she plucked weakly at his coat lapel. Her glazed blue eyes looked trustingly into his, and she whispered his name.

Erik was thunderstruck. No one had ever trusted him before, and for good reason. Erik knew, at that moment, against all his own powerful will and determination, he had come to care for this annoying harridan. Somehow, they had become friends. He would have been devastated to lose her. And that was then, long before he had grown to love her.

Erik was propelled instantly back to the present, the memories dissolving like mist, by the soft sound of a sigh from the still figure on the bed. Sylvie's hand, lying open on the mattress, moved a little, fingers closing on air, as though she were searching for something. Without conscious thought, he sat next to her on the bed and took her cold fingers in his warm hand. He whispered her name. With his free hand, he stroked her hair back so he could see her face. Her purple-shadowed eyelids, so fragile looking, fluttered slightly but she did not wake up.

He picked up the empty water glass next to the bed and smelled it, wondering what the doctor was giving her to make her sleep. A bitter scent made him wrinkle his nose. Clearly, she would sleep for some time, so he decided to go in search of his daughter. Bending, he placed a soft kiss on Sylvie's temple, and pulled his hand carefully from hers.

Celestine was waiting for him in her sitting room. She looked weary and distressed. Erik wanted to embrace her, but she surprised him by saying something completely unexpected.

"The night Sylvie…miscarried, we saw a newspaper article from Paris that upset her very much. It was about the murder of that diplomat…the one you were sent to…"

He stared at her attentively. "Is that why…is that why she lost the baby? From the shock?" He asked, dreading the answer.

"I do not know, but I don't think so. I have felt for some time this would happen. It wasn't going well, even before." Celestine gazed at him, her blue eyes earnest. "Sylvie thinks you killed that man, but I do not believe it was you, Erik."

Erik felt a swell of emotion at her words. He walked to the window and stood looking out, collecting himself. "What makes you think that?" He asked her finally, sounding subdued.

Celestine made a little clucking noise. "Because he was stabbed, *naturellement*. You would have used a rope."

Erik laughed mirthlessly. "You know me well, Celestine. Apparently better than my own wife does."

"What happened?" She asked anxiously.

Erik shrugged impatiently. He was eager to find Marie, to scoop her up in his arms. "I went there intending to kill him, whoever he was. I never knew his name." He glanced at her darkly. "I did have rope, as a matter of fact. But when I got there and let myself in, he was already dead. Someone beat me to it. I went to Moreau and made him think I did it, and he gave me this." He reached inside his coat and pulled out the envelope.

"*Mon Dieu*," she breathed. "That is your pardon? He believed you?"

Erik nodded, and slid the envelope back in place. "Now I am going to see Marie." He said firmly.

Celestine smiled a little shakily, and he saw her eyes were brimming with tears. "Sylvie will be so happy to learn your news," she said, not sounding as if she actually believed herself, and blew her nose delicately on a lace handkerchief.

They both glanced toward the closed door. "How long will she sleep, do you know?" He asked.

"Several hours — when she wakes, we must get her to take some soup."

"I will wait," he said reluctantly. "After I see Marie, I think a bath would be in order. I smell like horse."

CHAPTER TEN

"I consider myself somewhat of an expert on terrible husbands."

I awoke from my forced nap feeling groggy, ill and thirsty. I had no idea how long I'd slept this time. I was only thankful my sleep was dreamless. I realized I was not alone; there was a small, warm shape curled up next to me in the bed. When I cracked open my eyes and rubbed the bleary feeling from them, I saw that Marie had somehow toddled her way into Celestine's bedroom and was sleeping next to me. Watching her angelic little face, I felt a stab of guilt; I had been avoiding my own daughter along with everyone else since…since that horrible night. It was wrong of me, I knew. Marie did not understand what was the matter with her *maman*. To be honest, I wasn't certain I did, either. But it seemed as if I wasn't really present any longer; I felt dead inside, an observer rather than a participant in my own life. It was better than thinking, or remembering.

I rubbed Marie's back gently and leaned over to bury my nose in her tumble of spun-gold curls. She smelled so sweet, floral and baby-ish. When she woke and saw me watching her, she smiled widely and reached for me. I found myself hugging her almost fiercely, but it was the lost child I was thinking of as I held her. Was it a boy, as I suspected? Wouldn't Marie have loved a little brother to play with and care for? Sighing, I wondered how much she understood of what had happened. She had only a vague idea of what '*maman* is expecting another child' meant.

"*Maman*," she said brightly in her little-girl, bird-chirp voice, "*Papa* is home!" She was happy and vibrating with excitement, as though offering me a wonderful surprise.

My heart seemed to stop beating. "What?" I asked, feeling bewildered. I wasn't ready; it was too soon. When did he get here? What day was this? Was I expecting Erik to be home already? I did not want…

At that moment, without so much as a knock, the bedroom door opened. I knew who would be standing there, and I had to force myself to drag my eyes up. The large form of my spouse seemed to fill the doorway. He was dressed in his vineyard work clothes, hair pulled back with the leather cord. There were shadows under his eyes, and he looked tired. When his eyes met mine, I saw a flare of yearning in them; then it vanished into an unfathomable expression. I stared at him blankly; there suddenly existed between us a great looming distance, which seemed impossible to bridge.

123

Marie said brightly, "*Papa* brought me a doll! With hair like mine!" She tugged at one of her own blond curls.

"That is…that is nice, *Petite*," I said absently. My voice sounded rusty.

I struggled to sit up, pushing ineffectually at my tangled hair. It was odd, but I could not summon up any joy at seeing Erik again though I had been so anxious for his return only a few days before. I sent him a baleful glance, and whatever Erik saw in my eyes, it was enough to make his expression grow chill.

"I need to talk to you, Sylvie," he said quietly. "It is important. I will get the nurse to take Marie outside for a while." He paused, reached out carefully to ruffle her curls, and then he was gone.

I helped Marie to climb down to the floor, noticing as I moved how weak I felt. I peered at my wan reflection in Celestine's bedroom mirror. Was that me? How ill I looked! And I thought Erik's eyes looked tired! Absently I reached for Celestine's brush and began running it through my hair. I was shocked at how thin and pale I had become in such a short period of time. I turned away from the mirror in dismay, to see that Marie was watching me closely. I began brushing her hair too, forcing myself to behave as if I were a normal person.

"Come see my doll, *Maman*?" She asked hopefully.

"Soon."

"I missed *Papa*," she said confidingly. "I am glad he is home."

The nurse-maid came to collect Marie then, so I gave her a little kiss and sat down on the bed to wait for Erik. He was not long in coming, and right behind him was Berthé with a tray in her hands. I sighed resignedly. People were always trying to feed me.

"What is that?" I asked dully, while I watched her set the tray down on the side table. I was eyeing the tray as if there might be a live snake under the silver cover.

"Chicken soup, Madame," she responded. Smiling encouragingly, she withdrew, leaving me alone with my husband.

Erik lifted the cover to reveal a steaming bowl of creamy soup, and the fragrance of it filled the little room. He leaned over and smelled it appreciatively, and I was forcefully struck by the memory of seeing him do that many times in the past, when I was his cook.

He looked at me askance. "I have been informed that your appetite is poor, so I ordered this soup brought to you. It was made to your recipe, Sylvie, so you know it will be good. Eat it." It was a demand, not a request. I could tell by the sternness of his voice that he would not take no for an answer. Frowning, I took up the spoon and brought a little soup to my lips reluctantly. It tasted like dust, but I forced a swallow down.

Erik moved to stand a little away from the bed where I sat, and I was thankful he had not yet tried to touch me. I prayed he would not. He was watching me closely, however, so I forced down another small mouthful of soup. He drew a deep breath.

"I did not kill anybody, Sylvie, whatever you may think," he said bluntly and unexpectedly. "I did not break my promise to you." Startled, I almost dropped the spoon. It took me a few seconds to process what he had just said.

"But…we saw it in *Le Monde*…the diplomat was found…" I stuttered to a stop, staring at him uncomprehendingly. "That was what you went to Paris *for*, Erik. I do not understand."

"*Oui*, I know. But luck was with me that night. I went there fully intending to kill him. I wanted that pardon, Sylvie, and you know as well as I it was either that or hang. But when I got there, the man was already dead. He'd been stabbed. They have no idea who did it." Erik turned to the window as he spoke, lifting the curtain and staring into the distance. I shuddered, imagining what he had seen that night.

"But if you did not kill him, what of your pardon?" I demanded bitterly. "M. Moreau would not give it to you, would he?" The thought that M. Moreau had put us through all this for *nothing* made me feel sick inside.

In answer, Erik picked up an envelope that had been lying on the bedside table, near the tray. He held it for a moment, and then handed it to me. It was large and heavy. Slowly, my hands trembling a little, I fumbled to open the envelope and pulled out a folded piece of parchment. When I unfolded it, I saw there was a large official seal affixed to the bottom, next to the neat signature of President MacMahon. It was the pardon, and we were free.

"*Vous voyez*, Sylvie, I went to Moreau and told him I had done it, that I assassinated the man myself. He doesn't know any better, and he gave me the pardon without any questions." Erik paused and looked uncertainly at me. "It means I am no longer a wanted man. We don't have to hide anymore."

I carefully replaced the all-important document in the envelope and gave it back to him. Staring at the bowl of soup with loathing, I could think of very little to say. But I knew I must say something; Erik was waiting for me to do so.

"I only wish it never had to happen at all. I would rather none of this had happened. I am...glad for you, of course." My empty hand came to rest over my flat stomach with a small stroking motion. Erik's eyes followed the subtle movement, and then he made a sound, almost a hiss of sharply indrawn breath.

"Glad for me? What about...you blame me for the miscarriage, don't you? You think it was my fault." He sounded shocked. When I looked up at him, I saw his face had gone pale.

I stopped pretending to eat the now cool soup, pushing it away in disgust. "Of course I blame you. It *is* your fault. You know it is." I could see I had stunned him. But what could he expect?

"Sylvie," he began, his voice unsteady. I knew I had wounded him, and I didn't care. I did not care about anything.

"Please go now, Erik, and let me rest," I said quickly, to cut him off. I had to look away from him then, for the expression in his eyes was hard to bear. I climbed back into the bed, pulling the duvet over me. When I turned toward the room again, it was empty.

Erik

When Erik walked blindly out of the bedroom, he was not surprised to find Celestine in the hallway waiting for him. He realized she had been expecting something like this. But he hadn't. The homecoming he'd been dreaming about, imagining for days, had just evaporated before his eyes. He stood before his old friend, feeling gutted, and his whole body seemed to vibrate with emotion.

"She blames me," he whispered. "And she looks so..." his voice caught, and hot tears threatened to fall. Celestine put her arms around him and he found himself hugging her back, feeling idiotic and childlike in spite of the fact that he loomed over her delicate frame. Yet he felt comforted as well.

"I know, I know," she murmured. "It will pass; Dr. Olivier says it is common for a woman who has suffered such a loss not to be herself for a time. He called it a severe case of Melancholia. Some women have it worse than others, and apparently Sylvie's case is a bad one. He says we must be patient and it will eventually pass." She pulled away from him and continued, "She lost a great deal of blood, and it will take a few weeks to recover from that."

"But why won't she eat? She is so thin." He asked worriedly.

"I asked Dr. Olivier about that; he says a loss of appetite isn't unusual. He said if she doesn't start eating soon, to let him know." She frowned, knitting her brows together. "But I do not know what he can do that I have not tried," she added irritably. "Berthé, Mathilde… we have all tried."

Erik blotted his wet eyes with a sleeve. He drew in a long breath. Anger was suddenly coursing through him – anger at Moreau, at Christine whose actions set this nightmare in motion, at his own fragile and ill wife, for treating him this way. And at himself, for he knew in his heart Sylvie was right: it was his fault.

"I am going down to the wine cellars," he said, his voice taut with frustration.

Celestine plucked at his sleeve. "I have been so worried about Sylvie…for a while now. I think…I think myself there was something wrong with the baby."

Erik shot her a speaking glance as he moved toward the stairs. "Of course there was something wrong with the baby, Celestine. And we can both guess what that was." He frowned moodily. "Perhaps this was for the best." And then he was down the stairs and out the door, taking deep breaths of fresh air, the air of home. It had been his worst fear, and somehow, the loss of the baby seemed to confirm it. Could he bear to put Sylvie through this again?

It should not surprise him that Sylvie should take this loss so hard; after all, her greatest desire was to be a mother. Erik had never heard of Melancholia, but it sounded much worse than simply saying she was grieving for her loss. His boots crunched on the gravel drive as he strode down the hill.

The first person he saw as he approached the winery operations was Robert. His heart sank; Robert probably hated him now, too. The old curmudgeon had always been so protective of Sylvie. Limping noticeably, Robert saw Erik coming toward him and came to a stop, staring. Robert's vest was splotched with purplish-red stains, so Erik surmised he was checking on the red variety fermenting in oak barrels.

"You are back, Master?" Robert asked, looking incredulous. Always one for stating the obvious, Erik thought wryly. He spread his arms out from his sides.

"As you see, Robert. I arrived a little over an hour ago."

127

"You've seen Madame, then? You know what happened?" Robert asked almost reluctantly, his expression pained. Erik nodded without speaking, and Robert went on, "It was a terrible thing, Master. It happened in the middle of the night, Madame Giry says." He gazed up at Erik anxiously. "How is she today?" Obviously, Robert was not inquiring about Madame Giry.

"Resting," he answered shortly.

"Ah," said Robert. Pulling out a large handkerchief, he began wiping his hands with it, and then the back of his sun-brown neck. When he glanced up again there appeared to be a slight twinkle in his eyes.

"I am no Monarchist, me," he continued as if they had been discussing this all along. "Seems as though things are fine the way they are nowadays. One less King-lover won't be missed, is what I say. Look at the mess the last one got us in to." With that pronouncement, Robert touched his cap and went on his slow way. A little further on, Erik glimpsed one of the workers start up the path toward them, catch sight of Robert heading his way, and quickly duck back and vanish. In spite of everything, he found his lips curving into a smile. It was good to be home.

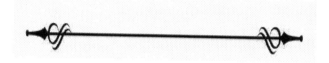

I knew I could not remain in Celestine's bedroom any longer; it wasn't fair to put her out of her own bed. The idea of returning to my own (*our* own) bedroom was repugnant to me, however. Although I knew that the room had been thoroughly cleaned, and a new mattress had replaced the old one, in my imagination I still saw it covered in blood. It was the place where I lost my baby, my Stèphane. And there was the other problem, which I did not wish to examine too closely: Erik was sleeping in that room, in that bed. He wanted me to return to our room, but I was not ready. I wasn't certain if I would ever be ready.

I caused our guestroom to be made ready for me, and after Erik's return, I made it my bedroom. Located closer to the nursery but farther from our room, it was where Dr. Gaudet stayed whenever he came for his summer holiday. It was a small, cozy room with a bookcase full of medical and physiology books, a chess set, and other little things designed for his comfort. Dr. Gaudet was never happy without some comforting disorder around him. Erik was predictably angry when he learned I was going to use it as my bedroom.

I was still too weak to pack things for myself, so I sent a housemaid to retrieve some of my nightclothes and bring them along. Erik came instead, bristling with indignation. I was sitting on the edge of the bed, playing idly with some fringed trim on the pillow and staring into space. I looked up as he came in, and as he met my eyes I could see the anger dissolve and concern take its place. I almost preferred the anger.

"Is it the bedroom, or is it me?" He demanded bluntly, his voice low and rough. I lowered my eyes and contemplated the bit of fringe. It was shiny and rather pretty. I enjoyed running my fingers over it; it was hypnotically soothing somehow. The silence stretched out while I considered his question.

"Both, I suppose," I answered finally. "I need…I just need time to rest. I do not want to go in that room again." My voice sank to a whisper. "I can't."

Before I knew it, Erik was kneeling next to me. He took my hand in his, pulling my restless fingers away from the fringe.

"I cannot bear to see you like this, Sylvie. I want to take care of you. I want to help if I can." He paused, perhaps waiting for me to make some response, but I could not think what to say.

"Please, Sylvie, look at me."

I pulled my cold hand out of his warm one and made a project of arranging the folds of my dressing gown. Finally I raised my eyes to his. He flinched a little.

"Will you tell me what happened?" He asked gently. I stared at him in burgeoning alarm.

"No! No; I…I don't really remember," I murmured. My fingers plucked at the fringe again. If I didn't think about it, if I kept everything neatly locked away, I would be alright. This not feeling things, I rather liked it. I had always felt things *too* much. I was like an empty vessel now.

Slowly Erik rose and stood looking down at me. I could feel the weight of his gaze on my head, but I could not bring myself to look at him again.

"I love you, Kitten, and I know you are not well," he said at last. "But I won't allow you to stay in this room forever." After a moment, I heard the door close after him, and I was alone again. That was good. When the maid came in with an armful of my things a few minutes later, I was still sitting in the same place, staring out at nothing, playing with the bit of fringe.

"Shall I bring you some tea, Madame?" She hesitantly asked when she had finished putting the clothing away.

"*Oui, Merci.* That sounds nice," I replied. After she left, I went to the *armoire* and retrieved a nightgown. By the time she returned, I was in bed, asleep. At least I assume I was, for the tea was quite cold when I awoke later.

I slept a great deal every day, *en fait*, after…my loss. Sleep was a blessed escape for me, but also I was exhausted all the time. I wondered how long I would feel this way. It was so unlike me. When I was awake, I felt as if I were wrapped up in cotton wool, only dimly perceiving life going on around me. I was ridiculously weak, to the point where I could not go downstairs and expect to climb back up again. This I learned the hard way, when I ventured downstairs only a few days after Erik's return so I could sit a while and see the garden outside. I did not really care very much about the garden, but it was something to do.

Celestine was glad to see me out of bed and downstairs, and she fussed over me relentlessly. But when it came time to mount the stairs again, I managed to get up three of them before I felt my head spin and I abruptly sat down on the tread.

Erik was beside me in a flash, no doubt summoned by Celestine.

"What is the matter?" He asked worriedly.

I shook my head in frustration. "I cannot get back upstairs. I am still too weak. I should not have…" before I could complete my sentence, I gasped as I felt him lift me up in his arms.

"Damn it," he muttered crossly. "You ought to have called for me to help you." He started up the stairs carefully. He turned his head to look at me, and I could not speak for a moment. I was filled with discomfort at the sight of his melancholy face so close to mine. I found myself looking away. It was too much, this physical closeness.

Erik carried me gently upstairs and down the hallway to my room. Hefting me in his arms as though testing my weight, he said in a disapproving tone,

"You are as light as a feather, Sylvie. I am not even breathing hard." And he wasn't. "Next time you wish to come downstairs, you need to let me help you back up."

Carefully he set me down on the side of the bed, and I sighed with relief. I felt immensely tired all at once. I started to reach down with trembling hands to remove my slippers, but to my surprise Erik knelt and performed the task for me. His hands were gentle. When he finished he sat back on his haunches and looked up into my face. His expression turned hard.

130

"How much longer will you continue to punish me, Sylvie?" He asked. I felt my mouth fall open in shock. Was that what he thought I was doing? *Was* that what I was doing? I frowned, not wishing to examine myself too closely.

"I...I do not know," I said finally, truthfully.

Erik's mouth set in a thin, firm line, a sure sign that he was vexed.

"Sylvie, I am sorry you lost the baby. I know you think it is my fault, but we don't know that for certain. It could just as easily have been something to do with you." With those cruel words, he rose and left the room, closing the door quietly behind him. I stared at the closed door for several seconds, while all sorts of rejoinders crossed my mind. Why had he said such a thing? It *was* his fault, and there was nothing to be gained by trying to blame *me*.

Erik

A month had passed since his return, and spring was giving way to summer. The sunflowers were growing in the fields, and tiny grapes were beginning to form. Erik thought that Sylvie was showing some improvement in little ways. She ate a bit more, and was able to mount the stairs without help. She behaved toward Marie as she always had, doting and affectionate. But she refused to return to their bedroom, and she avoided interacting with him unless someone else was also present. He regretted what he had said to her in the heat of anger, for he knew it only served to drive the wedge between them even deeper, but he refused to apologize to her.

He knew something was terribly wrong with her, something other than physical, and Erik felt helpless to do anything about it. He had summoned Dr. Olivier back to the *château* demanding that he do something to help Sylvie. Other than murmuring some platitudes and suggesting that she get more fresh air, he was no help at all. It was the Melancholia, Dr. Olivier explained, and 'Give her time', was all he could advise. Erik was entirely sick of hearing that phrase.

The spirited, brave, fascinating woman he had married was like a vacant house. Behind her lifeless eyes the windows were closed. She was

131

dulled, dimmed, absent. It drove him mad with frustration and he often used anger to conceal the real fears he had for her. It helped to work, and he threw himself into vineyard work and whatever else needed doing on the property. One day he even found himself digging post holes for a new fence. But Sylvie was never far from his troubled thoughts. What was the matter with her? He did not know how much more he could take. One afternoon, driven to his limits by her lifeless behavior at luncheon, he could not help but confront her as she slowly ascended the stairs to lie down.

"How much longer is this going to go on, Sylvie?" Erik demanded fiercely. Sylvie turned and gazed calmly down at him. Her preternatural calm was another thing that drove him mad.

"What do you mean?" she asked, sounding mildly puzzled. Frustrated, he flung his arms out wide.

"Isn't it obvious?" He growled. "You are avoiding me. We never talk any more. We haven't talked privately since my return from Paris."

She stared at him blankly, as though he were some peculiar stranger. "What do you want to talk to me about?" She asked.

Erik wanted to shout at her. Instead he took a deep calming breath and said, "You haven't asked me about the hospital, or Father Barbier. You don't seem interested in what happened to me while I was gone." He had been looking forward to telling her about his wild ride on the steam carriage. Sylvie's expression turned strangely cold as she listened to him.

"No, I suppose I haven't given much thought to that. I have been rather preoccupied, you see, with what happened to me here while you were gone." Her voice was bitter, angry, and she turned away from him and continued up the stairs. Stung by her words and frigid demeanor, Erik swore silently under his breath. She was never going to forgive him, apparently.

"I want you back in my bed!" He heard himself shout angrily. That wasn't what he intended to say, but it was foremost in his mind. Of course he wanted that, he wanted – craved - the heart-and-soul intimacy that had been theirs until such a short time ago. But he wasn't going to beg her for it.

Sylvie froze on the stairs, one hand gripping the banister tightly until her fingers went white.

"Is that all you can think about?" She hissed furiously. "Leave me alone!" And she was gone; lifting her skirts in both hands, she ascended the stairs as fast as she could and disappeared down the corridor.

Erik was left standing alone at the bottom of the staircase, mouth open, staring after her. In about five seconds, he was so searingly, blindingly furious it felt like he might spontaneously combust. He longed for someone to kill, preferably with his bare hands. And there was a part of him, the

132

untamed, feral part of him, that wanted nothing more than to go after his wife, follow her into her room and force himself on her. How dare she? How dare she deny him her bed? She had no right to refuse him. He would go to her right now, and…" He rubbed his hand over his face, groaning.

The tantalizing thought of lying with her made him hot all over, and in a flash another overwhelming emotion had replaced the anger: raging desire. But he would not ravish his own wife; it would only give her another reason to hate him. Besides, Dr. Olivier had yet to say it was safe for Sylvie to resume marital relations. Slowly Erik turned and went back outside. He found himself at the stables near the house, and here he dunked his entire head into a trough of water and came up dripping. He still wanted to kill someone, so he decided to go and take it out on Robert.

CHAPTER ELEVEN

"Too much self-inspection is bad for the soul."

I wasn't proud of my behavior, Reader. I knew full well it was petty and small of me to treat my husband in such a way. But it was only later, when time had done its work of healing, that I realized I was punishing Erik for the fact that I'd lost my baby. I refused to acknowledge that there might be some other, unrelated reason. But at the time, all I could think of was how everything was his fault. I suppose I needed to find someone to fix the blame on, and he was a very large and convenient target.

When I reached the bedroom after that dreadful exchange on the staircase, I expected I would indulge in a fit of weeping. It seemed imminent, after the hurtful things I had said to Erik, and he to me. But to my surprise, I felt nothing at all. Not even mild irritation. On some level, I knew this could not be right. On the other hand, this strange cottony insulation kept other, more painful feelings safely away. I decided not to investigate my inner workings too closely. Instead, I donned a soft nightgown and went to bed.

After a nice nap, I spent time with Marie in the nursery, helping her stack brightly lettered blocks (it must be a coincidence that the blocks spelled out 'doll', I thought to myself). Then she would not be satisfied unless I listened to her 'play' her miniature piano. I knew it would not be long before Erik would begin giving her official lessons, for she certainly possessed an aptitude for music.

I often regretted my complete lack of musical talent, but at least Marie had it. Obviously, she had inherited that from her father, not me. My mother loved music and played the pianoforte, but her abilities passed right over me. One always tends to over-estimate the talents of one's own children, but even so as I listened to Marie I thought she was a veritable prodigy. After this peaceful and pleasant interlude, I went back downstairs for tea with Celestine in my sitting room.

I did not want to tell her about my painful fight with Erik, so we kept to safe topics. There were fewer of those now, for I refused to look at the newspaper any longer and I did not care about the fashion pages. Today our cook had placed some *madeleines* on a pretty dish to go with the tea, knowing I liked them, and I could not resist dipping one or two into my cup. They were delicious.

And then Erik walked in. His hair looked slightly damp, as though he had just come from taking a bath.

Before I could feel the hot blush spreading across my cheeks, he spoke somewhat brusquely.

"The footman just brought me this." I saw that he was holding a telegram in his hand. He did not exactly meet my eyes, but rather glanced between Celestine and I. The memory of our recent exchange must be on his mind as well.

"A telegram?" I exclaimed, feeling a vague amount of interest. "Who is it from?" Suddenly a horrible thought came to me and I felt myself go pale. "It is not from Dr. Gaudet, is it?" I asked in trepidation. What if something had happened to Father Barbier? And I had not even bothered to ask Erik about him. The thought made me feel small.

Erik frowned, and I could see the same concern cross his face.

"I do not know; I haven't opened it yet." He tore open the thin blue paper and read the brief message while I waited with pent breath. A peculiarly blank expression appeared on his face, rapidly followed by a glower of annoyance. "*Sacré!*" He exclaimed. "I had forgotten about the Arlingtons!"

"Who are the Arlingtons?" Celestine and I asked at the same time, both of us sounding perplexed. I had never heard the name before, but it did not sound French to me.

Instead of answering at once, Erik looked at me helplessly. I watched a variety of expressions cross his face. Irritability gave way to chagrin, and finally embarrassment. Who were these people, that they could elicit such a reaction from Erik?

"Well?" I prompted curiously. Erik moved further into the room rather reluctantly I thought, and sat down, staring at the telegram as though he hoped the writing on it might alter.

"I met them while I was staying with Philippe at the hospital," he said slowly. "Philippe arranged a dinner so that I could meet them…him. Dr. Arlington is an American surgeon. He was in Paris to give a lecture."

"I see," I murmured, not seeing at all. "Why did Dr. Gaudet want you to meet, I wonder?"

There was a pause. "Dr. Arlington specializes in what is called plastic operations. He has a clinic in New York where he repairs the faces of soldiers injured in their war." Out of the corner of my eye, I saw Celestine sit up a little straighter on the *settee*.

"What does the telegram say?" She asked, fixing Erik with a gimlet eye.

Erik looked directly at me as he answered her question. "I...I invited them...him...to stop here on their way back from their holiday in the south of France." He paused, watching my face closely. "I am interested in speaking with Dr. Arlington further. He told me that if I came back with them to New York, he could make me a much better mask. It would be more natural-looking. *Et aussi*, he thinks his surgical techniques might improve my...appearance." His words fell like stones into a still pool.

"*What?*" I cried, astounded at this revelation. I leapt to my feet, and stood glaring down at him. "Why did you not tell me about this before?"

Erik gave me a speaking glance. "Because you had no interest in what happened to me in Paris, remember?" He answered acidly. "And besides, I had other things on my mind." I sank slowly back down on the *settee*. I felt my mouth open and close twice but nothing came out. Much as I hated to admit it, he was right, and I was rendered speechless. Not so Celestine.

"When do they arrive?" She asked briskly. "I must get rooms ready and order in more food." I suspected what she really wanted was to leave the room before the fight she sensed brewing between us exploded while she was still there. Erik gave her the telegram.

"They are apparently in Sarlat as we speak. They would like to know if tomorrow would be convenient." Erik answered flatly. He looked penitently at me. "I am sorry, Sylvie. I had forgotten all about Dr. Arlington. The timing is atrocious, I know."

Ignoring his half-hearted apology, I asked, "Who is 'they'? Is the doctor traveling with his valet?"

There was a minute pause before he answered. "*Non.* His daughter is accompanying him on his trip to France."

Celestine, already at the door, turned back. "His daughter? I was going to put Dr. Arlington in the downstairs bedroom suite. I wonder if she has a nursemaid with her." I could see her mentally ticking off what few extra rooms were downstairs.

Erik made a derisive sound. "No, Celestine, she is not travelling with a nursemaid. Edythe Arlington looks to be in her early twenties, and quite independent."

Now I do not pretend to know a great deal, Reader, but I do know my own husband. And while he was discussing the doctor's daughter he appeared uncomfortable, but he was trying to conceal it. Something about her discomfited him. I wondered what it was. It was of no matter now, for apparently we were about to have houseguests and there was much to be done. I rose, therefore, and straightened my skirts.

136

"Do you know how long they plan to stay with us?" I asked, not doing a particularly good job of concealing my vexation. It was an extreme understatement that this was not a good time to be entertaining strangers. Why could he not have warned us they would be coming? But I supposed he really *had* forgotten, what with everything that had happened upon his return. It wasn't fair for me to be upset with him about that as well.

"I do not know; it was never discussed. I only spent the one evening with them and Philippe. However," he paused, looking pained. "I intend to tell Dr. Arlington that you are ill and they must shorten their stay. A few days at the most."

"*Bien*, I will send the footman back to the village to let them know tomorrow is fine," I said, and left the room after Celestine. She had already taken herself off, no doubt to track down a housemaid with orders about airing out the guestrooms and finding clean sheets. I had no wish to be alone with Erik, for the uncomfortable memory of that heated conversation on the stairs still rang in my ears. And I must admit, I was so thunderstruck by his news that I needed to be alone to think about it.

After speaking to the cook and dispatching the footman with a shopping list and a message to deliver to our impending guests, I went back upstairs to my bedroom and sat on the side of the bed, pondering Erik's sudden revelation. I must acknowledge it had hit me like a bolt from the blue. I assumed that after all this time he had come to terms with his facial disfigurement, made peace with his appearance. But now, thanks to Dr. Gaudet (I scowled, wishing he had stayed out of it), Erik had been introduced to someone who might actually be in a position to offer him help.

I rose and went to the window, opening it and letting in the warm afternoon air of early summer. Leaning my elbows on the windowsill, I stared out, but I was blind to the beautiful view. I was thinking of Erik's face. I preferred my husband just as he was. I had always been thankful for his hideous visage, for I knew in my heart that if Erik had been born without it, his stunning good looks and genius for music and many other things would have made it possible for him to have any woman he wished. He would not have even met me, let alone choose *me* from among the many beautiful and interesting women who would want him. He would be so far above me, it was laughable.

What if this possible surgery improved his appearance to such an extent that he looked…almost normal? Would he still want me? A sigh escaped me then. Why should he want *me*, when I did not want *him*? Suddenly I felt overwhelmingly tired; how was I to manage when these strangers descended upon us tomorrow? I turned back to the bed and crawled under the covers gratefully. Thank goodness for Celestine, I thought as my eyelids drifted closed.

By the time our guests arrived the next day it was nearly teatime. I was thankful for the lateness of their arrival, for it gave Celestine and the household staff enough time to prepare rooms and stock the kitchen with necessary comestibles and wine. I was not much help in this regard, so I remained cloistered in the nursery with Marie in order to keep her out from under foot.

I was downstairs when the Arlingtons came rolling up in an elegant travelling coach pulled by four horses and driven by a smartly liveried coachman. It seemed a bit ostentatious to me. The need for such a large conveyance for only two people was readily apparent: the back and top of the coach were piled with boxes and trunks.

Erik was on the front step to meet them, as was only right considering they were his guests, but I thought he looked wary rather than pleased to see them. He was standing straight and unsmiling as the coach rolled to a stop. I noticed he had changed from his work attire into an elegant suit and waistcoat, a costume which always becomes his manly form.

I remained standing forlornly in the doorway. Though I had rested a good part of the day and managed to make myself fairly presentable, I was only too aware of my wan face and thin frame. For some inexplicable reason, one of the effects of my troubled pregnancy was a thinning of my hair. Usually thick and honey-colored, my locks were now noticeably thinner and drab-looking. Self-consciously I tucked a stray lock behind my ear.

The coachman descended and placed a step beneath the coach door. The first person to come out was obviously Dr. Arlington. I did not know what to expect an American physician to look like; I knew from Erik's brief explanation the previous evening that he had served on the side of the north in that country's civil war as a battlefield surgeon. I suppose I thought Dr. Arlington might look like photographs I had seen of General Robert E. Lee, sporting a full beard. This gentleman, however, was rather thin and reedy, and as he stood next to the carriage door I saw he had a slight stoop, as if he were carrying an invisible burden on his shoulders. He turned to assist the other occupant of the carriage out; this was rather a production, for her skirts were vast.

I beheld Edythe Arlington for the first time as she emerged from their coach and shook out an impractical traveling costume covered with lace and flounces and rather too low-cut for day wear. I did not know it at the time, *bien sûr*, but it was my first glimpse of the person who was to become my worst enemy. In fact, she already *was* my worst enemy, only I did not know it yet.

As my husband went down the steps and across the gravel to bow and shake hands with Dr. Arlington, I watched from the doorway as the young woman came to stand beside her father. She was but an inch or two shorter than he, and did not resemble him in any way. She was as dramatically vivid as he was faded. I could see that she was quite beautiful. Perhaps, I mused, she took after her mother.

She pulled a wide-brimmed hat from her head and began fanning herself with it, all the while looking into Erik's face with what could only be called a flirtatious smile. She was, I noticed, almost of a height to him. Something about her…several things, actually, reminded me of the Comtesse deChagny.

Erik was welcoming them and there were smiles all around, but I noticed that his attention was all for the doctor. He seemed to be trying to avoid interacting with Miss Arlington. It occurred to me that something must have happened between them during that dinner in Paris. I wondered what it was. Then my breath caught as she playfully swatted Erik on the chest with her hat in order to secure his attention. It was a blatantly flirtatious gesture. She said something to him, something amusing obviously, and I saw his eyes meet hers and a smile cross his face. He murmured something in return that brought an answering curve to her lips and then turned toward the house with a gesture of invitation.

They were coming toward me. I knew I ought to smile and come forward to make them welcome like a proper hostess, but instead I stood frozen in place, almost helplessly. Who were these people? Why were they intruding into my life? A feeling of uneasiness stole over me as I watched their approach, glancing around them at the *château* and grounds interestedly as they did so.

When Erik introduced me to Dr. Arlington, the American placed a pair of gold spectacles on his eyes before sweeping over me in a brief but thorough visual examination. Then he bowed over my hand. I recognized that look as purely professional in nature; as I knew from my own dear departed father, once a physician, always a physician. Dr. Arlington's voice was soft and there was something rather shy and kindly about him. He spoke French quite well, and I found I rather liked his flat American accent.

When his daughter stood before me, I had to look up in order to see her face. She was tall and slender, with a dark mass of hair piled on her head and curls spilling down the sides. Her black eyes surveyed me coolly. I thought I detected amusement lurking in them for some unknown reason.

"So this is Mrs. Bessette," she said, also speaking excellent French but with that peculiar accent. "I cannot tell you how pleased I am to meet you at last." Miss Arlington looked me over much as her father had, and then she smiled in a self-satisfied way. She slanted her head to look askance at Erik, and there was something sly and almost cat-like about her at that moment. In the quick glimpse I stole of *his* face, he was suddenly wearing a distinct scowl.

It was with great relief that I observed Celestine coming toward us in the foyer. I went through the proper motions of performing introductions, and suggested she show the Arlingtons to their rooms to freshen up before tea. She and I had both agreed that my sitting room would be the best place for this amiable interlude. It was comfortable and afforded the best view. After they departed with Celestine, Erik and I found ourselves standing alone together in the foyer. I looked inquiringly at him.

"Miss Arlington is quite lovely," I murmured. Erik scowled yet again.

"Is she? I hadn't noticed," was his completely untruthful response.

"She seems a bit forward." I added thoughtfully. We turned and began walking slowly toward my sitting room. I heard him snort softly.

"That scarcely begins to describe it. She is a rude, vulgar American." He said firmly. "I do not like her." Was he trying to convince me, or himself?

"Her father seems nice, however." I conceded.

At these words Erik said earnestly, "He is, Sylvie. He is completely devoted to his work and to helping people."

By this time we were in the sitting room, and automatically I went about fluffing cushions, checking the flowers were fresh and straightening what little disorder there was in this much lived-in room.

"And you hope he will be able to help *you*, do you not?" I asked.

"*Oui*, I told you that already. While he is here we will discuss it further. I have not yet made up my mind." He was standing in the middle of the room, watching me as I moved about. Seeing there was nothing more to do, I seated myself and arranged my skirts. A thought occurred to me, and I frowned.

"Erik, when they return to America is it your intention to go with them?" There was a brief, tense pause before he answered.

"I am leaning strongly in that direction. Would you object to my going?" Did I detect a challenge in his voice? We gazed at one another for a long moment, his eyes cool. I could make no reply to his question, and his lips set in a thin line of displeasure. My eyes dropped to my lap.

In the heavy silence that followed this fraught exchange, came the welcome interruption of Berthé and the rattling tea cart. Erik opened the door for her, and she smiled shyly at him. I saw that Celestine had ordered both coffee and tea for our guests, something I would not have thought to do. Being Americans, I had no clue which they might prefer. The cart was loaded with various delectibles like little crustless sandwiches, an assortment of delicate tarts and thin slices of cake.

"*Merci*, Berthé; that looks lovely." I only wished I had any appetite for the food, but I found that the misgivings I felt about our guests and their purpose here had taken my appetite away.

A few minutes later Celestine entered, escorting Dr. and Miss Arlington, who followed her into the room. Both had changed into fresh attire and Miss Arlington was now wearing a deep green dress cut *en princesse* that nipped in at the waist before flaring into draping skirts. Her thick black hair was caught up in an artfully arranged mass atop her head. Around her neck she wore a gold chain from which was suspended a large emerald. The square-cut stone nestled between her artificially plumped bosom, rather obviously I thought. I had to admit, however, that she looked positively regal, if a bit overdressed for afternoon tea. Her father was dressed much more conservatively, in a black suit and an odd little neck tie that looked like black ribbon. It must be some peculiar American fashion.

I felt my hackles rise as I watched the American girl deftly, efficiently but ever so innocently arrange it so that she was seated on the *settee* next to Erik. He looked as though he was not sure how he ended up there, but I saw how she beckoned as if to speak to him and then pulled him down beside her and quickly claimed his attention. By the time he looked around for a chair, they were all taken.

I might be feeling somewhat ambivalent toward my husband at the moment, but he was still my husband. I could not suppress a small flare of jealousy as I watched her attentions toward Erik. It was perfectly clear to me, and probably to him as well, that she had amorous designs on him. This explained his reluctance to remain in close proximity to her. But was it purely self-interest on her part, a real attraction to him, or was she only trying to draw Erik to her father's clinic as a potential client? Only time would tell.

Needless to say, I did not let my cogitations and concerns interfere with my duties as a hostess. With Celestine's help, I dispensed coffee and tea and passed the platter of *petite* sandwiches around. Once the formalities were attended to, I turned to Dr. Arlington and inquired about their journey through France and what sights they had seen. Before he could even open his mouth to reply, Miss Arlington, having declined anything to eat, began a spirited account of their travels. A demure and retiring *mademoiselle* she was not.

It was obvious that she was primarily interested in keeping Erik's attention fixed upon herself, for she scarcely took her eyes from him as she talked amusingly about their journey and the places they had seen in the south of France. Dr. Arlington leaned toward me confidentially.

"I cannot help but observe that you are not in the full bloom of health, Mrs. Bessette," he said in his gentle but oddly accented French. "While I am staying under your roof, I would be happy to assist you in any way."

Unfortunately, his quiet words happened to fall into a little lull in the conversation, and I became aware that all eyes, especially Erik's, were abruptly drawn toward me. I felt my cheeks glow.

"I…I have not been well, that is true. But I hope I am on the mend now," I replied, not meeting the doctor's probing eyes.

"Is that so?" Miss Arlington said waspishly. "That must explain why you appear so washed out and tired. I am so sorry for our inconveniencing you by this visit, Mrs. Bessette." She finished with a sweet, horribly artificial smile.

It was a good thing Miss Arlington could not see Erik's face at that moment. He looked as though he was only seconds away from strangling her. Celestine's eyes were flashing blue fire.

"Edythe!" Her father, sounding appalled, began to remonstrate. Miss Arlington turned appealingly toward him.

"But I was merely confirming your diagnosis, Father! I meant no disparagement, I assure you." She turned with a fluttering of her long lashes, not to me, but to Erik. "You see, I have spent so much time assisting my father, I have become perhaps a bit too…"

"Insensitive?" Erik snapped, scowling at her.

"But no…I was going to say, perhaps a bit too clinical." She turned to me then, saying "you take no offense; I am sure, Mrs. Bessette." She bared her teeth at me in a parody of a smile.

I did not deign to give her any reply; probably for the best for I was seething with anger. Instead I rose stiffly from my seat and turned to Dr. Arlington, who was clearly discomfited by his daughter's rudeness.

142

"En fait, I am not yet strong enough to spend much time with you, Doctor, so I will retire to rest before supper," I said, my voice remarkably steady. "I hope you will make yourself comfortable here. If there is anything you require, please tell Celestine and she will be happy to help you." I turned and glared down at Edythe Arlington.

"You see, Miss Arlington, I have but recently suffered a miscarriage." With my head held high, I walked out of the room with a swish of skirts. As the door closed behind me I heard Erik utter a choice swear word, Dr. Arlington begin to scold his daughter, and Celestine hastily inquiring if anyone wanted more coffee. In short, everyone began talking at once.

It wasn't exactly a lie that I required rest, for sometimes it felt as though I would never regain my strength. I could not yet move with my customary briskness, nor ascend the staircase with ease. So it was that I had just reached the stairs when I heard the sound of someone approaching me from behind.

The rustle of silk announced Celestine, no doubt coming to check on me. Imagine my surprise when I glanced behind and saw Edythe Arlington walking up to me. I had gained the first step, and there I stopped, eye to eye with her. She could not conceal the challenge in those snapping black eyes, but then her gaze fell, and she bit her lower lip contritely.

"I am to make my apologies, Mrs. Bessette, for my rudeness a moment ago," she said in her low, melodic voice. She returned her eyes to mine, and studied me speculatively. "I was surprised, is all," Miss Arlington continued, her voice losing its note of contrition. "I had rather expected that, since Mr. Bessette appears to be such a manly, virile sort, his wife would match him in strength. Instead...." Her chin lifted as she spoke, and she gave me a taunting smile.

I felt my own not unsubstantial chin go up as well. "Is that the way Americans apologize to someone? I cannot say it is very effective."

Edythe laughed a little, and looked chagrinned. "No, it wasn't, was it. Do forgive me for being so bold. I have always been an outspoken girl."

"No doubt. I can assure you, Miss Arlington, that when I am in health I am certainly the match for my husband. You are not exactly seeing me at my best." I tilted my head and pursed my lips thoughtfully, before adding, "While you are with us, you should ask Erik to tell you who he really is. You may find the information...edifying." With that, I turned from her and made my rather slow but dignified way up the stairs. All the way up, I could feel Edythe Arlington's dark malignant gaze on my back.

CHAPTER TWELVE

"You do not always behave like a lady."

The gauntlet had well and truly been thrown down. Between Miss Arlington and I, there would be no misunderstanding each other. I was not certain about Erik, however; he appeared quite obtuse as to the nature of her attentions to him, or at least was trying to appear obtuse. It occurred to me that his lack of experience with the female sex might make it difficult for him to see what she was about. One thing I knew for certain: Miss Arlington might be lovely, but her behavior and boldness would never endear her to Erik.

Resting in my room, I turned over in my mind the afternoon and Miss Arlington's behavior. Never in my life had I been exposed to someone like her, so bold and determined to get her way, nor so unscrupulous in her methods. The entire interaction seemed to me to be unreal, like a conversation one has in a dream.

After I stripped off my gown and underthings and put on a nightgown, I slipped into bed and lay for some time thinking. What if Miss Arlington's interest in Erik was quite genuine, and nothing whatsoever connected with her father and his clinic? My husband was, *après tout*, a striking man, as virile and manly as she described him. Moreover, she had seen him without his mask, and appeared unconcerned. But not only that….

I sat up suddenly. An unpleasant thought had just occurred to me. If Erik were to go with them to America, and he decided to have the surgery I knew Dr. Arlington was trying to convince him to have, his would no longer be such a hideous visage. The improvement might be enough to remove any lingering concerns she might have over his appearance. I knew in my heart this fear was the real reason I did not want him to have the surgery.

Sighing, I reclined again and tried to sleep, but a nagging thought kept intruding on my rest. I was certain that Edythe Arlington had her sights set on taking Erik away from me, but *why*? Why did she want him so badly? She barely knew him; they had spent one evening together over dinner with Dr. Gaudet and her father. Erik was a virtual stranger to her. It troubled me, for somehow I knew in my heart this was no passing fancy on her part; no wish for a casual dalliance with a dangerous and attractive man. She wanted him for herself.

One thing I recognized about myself, though. The arrival of Miss Arlington coincided with my long-suppressed emotions returning. It would appear that green fire was thawing me out.

She was strong, and I was weak. She was young and lovely, and I...well, the mirror told that sad tale. She was brash and bold and flirtatious, while I...was not. While Miss Arlington made eyes and sent her smoldering smiles toward my husband, I on the other hand treated him coldly, cruelly, pushing him away from me. I felt completely powerless to do anything to stop her. I found myself caught in a net of my own making, like a floundering fish, with no idea how to escape.

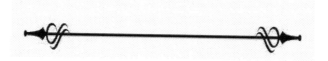

I remained cloistered upstairs until it was time to dress for dinner. I whiled away an hour in the nursery with Marie until Berthé came to assist me to bathe and dress. This time I took care to wear one of my most flattering gowns. It was a lovely blue-green silk with silver lace trimming caught up here and there by jeweled bows. Once, I could be assured upon seeing myself in the mirror while wearing it that I was looking my best. Not so today, however. The gown hung loosely on me, so Berthé found a white silk sash and tied it into a jaunty bow around my waist. That helped a little.

You understand, of course, Reader, why I was at pains to look the best I was able. I need not explain my motives. After arranging my hair, I thought of one last important detail to complete my *ensemble*. I sent Berthé to Erik's (and my) bedroom to fetch my diamond earrings from my jewel box. I owned very few jewels; my stunning heart-shaped ruby wedding ring of course, and a few old-fashioned pieces inherited from my mother.

On our first wedding anniversary, Erik had presented me with an exquisite pair of blue diamond earrings. The round middle stones were large and of a color similar to my own blue eyes, and surrounded by tiny sparkling white diamonds. Though I loved the earrings, I seldom wore them, for they were for more formal occasions. I felt certain that tonight's dinner would be one of those times. Once I had fastened the earrings on and examined my reflection in the mirror, I thought the blue stones seemed to bring out a bit of sparkle in my dull eyes.

A touch of perfume behind my ears and a little lip rouge completed my *toilette*, just as a peremptory knock on the door announced the arrival of

146

Erik to escort me downstairs to the dining room. When I opened the door to admit him, I saw that he was faultlessly attired in a dark evening suit with tailcoat; his long light brown hair was tied back with a strip of black velvet. My heart gave an unexpected leap of pleasure at the sight of him. He always ordered his clothing made to his specifications from a tailor in London, England. He preferred English tailoring and fabrics to French for some reason, and I could not deny they fit him well. He was a fine figure of a man, and I could certainly comprehend Edythe Arlington's interest in him. I had felt the same interest upon seeing him for the first time.

His eyes widened a little as he took in my appearance, and when he saw the diamond earrings, a look came into his expressive eyes that I did not really understand. They seemed to glow for a moment.

"You look lovely, Kitten," he said in a low voice. I felt a faint blush warm my cheeks.

"So do you," I murmured, looking down, feeling unaccountably shy.

"Are you ready?" He offered me his wool-clad arm and I took it.

"*Oui*, I am ready."

Stopping suddenly in the hallway, Erik paused and looked down at me, his expression serious. "That was unconscionable, the way Miss Arlington spoke to you this afternoon. I trust she made her apology to you? I insisted that she do so. I made it clear to her that I was quite displeased." I felt the muscle bunch up under his arm as he spoke, revealing the extent of his displeasure. It was never a good thing when Erik was displeased. I glanced up serenely into his face and smiled a little.

"Oh yes, she apologized to me," I replied truthfully.

"*Très bien*. Otherwise, I would have some choice words for her tonight." He responded, sounding vexed.

"I probably should tell you..." I said hesitatingly. "Do not be surprised if she asks you some time...who you really are."

"Why would she ask me that?" He inquired curiously. I shrugged as casually as possible.

"There is no reason why she should not know; you are no longer a wanted criminal. It occurred to me that perhaps if she knew the truth about you..."

"Ah! You think that might put her off? *Dieu*! I hope so!" He said fervently. "I will be sure to tell her something particularly bloodcurdling if she asks me." He lifted my hand up from where it rested on his arm, raised it to his lips and kissed it before replacing it. "Thank you, Sylvie; that was well done." We smiled conspiratorially at each other, and I was warmed by the thought that at least in the matter of Miss Arlington, we were united together.

We descended the stairs, and as I gripped his arm for balance I was reminded of all the times when we first knew each other, that he would pluck my hand from his arm if I ever had the audacity to place it there. He disliked being touched in those days. How much had changed since then!

Downstairs, we proceeded to the dining room. I was not looking forward to it, but with Erik by my side, I felt brave enough to face Miss Arlington and her flashing eyes. I could not help but wonder what insulting things the brash American girl would say to me tonight. She had quite a malicious tongue, to be sure.

However, dinner went off quite well; everyone, including Miss Arlington, was making an effort to be on their best behavior. She was relatively quiet and subdued throughout the meal. Mathilde had excelled herself in the kitchen and everything was both delicious and lovely to look at. I was certain she was thrilled to have guests in the house for a change. The first course was a delicate white soup made with asparagus, served chilled. It was followed by a fish course, something we enjoyed on a regular basis since we were so close to the river. Finally, there was late season lamb, roasted to perfection. I actually enjoyed the food, all the while feeling a little stab of envy for Mathilde. I once cooked every bit as well, but cooking for such a large household would have been beyond my capabilities.

At the conclusion of the meal, Dr. Arlington politely and apologetically expressed a desire to speak with Erik in private. I felt ice settle in the pit of my stomach, for I knew they would discuss Erik's coming with them, and the surgery. Erik agreed promptly; standing, he excused himself and suggested they retire to the parlor we reserved for guests. His instant acquiescence to the doctor's request told me that he was anxious to have this conversation. Passing my chair at the table, he rested his hand for a brief moment on my shoulder. I watched them go with trepidation, until Miss Arlington claimed my attention back to her. I tore my eyes from Erik's retreating form reluctantly.

I saw that her gaze was fixed upon my left hand. My fingers were wrapped around the stem of my wine glass, where I had been toying with it fretfully.

"That is a beautiful ring," Miss Arlington said. "Did he give it to you?" She was staring intently at my wedding ring, the large, perfect heart-shaped ruby Erik had placed on my finger the day we wed.

"Yes, on our wedding day." I replied cautiously. She tilted her head to one side.

148

"May I see it please?" She asked. Slowly, somewhat grudgingly, I released my hold on my wine glass and lay my hand down flat on the tablecloth so she could see the ring more closely. Miss Arlington studied it in silence for a few seconds, her gaze hot and interested, and then she raised her eyes to mine.

"May I try it on?" She asked.

I gaped at her, not expecting such a rude question. I responded without conscious thought.

"*Absolument pas!*" I exclaimed, "It never leaves my hand."

Miss Arlington gave her head a toss, and it seemed to me she was trying to school her expression. "Oh never mind! I do not really like rubies, personally. I prefer diamonds. But it is just such a fine stone." She drained the last few drops of wine from her own glass and set it down decisively.

"I would love to meet your little daughter, Mrs. Bessette," she said in an abrupt change of topic, patting her full lips with her napkin and then setting it next to her plate. "Might we do that now?"

I acquiesced willingly, thinking perhaps Miss Arlington regretted all her rude remarks to me and peculiar interest in my ring, and now wished to extend an olive branch.

"*Bien sûr,*" I said, pushing back my chair. "The nursery is upstairs. Marie will be getting ready for bed, but I'm sure she will still be awake." We walked together to the staircase, and I was conscious all the while of how she towered over me.

We had just reached the top of the stairs and were starting down the hallway when she turned to me and said,

"I expect you lost your baby because of Mr. Bessette. The baby must have inherited his deformity, which I understand is something he was born with. I make no doubt that you cannot forgive him for such a thing. I am sure I could not." These words were not spoken with any smugness, or even a hint of maliciousness. They were spoken calmly, as though she were only discussing the weather. She then turned and continued down the hall toward the nursery. I stared after her, rigid with indignation, breathless at her audacity. Did she really think I could not see through her machinations?

There was no proper answer I could make, however; for had I not believed the same thing myself?

Erik

Although it was too warm for a fire, Erik lit all the candles to bring the comfortable masculine room to life, and began the soothing male ritual of cognac preparation. Remembering that Dr. Arlington had smoked a cigar in his hotel suite, Erik offered him one, as he always kept a few on hand for the occasional guest. Dr. Arlington declined the cigar tonight. Seated in leather wing chairs, the men sipped the warmed brandy in companionable silence for a few minutes.

Finally Dr. Arlington broke the silence. "My daughter and I will not trespass on your hospitality for very much longer. I can see that your wife is still recovering her strength and it must be a trial for her to have us here. Also, both Edythe and I miss my son, and we are anxious to see him again." He studied Erik before saying earnestly, "I would be very pleased if you would consider returning to New York with us when we depart. We sail on the Oceanic from Liverpool, England, and if you will join us, I shall wire ahead for a berth for you. I feel certain…I know…that I could help you, Mr. Bessette. The better mask is one thing, but if you could see our clinic, meet some of our patients and see what has already been done to help them, I think you would be convinced."

Erik felt himself already convinced to make the journey, but the idea of leaving Sylvie so soon, when she was still weak and fragile, filled him with unease. It would be weeks before she was strong enough for such an undertaking, but Erik worried that if he waited for her to recover so she could come with him, he might change his mind about the trip. He swirled the cognac around in the wide glass and abruptly turned the subject.

"You have a son, Doctor?" He inquired. This proved to be a good diversion, for Dr. Arlington's long, somber face lit up.

"Yes, Matthew. He is just turned seventeen, and still in school. He is at home in New York. He intends to follow in my footsteps and take up medicine for a career." The fatherly pride in his voice was evident. That was an emotion Erik could well understand.

Erik raised his glass in a little toast, saying, "I will introduce you to my daughter, Marie, *demain*. She is two years old."

It still amazed him at times to think of himself as a father. He adored his daughter, and in some inexplicable way, seemed to possess the ability to be a good father to her. He had no idea where that ability came from, given his own horrible childhood.

Since returning home from Paris, Erik had tried not to think about the lost child. It had been his child, too, and a part of him felt his own form of regret for the loss. He rose and went to the windows, pulling the curtains together to shut out the night. Standing with his back to the window, he said, "Sylvie was hoping the *enfant* she lost would be a boy. She already had a name picked out." He looked down at the floor, feeling suddenly embarrassed at talking like this to a virtual stranger. But Dr. Arlington merely asked,

"Is it known why she lost the baby, Mr. Bessette?"

Erik shook his head ruefully and went back to his chair, taking up the cognac again. "You may as well start calling me Erik, Doctor. I expect we will be together for some time if I come with you." He released a long breath and went on. "*Non*, to answer your question, we do not know. It might have been, it could have been..." he made a helpless gesture toward the disfigured side of his face.

Dr. Arlington looked a little uncomfortable. "That is possible, I suppose, but in many cases this can happen for no apparent reason."

"We will never know for certain, but I do know Sylvie was unwell from the first. With Marie, she was so healthy, and she never looked more beautiful. She was fine. But this time..." he shrugged and sketched a frustrated gesture with his hand. "She lost weight instead of gaining, and she was sick all the time. And to have her lose the baby while I was away...I just do not know if I can leave her now."

"I understand," Dr. Arlington said, stroking his thin goatee absently. "And I cannot blame you. Have you spoken to Mrs. Bessette about this yet?"

Erik did not want to admit that he had forgotten all about the Arlingtons until the day before they arrived. "*Bien*, when I arrived back home the miscarriage had just happened, so I did not mention it to her right away. I do not believe she is particularly receptive to the idea, nor is she well enough to accompany me."

"Of course. Well, we will remain here for perhaps two or three more days before we return to Paris, so there is still time to consider. Tell me, er, Erik, have you any questions about our procedures or the surgery? I would be happy to answer them. I imagine you must have questions."

Erik did, and for the rest of their time in the sitting room, they discussed surgical procedures and some of the reconstruction work Dr. Arlington and his partner Dr. Buck had already performed. Dr. Arlington produced a copy of his brochure and explained in detail the work that had been done to each man's face. It was fascinating, if rather disconcerting.

When they finally emerged, everyone else had gone to bed, so Erik escorted the doctor to his own bedroom door and bid him *bonne nuit*. Then he made the rounds of the house ensuring the outside doors were locked and all candles were extinguished, as he did every evening. He loved this nightly ritual; this house, this *château* and everything in it, was *his*. Then he went slowly upstairs. His thoughts were in a whirl, and he knew sleep would not come to him for a long time.

He found his restless feet had carried him to Sylvie's bedroom door. All was silent within; he supposed she was asleep at this hour. More than anything, he wished he could talk to her, talk everything over with her, but even though she seemed somewhat receptive to him now, there was still such a vast gulf between them. Of course he could simply open the door and go in, and a part of him wanted to do just that – but instead, Erik turned away and went to his own room, feeling lonely and bereft. Just as he closed the bedroom door behind him, he thought he heard the rustle of a woman's skirts and the soft sound of a footfall in the corridor.

"Celestine?" he called, thinking it must be she, but there was no answer. The corridor was empty; no one was there.

Erik (continued)

At breakfast the next morning it was obvious to all that Sylvie and Miss Arlington had taken a strong dislike to each other. Sylvie was cool and reserved toward the young woman, and Erik could not blame her, considering Edythe's inexplicably rude behavior toward his wife. Edythe, for her part, mostly ignored Sylvie and concentrated all her considerable but unwelcome charms upon himself. She was faintly polite to Celestine, but no doubt thought of her as a mere servant and not worth her attention. Dr. Arlington appeared oblivious to the awkward situation. He sat next to Sylvie at breakfast and kept a solicitous eye on her as she nibbled at a croissant and some soft fresh cheese.

It was going to be a beautiful summer day, so Erik suggested an afternoon carriage ride around the estate and surrounding area to show it to the Arlingtons. It would get everyone out of the house and get Edythe out of Sylvie's hair for a while. The Arlingtons were amenable to the idea, but to Erik's surprise, Sylvie stated quite firmly that she intended to join the party.

"Some fresh air will do me good," she insisted. "I will make certain I am well wrapped up." Dr. Arlington seemed pleased that she would join them, and agreed that a carriage ride on a nice day would do her no harm. For his part, Erik was relieved that she was coming along; having his wife with him ought to dim some of Edythe's enthusiasm. He did not miss the livid look the young woman shot Sylvie, however. He would have liked to box her ears.

They agreed to leave directly after the noonday meal. Erik went to the stables to prepare the one open carriage they owned, while Celestine bustled off to organize water bottles and blankets and other things the wanderers might need. As he was about to go out, he saw Sylvie out of the corner of his eye, watching him. Her troubled expression caught at his heart. She looked a little lost.

Turning back to her, he asked, "Will you walk to the stables with me, Sylvie?" He would be glad to have a few private moments with her, and fortunately she acquiesced.

"Thank you," she said breathlessly as they went down the path together. She took his arm, even though the ground was level. Erik slowed his steps to match hers.

"I must speak with you, Sylvie," he said as soon as they were well away from the door. Her wide blue eyes shot to his apprehensively.

"You mean to go with them, don't you?" She said softly.

"That is what I wished to talk with you about. I would like to go, but I won't leave you unless..." suddenly he was interrupted as a voice hailed them gaily from behind.

"May I join you?" It was Miss Arlington, of course. She was proving to be quite a pest. Erik scowled, cursing under his breath. Sylvie gave his arm a sympathetic squeeze.

"Are you certain you wish to go to America with *her*?" she whispered just as that persistent young woman strode up to them. Sylvie had a point, Erik thought. Miss Arlington promptly went to Erik's other side and attached herself to his free arm in a gesture that was curiously possessive. Deliberately he inclined his head toward Sylvie.

"We will talk later, when we are in private," he said pointedly.

"Oh dear," Miss Arlington exclaimed innocently, "have I intruded upon a private conversation? I do beg your pardon." But she remained glued to Erik's side like a barnacle, her wide impractical skirts wrapping around his lower legs and almost tripping him on the way to the stableyard. Sylvie said nothing, but she radiated discomfort; she kept her eyes downcast and her mouth set.

"Why are we walking at such a slow pace?" Miss Arlington asked brightly. "I am looking forward to seeing your property, Mr. Bessette, but we will take all afternoon at this rate." Sylvie's breath hissed as she drew in a perturbed gasp. Erik withdrew his arm from the other woman's and gave her a quelling look.

"You know perfectly well why, Miss Arlington. You need not walk with us if you find the pace too slow."

Edythe tossed her head. "Oh, dear me, I was forgetting that Mrs. Bessette is poorly. I am always in the pink of health myself. Well, no matter, here we are!" And she tripped along ahead of them into the stableyard.

Sylvie glared after her in consternation. "She is…she is…"

"I know," he replied. "I do not understand what is wrong with the woman. Sit here, Sylvie, while I see that the carriage and horses are ready for us after lunch." He left Sylvie sitting on a stone bench under a shade tree and went inside, followed, of course, by the persistent Miss Arlington. Erik growled in frustration; it was going to be a long day.

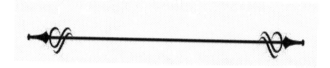

I knew what Erik had been about to say when we were so rudely interrupted by the brash American girl. No matter how much he desired to go to New York with Dr. Arlington, he would deny himself the opportunity if I were not well enough for him to leave me. I had come to realize that I did not want him to go, and the thought of seeing him again with an altered face made me feel almost…*afraid*. Even though I had been so angry with him, even felt on some days that I would *love* it if he would go away; I found that I no longer felt that way.

I possessed in my hands (figuratively, not literally) something that would permit Erik to leave me without worry or concern about my slowly improving health: a letter from my old friend and employer, Dr. Philippe Gaudet. The letter had arrived yesterday, but I was so taken up with our guests I had not found the time to read it until bedtime. Celestine had written to inform him of my loss, and kind man wasted no time in arranging time off from the hospital to come and see me. He was planning to come in about two weeks, once another doctor could be found to take his place at St. Giles Hospital. I knew that Erik would feel much easier about leaving if Dr. Gaudet was here watching over me, even if he could only stay a week or two.

If Erik did go with the Arlingtons, he would be gone by the time Dr. Gaudet arrived.

Now I pondered whether or not I should tell Erik about the letter. It would be tantamount to telling him he was free to go, I well knew. He would be gone a long time; months, perhaps. We never had been apart for more than a few days. *Sans doute*, I reflected ruefully, and with some shame, he would be delighted to escape from his shrew of a wife.

I longed to go to my room and rest after the noonday meal, but I was not going to lay about being an invalid while that shameless hussy worked her wiles on my husband. I tried to coax Celestine to come along on the carriage ride, but she steadfastly refused the treat. She already knew what the estate looked like, she informed me, and had better things to do. Which I could not deny was true.

After lunch and a quick visit to the nursery, I went to my room and changed into a simple gown of rose-pink *le velours côtelé*. The gown was *sans* a bustle, since a bustle made sitting for periods of time quite challenging. It came with a neat little jacket of the same material, trimmed with black cording. I donned my sensible walking boots, collected my straw hat and went downstairs to meet the others.

Erik was standing at the bottom of the stairs, appearing to be on the watch for me. When I reached him he surprised me by hesitantly bending toward me and kissing me lightly on the cheek. I realized with a sad feeling that it was the first time I had permitted him to kiss me since his return home. I felt my heart give a little jolt at the warm, moist touch of his lips, and I wanted…wanted…I wanted to kiss him back. But I could not, for at that inopportune moment the Arlingtons joined us.

Only partially concealing my disappointment at their untimely arrival, I forced myself to greet them politely. That was especially difficult in *her* case. She was the last person I wished to behave politely toward.

Miss Arlington was wearing another of her many inappropriately flounced, trimmed and low-necked gowns, and the matching hat on her head was so wide no one could get within feet of her. It was no wonder they had to travel with all those trunks and boxes. Catching sight of me, she looked me up and down disdainfully before following her father to the carriage.

"What a charming *ensemble*," she said sneeringly, her tone of voice indicating exactly the opposite. She obviously found my driving costume quite plain.

"Yes, it is," Dr. Arlington agreed innocently, smiling and bowing to me. "Mrs. Bessette, you are looking very well this afternoon." He added. Behind her father, Miss Arlington rolled her eyes. The fragrance of

155

honeysuckle trailed sweetly after her, and I discovered that I disliked that scent above all others. I vowed that no such vine would ever be planted here.

The carriage was an open one, and with Miss Arlington's voluminous skirts there was barely room for the four of us on the two seats facing each other. Her lacy flounces frothed against my knees as I sat opposite her. Erik had appointed one of his men to sit in the box and drive, leaving him free to talk and point out things as we went along. I confess I was privately amused to see my husband, the former Phantom and confirmed misanthrope, taking us all on a sight-seeing tour. It seemed incongruous somehow.

We began by proceeding down the road to the winery operations, which were Erik's pride and joy. We passed through rows of grape vines, young grapes already appearing in tight green clusters, and then through the strong upright stems of young sunflowers. Everything looked as beautiful as if it were a painting of itself.

"Who is that ridiculous-looking old man?" Miss Arlington demanded as we drew close to the first stone storage building. She pointed, laughing, and we all looked in that direction. It was Robert she was pointing toward. I felt a searing flash of heat pass through me at her cruel words.

He was standing just outside the wide wooden door, staring back at us, his grey hair sticking out from under his old cap in tufts. As we watched, he pulled off the disreputable cap and scratched his head in wonderment. No doubt, he was thinking *we* were the odd ones.

"That 'ridiculous-looking old man', as you call him, happens to be the most valuable employee in the winery. He knows more about vines than everyone else here put together." I said tartly.

Miss Arlington gave Erik a look from under her thick lashes. "Oh now really, Mrs. Bessette; you cannot mean that Mr. Bessette here knows less about this place than that…dear old fellow."

At that moment, bless him, the 'dear old fellow' chose to lean over and spit disgustingly onto the ground. The driver smirked, and both Erik and I burst out laughing, while the Arlingtons stared at us as if we were mad.

The rest of the outing was uneventful; we went along the river for a short distance, and then back up the hill to the main road, returning eventually to our estate. There was no usable road in the other direction, and at the back of the property was the steep hill that eventually led to the ruins of a medieval hill fort.

Dr. Arlington kept a kind and watchful eye on me, offering me water and fruit when we stopped to rest, and even checking my pulse now and then. He asked Erik interested and intelligent questions about grape growing and wine-making. Edythe Arlington, on the other hand, grew more and more bored as the afternoon progressed. It was clear that she had no interest at all in country life. Neither the profusion of wildflowers nor the beauty of the river could capture her attention. Presently she began to fretfully express a desire to return to the *château*. As I was feeling quite tired by then, I added my voice to hers, and we turned the horses for home.

Erik

Erik was more than happy to order the driver to take them back to the *château*; he was fed up with Edythe's sly glances and little flirtatious insinuations. If this kept up, he was going to have to take her aside and speak sternly to her. Her behavior toward him was absurd in the extreme; he was married, he had a child, he was a murderer and he was ugly. Why these foolish games she insisted on playing with him? He was also anxious to be alone with Sylvie, so they could talk.

Sylvie sat next to him on the seat of the carriage, and he studied her thoughtfully for a moment before looking away, across the fields. It was not like her to sit by passively while Edythe flirted outrageously with him and made unkind comments to her. Why did she not speak up? Grow angry or jealous? He scowled into the distance, pondering. One explanation that quickly presented itself was that she no longer particularly cared whether or not another woman found Erik attractive. It was not a pleasant explanation, but it certainly fit the facts, as well as Sylvie's treatment of him since his return from Paris.

He was relieved when they turned into the long drive toward the *château,* and ordered the driver to stop by the steps to let everyone out. When the driver stopped the carriage, Erik bounded down and assisted both the women out, taking particular care to put Edythe down with a heavy thump that knocked her impractical hat askew. For that, she rewarded him with an angry flash of her black eyes. He pretended not to notice.

A servant came from the house to collect the baskets and water bottles. Erik paused to talk to the driver – the man did not normally drive the carriage; his main work was caring for the horses and keeping the stables clean and tidy. He cared for Danté as well, and Erik had noted something amiss with one of Danté's shoes; a result of their long, breakneck trip from Paris. He wanted to be sure the hoof had been seen to.

Shaking out her skirts, Sylvie adjusted the becoming straw hat she wore and said, "I will walk on to the stable and get the doors open. I could use a chance to stretch my legs after sitting in the carriage for so long." She smiled at Dr. Arlington. "When I return I will see about some refreshments in the parlor." Turning, she went down the path to the stables. Dr. Arlington gazed at her retreating form with a bemused expression. Edythe hesitated for a moment, and then followed after Sylvie.

"I feel the same, Father. I will just catch up with Mrs. Bessette."

"Certainly, my dear," said Dr. Arlington, giving himself a little shake. "I myself feel a restorative is in order," and he turned toward the steps.

Erik gave the horse on his side a pat on the neck and started down the path after the women. He would not mind helping take the harnesses off and rub the horses down, and he wished to keep a watchful eye on Edythe. He felt uneasy leaving her alone with Sylvie for some reason; it was intuition, but he always trusted his intuition. It was one of the reasons he was still alive today.

There was a wide, tall hedge of dark, shining yew between the formal garden by the house and the stables beyond. It had been planted long ago in order to conceal the stableyard from view of the *château*. The path ran from the house to the stable and passed right beside the clipped edge of the yew hedge. Looking ahead, Erik saw Sylvie reach the hedge and then stop to watch the approach of the carriage and four horses. She paused there, obviously waiting to allow them to go by before she stepped back into the path. Behind her walked Edythe, and she, too, glanced toward the approaching carriage. She seemed to stiffen suddenly.

It happened too fast, and yet time slowed down so that everything seemed to take hours to happen. Edythe caught her foot, no doubt tripping over her own wide skirts, and fell forward with a cry. She fell directly against Sylvie, who was standing by the path completely unaware of her. The force of the blow sent Sylvie flying into the road while Edythe landed heavily on the grass. Unable to catch herself, Sylvie plummeted to the ground directly in the pathway of the approaching team. A piercing shriek rent the air. It was Edythe who screamed, as the horrible accident unfolded before her eyes.

158

CHAPTER THIRTEEN

"Bonne Chance, Erik."

O ne moment I was standing at the edge of the path waiting for the carriage to pass me by, and the next...the breath was knocked completely out of me as a hard blow to my back flung me to the ground. I could not possibly catch myself or arrest my fall; I landed full in the path of the lead horses, helplessly tangled in my own skirts, with just enough time to know what was about to happen. A shrill scream came from quite near, followed by a frantic yell from the driver. I was about to die a painful, ghastly death in the next second, and there was no time to even draw one last breath.

Suddenly there was a blur of movement; before I could comprehend what was happening, I felt myself being seized and dragged roughly across the dirt path. My cheek scraped painfully on a stone. Someone took hold of the harness of the lead horse and pushed for all he was worth. A familiar voice shouted something to the driver and somehow, the horses veered just enough to pass me by where I lay sprawled in the dirt. I saw their legs and hooves less than a foot from my head, followed by the wheels of the carriage. My eyes shut tight, and I felt the vibrations of the wheels where my body met the path, and then the carriage came to a grinding stop. Who had moved with such alacrity? Who had been close enough to save me? I had not seen anyone nearby. But I knew it was Erik; no one else possessed such strength and agility, not to mention quick thinking.

He was cursing in a steady stream, sounding shaken. He knelt over me and turned me gently on to my back. I opened my eyes to find Erik's white face peering into mine.

"Sylvie! Sylvie...*sacre*! Are you hurt?" His voice shook; his eyes were wide with terror. I could not answer, however, for I was gasping for breath. It felt like I had somehow forgotten how to breathe. I shook my head and tried to sit up. Erik's strong hands were gentle on my back, helping me to rise to a sitting position. Finally I was able to take a shallow breath, and then another.

The driver had jumped from the high seat and hurried over to us. His horrified young face was skull-white. And then I saw *her*. She was picking herself up from the grassy edge of the path. She reminded me of a sleek panther, gathering itself to pounce. Her enormous hat had fallen off and lay nearby, and her light silken skirts were marred by grass stains.

159

But instead of springing upon us, Miss Arlington hurried up as well. Her hands, I noticed when she wiped them on her skirt, were scratched and bleeding from her own hard fall. She seemed almost as breathless as I was. Surprisingly, my own hands were only lightly scratched.

Both she and the driver began talking at once, apologizing profusely for their part in the accident. The young man was, I knew, afraid he was about to be sacked. Before I could speak, Erik assured him he had seen everything and it was not his fault. Miss Arlington knelt on the ground next to me, her dark eyes so black no pupils were visible. She appeared to be in shock.

"Oh, Mrs. Bessette, I am so sorry! I tripped just as I was about to speak to you, and I cannot tell you how glad I am that you were not hurt. I've never been so frightened in my life!" She put her hand on Erik's arm and gazed admiringly at him. "You were just amazing, Mr. Bessette!"

Erik, ignoring her, gathered me carefully into his arms, lifting me effortlessly. "Come, Sylvie. I will carry you back to the house. You have not caught your breath yet." I curled both my arms around his neck, truly glad for his help. I was so shaken by my close call walking was out of the question. I could feel uncontrollable tremors running through my body, but here in Erik's strong arms I felt safe.

I turned my head and glanced back over Erik's shoulder at Edythe Arlington as he started walking with me up toward the house. She was standing in the path glaring after us, holding her hat in one hand. Her entire expression had changed in an instant; the face of concern was wiped away, replaced with such a hate-filled scowl that if looks could kill, I'd already be dead. That look told its own tale.

As we made our way upstairs, with Celestine fussing along behind us, I murmured, "You seem to be carrying me around rather a lot lately." In response Erik tightened his grip on me. Carrying me into my room, he lowered me carefully to the bed and turned to Celestine.

"Fetch Dr. Arlington. I want him to examine Sylvie. *Maintenant.*" She nodded and bustled out.

"I am fine, Erik. There is no need..." I began. But he suddenly sagged on to the bed next to me and buried his face in his hands.

"*Mon Dieu*, Sylvie!" He exclaimed in a muffled voice. "I feel as if I aged ten years in the last five minutes! I thought I was about to witness your death right before my eyes!"

I touched his arm gently. "But you saved me. I did not realize you were even there, but I am very glad you were."

"I was almost too late," he mumbled from behind his hands.

160

"I am not sure what actually happened, to be honest. How did Miss Arlington come to be so close behind me?" I was hoping to distract him, and it worked.

"She decided to come with you down to the stables after her father went into the house. She was following behind you, and she had almost caught up with you when you stopped there." He drew a shuddering breath. "She tripped on something; probably her own damned skirts, and fell into you on her way down. I was coming down to help with the horses."

I regarded him seriously. "Erik, just think what would have happened if you had not been there."

"No." He said firmly. "I do not want to."

"You saved my life," I reminded him. "Again."

"You *are* my life," he said simply.

I felt tears brim in my eyes at his words. It was true, and it had always been true. It was I who had changed. I came to a decision right then. I would cease my selfish behavior and do the right thing.

"Erik, on the *coiffeuse* over there, is a letter from Dr. Gaudet that came for me yesterday. I…I forgot to tell you about it what with one thing and another. Will you read it?" He gave me a perplexed look, and picked up the letter. I watched him as he opened it and began to read. The die was cast, I thought, for good or ill. He was still reading when Celestine entered the room with Dr. Arlington on her heels.

Dr. Arlington had a busy time of it that afternoon. First he examined me, finding nothing wrong other than bruised knees and a scratch on my cheek from a stone. The way he fussed over me, you would think the carriage must have hit me. When I thanked him and told him how kind I thought he was, he actually blushed almost to the color of his rusty red hair.

His daughter required her hands to be cleaned and bandaged, and then we all met in my sitting room where Dr. Arlington administered medicinal glasses of brandy for the men and sherry for the ladies. I do not mind admitting I felt the need of something stronger than tea after my brush with death.

Edythe Arlington had changed into a clean gown, as had I. She was so solicitous and apologetic about the accident that I began to wonder if I had imagined that hate-filled look. She even neglected to flirt with my husband.

It was decided to have an early supper and retreat to our various rooms. We were all rather tired, partly from the carriage ride and partly from the excitement of the near-accident. During supper I surreptitiously cast the occasional glance at Miss Arlington. Her expression remained quiet and subdued. She did not look at me.

It was not until after supper when we were preparing to retire that I had an opportunity to speak with Miss Arlington alone. Catching up with her as she left the dining room, I gripped her by the arm and pulled her around to face me. Startled, she clearly hadn't expected to see me there.

"I just want you to know, Miss Arlington, I am well aware that what happened this afternoon was not an accident," I said calmly, looking up into her black eyes. "You pushed me deliberately."

The black eyes widened. "Why my dear Mrs. Bessette, your unfortunate illness has apparently affected your mind. You are imagining things. Why on earth would I do something like that?"

I continued as though she had not spoken. "I do not intend to tell my husband of my suspicions, because I know he very much wants to come to America and learn more about the surgery. I do not want to stand in his way, especially since he desires this so much. But I advise you to have a care, Miss Arlington. You will never take him away from me."

Miss Arlington regarded me for a moment in silence. There was a dangerous glint in her dark eyes and her hands were tightly clenched. I felt a momentary qualm of fear. She was in a difficult position, to be sure: to challenge me openly could mean the difference between Erik coming with them or remaining at home with me. Finally her lips parted.

"Why, I do not know what you mean, Mrs. Bessette, I am sure." With that, she turned and flounced away to her room. I squared my shoulders and turned to the stairs. At least, I thought, we both know where we stand.

The next morning Erik told Dr. Arlington that he had made up his mind to go with them to America. Dr. Arlington was quietly pleased; his daughter exultant. Dr. Gaudet's letter gave Erik the assurance he needed that I would be in good hands, at least for a while. It was what I expected he would do. I knew that in giving Erik the letter, I was tacitly freeing him to go. It was for his sake, not mine. I hoped I would not regret it.

We gathered outside for the mid-day meal, for it was a lovely day. With the journey now imminent there was much to discuss. Dr. Arlington was eagerly explaining the stages of the trip to Erik. I listened in resigned silence.

"We will travel by train to Calais," he was saying, "and take a steamer from there to Liverpool. It is much faster than travelling overland across England, which would take days. At Liverpool we will board the RMS Oceanic, which I must say is a fine, modern vessel. We enjoyed the trip over very much, didn't we, Edie?" He smiled reminiscently at his daughter. "As I think I mentioned to you before, it takes eight or nine days to make the crossing, depending on the weather."

Miss Arlington made a project of slipping a red grape between her lips, and then said smugly to Erik, "I don't suppose you have done much travelling, Mr. Bessette. This will be quite an adventure for you."

Erik took a sip of wine and sent a rather feral smile in her direction. "I have done a great deal of travelling, as a matter of fact. But my travels took me east, rather than west." He slanted a sly look in my direction as he replaced his glass on the table. If she only knew, I mused to myself.

The conversation shifted to a discussion of how long Erik might need to remain in New York, what the weather would be like, and what garments he should bring. Miss Arlington was particularly emphatic on his packing evening attire.

"We always stay at the 5th Avenue Hotel," she said, her eyes lighting up. "It is such a fine hotel, with a magnificent ballroom and there is dancing every evening. There are many floors, and the hotel has a perpendicular railway so guests can ride up and down in a little car rather than climbing all those stairs." I tried to imagine a vertical railway running up the side of the hotel, but failed in the attempt. What would keep people from falling out?

"I attended a reception for General Grant held there in 1865," added Dr. Arlington. He shook his head in dismay. "It was such a crush, and very poorly organized. I was unable to even draw near the general. But Edie is right; it is a beautiful hotel."

"So you see, Mr. Bessette," Miss Arlington continued as though her father was not even there, "some finery is definitely called for. I warn you, I will be expecting you to dance with me while we are there." She leaned toward him, her eyes signaling a challenge. "You *can* dance, can't you?" She was, I realized with consternation, acting as if I were not even there.

Stony faced, he replied, "I dance only with my wife." My heart gave a little leap of joy. Miss Arlington sent me a quizzical look, clearly wondering at Erik's attachment to a woman so devoid of charm or looks.

It was decided that the travelers would depart in three days, early in the morning. There was so much packing to do, so much to set in order on the estate, the time passed in a trice. Erik spent as much time as he could with little Marie, and did his best to avoid Miss Arlington. In the process, he also seemed to be avoiding me.

Miss Arlington expressed an interest in visiting Sarlat again to do some shopping, and made arrangements to have their driver take her there in their barouche. Since there was not much to shop for in Sarlat, I suspected her real desire was to get away from the *château* for a while. There was, after all, nothing to do here that would interest her. I half expected she would try to talk Erik into accompanying her, but she did not.

She was gone most of the day, and it was certainly a relief to me to not to have her dark presence hovering about. Erik was glad of it, too. There was so much to do to prepare for the journey, and she would be of little help.

Celestine and I were busy morning till night; and though I hated to do it, I knew I must ask for advice from my arch enemy, Edythe Arlington, when she returned from town. I had no idea what items to pack for Erik, or how many of them, but she clearly had a very good notion of what men required in the sartorial way.

Miss Arlington did not return to the *château* until late afternoon. She seemed quite pleased with herself. With much fanfare, she produced a large shopping bag and proceeded to distribute an assortment of gifts she had bought in town. Her parting gifts to us, she explained. For Marie she had bought a little Victorian style picture book, with extra pages that could be pulled open with a bit of ribbon, to reveal a hidden picture within. She had found a pair of soft leather gloves for her father. For Erik she produced a book of English (and American) words and phrases so he could begin to study for his time in America. She brought nothing for Celestine, for she considered her a servant and beneath her notice. And for me? With a flourish she produced an ornate silver backed hand mirror, which she presented to me with a cool, cruel smile.

"How thoughtful you are," I murmured, and handed the mirror to Celestine. Miss Arlington gave me a smug look before turning away.

Her father, having completely missed the underlying implications of her gift to me, turned to her as he tried on one of his brown leather gloves, asking,

"Didn't you get something for yourself, Edie?"

"Why of course, Father! How could you ask?" From the bottom of her shopping bag she extracted a dark brown fur muff and placed her hands inside it, twirling a bit to show it off. It looked like mink.

"Why did you buy that?" Erik asked disdainfully. "It is summer, in America as it is here."

Miss Arlington shrugged in an off-hand way, pulling her hands out of the fur muff. "The winters in New York can get awfully cold," she explained. "I will be glad of it come wintertime."

Miss Arlington turned to the large mirror in the foyer where we were standing and patted at her rather disarrayed black locks. She smiled smugly at her own reflection. Regarding her in venomous silence, I vowed that the minute she was gone, I would give the hand mirror to Berthé.

Those few remaining days passed far too quickly. I saw little of Erik, and when I did see him, usually at meals, he was quiet and withdrawn. Once or twice I caught him watching me with a perplexed expression, as though he were trying to penetrate my thoughts.

The night before Erik and the Arlingtons were to depart for America, I brushed and braided my hair for the night, put on my dressing gown, and slipped down the hall to peek at Marie in her little bed. Finding her angelically asleep with her pink rosebud mouth slightly open and her beloved doll clutched against her side, I quietly slipped out again and closed her door. I was on my way back to my own room when I paused in the hallway, listening.

I was arrested by the faint, mournful sounds of a piano coming from Erik's music room downstairs. What haunting tune was he playing tonight? I did not recognize it. To my knowledge, he had not sat down and played his grand piano since his return from Paris.

The music floating up the stairs sounded poignant and melancholy. I stood, holding my robe tightly around me, and listened intently. Erik always played according to his mood. He was leaving on the morrow, and when would we see each other again? He was journeying into the unknown in more ways than one. What must he be feeling tonight? I was sorry to realize that I had not cared one bit for his feelings for some time now. Only for my own. My selfishness brought a bitter taste to my mouth.

I turned and started hesitantly toward the stairs, then stopped and started back to the bedroom again. I did this at least twice. I am not normally so indecisive, but words were bottled up inside me needing to come out, and I was not certain of my welcome. Why should Erik welcome the horrid shrew his wife had become? That had been a little joke between us, him calling me a shrew, but even I had to admit I was living up to the name. Finally I scolded myself for my cowardice, screwed up my courage and descended the stairs. How could I let him leave tomorrow without speaking to him?

Erik looked up when he saw me enter the music room, and his fingers lifted from the keyboard. Once the music stopped, the silence was deafening. The room was rather dim, only one candelabra on the top of the piano to light the ivory keys and his face. We stared at one another without speaking for several seconds, his eyes glittering in the candlelight. His face was unreadable but not unwelcoming, so I came fully into the room and closed the door behind me. I did not wish Miss Arlington to overhear what I had to say, and I would not put it past her to follow me downstairs, or come herself in search of the music (or the man playing it).

As I approached Erik, coming to stand near the piano, I realized I was trembling and wringing my hands together in a ridiculous manner. I forced myself to stop doing that, and took a deep breath. How difficult this was! It was like talking to a stranger. But he was not a stranger, I reminded myself. He was my husband.

"I...I need to tell you something," I said, forcing the words out. "You are leaving tomorrow and I cannot let you go without..." Suddenly he was standing, and his hands were on my shoulders, his grip just short of painful. The movement was so quick that I caught my breath and fell silent, startled.

"Without what?" He asked; his expression tense and wary. I found it was easier to speak my piece if I did not look at him, so I focused my eyes on the front of his brocade waistcoat.

"I realize it is inadequate, but I want you to know that I...I am sorry for all those things I said to you when you came back. I didn't mean any of it. I wanted to hurt you. I was so...when I lost the baby...I wanted that baby s-so much, and..." I became aware that tears were flowing down my face, and my voice broke on a sob.

"I'm sorry...this wasn't what I..." I pressed my hand to my eyes and tried to move away from him, but he held me fast.

166

"Shhh, Kitten," he murmured, and his arms went around me. "Come here." He cradled my head with one hand and guided it to his shoulder. That felt amazingly good. Presently I stopped crying and wiped my eyes on my sleeve, but I stayed there, against Erik's warm chest. Had I actually forgotten how good it felt when he held me? Somehow his gentle support gave me the courage to continue.

"I did not want you to leave tomorrow without telling you…that I love you, Erik. I still love you. Oh, I wish…" Here I stopped, hesitating to go on. His arms tightened around me and I felt his face against my hair.

"I love you too, you difficult and annoying creature. What is it that you wish?" His voice sounded rough with pent emotion.

Slowly I pulled away so that I could look into his face. He wore a softer expression than I had seen for a long time. "I ought to have told you this before, but I wish that you were not going to America, Erik. I…I do not want you to change your face." At my words he looked startled, and then confused.

"But why, Sylvie?"

I felt my cheeks color, for I could not tell him what was in my heart: my secret fear. "I do not know; I just like you the way you are." Struggling to explain, I went on, "If you have this surgery Dr. Arlington is talking about, when you come back you won't be…won't look the same. You will be different."

He sighed. "I will still be the same man, you know that perfectly well. Sylvie, think what it would mean to me, if the surgery…if I could look just a little less hideous. I've lived with this face all my life, never dreaming anything could be done about it. But what if something *can* be done?" He said earnestly. "I need to at least pursue this."

Reaching up to place my hand against his cheek, I said, "You know you have never been hideous to *me*, Erik. Must you do this? You will be away such a long time…."

"I *want* to do this. At the very least, Dr. Arlington can make a better mask for me. But for that to happen I have to be there, at the clinic. No one else is doing the kind of work he is doing, apparently. I know it is a long time to be away from you and Marie, but I will write you often, I promise. Philippe will look after you while he is here. I won't make any decisions or take any actions about surgery without telling you, Sylvie." He gave a self-deprecating little chuckle. "And if my recent absence is any indication, René and Robert between them can manage the winery operations without any help from me."

By now our positions had somehow changed; Erik was seated on the piano bench and I was on his lap. I could not recall how he managed that, but I did not mind.

"*Oui, vraiment*, though their discussions can grow rather heated; but I will miss you, *mon mari*." I murmured.

Erik stroked my hair and gave my braid a gentle tug. "I will miss you as well, Kitten. More than you know. I want you to do something for me while I am gone." He said, his voice becoming serious.

"What?" I asked warily, caught off guard by his sudden change of tone.

"I want you to try to take better care of yourself. You need to regain your appetite, and get your strength back, Sylvie. You are too pale and thin." He gave me a squeeze around my narrow midsection. "You know I prefer you to be a little more...more."

I felt a flare of resentment at his request, but could not really argue with him, for I knew he was right. He was thinking only of my own good. I nodded my head.

"*D'accord*." I said finally.

"Good. I thank you for that." I felt his lips brush my cheek, and then he said, sounding strangely uncertain, "Kitten, I want...I need...would you allow me... to come to your bed tonight? It is our last night together for some time, after all." He must have felt me stiffen slightly, because he added quickly, "Dr. Olivier has said we may resume our...relations. I'll be gentle, Kitten. I won't hurt you. It's just that...*Mon Dieu*, I've missed you so!"

And suddenly his mouth was on mine; not that gentle really, in fact, quite insistent. Although I was taken somewhat unawares, I found I could not stop him. How could I, when I was twined around him like a vine, kissing him back ardently, my fingers tangled into his hair?

We had one difficult moment in the hallway, when he would lead me to our own bedroom but I balked. "No, I do not want to go there...please, Erik..." He understood, so we went to the guestroom I had been using instead. To be honest, I think he would have been happy with the hallway by that point.

Oh, Reader, it was as if the past horrible weeks had never been! I forgot all about, well, everything really, even that diabolical girl. True to his word, Erik was gentle and patient with me. After we had sated our physical desires (which took some time), we satisfied other, more intimate needs: the emotional connection we both craved in our hearts. I did my best by word and deed to demonstrate my feelings for my husband, and he certainly seemed to appreciate my efforts. We lay together talking long into the night,

Erik telling me stories about his time in Paris. It was wonderful. His tale of catching a ride on some sort of steam-driven horseless carriage, however, I stoutly refused to believe. It was too far-fetched.

I tried not to show how aghast I was when he told me of hiding for the night in his old cavern, far below the burned out shell of the opera building. The thought was utterly depressing, and my heart went out to him. Though he made light of it, I knew it must have been too depressing for words.

We promised each other, perhaps naively, that nothing would ever come between us again. I believe I even quoted Shakespeare, to Erik's disgust. That night, before Erik left for America, I felt in my heart that he was still mine, and that I was forgiven for my cruel behavior toward him.

CHAPTER FOURTEEN

"Somehow I rather hoped there might be a little adventure ahead, even if just in a small way."

W e were forced to hire an extra wagon to follow behind the Arlington's overloaded carriage in order to accommodate Erik's single trunk and a portmanteau. With all Miss Arlington's trunks and boxes (for most of them were indeed hers), there was scarcely room for the driver on their carriage, let alone any other cases. She could have used a ladies' maid to help her with all her things, but I learned from Celestine that Miss Arlington could not keep any — they all left her service after a day or two. Somehow this information did not surprise me.

The travelers were unable to depart for Paris until late morning because of all the packing. The Arlingtons were chafing to get underway, for they were eager to return home to Matthew, Dr. Arlington's young son. I was glad for the delay, however, for it gave Erik and I a few more precious moments to be together with Marie.

I had my private reasons for not wanting him to make the trip, but I reminded myself that it was not dangerous; it wasn't as if he ran the risk of capture and death. He was committed to the journey now, and eager to go. I could see the idea of the surgery was growing in him.

At last it was time, and all was ready. We could delay this moment no longer. We left Marie in the nursery and went down to the carriage together. Thankfully, she was too young to really comprehend the length of time her *papa* would be away, and so there were no tears. Not from Marie, I should say.

Celestine was waiting for us near the carriage, and I saw that she was attempting to press a basket of sandwiches on Miss Arlington, who accepted them rather reluctantly. Celestine, turning to Erik, embraced him warmly and then pulled out her handkerchief and blew her nose. I noticed even Robert was there to see 'the Master' off, lurking about by the wagon loaded with trunks. I hoped he wasn't thinking of hiding in the wagon and going along, but apparently he just wanted to say goodbye.

Catching sight of Robert standing awkwardly by the wagon, Erik went to him and, to Robert's obvious surprise, shook his hand and then murmured something for his ears only. Robert, flushing a little, tipped his cap to him, gave the Arlingtons a surly glance, and stalked away to the winery. I decided I would have to pay a visit to Robert later and make him tell me what Erik whispered to him.

"Well!" Miss Arlington huffed, having intercepted the surly look.

Before I knew what he was about to do, Erik returned to me, took me in his arms and kissed me hard, in front of the others. Although I enjoyed his spontaneous demonstration of affection, I wished it was not in front of an audience. I could feel a hot blush spread across my cheeks. While Miss Arlington watched us with narrowed eyes, Dr. Arlington wore a rather wistful, sad expression on his long face. He approached when Erik released me and to my surprise, took my hand and kissed it, bowing in a courtly manner.

"Thank you for your hospitality, Mrs. Bessette," he said softly, holding my hand a little longer than was necessary. "It was indeed a pleasure to make your acquaintance, and one I shall long treasure." A quizzical expression passed over Erik's face when he observed this exchange, but he turned away quickly. It was time for them to go.

Miss Arlington was the first into the big carriage, as usual wearing one of her feminine but impractical gowns, a fur trimmed jacket, and a matching parasol, also trimmed with fur. She did look lovely, I admitted to myself sourly. I hoped fervently that all that impractical fur would make her hot and cross before too long.

She spoke not a word to me, nor I to her. I considered myself under no obligation to behave politely to someone who had recently tried to kill me.

Standing with Erik before the open carriage door, I took his hand in mine and pressed something into his open palm, carefully closing his fingers over the gift. He put his other hand under my chin and tilted my face up to his.

"What is it?" He asked. Erik did not care for surprises.

"Look and see," I answered, smiling and blinking back tears. Unwrapping the little gift wrapped in tissue paper, he revealed an old fashioned gold locket on a long chain. He had never seen it before, for it was my mother's. I had removed the very old *daguerreotype* likeness of my father the locket once contained and replaced it with a lock of my hair, and one of Marie's.

"Open the locket later, when you are alone." I said. "It will bring you luck."

171

He looked into my eyes with such a burning expression, it almost took my breath away. "We will be all right, Sylvie," he whispered, and I knew he was not referring to himself and the Arlingtons.

"*Oui*, my love, we will."

Celestine and I stood together and watched the carriage roll away down the gravel drive, followed by the loaded wagon. It was odd indeed to be doing this again, under very different circumstances. This time there were no mounted soldiers with rifles and bayonets. Nevertheless, I felt sure that in her own way, Edythe Arlington was just as dangerous.

When they were out of sight, almost as one we turned and looked at one another.

"Rather gives one a sense of *déjà vu*, does it not?" I asked her with a small, tight smile.

Celestine put her arm through mine and we turned back to the house.

"It does, I suppose, but...this feels different somehow. Sylvie..." she paused, looking troubled. "Do you trust that young woman? There is something about her..." her voice trailed off. I felt my gaze wander out across the verdant valley to the glitter of the river far below.

"No, Celestine, I do not. There *is* something about her." I glanced at her thoughtfully. "She is, in my opinion, a very disturbed young woman. You know what she wants, don't you?"

Celestine frowned. "It is patently obvious what she wants, but why?"

I turned to her almost eagerly.

"I have asked myself that same question almost from the first! But I cannot answer it. Unless..."

"Unless what, *Ma Chère*?" She prompted when I paused uncertainly. If Celestine but knew, I hesitated because I was not ready to confess to her or anyone my suspicion that the young woman had tried to kill me.

"I hesitate to say it," I said at last. "But I cannot help wondering if Miss Arlington is a stable person. She seems to have formed a decided preference for my husband, even though she scarcely knows him. And knowing he is married and a father! That, to me, is not natural."

"She is also quite spoiled, and accustomed to having her way in all things. You must have observed the way her father allowed her to get away with such rudeness." Celestine gave a little huff of annoyance. "I would never have allowed Meg to behave in such a way."

"Poor Dr. Arlington is so taken in by her, I do not think he realizes her true nature." I sighed, and continued on up the steps into the cool of the foyer. I was glad that Celestine and I were *en rapport* in regards to Miss Arlington. "Well, I could not bring myself to prevent Erik from taking this trip, it would not have been fair, Celestine, after all I have put him through. I have to trust...trust him."

Celestine gave me a fond look. "You can, you know. He is the most loyal man I've ever known."

"I hope you are right," I murmured. Although I did not say so to my friend, it was Miss Arlington I did not trust. I turned toward the staircase, thinking longingly of my bed. The morning's rushed activity had made me weary. And I was feeling quite melancholy. Celestine, however, had other ideas.

"*Non*, my dear, do not go up yet, it is still *le matin!*" She exclaimed, taking my arm again determinedly. "Let us walk through the kitchen and have a look at the *potager*. I want to see what is ready. After all, Dr. Gaudet will be here soon and I must prepare for his visit. Mathilde has planted a beautiful vegetable bed this season, and you have not even seen it yet." Reluctantly, with a wistful backward look at the stairs, I allowed a stronger will than my own to prevail. We went to the garden. Celestine's smile held a trace of smugness, it seemed to me.

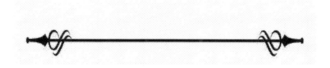

Erik

For a change, Erik kept his overflowing emotions in check, which was a good thing considering he had just discovered Dr. Edward Arlington carried a *tendresse* toward his wife. He was glad they were leaving; he knew there was no cause for jealousy, but the knowledge that the other man coveted his wife was enough to bring out his deep streak of possessiveness. It was a trait he endeavored to bury, for it did him no credit.

Glancing bemusedly at Dr. Arlington, he wondered if he had formed any other romantic attachments after the death of his wife. Erik supposed not. He really could not blame him for finding Sylvie attractive; even as thin and washed out as she was now, she was still a warm, lovely creature, kind and generous. How he would miss her!

He felt the gold locket heavy in his pocket, and touched it softly through the fabric of his coat. This leave-taking, to his relief, was not as fraught with misery as the last one. There was hope, and the interest of new things, new discoveries to be made. And at home, the knowledge that Philippe would be there soon. Erik felt he had done all that he possibly could to see that Sylvie was well cared for in his absence. One at a time he had taken Celestine, Robert and even René aside and given them explicit instructions on what ought to be done for her. He could be at ease on that account, at least, for none of them would dare disobey his orders.

They reached the road; then they were on it and driving toward Sarlat, where they would connect with the main thoroughfare to Paris. Behind him was all he knew and loved, ahead all was shrouded in mystery. But Miss Arlington obviously wished to make all known to him, for she began to talk engagingly about the journey and what they would see and do along the way. Her father sat in silence, gazing at nothing. Presently he brought out a notebook and pencil, and began jotting down notes. Erik stared out the window and allowed Edythe's melodic voice to fade into the background.

The journey to Paris seemed interminable to Erik. It was all too familiar – hauntingly so. The same roads, the same inns along the way, as his only too recent journey taken with Moreau. Only this time there were no soldiers on horseback surrounding their carriage. In some ways, however, he felt just as trapped. On occasion, to escape his captivity in close quarters with Edythe Arlington, he rode in the wagon that carried his belongings. He didn't mind sitting up on the bench with the driver, although Miss Arlington was scandalized. She thought it was an extreme breach of etiquette for him to 'hobnob', as she put it, with a servant. He wondered if all Americans were so snobbish.

Fortunately, Erik happened to discover a deck of playing cards in a pocket of the carriage door, and made use of them to keep the Arlingtons amused during the long stages between stops to change horses. When he was a child, he ran away from home with a band of gypsies. It was a harsh, cruel existence for a child, but in the process he learned to perform card tricks, magic tricks, and to tell fortunes by palm reading. The gypsies had taught him many useful things, some of them unpleasant, but card tricks were innocuous at least. Edythe Arlington was fascinated, and spent hours observing the deft movements of his hands to see if she could detect the *tour de main* involved with each trick. Dr. Arlington did not find them quite so amusing, and would soon bury his nose in a book.

In the evenings Erik found he enjoyed sitting in a private dining room of whatever inn they had stopped for the night, talking to Dr. Arlington and getting to know him better. He seemed a gentle, quiet soul, in spite of his experiences in the War Between the States, as he called it. His company was restful, exactly the opposite of his daughter's. He talked about many things, including the war, dwelling especially upon how he had learned his surgical techniques from work in the field. The one subject he would not bring up, however, was his late wife. In turn, he encouraged Erik to talk about his life on the *château* and his music. He appeared genuinely interested in hearing Erik play one day. He was not himself musically inclined, but appreciated it in others.

Their time in Paris was by necessity short indeed, and Erik was not sorry for that. He was uncomfortable being back in the city; with no bolt-hole to hide in, he felt exposed. He was not yet accustomed to the fact that he was a free man. Even before the crimes he committed at the Opera House, he had behaved as if he were a hunted man. He could not seem to help it. He trusted no one. How could one shake that off after so many years?

They lingered only long enough for Dr. Arlington to send a few telegrams; one to his son in New York, another to their housekeeper, and one to Dr. Buck, the surgeon and partner in charge of his clinic. After these tasks were accomplished, they drove straight to the *Gare*.

Erik had never been on a train, or had cause to visit a train station. Arriving in the carriage at the station to catch the *Chemins de Fer du Nord*, the train that would carry them to Calais, he was aghast at the crush of people, baggage carriers, horses, and so much noise. It was a waking nightmare for him. This trip to America suddenly seemed that it would go on forever. First this hellish train station, then the dock and a steamer to ride, then Liverpool and another steamer. The thought of all that lay ahead exhausted him. And here in the *Gare*, even with his mask in place, he felt as exposed as he had the night Christine removed his mask and wig in front of an entire audience. It was all he could do not to bolt away from the station at a run.

The Arlingtons must have seen the panic in his eyes, for almost as one they converged on him, as did another man who was apparently Dr. Arlington's valet. He had been staying at the hotel until their return from the south of France. Between the three of them, they shielded Erik from the prying eyes of their fellow passengers until they were at last boarding their train carriage. Erik did not take a full breath until he was safely ensconced within. His relief at finding himself in a private berth was indescribable, and he vowed not to leave it until the train arrived in Calais. Desperate to be alone with his thoughts, he declined the Arlingtons' invitation to join them in the dining car for luncheon. He drew the shades at the windows, rang the bell to order his own meal, and heaved a long sigh of relief.

Having fortified his frayed nerves with a glass of wine and something to eat, Erik took out the gold locket and opened it carefully. Inside, held beneath the thinnest little ovals of glass, were two tiny locks of golden hair. The one that resembled angel floss was his daughter's, *sans doute*. The darker gold ribbon of hair belonged to his wife.

He stared at the golden curls for some time, and then closed the locket with a snap and replaced it in his pocket. He considered putting it under his pillow when he retired for the night. He hoped Sylvie was right about it giving him luck, for he felt he would surely need it.

CHAPTER FIFTEEN

"It is not my nature to be miserable when being optimistic and cheerful will do instead."

Imagine my surprise when, only two days after Erik departed with the Arlingtons, a cheerful and smiling Berthé appeared at my bedroom door first thing in the morning to help me dress. I seldom required anyone to help me dress in the mornings, except during that time I was still very weak from my loss. I stared at her, mystified. Even more perplexing, she pulled from my *armoire* a casual riding costume that I seldom ever wore.

"Berthé, I can dress myself," I said firmly. "I want one of my day gowns. I am not going outside today."

"Madame," she murmured shyly, not meeting my eyes, "I am instructed you must wear this today." Instructed? I frowned.

Rather than argue, which I had no energy for anyway, I shrugged and let her help me into the dress. It was much less voluminous than my normal gowns, if a rather unflattering shade of olive green. Once downstairs, carrying the straw hat she insisted that I bring, I found Celestine in the breakfast room ahead of me. She beamed happily at my appearance, and handed me a cup of *café au lait.* Clearly my costume was no surprise to her.

"Did you…" I began.

"You look lovely this morning," she said brightly. Since this could not possibly be the case, I wondered if everyone had gone mad in the night.

"What…" I began again, but got no further. Celestine sat me down in front of a plate, upon which rested a piece of buttered toast and a boiled egg.

"Have your breakfast, my dear." She said earnestly, her eyes sparkling. The direst forebodings were aroused in me by her behavior. However, I *was* feeling a bit hungry, so I sipped my coffee and nibbled at the toast. Finishing my egg, I was about to inquire as to what on earth was going on, when someone began hammering loudly on the front door. The sudden noise made me jump and spill my *café.*

"What…"

René stood in the doorway of the breakfast room like a breath of fresh air, a broad smile on his tanned face. He was wearing riding boots and breeches which I must admit were very becoming to his long legs.

"Come, Madame," he ordered. "We are going for a ride." He flashed a toothy grin toward Celestine and winked at her. She blushed, and I rolled my eyes in exasperation.

Well, this was simply too much. Who were these people, and what had happened to the ones I knew? I very carefully placed my napkin on the table next to my plate. Very carefully I rose and turned toward René. Beginning to feel quite vexed, I drew breath, but before I could speak, he reached for my arm and I found myself being gently but inexorably tugged toward the door. Sputtering in dismay, I heard Celestine give a little chuckle as I was towed outside.

On the gravel path at the foot of the steps were two horses – Danté, Erik's big black, and another, much smaller horse. She was a lovely mottled silver-grey. I had never seen her before.

"René…" Gesturing toward the little mare, I began to expostulate, concerned that he had stolen the horse.

"I borrowed her from the neighbors. She is quite gentle." René explained. I turned and looked askance at him. He wore a brilliant smile.

"I sense a conspiracy," I said, frowning. He threw his head back and laughed.

"Come, Madame, I am taking you for a little ride. M. Bessette said before he left that you must take some fresh air. His wish is my command."

"And did he also give you permission to ride his horse?"

René shook his head. "Ah, no, Madame. Danté gives his own permission. If he did not wish it, no one could ride him." Having said that, he proceeded to lead the pretty little mare alongside the lowest step, and I could not resist approaching to stroke her soft, silky neck. She seemed quite gentle. She turned her head to examine me curiously and René handed me a sugar lump from his pocket.

"What is her name?" I asked, as I felt the mare's big warm lips working on my palm to gather up the sugar lump. There was a delicate crunch as she ate it.

"*Ballerine*, Madame." He said. "Her owner named her that because she is so graceful. She is five years old and well trained. Now she has taken the sugar and been introduced to you, you may mount her."

Oh, I could, could I? Reminding myself that I had given Erik my promise I would work at recovering my strength, I reluctantly consented. With some help from René (a great deal of help in fact), I was soon sitting aside on *Ballerine*, one foot in the stirrup and my hands holding the reins. I seldom rode horseback except seated in front of Erik, and at those times, I rode astride, which I found to be much more comfortable than side-saddle.

It is improper for a woman to ride astride like a man, for inexplicable reasons. No doubt it is one of those strictures placed on the female sex by men in order to make life more difficult for us. They are very good at that.

With some trepidation, I asked in a voice that quavered embarrassingly, "We won't be riding far, will we, René?"

"*Non*, Madame. I thought for today, we would ride down the drive as far as the gate and back."

"For today?" I asked uneasily. The plot was thickening.

Having seated himself astride Danté and taken up his own reins, René turned the great black horse toward the drive. But before he would condescend to move, Danté stretched out his long glossy neck and sniffed me thoroughly, nibbled a bit on my sleeve, and gave me a searching look with his great dark eyes.

"He is happy to see you," René explained. Staring back into those unfathomable eyes, I felt tears sting my own. Unable to speak for a moment, I stroked my fingers down his long silky muzzle and smiled.

"I am happy to see you, too, Danté." Danté seemed satisfied then, and turned toward the drive.

"Fresh air and a change of scene are what you need, Madame Sylvie," René said confidently.

Ballerine fell in step behind the black horse obediently, for which I was thankful. Although I couldn't bring myself to admit it to René, I had no idea how to steer my horse with the reins. Riding lessons were never considered necessary in the *milieu* I was raised in; my father was a family physician with limited means. Watching René closely, I thought perhaps I might pick up the essentials from him.

It was a lovely morning, to be sure. The gravel drive from our *château* to the road was fairly long, and lined with old sycamore trees most of the distance. In places their branches met in the middle, creating a shady bower pleasant to ride or walk through. The land to either side was uncultivated, and so consisted of meadowland and a profusion of wildflowers. Bees and bumblebees were busily working over the flowers, and now and then a laden bee buzzed right past my head.

I found that to my surprise, I was enjoying the experience vastly, and at least for a short time, forgot my worries about Erik alone in the company of those peculiar Americans. It was a relief, in fact. And, I had to admit, it was a relief to be out of the house. The dainty little mare lived up to her name, stepping along as gracefully as a doe.

René rode on without speaking; allowing Danté to set his own pace, which for a change was measured. Every now and then, the black horse turned to glance behind, as if checking on his followers. I felt my heart expand with affection for him. I vowed I would venture to the stables and bring him a carrot or an apple soon. He deserved it.

After perhaps ten minutes of slow riding, we approached the two old stone pillars that marked the entry to our estate. When I first beheld them, they were covered with lichen and ivy, but now they stood proudly, clean and white. Beyond them was the road. To be honest, this was in fact more of a farm cart path than a road, fairly rutted and a bit overgrown. As it wound its way down from the hills toward Sarlat it eventually grew into a well-maintained thoroughfare wide enough for two carriages to pass each other.

We rode out between the pillars and stopped in the road, but when René would turn to retrace our steps I found myself unwilling to follow him, at least for a moment. My eyes were drawn away, down the empty ribbon of dirt road that led to the village and beyond. This was the way Erik and the Arlingtons had taken only a few days past. It was hard to imagine the chain of events that would somehow take them to England and from there across the ocean to America. Erik would experience places and people that I would not; a part of me suddenly yearned to ride that way myself. My heartbeat sped up as I gazed with longing into the hazy distance.

"Madame? Madame Sylvie, are you all right?" René asked, sounding concerned. "Did you wish to ride further today?"

Abruptly called back to reality, I pulled gently on the reins and turned *Ballerine* back toward home. "No, I was only looking. I have not been this way for some time," I said, repressing a sigh.

Too soon we were approaching my front steps again, and René was reaching up to help me dismount. Grinning piratically as he lowered me to the ground, he said cheerfully, "*Eh bien*, M. Bessette may be away for some time, so I will take you out riding each morning." Leering at me absurdly with his one eye, he pretended to twirl a nonexistent mustache and added, "He may be sorry he asked me, for perhaps you will fall in love with me instead!"

"As have all the other susceptible ladies in my household, you mean?" I asked, unable to keep from smiling back at him. It was a good thing René lived in the country; what a heartbreaker he would be if he resided in Paris! Giving him a mock stern look, I added, "I certainly hope all this riding will not keep you from your job, René."

"Oh no, Madame Sylvie, not at all. I will be here tomorrow at the same time, so best you be ready." Sweeping off his wide-brimmed hat, he gave me a deep bow and then prepared to mount Danté again. "*Et maintenant*, I must return the horses to the stable. *Bonjour!*"

180

"And good morning to you, Danté," I added cheerfully. The horse whickered at me as he was led away along with the lovely *Ballerine*. I watched them depart toward the stables on the other side of the *château*, and I suddenly became aware that I was smiling. For the first time in many weeks I felt rather happy, in fact. Although I was a trifle weary from the exertion, slight though it was, I found I was looking forward to riding out again on the morrow. It was a pleasant change to have something nice to look forward to. I wondered how long our neighbor would be willing to lend us his little mare.

Although Dr. Gaudet would arrive in a few days, and I loved him dearly, I was not looking forward to certain aspects of his visit. He would wish to ask me questions, and I would have to remember all that I was trying to forget. I would have to steel myself against having to relive the most painful experience of my life. Well, at least he would be good company for Celestine, and little Marie considered him to be a grandfather to her.

As it turned out, however, my misgivings about Dr. Gaudet proved to be unfounded. Although he was a physician, his specialty was leprosy and caring for the elderly, not women of childbearing age. He knew next to nothing about my own situation. It would have been difficult to miss his troubled expression, however, when we greeted each other in the foyer upon his afternoon arrival. Fortunately, Marie was there too, and provided a welcome distraction.

Dr. Gaudet and I had known each other for several years. Until I fled Paris with Erik, I provided meals for his patients at St. Giles Hospital from my professional kitchen. We had grown fond of each other, but I would have to say that between Erik and Dr. Gaudet an unexpectedly close relationship had developed. The good doctor seemed to take an almost fatherly role toward my spouse. The two men had nothing in common, and Erik was probably not even aware that Dr. Gaudet's warm affection for him satisfied some deep unspoken need.

Dr. Gaudet and Celestine seemed to enjoy each other's company, as well. They never met when we all lived in Paris, but since the doctor began spending his annual holiday with us at the *château*, they were thrown together regularly. I could not help but notice that Celestine had an extra sparkle in her eyes as she escorted Dr. Gaudet to his room (the one recently vacated by Dr. Arlington, in fact, for I was occupying his usual room). Dr. Gaudet smiled and twinkled at her in response. Hmmm...I wondered, and then shook my head. People their age surely would not develop romantic feelings for each other, would they?

Once Dr. Gaudet was comfortably settled and rested after his journey, we gathered in the dining room for the evening meal. After the usual questions about how we were, and how the patients at the hospital were getting on, I broached a subject that had been in the back of my mind for some time. I turned to Dr. Gaudet and, concealing the resentment I felt, asked,

"I understand that it was you who introduced Erik to the Arlingtons. What do you think of them?" Celestine and I both waited with interest for his response.

Patting his lips with his *serviette*, he replied, "I first met Dr. Arlington when I attended his lecture on his pioneering surgery techniques. We have invited him to return and give a teaching course on his techniques for facial repair. He was very interested in meeting Erik." He paused and looked askance at me. "As for the daughter, she is very lovely, *vous comprenez*, but she appears to be unduly headstrong and rather...experienced, I should say."

"That is one way of putting it," Celestine said wryly.

"She seemed quite taken with Erik," Dr. Gaudet added, a slight frown notched between his brows. "I recollect she had an extraordinary reaction when she learned that he was married...almost as if she were angry." He sounded mildly perplexed. "We both thought it was rather odd."

A tense silence ensued at his words, while Celestine and I exchanged pointed glances with each other. I took a small sip of my wine, and Dr. Gaudet looked inquiringly from one to the other of us.

He said slowly, "Am I to understand that something, er, untoward occurred while the Arlingtons were staying with you, Sylvie?" I cleared my throat.

"Dr. Arlington was, is, a very kind person, and Erik liked him a great deal, as did I," I said quietly. "But his daughter, Edythe...she took a dislike to me from the first, and I think...we both think, Celestine and I, that she has designs on Erik. She flirted with him outrageously, in front of us all."

"*Et aussi*, she was quite rude to Sylvie, on more than one occasion," Celestine chimed in, her eyes flashing. If she only knew!

Dr. Gaudet shook his head sadly. "*Bien*, I am sorry to hear that. I begin to regret introducing them to Erik, but I had no idea they would actually invite themselves to come here."

182

I was not certain that I had heard him correctly. "They would... *invite themselves*...do you mean to say, Erik did not invite them to come stay with us? They invited themselves?" I asked incredulously. "How did that come about?" All this time, I had been blaming Erik for something that was not his fault. Here was another reason to feel guilty.

Dr. Gaudet found himself suddenly the center of our attention. He did not seem to mind. He removed his pince-nez, polished them a little, and replaced them carefully on his nose.

"*Oui*, that is so. It was all her doing if I remember correctly. We were just leaving the Arlingtons' suite at the hotel. Erik told them that he could not be certain when he would return home, and so did not know if he would see them again. And all at once, Miss Arlington said... let me see...she said why could they not stop here on their way back from the south. Dr. Arlington said it was too far out of their way, but it was obvious that Erik was torn. Finally he said yes, but I could see that he was troubled." Dr. Gaudet toyed with the stem of his wineglass. "I can understand that now, I think. Then, I did not realize her interest in him, but, *sans doute*, he must have seen it for himself. He is a very observant young man."

Celestine leaned forward. "Sylvie feels that there is something not quite right about Miss Arlington," she confided. "And I tend to agree with her. We are both concerned, but it is like trying to grasp a shadow. We have only our intuition to guide us, I am afraid." She subsided back in her chair with a frustrated gesture. Dr. Gaudet looked distressed.

I patted his hand reassuringly. "It was not your fault, Doctor. Do not take responsibility upon yourself." I gazed thoughtfully at my plate and realized with no little astonishment that I had eaten almost everything on it. "I think I will write to Erik and warn him of our suspicions. He promised me that as soon as he reaches the hotel where they are to stay in New York, he will send me a telegram with his address."

"But will that not take a long time?" Celestine asked.

I shook my head. "*Non*, Dr. Arlington was telling me about the transatlantic cable which was strung all across the bottom of the Atlantic Ocean, if you can believe it, just after their war ended. He says Erik's telegram will be here within a day." It seemed an amazingly short time for a message to cross the entire ocean.

"Oh, yes," Dr. Gaudet said, smiling. "I recall reading about that. It is marvelous, is it not? What will they think of next?"

Berthé came in then to take away the plates and bring dessert: a sweet cherry clafoutis and a pitcher of thick cream to pour over it. It was made from one of my mother's recipes and I remembered making it for St. Giles

Hospital more than once. For the patients, I would always pit the cherries before baking them, even though it is not traditional to do that. I thought Dr. Gaudet would appreciate it, and he did. Berthé's plain round face lit up when she saw how much I had eaten of my supper. Once she left the dining room to bring the *café*, I turned to Dr. Gaudet.

"Tell me about Father Barbier, won't you, Doctor? I am very concerned about him – his letters are much shorter than in the past." With that, the subject turned to hospital matters for the remainder of our amicable evening.

CHAPTER SIXTEEN

"I was having a lovely dream."

Erik

Though Oceanic was every bit as comfortable as Dr. Arlington assured him it would be. But he had not expected it to also be beautiful. No expense had been spared in its stylish rooms, both public and private. But what Erik found most attractive about the liner was the full set of masts. The Oceanic used both steam power and sails to carry it across the Atlantic, enabling it to make the journey in an astonishing eight or nine days. This was a vast improvement over ships of the past, and he found the billowing white sails elegant and beautiful. The entire experience inspired him to write a piece of music, but unfortunately he had no sheet music paper with him. His fingers practically itched to play something, and every morning he awoke with music rolling through his mind.

The first class staterooms that Dr. Arlington secured for them were located amidships, away from the constant noise and vibration of the engines. Even so, the rooms were by necessity small, and somewhat cramped. He wondered half-seriously if all the baggage brought aboard by the Arlingtons was the reason the ship seemed to lay so low in the sea. It was a disconcerting sight to someone so unused to either the sea or sailing.

In spite of his pleasant surroundings, Erik found the confines of the ship to be claustrophobic. It was his first time on the ocean, first time on a ship, and the saloon was filled with men smoking and drinking and ladies gossiping the days and nights away. Their vapid conversations were remarkably similar to those he had occasionally overheard from theater-goers in Paris. From the ship's portholes all that could be seen was water, and more water. He craved the sight of something green.

He took to prowling the deck at night, while most other passengers sat in the saloon playing cards. The fresh sea air and sense of openness gave temporary relief from the feeling of being trapped in a small shell bobbing along on an infinite ocean. At night, the sky was a vastness of stars, but all that could be seen of the sea itself was the white froth cut by the Oceanic's bow. Though the nighttime air was fresh and cool, it was comfortable enough since they were making the crossing in high summer.

Edythe Arlington joined him occasionally on these nocturnal forays, claiming that she was also in need of fresh air. Erik doubted this was her true reason, but as she did not flirt with or annoy him, he permitted it. Not once did she behave in such a way that he might object to it, and she seemed to go out of her way to be pleasant company.

Edythe told him of her life: about her adored and spoiled younger brother Matthew, and of her vague memories of her mother. She had been eleven or twelve when her mother died in a tragic accident: falling down a flight of stairs at their home in New York. Edythe was old enough at the time to remember things about her mother, but Matthew had been too young. Her father, she explained, did not like to talk about his late wife, but Edythe had told Matthew as much about her as she could remember.

It took Erik a while to become accustomed to her height as she walked next to him, her heels clicking on the wood of the deck. He was used to looking down at Sylvie when they walked together, but he and Edythe were almost of a height.

One night when they were strolling the deck together, Edythe unexpectedly turned to him with a question. "I almost forgot about something I wanted to ask you. Your wife suggested that I should ask you to tell me who you really are."

Edythe glanced at him curiously, shifting the silk scarf she wore over her head a little so she could see into his face. Erik was only momentarily taken aback; he recalled Sylvie telling him of her conversation with Edythe. He wondered if knowing the truth about him would change anything, but somehow he doubted it. Edythe gave a little chuckle and shook her head.

"I did not understand her, I don't mind telling you. I was under the impression that you are a winemaker and a sometime composer of music." Her tone of voice made it sound as if Sylvie were imagining things.

Walking along with his hands in his pockets, Erik smiled to himself. He looked askance at the confident young woman striding along next to him.

"That much is certainly true, Miss Arlington," he began, but she interrupted him with an impatient gesture.

"Do call me Edythe, please! We need not stand on such formalities now."

Erik made her a small mocking bow. "I am honored, Mademoiselle. But I prefer the formalities; *je regrette.*" Edythe pouted at him prettily but made no reply to this. "To answer your question," Erik went on, "I am a winemaker, and have been since we moved to Sarlat from Paris. But I have been many other things in my past."

"Such as?" She asked interestedly. They had reached the stern of the ship and turned to retrace their steps. Erik was silent for a moment, considering what he ought to tell her. He must assume that once Edythe

186

knew these things, Dr. Arlington would know them as well. Finally, he decided to simply tell the truth.

"I was once a paid assassin, I used to participate in blood sports, as they might be called, I have been a building contractor, a magician, a gypsy, and I have killed three men since my return to France from the East." He glanced casually at Edythe, who was listening to his recital in stunned silence. "Would you like to hear more?"

"More?" She asked incredulously, her voice a whisper. "There is more?" Unable to resist, he gave her one of his most feral smiles, showing quite a lot of teeth. Perversely, he found he was enjoying her discomfiture.

"I don't suppose your newspapers would have carried the story," he continued conversationally, "but I also burned down the Paris Opera House and kidnapped one of the female singers. In those days, I called myself the Phantom of the Opera, or sometimes just the Opera Ghost."

Edythe turned wide, startled dark eyes on him.

"Phantom...but...your wife...she knows all this about you?"

"Oh yes," he replied with a shrug. "Sylvie has been working at redeeming me from my evil ways ever since we met." He could not resist adding, with a sly glance at Edythe, "not always successfully."

They walked along in silence for a few moments, while another couple promenaded past them going in the opposite direction. Once alone again, Edythe spoke. The question she asked caught Erik off guard.

"What happened to...the girl you kidnapped?" She inquired breathlessly.

"Nothing," he answered curtly. "Her fiancé came to her rescue before anything could happen to her." He frowned at the gnawing memory. Sylvie always believed better of him than he believed of himself, but even Erik had to admit that he would never have forced himself on the young, innocent Christine. Unfortunately, Christine seemed to think he was capable of such a despicable deed at the time.

Edythe gave her head a toss, and smiled at him. "So, you are not a ravisher, Mr. Bessette, although it sounds as if something interesting might have happened had you not been so rudely interrupted." She laughed, as though she found this idea amusing.

Erik stared at her. He was beginning to feel active dislike for Edythe and her forward behavior. He was no longer enjoying himself now that he was the one being discomfited.

"I would not have taken her innocence, Miss Arlington, whatever you may think of me." He said coldly. Turning, he walked away from her and made his way alone back to his stateroom.

She called out to his retreating back as he stalked away, "And did you kidnap Mrs. Bessette, too?" To this idiotic question he made no reply, just kept walking. And Edythe Arlington? She stood for a moment watching him, a smug little smile playing on her lips.

One afternoon perhaps a week after Dr. Gaudet's arrival, I was sitting in the garden waiting for Celestine to join me for tea. Dr. Gaudet often retired to his room for a nap in the afternoon, so our tea would be *tête-à-tête*. Celestine was unusually late today; I hoped some household calamity had not occurred.

Since cherry season was still here, our cook had thoughtfully included a bowl of bright red cherries on the tea tray. After pouring my own cup, I helped myself to a few, tossing the pits into a nearby flower bed. Since I began riding every morning with René, I had to admit the exercise seemed to stimulate my appetite. The fresh, sweet taste of the fruit was irresistible to me. I allowed my mind to run through my favorite cherry recipes as I waited for Celestine. If we had enough fruit this year, some jam might be just the thing.

A movement inside the room caught my eye. I glanced up expectantly and saw Celestine coming toward me, a bemused expression on her face. She carried a letter in her hand. Our footman must have returned from the village with the mail. My heart did not leap in anticipation, for Erik had told me how long the journey to England would take, and that journey would be followed by a nine-day sea voyage. I could not expect to receive the eagerly awaited telegram for at least another week.

"What is the matter, dear?" I asked. "Not bad news from Meg I hope."

She shook her head at my inquiry, saying slowly, "It is not from Meg. It...it is from Christine, writing from the deChagny estate." She sat down at the white iron garden table and accepted a cup of tea from me, with extra sugar as I knew she liked. Sipping from it, she met my curious eyes over the rim of the china. She appeared troubled. "There is nothing wrong but...it is...most unexpected. I am wondering if I ought to let you read it, *ma chère*."

188

It wasn't like Celestine to be so reticent, and yet…. "Well, if it is a letter for you, I do not think it would be appropriate for *me* to read it," I said reluctantly but properly. Now, of course, all I wanted was to read the blasted letter, but I couldn't say so. "I do hope she is not planning on favoring us with another visit. Her first one caused more than enough trouble."

"*Non;* it is not that. At least part of it seems to be an apology of sorts, for being the cause of the trouble."

"Oh. I did not realize she was aware of the outcome of her visit here." I said, rather snappishly. Although I would not speak so out loud, I assumed that Christine, having identified Erik as the Phantom, had gone blithely back to her elegant, pampered life on her own, much larger estate. After satisfying herself on a deed well done, she would perhaps send for someone to make her a new gown.

Celestine looked slightly abashed. "Well, I wrote to Meg and told her what had happened, and I imagine…"

"Meg wrote in her turn to Christine," I finished for her. "Never mind, they are friends, so it was to be expected. And if her letter to you contains an apology, it ought by rights to be directed to *me.*"

"I rather think, having read it, she was hoping I might pass it along to you." Said Celestine wryly, handing me the letter.

It was several pages long. The paper was, *naturellement,* the most expensive and fine money could buy, tinted a soft shell pink. The pages were covered in a feminine, rather girlish hand. Without hesitation I spread open the letter and began to read.

"*My very dear Madame,* (it read)

You will forgive my writing you in this way, but I am in haste and so cannot manage the thing properly. If my darling Raoul should discover I am writing to you, he would be disappointed in me. I hope you understand.

I cannot tell you how wonderful it was to see you again. You look exactly the same! It is amazing. I know I look much different to you, do I not?

I hope you will appreciate how difficult it is for me to write this missive to you — I must confess some truths that I admit I would rather not. But I will not be cowardly, as I have been too many times in the past. You know of what I speak.

189

I received a letter from Meg only yesterday, telling me of everything that occurred after (here there was a splotch of ink and a word or two scratched out) my unexpected visit to you. This news has pained me greatly. Raoul, I am sorry to say, does not agree with me on this and so I take up my pen in secret. I pray you will keep my secret, Madame Giry. What I am about to write makes my cheeks flush with shame, but so be it.

I hope you and Madame Bessette, and…and Erik, understand that I never intended harm to come to either of them. I was told that the police only wanted confirmation of his whereabouts in order to keep a watch on him. Raoul convinced me that it was right to cooperate as much as I could, because no one else (or so I thought) would be as well-placed to identify him as I. I would not have consented to any of this if I knew it meant Erik (I still have a difficult time thinking of him by that name. He was always the Angel to me you know) would be arrested like that.

But I cannot rest until I tell you, Madame Giry, the complete truth, for ever since it has been eating at me that I did wrong.

The truth is, I did wish to see him once more. I always wondered what happened to him when we left; how he had escaped pursuit, where he was all this time. I blush to write this, but in the back of my mind I sometimes expected he would return to find me some day. I thought he might try to win me back to him, for I thought that his love for me would never die. I suppose in a way I took that for granted. You see, I missed him — I missed his advice and kindness to me all those years, and the lessons. He was such a good tutor. I remember my days at the Opera Garnier, oh so fondly. The performances, the footlights, the excitement of it all. I was but a girl and it was all so thrilling; and for the silly girl that I was then, it seemed romantic to have two suitors vying for my affections.

One day I received a letter from Meg, telling me all about a visit she made to you. She probably told me more than she ought, for she said that Erik was there, and that he was married, and appeared to be very happy. I was stunned to realize that in fact, he probably never even *gave me a thought, let alone be planning to try and steal me away from Raoul. And Madame I must confess, though it pains me, that I was jealous of this woman who had somehow met and married Erik. I believe I felt she had taken him away from me. I felt so foolish after I met Madame Bessette, for she is the nicest creature, and I could see for myself how happy they were together. I felt then like a low worm, I can tell you.*

It was so extraordinary for me to see him again – he looks so different, healthy and vibrant. And he seems to be much calmer in his mind than when I knew him. I must tell you, I do love my husband, for he takes such good care of me, but I admit to you now that I did love Erik also. I loved them both, Raoul and Erik. How could I not care for the Angel, when he meant so much to me for so long? I trusted him implicitly. If things had been different… but he grew so unpredictable, and then he did those horrible things. His violent behavior turned me away from him, and I grew to fear him instead.

I was truly glad to see how content and happy he has become, but it was also painful to see because I could not help but think that this might have been my life, if things had ended differently. I cannot tell you how small I feel as I write these petty words.

I hope, Madame Giry, that Erik and Sylvie, and yourself too of course (you were as a mother to me, and I am so fond of you) will find it in your hearts to forgive me for the damage I have caused. If I could go back and change things, believe that I would.

Before I close, I wish to share some joyous news with you – I have learned just a few days ago that I am expecting a happy event in perhaps seven months' time. I am so looking forward to becoming a mother for the first time. Seeing Marie Petite made me envy them all the more, but now I shall have my own little one to raise. I believe it will give me much pleasure and joy, and also offer the stimulation that has been lacking for me since we moved to the deChagny estate. Perhaps I will not dwell so often on memories of the past.

I hope you will write Meg soon, and she can then pass along your information to me. I long to know that all is well with you and the Bessettes (as I must think of them now).

Much Love, your Friend, Christine

After reading Christine's letter, I had the uncomfortable sense of invading someone's most private confessions. Did she really intend for Celestine to allow me to read her letter? I wondered if she would have wanted me to see her innermost thoughts in that way. I wasn't certain, but I carefully folded up the delicate sheets and returned them to Celestine. It seemed to me that some of Christine's behavior when she visited us was now explained, in particular why she appeared hurt or resentful that Erik had never told her his name. What would Erik think if he could read her words? I did not realize I'd spoken the thought out loud until Celestine answered me.

"It is too late now; I do not think he will ever forgive her for this."

"*Oui*, perhaps you are right; but you know, Celestine, she has such a malleable nature. A stronger personality than her own can influence her easily. I believe she truly is sorry, and as we have said before, none of this would have happened in the first place if Erik had…made better decisions. Have some more tea."

"Thank you, my dear." Celestine accepted the refilled cup I handed her rather abstractedly. She was still pondering the letter, I could tell. "I always wondered how Christine really felt about Erik. I used to wish…" she hesitated, looking chagrinned.

"That she would choose him; I know that, Celestine. I have always known that." I told her gently.

"*Oui*, it is so, or it was at one time. But I have felt for a long time that Erik made the right choice for *himself*. Whether Christine made the right choice for herself or not, no longer matters. She made her decision and she must live with it. I sincerely doubt she could have made him as happy as you have, *ma chère*." I shook my head remorsefully as she finished speaking.

"I have not made him very happy of late, Celestine, and well you know it."

"You had your reasons, dear."

I sighed, and gazed down toward the river, sparkling in the distance. "So she is expecting a happy event; I hope it will go well for her." I murmured, attempting ineffectively to suppress a flare of envy. I felt Celestine's hand cover my own.

"You will have another baby, Sylvie," she said warmly. "A perfectly healthy one, just like Marie. I am certain of it."

Gently I pulled my hand from under hers and picked up another cherry to eat. I thought about her words. There was something almost frightening in the contemplation of another pregnancy – no, let me be perfectly honest, Reader. At that moment, the idea terrified me. I knew that I would live in fear of suffering another such loss, and I did not believe I could survive that if it happened again.

Erik

Something about the unfamiliar motion of the steamer at night as it plowed through unrelenting waves, the faint but ever-present vibration of the engines, and the scent of the sea propelled Erik into strange dreams almost every night of the voyage. Some were the old, evil nightmares, but others were just peculiar dreams.

This night he came awake in the dark of his berth with the image of a man's terrified face staring wide-eyed into his. It took a moment of cogitation to remember to whom the face belonged; it was an unshaven, dissipated face, still clinging to the vestiges of handsomeness. Once he had identified the man, he relaxed back on the pillow with his hands behind his head, and spent a few minutes gloating in satisfaction. It had been a deed well done, and the memory was a happy one, at least for Erik. The man was Sylvie's first husband. He smiled into the dark, reliving that incident with relish.

It occurred not long after he and Sylvie had engaged in a heated argument over (what else?) his unhealthy relationship with Christine. But even though Erik was angry with Sylvie after their tense conversation in the cavern, when he was alone there he found himself dwelling on something she had told him earlier that night. They were sitting quietly in the boat, just talking. This experience, sitting quietly and talking of many things, was as alien to him as flying to the moon, but he had enjoyed it nevertheless. It seemed like something friends might do.

But when Sylvie talked briefly and reluctantly about her marriage, and her former husband, he found himself growing increasingly upset and angry – not at her for a change, but at that worthless man. Sylvie's face really was like an open book to Erik, and he read there much more than her reluctant words revealed.

This man, this *officer*, had wed Erik's gentle little cook and then abused her unmercifully when she was in his power. Erik could imagine him, oh yes. He would be tall and slim, handsome in his glittering uniform, with a high white brow. Erik found he hated this unknown man almost as much as he hated...well, never mind that; what was the damned man's name, anyway? He was determined to find out.

About a week after that argument, something occurred to thankfully thaw the ice between Erik and his tiresome cook. She happened to encounter Daroga in the alley, while he was making a delivery of the fireworks chemicals Erik found so useful. Erik had just collected his dinner tray from Sylvie and sent her on her way, when he heard her utter a panicked scream just outside the window, a cry of real fear. He found himself flying to her rescue without a thought. It was not a normal activity for him, to be sure, but he found he could not help himself. After reassuring her there was nothing to fear, somehow or other the experience put them back on good terms again. Was it because he so willingly came to her aid?

A few days after that, he ever so casually asked her one evening: was Bessette her married name? Sylvie said no, it was not. Looking a little shamefaced (as if somehow the divorce from that wife-beating drunkard was something to be ashamed of, and her fault), she had taken her family name back after the divorce.

As he helped Sylvie back through the window and handed her out the empty tray, he oh-so-casually asked her, what was her husband's name, then? Was it something really ugly, *la verrue* perhaps? He tried to make it sound like a little joke; that he did not really care about the answer. Sylvie had stopped and stared at him, nonplussed, but he did not look at her; he pretended bored disinterest.

Rather reluctantly, but unable to resist telling him, she answered in a low voice, "Saint-Ange. His name was Denis Saint-Ange." And then she closed her lips tightly and it was clear she would not utter another word about him. What a name, Erik thought. It surely fit the officer of his imagination. The saintly name, however, did not in the least suit his irritating harridan of a cook; he could not blame her for resuming her family name.

Back in the cavern, thoroughly enjoying the tender piece of fish wrapped in a pastry crust that she had lovingly prepared for him, Erik turned his thoughts to Sylvie's former husband. Was he still in Paris? He set himself to making plans, and then he set those plans in motion. And then he set himself into motion. The result was quite satisfying.

Smirking to himself at the memory, Erik rolled over onto his side in the berth, pulled the blanket up over his shoulder and sought sleep again. It would be hours before dawn arrived. Only two more nights and the Oceanic would at last reach New York Harbor. He was just about ready to swim the rest of the way.

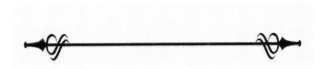

I very seldom dreamed of my mother, and never my father. He died too many years in my past to feature in my dreams at night. Not that I would not have welcomed such a visitation, for he was a dear man. Once or twice my mother made a casual appearance in my dreams, usually something to do with the cooking we always did together. She would be stirring a pot and giving me advice – to do with cooking, not life in general you understand.

So it was really quite extraordinary – very extraordinary – that I had an – well, extraordinary sort of dream featuring my dear departed mother, and one other. This was unlike any dream I'd ever had. It took place in the early hours of the morning, perhaps four or five a.m., and it shook me to my very core.

In my dream, I was climbing the five brick steps to the front door of my old family home, the home that I was forced to sell after the death of my mother. It was day time, and the sunlight was bright and cheerful. It was spring, or early summer, for the ash trees were twirling their narrow dark leaves over the walk. Even today, I could walk through the door of that house and know every corner and nook. I was born and raised in that modest two-story brick structure.

I walked down a short hallway, and with eager steps entered a parlor, knowing, in the way of dreams, that my beloved mother was in that room, waiting for me. Filled with happy anticipation, I pushed open the door and entered the parlor. Not much came to my attention other than the rooms' occupants, but I knew it to be furnished exactly as it always was. The furniture of my mother's parlor was not the comfortable, cozy sort; rather, it

195

was the spindly, white and gold delicate sort that was popular some years in the past. She loved it, so she did not care if it was no longer *dans le mode*.

It often happens that when one dreams about a departed relative or friend, even if a very beloved and missed one, the chance of a warm reunion never takes place. In dreams, they are simply there, as if in life. But in this case, to my wonder and joy, I was in complete understanding that my mother was dead, dead these four years or more, and yet she reclined on her ridiculously fragile *settee* in one of her old fashioned gowns with beads across the bodice, smiling at me in warm welcome. I cannot express my happiness at the sight of her, and the knowledge that on my lips were the words I longed to say.

"*Ma Mère...*" I whispered, but before I could utter another word, my attention was arrested, totally and completely, by her small companion.

Nestled against my mother's side was a child. Her arm was around the little girl, holding her close. The babe was, perhaps, two years old; she looked about the age of Marie. My mother, also named Marie, glanced warmly down at the tousled head of the child and then up into my eyes. My mother's wide blue eyes, so much like my own. She did not speak, but she was clearly trying to tell me something. I looked quizzically from her to the child, and then my heart seemed to stop.

The little girl watched me with an oddly knowing expression. Her fine, glossy locks were light brown, and her eyes were a pale blue, almost gray, and rimmed with dark lashes. I recognized those eyes: she had her father's eyes. She was beautiful, an angelically beautiful child, wearing a white lace nightgown that resembled a christening gown. And she had no visible disfigurement; indeed she was perfect. She was gazing at me intently. She smiled a childish little grin and reached her chubby arms toward me. She knew I was her mother, just as I knew she was my own lost *enfant*.

Slowly I advanced toward her; stumbling, I fell to my knees before the *settee* and without hesitation pulled the little girl into my arms. I *knew* her; I knew she was my own. Can we weep in dreams? I wept in mine that morning so it must be possible.

I felt my mother's hand caress my shoulder gently, but she never spoke. There was no need. I held my lost daughter tightly, knowing that soon she would vanish and be gone forever, because this was a dream. But she felt warm and solid, as real as Marie felt when I embraced her. What was her name? I remembered that I wanted to name the baby Noëlle if she was a girl, and the name came out in a whisper.

196

"Noëlle, Noëlle. I love you so much, my little one. Do not forget." Just as I said the words, I felt her small warm hand press against my cheek. And with that soft touch I was propelled out of the dream into wakefulness.

My cheeks were wet with tears, and my empty arms still seemed to feel the slight weight of a child.

With a gasp I threw off the blankets and sat on the edge of the bed. The dream was so real; I felt in my heart the truth of it. Belatedly I realized I had not said one word to my mother, but I must suppose she already knew what I would say if I could. How grateful I felt, knowing my own mother had taken my baby, *our* baby, under her wing. This vision was the greatest gift she could ever have given me. A little sob escaped me, because my heart was so full.

I rose from the bed, pulled on my dressing gown and stepped into my slippers. Quietly I stole from the room and down the dark hall. No one was awake yet; it was still quite early. Like a ghost I drifted along, until I came to the closed door of the room I had begun to think of as Erik's bedroom. But it was *our* bedroom. Reaching out slowly, I opened the door and stepped inside.

No one had been in the room since Erik left for America, except a housemaid to tidy up after him and clean the fireplace grate. The room was chill with the cold air of early morning. I lit all the candles and the room sprang to life. I walked around, looking at everything, including the big canopy bed. The *armoire* was all but empty; Erik had taken most of his clothing with him in a large steamer trunk. On top of his chest of drawers sat a familiar little object: his brass incense burner. At some point he had rescued it from his old home along with the mosaic box given to me as a gift. These were the only personal items he had brought with him when we left Paris. I picked up the small brass dish and lifted it to my nose. The small burned stub of incense had lost its fragrance. I set the dish back down and continued on my journey about the room, reacquainting myself with it.

Finally I stopped at the windows, and peered outside. It was still dark, and all I could see was my reflection and the points of flickering candlelight behind me. Gazing at my pale face in the glass, I felt that although nothing had changed, everything was different because of that dream.

I understood myself so much better now; when I refused to sleep again in this room, it was not in rejection of my husband, but because I was trying to hide from what happened here. There were so many things I was wrong about, I felt supremely stupid. Wishing to put the blame for my loss on Erik, I had convinced myself that the *enfant* must have inherited his disfigurement to such a degree that it could not survive. I was even wrong about the sex of the child! How certain I was that it would be a boy. Now I was absolutely positive it was a girl, and would have been that lovely little Erik-lookalike in my dream. Dr. Olivier was right; sometimes these things just happened.

I wiped away a few stray tears; I would always miss that beautiful child, would always regret that I lost her. What would she have been like?

Shaking my head ruefully, I turned from the blank window and went to the bed. As of this minute, I was moving back into our bedroom. Drawing back the sheets and blankets, I crawled into it and curled on my side, waiting for heat to collect beneath the sheets. The bedding had not been changed since Erik was here, and his scent lingered faintly on the pillow. He had such a delicious, spicy, masculine scent, I would recognize it anywhere. I burrowed my nose into the pillow searching for more of it, and then I sighed and fell asleep again, a contented, dreamless sleep.

CHAPTER SEVENTEEN

"I am afraid you will vanish into thin air."

Erik

"There it is! There's the hotel!" Edythe bounced up and down on her seat, pointing out the carriage window. Following her pointing finger, Erik beheld an enormous, glowing white square, the size of a city block, rising several stories into the New York sky. His first impression was of cold, hard ugliness, and what he would consider American pretension. Was it really necessary for a hotel to be so big? Then he remembered his visit to the Le Grande Hotel in Paris. It might not be as prepossessing as this glowing edifice, but it was certainly *de trop*.

Edythe turned to her father eagerly. "Will Matthew be here yet, Father?" Dr. Arlington had explained to Erik during the crossing that the Arlingtons had a house located near his clinic and surgery in White Plains, where his son Matthew lived when not in school. Matthew was expected to meet them here at the hotel.

"I hope so, Edie," replied her father. "There wasn't time for him to answer our telegram."

The wide street upon which they travelled was crawling with wagons, carts, carriages, and people on horseback or on foot. As they approached the pillared portico of the Fifth Avenue Hotel, Dr. Arlington leaned toward Erik.

"I should warn you that you must be on your guard at all times from pickpockets when you are out of the hotel. Pickpockets are the scourge of the city these days."

"How long do you intend to remain here?" Erik asked warily. He disliked what he had seen of New York thus far, and was anxious to visit the clinic. It was located in a less populated part of Manhattan Island, though reachable by train.

The doctor exchanged glances with his daughter. "Well, hmmm. I know Edie would like to spend some time here and see her friends…"

"And I want to show Erik the sights of the city while he is here!" Edythe added. Inwardly, Erik groaned. He hoped yet again that he was not making a dreadful mistake by coming here. He could always go home, he reminded himself grimly.

The first thing he did upon checking in to the hotel was ask where the nearest telegraph office might be. It turned out that the hotel had its own small telegraph office, located near the front desk on the ground floor.

"I promised Sylvie I would send her a telegram as soon as we arrived," he explained. Both the Arlingtons came along to show him the office and help the clerk understand what he needed. Despite careful perusal of the book on English Edythe had purchased for him and practicing in the privacy of his stateroom, Erik was far from fluent. "I will write her, but for now, this will at least let her know we arrived safely." He added.

"She will have your address that way too," said Dr. Arlington. "It will be printed on the telegram." Edythe said nothing. She busied herself straightening her skirts and adjusting her hat, looking slightly bored.

"I am going to ask at the desk if Matthew is here yet," she said, and strode briskly out of the telegraph office toward the desk.

Erik would rather have walked on hot coals than admit it, but he was glad for Dr. Arlington's help with the telegram. Not only did he not understand English particularly well, but he had never in his life sent a telegram. He felt a bit like one of the Bedouins who lived on the Arabian deserts – uncivilized, out of touch with the modern world. Apparently cost was determined by the number of words you wished to send. With Dr. Arlington's help he dictated a brief message.

'Arrived safely, address above. Letter to follow. Love, E.' It was terse, but he was not sure what else he ought to say. Tonight he would sit down with pen and paper and write Sylvie a long letter. She would write back quickly, he was certain. Letters could not travel anywhere near as fast as a telegram, *sans doute*, but perhaps he could hope to hear from her in a fortnight. He sighed quietly, feeling unaccountably melancholy. The distance between them seemed suddenly insurmountable. He did not want to remain here one minute longer than necessary.

Dr. Arlington's son Matthew, when he finally turned up at the hotel, proved to be a younger, slighter version of his older sister Edythe. He had the same dark, wavy hair, worn short. He had a decided tendency toward dandyism, and had obviously been attempting to grow a mustache during his father's absence, with lackluster success. Edythe teased him about it gleefully when they, including Erik, gathered for afternoon tea and coffee in the Arlington's suite. Matthew seemed a high spirited, good natured young man, who addressed his sister as 'stork' in response to her jibes about his dirty upper lip. The siblings were clearly very fond of each other.

Matthew expressed little interest in Erik or his mask; he seemed to take it for granted that Erik was merely another potential surgery patient for his father. He was far more interested in the sights and excitements of New York, and the tea dances held daily in the hotel.

When the Arlingtons pressed Erik to join them for dinner in the Fifth Avenue Hotel's opulent dining room, he declined.

"I intend to dine in my room," he informed Edward firmly. "I promised my wife a letter *tout de suite*, so I will stay in and do that." It was an excuse of sorts; in truth he was not comfortable wearing his mask in the crowded dining room.

Dr. Arlington looked concerned. "Is it because you do not wish to attract undue attention that you stay in your room?" He asked in a kindly voice.

Erik gave him a sharp look. The surgeon was perceptive indeed. Erik nodded once, without speaking. There was no point in making up some excuse.

They were standing in the carpeted corridor outside Erik's hotel suite. Dr. Arlington was already dressed for dinner in a formal suit of dark cloth. Now he tilted his head to one side, regarding Erik gravely.

"I wonder..." he said after a moment. "Perhaps it would be best for you and I to proceed to my clinic tomorrow, rather than remaining here in the city. We could get to work on creating a new mask for you – there is no reason we cannot begin that at once."

"I would prefer that," Erik said, relieved. The sooner they departed for the clinic, the better as far as he was concerned.

"I am sure Edythe and Matthew will be happy to remain here at the hotel for a few days." He smiled with satisfaction. "Yes, this will be excellent. I look forward to giving you a tour of our facilities." They parted in perfect accord, and Erik entered his elegant, wood-paneled suite. Looking around, he noticed a brass plaque on the wall, with a button to push when one wished to summon the servant who worked on that floor of the hotel. He pushed the button and then began the arduous task of using the correct English to order his dinner and some wine, and the necessary writing materials.

Once that was over, he discarded his coat, waistcoat and cravat, unbuttoned his shirt, and pulled out the gold locket he had been wearing under his clothes. The heavy gold was warm from his skin. He pried the locket open and placed it on a night stand by the bed, where he could see it. Here in this strange place, it was comforting to have a little reminder of home.

In the morning, he went directly to the lobby downstairs and presented to a young man behind the counter his letter for Sylvie. It was thick; several pages in his tight, firm handwriting on expensive cream colored notepaper. He had told her about the sea voyage, about his first glimpse of America, and of the hotel. He also told her he was going to the clinic to address the possibility of the new mask. He had avoided any mention of surgery, except to say that he would write again with more information when he had it. And of course, he told her how much he loved her, missed her, and sent his love to Marie *Petite*. The young man behind the counter, giving him a frankly curious stare, accepted the heavy envelope and dropped it unceremoniously into a box behind him.

Much to my regret, *Ballerine's* rightful owner claimed her back, so I began taking a walk in the morning instead. I missed the sweet little mare (and so did Danté) but as Dr. Gaudet pointed out, walking was better exercise for me anyway. Still, I thought it might be nice to have my own mare, so Erik and I could ride together when he came home. Now that I knew how to ride, I would not have to always sit in front of him on Danté.

I often walked the same way René and I rode: up the drive beneath the shade of the sycamore trees to the main road and back again. Sometimes I walked down through the vineyard and sunflower field toward the river. I was not yet able to walk all the way to the river and back, for the return trip was all uphill. I was getting better at it, though.

I had just entered the foyer and was untying the ribbons of my straw sun hat when Celestine came hastening toward me. In her hand was the unmistakable thin blue paper of a telegram. My heart gave a little leap and my eyes flew to hers. The long-awaited telegram!

"It was just delivered by the footman," she said, handing it to me. "It is from New York." I took it eagerly and tore it open without preamble. Scanning it quickly, I saw that it was, indeed, sent from Erik's hotel in New York. The message was brief to the point of terseness, but I was buoyed by the anticipation of a letter to follow.

Handing the telegram to Celestine, who was obviously anxious to read it, I began silently counting how many days it might take a letter to arrive here. It would take eight or nine days to cross the Atlantic, then by boat or train across the channel to France, and no doubt by some sort of public transport to Sarlat. It would be a fortnight at the very earliest. I sighed, feeling a trifle melancholy. Erik was so far away from me. What things would he have to tell me about, I wondered. The adventure of a sea voyage, his first sight of America? What was the Fifth Avenue Hotel like? And what of Edythe Arlington?

As I made my way toward my sitting room, I recollected my decision to write to Erik with our concerns (suspicions?) about Miss Arlington. But what should I say? That Celestine and I suspected she might not be quite right in her mind? How could I suggest she might actually be dangerous without telling him my suspicion that she tried to kill me? Frowning over this dilemma, I opened the door and went in.

Dr. Gaudet was in my sitting room with Marie; she was showing him the picture book Edythe Arlington had given her. The patient man had been attempting to read a book of his own but was forced to set it aside. Marie's little picture book had become rather sticky with jam and a few of the little pull-out pages no longer pulled out. She was still charmed by the book, however.

Dr. Gaudet, having satisfied himself that I was making good progress on my recovery, would be leaving soon, returning to Paris and his charges at the hospital. I would miss him when he departed. I knew Celestine would miss him, too. They had got into the habit of taking a turn around the grounds together after supper.

It occurred to me with a jolt of shock that if I wished to, *I* could go to Paris and visit Father Barbier. There was nothing to stop me now that we were free from the constant fear of discovery and capture. The idea was arresting. The sounds of Marie's chatter and Dr. Gaudet and Celestine's voices faded into the background while I contemplated the idea of traveling on my own to Paris. I was born and raised there, but until now, I could never go back. At first the mad idea felt exciting, even possible, but then I thought about the rigors of the journey, of travelling alone, staying in strange inns along the way…it sounded utterly exhausting. I shook my head regretfully, allowing reality to return. I handed Dr. Gaudet the telegram from Erik.

His face brightened. "Ah! So you have heard from the wanderer at last!" He said, reading it and handing it back to me.

"*Oui*, but I could wish for a little more," I replied, placing the telegram in the pocket of my gown. "However, his letter is already on its way to me, *sans doute*." I glanced at Marie and, since she was still absorbed in her picture book, added softly for his ears only, "Celestine and I are of a mind

203

that I should write Erik directly…about Miss Arlington, so it is likely our letters will cross in the mail." Although I did not say so out loud, I did rather hope Erik would tell me about the hotel's perpendicular railway. I found it quite impossible to imagine such a thing, or how it could operate safely.

Dr. Gaudet nodded approvingly. "*Une bonne idée*, my dear. When you do so, please convey to him my warmest regards, and assure him for me that I find you making great improvements every day."

I smiled at him warmly. "I will be certain to do so."

That evening after supper I retired to the bedroom and my little *secretaire* and spent over an hour struggling to compose a letter to Erik. I wished to convey a warning to him, but I did not want to sound unreasonable. Nor did I want him to think I was imagining things. It was a challenge, to be sure. In the end I simply told him that the three of us (because the suspicions of *three* people rather than just one might hold more weight) were concerned that Miss Arlington might have a potentially dangerous personality defect. He must beware of her, and try to keep her at arm's length. I frowned over that part, and chewed on the end of my pen. Did it sound as if I were trying to keep him away from her because I was jealous? Well, if I were being perfectly honest, I was a little bit jealous. He was now thousands of miles from home, alone in a strange city, and potentially vulnerable to her attentions.

In the morning the footman carried my letter to town. I imagined that our letters to each other must cross in the mail. But it was odd; Dr. Gaudet went back to Paris, life settled back into its normal routine, the days sped by, but there was no letter from New York.

CHAPTER EIGHTEEN

"He doesn't want to always have to hide his face!"

Erik

Later that morning, he packed a small valise and took a train to the village of White Plains with Dr. Arlington. He was ready to leave New York; it was such a noisy, dusty, brash place. He was accustomed to a city being like Paris, or Constantinople. Here there were few trees, and what trees existed were but saplings compared to the beautiful trees of Paris. Edythe expressed regret at his sudden departure, but declared she would remain with Matthew at the hotel to 'keep an eye on him'. Erik was not sorry to spend a few days away from her; he had taken to treating her in an aloof, distant manner, and it seemed to have cooled her ardor somewhat.

Dr. Arlington explained that his clinic was located in an older, historic building outside the Village of White Plains. On the train ride he told Erik that during the Revolutionary War, a battle between George Washington and the British took place in that area. Farmers were still turning up musket balls and other evidence of the battle when they plowed their fields. This lesson in American history was of absolutely no interest to Erik, and he listened with only half an ear.

As the train progressed, the landscape grew flatter and sparsely populated. The houses he glimpsed out the window were strange looking to his eyes: narrow, two story affairs with wooden walls invariably painted white and with steeply pitched roofs. This, Dr. Arlington explained, was because during the winter a great deal of snow fell here. This was difficult to imagine, for when they emerged at the train station in White Plains, the hot humid air hit him like an assault. Seeing him pull out his handkerchief and wipe his face and neck with it, Dr. Arlington gave him a rueful smile.

"The humidity does take a bit of getting used to," he said apologetically. Erik was thinking, meanwhile, of how much he wanted to rip the cravat off his neck and throw it away. Bien sûr, in the summer at home they sometimes had rather humid days, with the river being so close, but this felt like...like the air he breathed was more water than air.

While they waited for the valet to gather their belongings and summon a carriage, Erik looked about him with a growing sense of dismay. White Plains was a village indeed; it did not look to be even the size of Sarlat. It was the end of the line for the railroad, and the unprepossessing station was a squat red brick building set directly by the tracks. This seemed an unlikely place to have a clinic and surgery. He hoped he would not regret his decision to come here.

Dr. Arlington, on the other hand, grew more animated than Erik had ever seen him as the carriage made its sedate way down the wide dirt road. His grey eyes behind the gold spectacles brightened, and he even seemed to sit up straighter. He turned on the seat and looked at Erik.

"I have been away too long. I never intended to stay so long in France, but Edie..."his voice trailed off, and he peered ahead eagerly. "See there – that wide ring of elm trees? That is our destination: the Arlington/Buck Surgical Clinic for Civil War Veterans."

The carriage turned down a long drive between rows of trees. There were many trees, but no shrubs, flowers or bushes; the effect of the tall trunks of elm and maple trees against the flat green of the grounds gave it a park-like appearance. Glimpses of their destination could be seen between the trunks of the trees. Erik found his own heart beating a little faster as they approached the unassuming building.

Like everything else he had seen thus far, it was painted white, but this building was a long, two story structure of brick, solid looking and yet ethereal in its white perfection. Precisely in the center of the building was a covered porch, and there were many windows, all with dark green wooden trim and shutters. In front of the clinic was a wide, neat space covered in some sort of golden colored gravel. Crunching over the gravel, the carriage stopped before the covered porch, beneath which were double doors of some sort of hard wood. Everything looked pristine, clean, yet peculiarly impersonal.

Jumping down from the carriage seat, Erik studied the building in silence; he had a strange sensation that here in this place his life would change – either in a small way, or a very great way. What would he learn inside those doors?

Another week went by, and though each day I eagerly anticipated Erik's letter, still it did not come. Celestine suggested that perhaps it was lost or misdirected, and I ought to write him again and let him know.

"I will wait one or two more days, Celestine," I said when she proposed this possibility. "If it hasn't arrived by then, I will do as you suggest." I was not worried about him; surely if something were the matter – if he were ill or…I would hear from Dr. Arlington if not Erik himself. So I assured myself, at any rate. I was conscious of a growing sense of unease, however. He would have had my own first letter by now; what was happening there?

Celestine approached me in the hallway as I was leaving the nursery after spending an hour with Marie. She carried a letter in her hand, and I could tell by the expression on her face that this was not the long-awaited letter from Erik. There was a little notch of worry between her fine brows.

"It is from Phi…that is, Dr. Gaudet," she said in a subdued voice. When she handed it to me I did not want to take it. I think we both knew it was bad news.

Father Barbier had passed on to his reward, in his sleep, quite peacefully. One of the nuns had discovered him when she went to his room in the morning to bring him some *café* and a roll. He was lying on his back in bed, hands folded, his black eyes looking heavenward (most appropriately), and a small half-smile on his lips. The letter I had sent with Dr. Gaudet for him was lying nearby; he had read it several times apparently.

Due to the strict secrecy necessary in having a leprosarium in the city of Paris, the Hospital had its own small graveyard, and Father Barbier had just been laid to rest there, after a small ceremony. They had planted some crocus and *muguets de bois* bulbs over his plot, Dr. Gaudet explained, because he loved those flowers. There was, Dr. Gaudet explained, something on its way to me in the mail: a token of the esteem and affection that Father Barbier felt for me.

I was rather expecting this unhappy news. Dr. Gaudet tried to prepare me for it when he was here. But we always *think* we are prepared to hear impending bad news, until we actually hear it. Father Barbier had been more to me than merely one of the patients I cooked for at St. Giles Hospital. We took to each other from the first, and somehow it was as if we created a father-daughter relationship, even though he was a priest and I absolutely no relation to him.

He was small of stature, with bright black eyes like a bird's. He possessed a deep, sonorous voice and was often called upon to read an excerpt from the Bible before the beginning of the noonday meal. His face had been covered with the awful disfigurement that comes with Leprosy: painful red nodules and a distinctive flattening of the nose. He had been a missionary somewhere in Africa, and this was where he contracted the disease. In spite of these afflictions, Father Barbier had been an optimistic, happy man who always saw the good in people – including my future husband. I remembered his telling me, the day he married Erik and I, that we would never see each other again once I left that place. And he had been right. I wondered what it was that he wished me to have. I would be glad of something tangible to remember him by.

Without speaking, I handed the letter from Dr. Gaudet to Celestine so she could read it. Although she never met him, she knew what Father Barbier had meant to me, and to Erik as well. When we met in Paris, I had told Celestine that the patients at the hospital were burn victims, since I could not tell her the truth about them. Having met Dr. Gaudet, of course, she now knew what they really were. After quickly perusing the letter, she returned her concerned gaze to my face.

"I am sorry, *ma chère*," she murmured gently. "It sounds as if...he passed quite peacefully."

"Yes," I said abstractedly. "I am going out for a few minutes." Turning, I went downstairs, leaving Celestine staring after me. I collected my straw hat from where it hung in the foyer and went out into the warm summer sun. Tears stung the corners of my eyes, and I dashed them away. I walked slowly down the path toward the vineyard; there was someone else who needed to be told about this loss – the only other person here who actually knew Father Stèphane Barbier beside myself. Robert.

That night, after supper and a last check on Marie, I sat down at my desk and wrote Erik another letter.

'Mon Cher Mari,'

But here I paused, and sat lost in thought for a few moments. Outside the open window I could hear the last calls of doves to each other as they came home to the dovecote at the back of the garden. Had Erik's letter simply been lost in the mail, as Celestine suggested? Or had it even been sent? Could he perhaps have become so busy with activities in that strange, exotic place, New York, or perhaps caught up in the alluring charms of Miss Arlington, that he could not find time to write me? Pushing these disagreeable thoughts aside, I gave my head a shake and picked up my pen again.

'This is my second letter to you; I write to tell you that yours to me has never arrived. We fear it has gone astray in the mail, though I hope it will find its way here eventually. I am anxious to hear how you

208

get on, and what you are doing. Please write to me again as soon as may be, and tell me how you are and what is happening there. Have you been to Dr. Arlington's clinic yet?

We are all well here, and Marie petite sends her love. You will find she has grown a good bit when you see her again. She sleeps every night with the doll you brought her from Paris. I also am fine; I believe my strength returns more each day. I walk almost every morning, and Celestine tells me that my gowns are fitting better.

I do have some sad news to impart: Dr. Gaudet writes to tell me that dear Father Barbier has passed away, peacefully in his sleep. When I told Robert the news, he came as close to crying as I have ever seen him. I did cry, quite a lot. How I will miss him! Dr. Gaudet is worried that the Church may close the hospital, for there are now only three patients left. I do not know what will happen to them, but he hopes that Dr. Hansen in Norway might accept them at his hospital.

Please write soon, mon amour, with all your news. And remember your promise to me, that you would not make any decisions without telling me first.

I miss you so much. I wanted also to tell you that I have moved back into our bedroom, but it feels very empty without you.'

I paused at that point and blew my nose on my handkerchief, which by some miracle was on my person. Then I finished the letter, signed it and sealed it, ready to go out on the morrow.

Rising, I went to the window and stood looking out at the gathering gloom of night. A whisper of cool air lifted the lace curtains and brushed them across my face. I shivered, and drew the windows closed. Where was Erik, and what was he doing right now? I did not even know what time it was in America. Did he think of me, or Marie, at all?

CHAPTER NINETEEN

"I saw the stairs going down into darkness."

Erik

It was night time. Back at the hotel and bedeviled by all that he had learned during his week-long stay at the clinic in White Plains, Erik tossed and turned restlessly. Sleep was long in coming, and when he did sleep, he woke with a start, damp with sweat, from another nightmare. His nightmares were becoming more frequent, but this one was different. Instead of the usual evil memories returning to plague him, he dreamed about the clinic.

He had been there for several days while the new mask was being made for him, and there was at times nothing to do but explore the building and examine the surgical facilities. He was shown Dr. Buck's before and after photographs, which were much like the ones in Dr. Arlington's brochure. Both surgeons seemed to have a high rate of recovery and improvement from their special techniques, called 'plastic operations'.

One afternoon, shortly before sunset, Erik had found himself prowling about aimlessly on the ground floor at the back of the building, a little-used area that appeared quite old and untouched. There was a heavy wood door at the end of the sloping hallway, and he was unable to resist opening it to see what lay beyond. He had some idea that it must lead outside, to the back of the clinic building. But instead, the door opened upon a set of wide wood stairs, leading down into darkness. The walls on one side were of brick, dusty and cobwebbed. The black within was absolute; the air wafting up smelled peculiar. What was down there?

He had always possessed an uncanny ability to see in the dark, and descending into stygian depths held no fears for him. But before Erik could give in to his curiosity (he was getting to be as bad as Sylvie, he thought to himself wryly) and take a few steps down into the unknown room, Dr. Arlington had come upon him.

"Oh, there you are!" He had exclaimed, sounding perturbed. "Come away from there, Erik; that is an old basement we used to store supplies in. There is nothing to interest you there and I believe it is quite dirty." Taking Erik by the arm, he escorted him back to the main clinic area for a fitting of the new mask.

Now lying in his soft hotel bed, Erik tried to shake off the nightmare but the horrible dream images lingered. In the dream he had found himself standing before the wood door, and again he could not resist pulling it open to reveal the stairs descending into a deep darkness. When the door opened, frigidly cold air hit his face. In the dream, something about the stairs reminded him of the descent into his old cavern, and yet there was something wrong. Despite a growing sense of unease, Erik took the first step, and then the second. He felt drawn downward, pulled toward he knew not what. He became aware of a foul odor rising up to meet him.

By the time he neared the bottom of the stairs, the darkness was absolute. He suddenly held a candle in his hand, and when he passed the palm of his free hand over the candle, the wick burst into flame. A nice trick, but only possible in a dream. Holding the candle aloft, he looked around him.

Just as Dr. Arlington had said, it was a storage room of sorts - it was a morgue. The frigid cellar was filled with gurneys, and on each one lay a still form covered in a white shroud. Horrified, Erik at once turned to go, but even as he moved, the bodies began to stir. He could not look away. One by one they slowly sat up, and the shrouds fell away to reveal horribly mutilated faces. All the ghastly faces turned as one toward Erik, as though he had interrupted their endless sleep. One of the corpses slowly raised an arm toward him. He actually opened his mouth to scream, something he never did in his life, but no sound came out.

He forced himself to turn, but his body responded ever so slowly, and it seemed to take an hour to place one foot in front of the other and mount the stairs again. He saw above him the open door, and something white glimmering on one of the stairs near the top. It was his mask. How did it come to be there? Then the mask appeared to be much farther away, and there were many more steps. His feet seemed to be glued to the stair treads. He heard rustling sounds behind him. And that was when he bolted awake, sweating and filled with horror. He sat up so suddenly his head swam. He was here, safe in the hotel.

"Curse these damned nightmares," he muttered, rubbing his fingers over his eyes as if to wipe away the hideous dream images.

Damn it, he needed to get a grip on himself. It was only a nightmare, brought on by seeing all those photographs at the clinic, *sans doute*. He knew sleep would not return for a long time. He forced himself to think of something else; not difficult, for there were many things on his mind. How he wished Sylvie were here – she would have known what questions to ask about the surgery, and he could have talked everything over with her.

He sighed, and punched his pillow in a vain effort to make it more comfortable. In the morning, he decided, he would sit down and write her another letter, and tell her about his meeting with Dr. Buck, and about the new mask. He would lay it all out for Sylvie, and perhaps in that way, make it clearer to himself.

Erik stared up at the dark ceiling. This was another thing that was worrying him. He had been impatient to return to the hotel because by now, she would have received his letter and responded back to him. But when he asked at the front desk in the lobby, the boy behind the counter checked his box and found it empty. He had been so certain there would be a letter, he demanded the boy look again. It must be there. Unfortunately Edythe had chosen that moment to approach him, all smiles and questions about his trip to the clinic. She turned her big black eyes and smile on the boy behind the counter, causing him to flush and straighten his necktie.

Feeling irritated and worried, Erik had greeted Edythe somewhat brusquely. Too upset to speak to her, he gave her a stiff bow and excused himself. As he stalked away, out of the corner of his eye he saw Edythe and the boy exchange looks with each other, and Edythe shrugged. Damn her! Frustration and concern bubbled inside him. He ended up back in his hotel suite, pacing back and forth across the thick carpet, feeling like he might jump out of his skin at any moment. What he would have given for a piano!

It was at times like this that he missed his wife the most. He had always been able to rely on Sylvie to listen to him, to soothe his soul, and to offer sensible advice. She had been his one true friend, but now he could not help but wonder if the close bond they had shared was still intact. Why did she not write? Was she still, in spite of that last night together, angry with him?

A low groan escaped him, and he rubbed his weary eyes again. A sense of guilt crept over him, and he could not push it away. He could never be sure, but he strongly suspected that it was his fault that his wife had lost the baby. Sylvie believed it, and that was the reason behind her cold behavior toward him after his return from Paris. The loss could have been precipitated by her fears for him, or by his own disfigurement being passed along to the child. Such an evil choice had been forced on him: to let himself be taken away and hanged, leaving his family alone in the world, or to do what was asked of him and receive a full pardon. Of course the job had been dangerous, and of course Sylvie worried about him. It didn't matter which thing caused the loss, because the outcome was the same. He had hoped, believed, she had forgiven him, but was this silence on her part another way to punish him?

Or what if she had taken a turn for the worse, become ill again? No, no, Dr. Gaudet had been there, might still be there, and he would surely have alerted Erik if something was amiss at home.

There was a cut crystal decanter of water by the bed, with a crystal glass that fit over the mouth of the decanter to help keep the water clean at night. Erik lifted the glass and poured water for himself. He sat on the edge of the bed sipping it, ruminating morosely. Nothing was going right, nothing had gone right since the day Moreau, curse him, had appeared at the *château*.

Erik rose and went to the window. He was three stories up, and his room overlooked busy Fifth Avenue. Gaslights lit the street and even at this hour carriages and people still moved up and down the wide street. He watched this activity for a few moments, bemused. It was a good thing that he had a few years of civilized behavior under his belt, so to speak, or all this humanity surrounding him would have driven him mad.

He needed to push all the nagging worries about home and Sylvie aside so he could concentrate on all he had learned during the days spent at the clinic. He ran his hands through his hair, released his breath in an explosive sigh, and came back to the bed. Crawling under the blanket, he lay staring up at the dark ceiling, forcing his mind away from Sylvie and back to his experiences at Edward's clinic.

The first person he met upon arrival at Dr. Arlington's clinic had been the doctor's partner and fellow surgeon, Dr. Gurdon Buck. He was physically very much Dr. Arlington's opposite: shorter of stature, stocky and sturdily built, with a balding round head, round face, and a small pair of pince-nez perched on his long, prominent nose. His eyes were cool blue, narrow and with a slight squint. He had been expecting them, thanks to a telegram Dr. Arlington had dispatched prior to their departure from the hotel.

The two surgeons were clearly pleased to see each other again, exchanging warm greetings. He understood very little of what was said between them, although his English was gradually improving. Feeling awkward and out of place, Erik waited to one side until Dr. Arlington brought him forward to be introduced.

While he waited, he glanced about surreptitiously at his surroundings; to one side of the entrance there was a large open room, with light pouring in from the long row of tall windows. The walls were painted white, and the floor was of some dark polished planks of wood. There were tables and chairs, and a row of benches beneath the open windows. Several men occupied the room, playing cards or an odd looking game that seemed to take place on a chessboard, only the pieces were all the same – little flat disks in red or black. The purpose of the game was a mystery to Erik however. Upon closer inspection, he could see that the men were in various stages of recovery from facial reconstruction surgery. A few nurses in starched white uniforms flitted about.

Erik tore his gaze away from a soldier who obviously had suffered a bullet wound that went in one cheek and out the other, when he heard Dr. Arlington say his name. Turning back to him, he saw the doctor was beckoning him forward. He smiled at Erik reassuringly, saying,

"I have warned Dr. Buck that you do not speak very much English, and I am afraid he does not know any French, but I will be your translator."

Dr. Buck possessed a strong, firm handshake, and an obvious curiosity to see what was behind the mask Erik wore. His narrow eyes went straight to it. Turning to Dr. Arlington, he said something in rapid English. Dr. Arlington nodded and said,

"Dr. Buck is very interested in examining your face, Erik. I have just told him it is a birth defect of some kind. I also told him you were interested in having a better mask made. He understands you have not yet committed to having any operation performed."

Erik followed the two surgeons to an exam room, a clean, efficient, well lighted room that was a far cry from Philippe's small clinic room. There were various pieces of medical equipment and an exam table covered in stiff white sheets. Erik sat on that while Dr. Buck turned a bright light on his face and brought forward one of the pieces of equipment.

He studied Erik's disfigured face for several minutes, finally asking, "May I?" before touching his face with careful fingers.

Holding patiently still, Erik glanced at Dr. Arlington, who nodded encouragingly. It occurred to him at that moment that the hands that were gently pushing and pulling at his face were the same hands that might, at some future point, be operating on him. He felt a strange lurch inside, as if his equilibrium was suddenly off. What had seemed a far-fetched dream when he was still in France now loomed before him as a very real possibility. Was that excitement he felt surging up inside him, or fear?

After finishing his impromptu exam, Dr. Buck perched on the edge of the exam table, removed his pince-nez and absently began to polish them. Dr. Arlington asked eagerly, "What do you think, Gurdon? Can we help him?" They were conversing in English, but Erik found he was able to follow them reasonably well. Erik, watching the other man's face closely, felt his fate, and his face, hanging in a balance. It was clear that the final word would belong to Dr. Buck.

"I am afraid that the technique we use here, which is to use a flap of healthy skin close to the wounded area, cannot be performed on this man's face. There is too much of the disfigurement covering that side. The only thing that we might try..." here Dr. Arlington leaned forward, seeming to hold his breath.

"We could try taking healthy skin from another, less visible part of the body and attach it to a part of the face and see if it would survive there. This could work, for example, here where the eyelid has sagged away and exposed so much of the eye itself." As he spoke, Dr. Buck gestured toward Erik's ghastly right eye.

Dr. Arlington frowned. "But we have never attempted anything like that, Gurdon. I do not know if it would work, and if infection were to set in...because it is so close to the eye itself, he could lose his sight." Seeing that Erik was no longer able to follow their rapid English, he paused to translate for him. When he finished, both surgeons turned toward him, waiting for his response.

To Erik it sounded like a tremendous gamble to take, with no certainty of the outcome. His thoughts settled for a brief instant upon his wife, as a butterfly might stop at a flower. She did not, he recalled, want him to have any surgery on his face. An idea occurred to him.

"There is no need for me to make a decision this instant, Edward." He said. "But I am very interested in pursuing the idea of a new mask." Dr. Arlington nodded; Erik had the fleeting impression that he was relieved.

And so it was decided that the next day, the plaster cast of the left side of his face would be made. It would take another day to dry, and then it would be used to create a flexible mask. The process would take several days, and Erik resigned himself to staying there longer than he would have preferred. During Erik's time in White Plains, it was arranged that he would stay in Dr. Arlington's own house situated nearby, rather than at the clinic itself, which was almost full with veteran patients. There was a guestroom at the house, and Edward's housekeeper, Mrs.McKendrick, would make him perfectly at home.

The new mask, composed of some sort of cellulose material combined with an amount of soft rubber, now rested on the table next to his bed at the hotel. The mask had been worth the wait, cooling his heels at the clinic during the process of having it made to his exact facial conformation. It fit perfectly, had been tinted somehow to match his skin tone, and was much thinner and more flexible than any of the leather masks he had made for himself in the past. The surgeons were hoping that by developing a mask that was more skin-like in appearance, they could be made for use by veterans whose injuries could not be improved by surgery.

His new mask was so much more natural in appearance, he was able to wear it in public. He had experimented with this when they returned to the hotel from White Plains. Even if he decided surgery was not in the cards for him, it was worth making this trip for the mask alone. When he wore it, he felt transformed.

And now, there was time for him to consider everything; Dr. Arlington was traveling to Washington, D.C. to conduct a teaching course at a military hospital there. He would be away for some time, and Erik had agreed to make no definite decisions until his return. Edythe and Matthew had promised to keep him occupied until their father returned to New York. But he had to admit to himself that he was beginning to regret agreeing to wait; he longed for home, to be back in France where people spoke his language, longed to see his wife and daughter again. He resolved he would rise early in the morning and write Sylvie another letter. It would help him to sort out his thoughts, if nothing else.

I was completing the final preparations for taking Marie out for a picnic in the sunflower field. As anyone with a small child can attest, preparations for going anywhere can be quite time-consuming. Yes, she could bring her doll. No, she could not forgo her shoes. And so on, *ad infinitum*. We were finally ready to go when our footman met me in the foyer, carrying a long, rectangular package. It appeared rather heavy for its size. The direction on the box showed that it was from Dr. Gaudet at the Hospital.

The footman procured a sharp knife and cut through the wrappings to reveal a solid-looking wooden box. No wonder it was so heavy.

"Shall I open it for you, Madame?" the footman inquired.

"No, I will," I said. It must, I knew, be the final gift to me from my old friend and father-figure. Marie tugged on my dress, demanding to know if it was a present for her.

Carefully I lifted the lid of the box and looked inside. There was something wrapped in tissue paper. Keeping the curious child at bay, I

216

pushed the paper aside, to reveal an old, carved crucifix, painted and gilded and very beautiful.

"Oh," I murmured on an intake of breath. I recognized it, remembered it, quite well. The few times I had been in Father Barbier's small, austere room, this venerable old crucifix had hung on the wall over his fireplace mantel. When I asked him about it once, he told me that he had purchased it long ago, during his only visit to Rome to see the Vatican. It was certainly an antique and quite valuable. It had meant a great deal to Father Barbier, and now it was mine. With a hesitant, reverent finger, I stroked the carved wood, and then carefully replaced the tissue paper and the lid of the box.

"What is it, *Maman*?" Marie asked curiously. "Can I play with it?"

"*Non, mon petite chou*, it is not a toy. It is a…a relic and very special." Turning to the waiting footman, I placed the box in his arms. "Please take this to the bedroom for me." A sigh escaped me as I watched him mount the stairs. What was I to do with this gift? I wanted to put it somewhere safe, but where I could look at it sometimes and remember that kind old man who had been like a father to me. Pondering this, I took Marie's hand and we proceeded outside to meet René.

It was a beautiful summer's day, ideal for our excursion into the sunflower field. René took Marie up to perch in front of him on Danté, and she looked very small atop the big black horse. I walked alongside, watching closely even though he held Marie in a tight, secure grip. I carried a basket of delicious things to eat, because as far as Celestine was concerned, any venture out of doors called for a basket of food. But I did not mind.

We rode and walked at a slow pace down through the rows of flowers. They were taller than me now, and the enormous flower heads were forming. When they ripened, it was always a race to see who could harvest more seeds, us or the birds. It was for their valuable oil that we raised them; Erik sold the sunflower seeds on to be pressed elsewhere. It was a way to help make the estate pay for itself while we waited for the grape vines to mature and begin producing a good amount of fruit.

Marie chattered and pointed at things; it was not always possible to tell what she was saying but for the most part, she spoke well for her age. I thought her quite precocious. I did wonder if I had been as much work to raise for my own parents as Marie was to me – she was never still. She liked René very much, and today on the ride loudly announced her intention of marrying him when she grew up.

Suppressing a sudden laugh, I looked up at her and without thinking exclaimed, "Not you, too, Marie!" René glanced down at me with a rakish grin, the black eye patch and dark hair falling over his brow contributing to his piratical attractiveness.

"*Non*, Marie *Petite*," René said with a pretend-rueful expression. "Your *papa* would never permit it. Besides, when you are old enough to marry, I shall be far too old for you."

Marie frowned adorably, considering this. "You are not as old as *Papa*," she said, as though that settled the matter. Then her little face sobered, and she added in a sad, quavering voice, "I miss *Papa*. I wish he would come home." René and I both went silent for a moment, while my heart twisted in my chest. René gave Marie a comforting squeeze.

"Ouch." She said. "You are holding me too tight."

Swallowing hard against a strong desire to both laugh and cry, I reached up and patted her on the leg.

"I know you miss *Papa*, dearest. So do I. But...I am sure that soon..." I stopped and shook my head. Because I wasn't sure, not sure of anything. We proceeded in silence for a few minutes, and I could sense a wave of kindly sympathy emanating from René. He and I stole a glance at each other, a silent communication that said much.

Once we reached the chosen destination for our picnic, he handed Marie down to me and then dismounted. She felt heavier all of a sudden, and I realized with a little jolt that she was growing right before my eyes. In late autumn, she would turn three. The last of her teeth had just come in. I fought away a wave of anger and frustration directed toward my absent spouse, who was missing all these days of his daughter's life.

Taking her by the hand, I led her into an enchanted circle of sunflowers. Erik had planted the circle on purpose, to make a magical place we could visit with Marie when the plants were tall enough. Now, they towered over us, and even though the flowers were not fully developed yet, it was still a beautiful place. He had left a small gap to walk through, and once inside the circle, with the large flower heads bobbing above us, and golden light sifting through, it was indeed magical. I sighed, wishing he were here to share this moment with us.

René pulled a blanket from the back of his saddle and spread it on the grass. Gathering my skirts underneath me, I sat on the blanket and unpacked the basket. René joined me, settling down with long-legged ease. Marie was utterly entranced by the sunflower circle, and all her previous sadness was forgotten, at least for now. She toddled all around inside the circle, gazing up and down and through the green stalks. I had previously mentioned the possibility that we might glimpse fairies there, and she was much taken with this idea.

From the basket I removed an apple, cut it in half and went to feed the halves to Danté, who accepted them graciously. His big teeth made short work of the apple. In thanks, he snuffled and blew gustily on the front of my gown.

Taking a sandwich of thick roast beef slices from me, René said in a soft voice, "Robert tells me there has been no word since the telegram, Madame." We both turned our heads to make sure Marie was not paying any attention to us. I examined my own sandwich, consisting of thin slices of pink lamb on a croissant, as though it were of vital importance.

"There has been no word. Robert is correct." I said in an equally soft voice.

"That does not sound like M. Bessette," René said thoughtfully, before taking an enormous bite from his sandwich. He was correct about that, but as there seemed nothing for me to say in reply, I pulled from the basket a baked custard spiced with nutmeg in a porcelain ramekin – Marie's lunch, and called her over to me.

"*Merci, Maman*," she said once she had devoured the last sweet, creamy spoonful. I watched her as she got up and began to wander about again. Marie seldom remained still for long.

"It is beautiful here," I murmured, leaning my head back and gazing upward through the tall plants. "You could almost expect to see fairies."

Sandwiches finished, we shared a bottle of cold tea and sat quietly, listening to birdcall and watching the sunlight sifting through the tall plants. Then Marie began to yawn and look sleepy, so René repacked the basket. He sent a sidelong look my way, saying quietly, "Well, Madame Sylvie, just remember that if M. Bessette doesn't return, you always have me."

Utterly shocked at his even expressing the idea to me that Erik might never come home, I whipped my head around and stared at him in horror. "What a thing to say!" I exclaimed.

He was regarding me seriously for once, and no twinkle lit his dark eye. "There is no one quite like you, Madame. M. Bessette is a lucky man. I would not mind being in his shoes." My jaw fell open at his words, and I was rendered speechless. Bright, hectic color flooded my cheeks, making my face hot. René chuckled at my stunned reaction.

"You have not looked in a mirror lately, have you?" He asked, standing up and reaching for my hand to pull me up. Once I was standing next to him, unable to meet his eye, he said cheerfully, "I beg you will not tell M. Bessette I said that to you. He would have my head on a platter." He paused before adding ruefully, "So would Robert, for that matter."

"That much is certain," I replied tartly, shaking out the blanket. "Besides, you are too young for me." René burst out laughing.

It was time to go back to the *château*. Unsurprisingly, Marie fell asleep in René's arms on our return trip. Without her cheerful childish chatter, it was a rather quiet, constrained journey. I had been completely taken aback at his unexpected words. He was aware that he had shocked me, and made no further mention of such personal matters.

Entering the foyer after René, who had agreed to carry the still-sleeping Marie upstairs to the nursery, I paused before the mirror above the hallway table to remove my hat and check my hair. Smoothing a few windblown wisps back into place, I stopped and stared fixedly at my own reflection. René's words came back to me: 'You have not looked in a mirror lately.' It was true that I had not, but now I met my own gaze and studied my reflection thoughtfully. I actually *looked* at myself , and realized that at last, I was again looking *like* myself. My face and body had filled out again, and the bloom of health was in my cheeks. My eyes were bright, and my hair was thicker too. The transformation had been happening all along, but I simply wasn't aware of it.

René took that inopportune moment to come bounding down the stairs and thence into the foyer, where he caught me gazing at my own face in the mirror. He came to stand behind me, and our eyes caught in the glass. He smiled, while I blushed furiously.

"You see, what did I tell you?" He said, and then left to return to his duties in the winery.

I made my way slowly upstairs to change and tidy up.

'Today René and I took Marie for a picnic inside the enchanted sunflower circle that you planted this spring. It was such a perfect, warm day. She was fascinated, bien sûr. I so wished that you could have been here, rather than René. Do you remember when you planted the seeds, and we talked about bringing Marie there when the sunflowers were tall? She asked me when you were coming home; she misses you, as do I. I did not know what to tell her.

I do not understand why you do not write to us. What can possibly be happening there that would prevent you from sending a letter, or even just a telegram? You must know that we are all worried about you, mon amour. I do not understand this cruel silence you are imposing on us here. I confess I am growing afraid. I hope and pray your continued silence does not have anything to do with Miss

Arlington. I would rather know the truth even if it is painful, than endure this not knowing.'

CHAPTER TWENTY

"I was suddenly seized with a mad idea."

Erik

It was late evening at the Fifth Avenue Hotel, and Erik was alone in the large ballroom where tea dances were held every afternoon. He had spent a good part of the day wandering the city, wearing his new mask. He had found art supplies at a shop and occupied himself with making charcoal sketches of some of the citizens of New York. Keeping his hands busy helped to pass the time.

Thanks to Edythe dragging him to an afternoon tea dance at the hotel, he had made the happy discovery that there was a grand piano in one corner, and at night, after most of the guests were in bed or in other parts of the hotel, he had taken to coming downstairs to this piano and playing it quietly. There was never anyone else in that room; it was not the main ballroom, but only a salon of sorts. Most of the sheet music he found was for the dances, waltzes and so forth, but there were some classical pieces as well. When he could not sleep, playing and working on his latest composition offered a measure of comfort. He was working on a composition inspired by his ocean voyage. Work kept his mind engaged; something he desperately required.

Edythe, returning from attending a ball at another hotel, found him there. She entered the ballroom and crossed to where Erik sat at the piano, her chiffon skirts swishing and rustling with every step. She was wearing a red gown cut low across the bodice, revealing the smooth white tops of her small breasts. The vivid red color of the gown set off her pale skin and dark hair to perfection. A diamond necklace sparkled around her neck. Most of her very fine jewels had been inherited from her late mother, she had explained to him one day. He had assumed they must be gifts from her doting father, but such was not the case.

Approaching the piano, she removed her hat and fur wrap and leaned on the instrument. A sweet scent of honeysuckle wafted around her.

"What are you doing down here at this late hour?" She asked, smiling at him quizzically.

Erik did not want to tell her the truth, that his nightmares were plaguing him regularly now. He shook his head and turned his attention to the sheet music in front of him, pretending to study it.

"I was looking for you because I had a note from Father today," Edythe explained. "His training course is going very well, and they have asked him to stay on a little longer. He does not expect to be back for two weeks."

Erik scowled in irritation. It was the worst possible news.

"What on earth is the matter with you tonight?" She asked, her black eyes surveying him intently.

"I could not sleep," he replied finally.

She studied him, tilting her head to one side. "Is it because you are worried about the surgery?" She asked.

"No. There are...other reasons."

"I know what you need!" She straightened and slapped her hand on the piano. "Fresh air and some exercise. Let us take a walk around the block. It will do you good." The hotel occupied an entire city block, and to walk around it took some time. Erik agreed half-heartedly. Perhaps she was right. He was feeling sulky and morose, and some fresh air might clear his head.

It was a warm night, slightly humid, but a soft breeze flowing down Fifth Avenue helped to freshen the air. Erik was familiar with his surroundings now, having taken a few walks and carriage rides in company with one or the other of the Arlingtons. He turned right when the doorman bowed them out of the hotel and shoved his hands into his trouser pockets.

As they walked Edythe told him, in her sprightly manner, about the ball she had attended that night. After lifting her skirt to display a good bit of slender ankle clad in a ridiculously frail-looking evening slipper, she requested the assistance of his arm to walk. Several men passing by in evening dress practically twisted their heads off to catch a glimpse of her ankle. Ever since he began spending time with Edythe in New York, he had been acutely aware of other men's admiring gazes, and their envious or speculative looks toward him. There was no denying her striking beauty, but he knew there was no innocence in Edythe Arlington.

"I am sure I shall turn my ankle in these slippers, the sidewalks are so uneven here." She said, taking his arm in her grasp. Which of course, was not true. The sidewalks around the hotel were practically new.

Thinking of all the absurdly over-dressed women he had seen over the years at the Opera House, Erik said, "I shall never understand why women wear such foolish attire. I am thankful Sylvie does not dress in such a manner." He added this last as a reminder to Edythe that he still had a wife at home. She glanced up at him, a little smile playing on her full lips.

"And how are things at home, Erik? How is your poor wife getting along? I do hope she is feeling better." Edythe surprised him by asking, in an

223

innocent voice. Erik felt himself tense at her words, and shrugged his shoulders in an effort to relax his taut muscles.

"That is part of the problem," he said grimly. "I've written her several times, but I have heard nothing from her; not one word since I sent my telegram." He had not intended to confess this, but perhaps he needed someone to talk to, and for once Edythe was behaving sympathetically. "There has been more than enough time for a letter to come to me by now. I am worried about her," he confessed.

He felt Edythe give his arm a squeeze. Then she chuckled softly and said, "I am sure you need not worry about Mrs. Bessette. You know perfectly well you would have heard from home if something was wrong." She gave her head a toss. "Depend upon it, I am sure Mrs. Bessette is far too timid a country mouse to get herself into any trouble."

Erik gave a short bark of laughter at hearing his wife described in such a way. If Edythe only knew of the trouble Sylvie had gotten herself into in the past!

"Perhaps you are right," he murmured, and they rounded the corner of the block and started down the other side. Edward had been right about the prevalence of pick-pockets; they lurked everywhere a careless victim might be found. However, after one such hapless creature approached Erik, the others knew to keep away from him. Thus he and Edythe could walk the streets in perfect safety.

Changing the subject abruptly, she turned to him and asked, "How do you like the new mask Father and Doctor Buck made for you?" They talked of that and other inconsequential things until they arrived back at the main entrance to the hotel. Much to Erik's surprise, the walk had done him some good, and he was able to sleep at last.

Unfortunately, the next morning, he awoke in a foul mood, aggravated by forced inactivity and frustration. It was taking forever for Edward to return; nothing was going right, and there was no one to take his anger out on here. In this dangerously malicious frame of mind, Erik took up pen and paper and wrote what he swore to himself was the last letter he would post to his wife.

Concern, frustration and, dare he admit it, hurt, had transformed into anger, not an unusual circumstance for him. He wrote so vehemently that the tip of his pen tore the paper. He knew he was writing unkind, even cruel things, but he could not help himself, could not stop pouring out his helpless fury toward Sylvie. While he was writing all that vitriol directed at his wife, he felt it was what she deserved. He wanted to punish her. Perhaps, he wrote in closing, since she so obviously had no interest in him, he might never come back at all. It was doubtful she would miss him. He did not miss her, either.

He did not mean any of it, of course. He wanted to strike out at her, hurt her as she was hurting him. He closed the envelope and sealed it, and decided to mail it at once, before good sense would make him change his mind and burn the letter instead.

When he took the letter downstairs to the front desk there was a different hotel employee there; an older man with a large mustache. Erik was pleased and surprised to find that the man spoke a little French. Handing him the letter to Sylvie, which ought to burn her fingers when she opened it, Erik inquired about the boy who usually worked the desk.

The older man held one hand to his cheek by way of explanation, saying, "Toothache. He is seeing a dentist this morning." Almost as soon as the letter dropped into the box, Erik began to regret sending it. But the seething anger he felt, as well as his wounded pride, prevented him from asking for it back.

Erik was meeting Edythe and Matthew in their suite for breakfast, after which they were apparently going to hire a carriage and take him sightseeing. He supposed they were trying to keep him occupied while Dr. Arlington was away. He took the perpendicular railway upstairs, no longer marveling over the view from the glass box as it made its slow way up the side of the building.

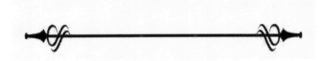

Another day with no word from Erik; another frustrating day just like all that had come before it. I excused myself from taking tea with Celestine, claiming I was tired and wanted to rest. *En fait*, I could not bear to face her with the disappointment that was becoming harder and harder to conceal. I wished that the daily flare of hope could be permanently extinguished, so that each day's disappointment would not hurt me so much.

Upstairs in the quiet haven of my bedroom I seated myself at my *petite secrétaire*. For a bit, all I did was sit and brood. Eventually I forced myself to pull a sheet of stationery from the drawer, fill my fountain pen and begin to write. It was yet another letter to my absent spouse, to ask him why he would not take the trouble to write back to me. It was sheer stubbornness that made me do it in the first place; my patience with him was

225

wearing thin. Nevertheless I tried to think of pleasant things to tell him: what Marie had said today, about how Robert and Celestine were, and about the vines and the weather. But I could think of nothing to write about myself, for I could not think what to say that would not sound bitter and resentful. And angry.

It was now well over a month since Erik's telegram had arrived to say he was safely ensconced in his hotel. Over a month and four letters sent with not another word from him. Part of me feared some calamity must have befallen him, but if that were the case, surely Dr. Arlington would let me know, or so I assured myself.

I feared I was partly to blame for Erik's current disinterest in me, but only partly. Yes, I had been distant, I pushed him away, had even, I admitted guiltily, been cruel to him - but that last night we spent together, it had seemed as though we might put the past behind us and start afresh. Had I not been forgiven?

But there was also Edythe Arlington. Thinking of Miss Arlington filled me with such blind fury, I realized I was gripping my pen so tightly a blot of blue ink dropped onto the thin paper. I put the pen down carefully and reached for a piece of blotting paper, scowling. Erik had been with Miss Arlington all this time, and it was more than enough time for her to work her wiles on him, alone and lonely as he must surely be. Erik was a man of strong appetites, he would not be able to go long without satisfying them, and Miss Arlington, I knew for a certainty, would be more than willing.

But how could he? How could he forget me so quickly, how could he turn his back on me, Marie, and on our winery, and the life we had forged here? I rested my head in my hand, and groaned in despair. What had happened to us, and to our love for each other? How had it come to this?

At that moment there was a knock on my bedroom door, and I looked up quickly, not wishing anyone to see me with my head bowed in despondency.

"Come in," I called, thinking perhaps it was Berthé bringing me the tea I had missed. But when the door opened, it was our young footman. He had a letter in his hand. My heart gave a leap of excitement – could it be?

"Is it...is it from..."

"It is from New York, Madame," he said with a wide grin. Everyone in the household knew of my daily anxiety and disappointment, though they said no word and pretended all was well. No doubt the footman was quite pleased to bring me what I had been waiting for so long. I tried to keep my hand from trembling when I took the letter from him, and dismissed him quickly. At last, at last! The long-awaited letter from Erik. I would tell

Celestine she was right *après tout*; his first letter had gone astray, just as she had suggested.

Grasping my letter opener, I carefully opened the thin paper, not wishing to tear it in my eagerness. With a leap of my heart I recognized his bold handwriting covering the paper, although for some reason his pen had made several tears in it. Perhaps he had been in a hurry. I was overjoyed; this long-awaited letter was like having Erik near me again. Eagerly I began to read.

I read that letter three times through, for each time I could not believe my eyes. But the words were always the same. Finally, I let the paper fall from my fingers in shock and dismay. My shoulders sagged. Fury and something akin to hatred flamed on the page and scorched my heart. What did it mean? Why was he so angry with me? How could he have said those things to me? My hurt and confusion was such that I could not keep from crying. He had not even sent a kind word for Marie, or asked after her.

After a while I pulled myself together and went blindly in search of Celestine. She was in my sitting room poring over a list of household supplies. One look at my distraught face told her something was very wrong. Wordlessly, I extracted Erik's vitriolic missive from the pocket of my gown and handed it to her. She took it from me without speaking, a little crease of worry notched between her brows.

I watched Celestine's face as she read it, and saw the color drain from her cheeks. Finishing, she let the paper fall into her lap and stared at me in shock.

"What does this mean?" She asked, sounding as confused as I felt. "What is he talking about?"

"I wish I knew, Celestine," I replied, sitting down numbly next to her. "Your guess is as good as mine."

"He sounds as angry as I have ever known him to be," she murmured, hesitantly touching the paper. "Look how he has made these tears in the paper."

"He seems to be…accusing me of something. Almost as if he thinks I have abandoned him. Why would he ever think that? He writes as if he hates me, Celestine." A small sob escaped me and I blotted my wet eyes on a corner of my skirt.

I clasped my hands tightly in my lap, frowning. If there had been a fire in the grate, I would have tossed Erik's letter into the flames without a second thought. But it was high summer, too warm for a fire.

"He accuses me so wildly, Celestine; he does not sound at all like himself. I think…I think it is that woman's doing!"

Celestine was taken aback. "Do you mean Miss Arlington?" I nodded vigorously.

"Yes, yes. I am certain she has been saying vile things about me, filling his mind with wickedness. I hate her!" This last came out in a high voice, as my own anger flared. Celestine patted my arm.

"You need a cup of tea, Sylvie, and perhaps a rest. This letter has upset you." Indeed it had. I was not certain I could rest, I felt so distressed, but I went back upstairs as she suggested. I brought Erik's letter with me, and ritually set fire to it in our fireplace grate using a match for the candles. I would not condescend to answer it; it did not deserve any response.

Slowly I removed my slippers and sank into bed, where I lay staring up into the canopy wondering what on earth had happened to my husband. Celestine was right about one thing: he sounded as angry as I had ever seen him. The venomous, hurtful tone of his letter reminded me of the bitter, misanthropic man he had been when I first met him. It was as if we had suddenly become enemies, when I had done nothing to deserve it.

I did eventually sleep, surprisingly. While I slept, I dreamed again, but not of my lost daughter this time. In this dream, I was climbing the path up through the dense forest behind the *château*. The trees seemed thicker somehow, closing over my head. My feet were soundless on the path, covered as it was in moldy leaf litter. I wanted to reach the top of the hill, where the ancient ruins stood, and where I could see out over the valley. But I was not alone.

He was walking behind me, keeping a yard or two back, walking as soundlessly as I. I did not turn my head to look at him, but I knew he was there. The distance between us was profound, significant. Neither of us spoke.

Once a lock of my hair caught on a bramble, and as I struggled to untangle it, he approached me and carefully unwound the lock from the thorns and freed me. His touch was impersonal. Then, as I gazed unwillingly at him, he continued up the path without looking back at me, and I followed him. I saw in surprise that he was wearing a cape, a heavy winter cape like the ones he wore when I first met him. I wondered why, since it was summer.

After what seemed an interminable time, we arrived at the remains of the hill fort, and we both approached the edge of the hill. Long ago a low stone wall had been built here, and some of it still stood, wound about and held in place by many green vines. We stood side by side at the wall and gazed out across the valley. Far down below was our house, but it was snugged up too close to the hill to be visible from here. I turned my head and looked longingly at him.

"Where are you?" I asked, my voice filled with anguish.

He turned to face me, and I was struck anew by his handsomeness; his profligate male beauty. His pale eyes looked sad.

"I am right here next to you, Sylvie," he said gently. "This is where I always am. I thought you knew that."

Was it true? Unable to resist, I moved to close the distance between us. I longed to feel his arms about me. I reached out to him.

And then, he leaped lightly to the top of the old stone wall, spread out his arms and the cape became wings, and with one push he flew away from me. I reached for him, but my hand caught only air, and I was pierced with despair.

"Wait!" I cried, "Take me with you!" But it was too late, he flew like a large black bird across the valley and vanished toward the west, dwindling as I watched into a tiny dot in the sky and then gone altogether. I woke up then, and realized that I was lying on my bed still fully dressed, and crying, crying in my sleep.

I sat up and scrubbed my face with my hands furiously. I was tired of crying, tired of being left behind like a forgotten bundle. Ignore me, would he? Send me curses by post? This was too much! Throwing off the quilt, I got out of bed and found I was pacing around the room, growing angrier by the moment. A mad plan was forming itself in my mind. With that strange dream fresh in my memory, I realized that *I* wanted to fly, too. And I would – I would fly to Erik. Right next to me, indeed! He was going to wish he had stayed next to me. When I was finished with him….Who was it said, 'Hell hath no fury like a woman scorned'? Well, whoever it was, I was feeling extremely furious now.

Glancing at the clock, I saw it was not particularly late, only a little after nine. I must have slept for several hours. Impetuously I donned my slippers and padded down the hall to Celestine's small suite of rooms. Without preamble, I knocked vigorously on her door. There was a rustling sound within, and I pictured her putting on her own dressing gown. She would be getting ready for bed at this hour.

In a moment, she opened the door, looking concerned. Her hair was in a long red plait down one shoulder.

"Is anything the matter?" She asked worriedly.

"No, nothing is wrong; that is, I am not unwell. I am sorry to disturb you, Celestine, but I must speak to you. May I come in?"

"Certainly, my dear," she said, moving aside to let me enter her cozy little sitting room. She paused to light a couple of lamps and then, with her usual acuity, poured us each a small glass of sherry. Tossing mine off in a single swallow, I began pacing in a tight circle around a floral rug in the middle of the room. Celestine watched me warily.

"Celestine," I said abruptly, stopping in front of her. "I am going away. Tomorrow, if possible. I will rely on you to take care of Marie for me and manage things until I return." I frowned, feeling guilty. "I hate to leave her like this, so suddenly, but I cannot remain here another moment!"

At first my declaration was met by a strange stillness in her. I must have shocked her tremendously. Then, to my amazement, she set her glass down and stood, and embraced me firmly. As she stood back from me, her hands still on my shoulders, I saw she was smiling and her eyes were bright.

"At last! What a relief!" She exclaimed. As I gaped at her in confusion, she continued, "I was wondering when you would come to your senses and go after him. I was beginning to think I would have to speak to you about it. I suppose it was reading that letter today that was the final straw."

"How…how do you know that is where I intend to go?" I asked her wonderingly.

Celestine gave a little laugh. "You should see your face, *ma chère*. It is written all over. You…you look alive again."

I shook my head and sat down. "I imagine I look angry, Celestine, because I am. But I think perhaps I will have another sherry," I said bemusedly. "It was the letter, I suppose. I have to get to the bottom of this."

"What is your plan?" She demanded briskly. "I will help you pack tomorrow if you wish. You know you need not worry about anything here."

Sipping my sherry more slowly this time, I pondered her question. I knew I could not rush off willy-nilly to catch a steamer to America, though I was on fire with the urge to find that black-haired witch and slap her smug face. For what I had in mind, preparations would take several days.

"I will go first to Paris." I looked at her pointedly. "I will need a few new gowns, and perhaps a new hairstyle."

Celestine's eyes glowed. "*Parfait!*" She exclaimed delightedly. "I agree; you must present yourself in all your beauty. Oh, I can see it now! But you must know, Sylvie, Erik would never look at another woman. This distance that is between you, it will vanish when he takes one look at you, I am sure."

I made no reply to this remark; I did not have her confidence in my husband. No, that was not right. It was my fear that I had pushed him too

230

far. And I knew in my heart that Edythe Arlington would stop at nothing to get her claws into him. It was as though the heartfelt words of longing and love in my letters to Erik meant nothing to him. Could he possibly have meant it when he said he might not come back home? But there was another thing I worried about.

"I only hope...I hope that he will not have agreed to have surgery on his face before I get there, Celestine," I said with a shudder. "That was another of our disagreements. I did not want him to change his face. It was selfish of me." I gazed at the rug as I spoke. "I won't stand in his way any more if he wishes to go through with it, but...but I would like to see him just once more as he is. As the man I fell in love with."

I was not, *bien sûr*, able to leave the next day, for such things can never be accomplished without some planning and packing. So I left the day after. In the midst of packing a case for myself and trying to arrange for a carriage to take me to Paris, the day flew by. Robert, having learned somehow of my plans, insisted on talking to me. It was urgent, he said.

"Why are you taking a carriage to Paris, Madame?" He asked, hands on hips. "It will take days to get there, and you will have the expense of staying at inns along the way. And those places are not safe for you. No, you must take the train."

"The...train?" I stared at him blankly. "I never thought of that. But where would I board a train?" The idea was growing in me – it sounded exciting. I had never been on a train before. It would be like flying. But I knew there was no station near Sarlat. Robert looked at me as if I were demented.

"Toulouse. There is a station there...don't you recollect seeing it when we went to the market faire last year? You catch that train and then change in Tours, and from there you may travel directly to Paris. It will take only one day, Madame."

"*One day?* How marvelous!" I was thrilled, but also amazed that Robert of all people knew so much about trains. "I will go and order the carriage to take me there in the morning. Thank you, Robert."

That evening Celestine came into my bedroom to help me finish packing and make sure nothing important was left behind. We sipped our sherry companionably, as we had always done together. I was thankful to have her for a friend. Folding up a nightgown, she asked,

"What will you do when you get to Paris, Sylvie? Where will you go, to the Hospital?"

I had thought of that to begin with, but now I had something else in mind. I shook my head, taking the folded nightgown from her and carefully placing in my small case. I glanced at her slyly.

"*Non*, my dear. I need to be closer to the shops. And I need to find some lady who knows the best places. I intend to call upon M. Moreau." Closing the case with a snap, I added, "that man owes me his help, and he is going to give it to me. And hopefully so will his wife."

Considering this, Celestine sipped her sherry and smiled. "What an excellent idea! You must write me and let me know how you go on."

I looked earnestly at her. "I do not intend to be away for very long, you know. I do not want to be away from Marie for very long. I intend to go directly to the Fifth Avenue Hotel, find Erik, and convince him to return with me to France. If he will not come..." I smoothed my hand over the quilt on the bed. "Well, I do not intend to leave without him."

Celestine toyed with her braid absently. "I cannot imagine, Sylvie, that Erik could have any interest in Miss Arlington, as you seem to think. It must be something else that is causing him to behave so out of character. I wonder...suppose he has had some surgery, and is recovering from it? Perhaps something they have given him for pain has made him delirious. For I cannot believe for one minute that he meant those things he wrote."

That had occurred to me as well, but I did not think it could be the case. "No, Celestine, I am certain he would not have done that without telling me. He promised..." I sat heavily on the side of the bed, feeling discouraged. "He said he would take no actions until he told me first, and there was no indication of that in his letter. I feel in my heart that Miss Arlington is at the bottom of this, and when I find her, she will regret it."

Brave words, no doubt, spoken from the safety of my bedroom. But it was I who would regret it, *en fait*.

CHAPTER TWENTY-ONE

"My thoughts clear, my plans made, and the determination to carry them out."

I will draw a veil over my goodbyes to Marie and Celestine, and my departure from the *château*. I imagine leaving my daughter behind was harder on me than on her, for Celestine offered to take her to the kitchen for milk and biscuits. This brought about a miraculous end to her tears, but not to mine. In addition, I had to promise to bring her another doll, for her old one had mysteriously lost all its hair.

It was my intention, once I arrived at the *Gare* in Paris, to make directly for the Hospital. I could stay in the place that had always been a refuge, and get my bearings before making my way to M. Moreau's house. It did not seem quite right to descend on M. Moreau and his wife without any advance notice. I telegraphed ahead to let Dr. Gaudet know of my imminent arrival. I knew he would be quite surprised.

I must admit my excitement over riding on a train for the first time in my life quickly faded next to the reality. Adventure soon palled, once the novelty of such amazing speed wore off. The train cars were hot, the seats hard wood with no cushioning on them, and smoke from the engine kept blowing into the open windows. People had to open the windows else suffocate in the heat. As far as food was concerned, you were expected to bring your own, but Celestine had seen to that, *bien sûr*. It was only after we had arrived in Paris that I learned the train had first class compartments, but it never occurred to Robert to inform me of that fact.

It was a long, arduous journey to Paris, and we did not arrive until nightfall. How thankful I was to exit that uncomfortable train car and set foot on the soil of my native city!

When I emerged from the noisy, crowded *Gare,* an old familiar friend was waiting on the street nearby: Dr. Gaudet had thoughtfully sent the Hospital's brougham to meet me. I would have recognized it anywhere. I could have wept with joy when I climbed into the venerable old coach with its cracked leather seats and cloudy glass windows. The driver was a young man I did not recognize; his wooden leg identified him as a veteran of our recent war. It had been Robert who drove the Hospital carriage back in my day. Night had fallen, and I could not see out the windows, so I settled back to enjoy the journey to the Île de la Cité. Someone had made an effort to make the carriage seats more comfortable: a soft fur throw covered the hard old leather.

I listened raptly to the sounds of the creaky brougham, the jangling of harness and clop of the horses' hooves as though it were the most beautiful *aria*, and permitted myself to wallow in nostalgia.

The Hospital's old carriage had reached the Pont Royal Bridge, and was making the crossing. I was sorry that it was dark outside the windows, for this was a view I would dearly love to see again. It would have to wait until the morrow, however. Once across the bridge, it was only a mile or so to the Hospital.

That place held many happy memories for me, but wistfully I reminded myself that one who meant much to me was no longer there. I could visit his grave and lay a flower there for him, but I would never again see those eyes that were as black as a bird's, nor see that kind smile. It was disconcerting to think that of the nine patients residing at St. Giles when I first came there, only three were now left. I felt sorry for Dr. Gaudet; the big old building must seem very empty now. Even the quietly efficient Sister Chantal had retired a few months ago to spend time with her brother and his large family.

The young driver delivered me directly to the front door of the Hospital. Although I could not see it, in my mind's eye I pictured the venerable three story red stone building, several centuries old. It had been a nun's cloister for many years, before the Catholic Church gave it to Dr. Gaudet for his secret leprosarium. It was ideally situated for its purpose, being in a part of the city where the air was always fresh, and set back far from the road, surrounded by a high wrought iron fence. Dr. Gaudet told me once that the hospital had been named after St. Giles, the patron saint of lepers.

It was Dr. Gaudet himself who opened the heavy wood doors for me, while the young man, obviously their man-of-all-work replacement for Robert, brought down my one case. I deliberately packed lightly since I planned on doing quite a bit of shopping while in Paris.

Once inside the building, I understood why Dr. Gaudet opened the door; with only three patients remaining, most of the nuns had moved on to other, more active Catholic hospitals. He was all but alone there now. A wave of melancholy swept over me when he explained this while guiding me to the refectory, a large, well-proportioned room with a small, hideous old kitchen next to it. How much had changed in such little time!

On one of the long wooden tables was a tray with something for me to eat after my train trip, and a small glass of the doctor's own very good red wine. I wasn't really hungry after finishing off the basket of food Celestine had sent along with me, but I did not want to hurt his feelings, so I made an effort to pick at the contents of the tray. There was only some cold sliced ham with cheese and a little salad. Meeting my eyes across the table, Dr. Gaudet shrugged, looking somewhat chagrinned.

"*Bien*, we were never able to find anyone to cook for us who was half as good as you, Sylvie." His eyes wandered over the empty refectory with a wistful expression, as though populating it with patients and staff as it had once been. "And of course, the Church has seen fit to reduce our funding since we have only three patients now."

"I am sorry, Doctor," I said. "I wish there was something I could do to help."

Dr. Gaudet forced a smile that did not reach his eyes, and changed the subject. "*Eh bien*, there is one happy thing to come. Your estimable husband has promised to provide us with a better carriage and a new team to pull it. He said he would see to it once he returns from America." It was the first I had heard of that, but I could not argue with the need. That brougham had been ancient when I used to ride in it on occasion.

"Have you heard from Erik, by the way?" He asked innocently. "I myself wrote him a letter to tell him about Stèphane's passing. I had not heard anything from you and to be honest, I was curious about how he was getting on over there. I have received no reply however. I imagine he is quite busy." While Dr. Gaudet was happily chattering on, I was staring rather grimly at my plate, pondering what he was telling me. So Erik had not written to Dr. Gaudet either?

After a moment I came out of my reverie to realize that he had just asked me a question. "What, Doctor?"

"I was just wondering what brings you to Paris, Sylvie? I was surprised to hear that you were coming. But I must say, you look much better since I saw you last. You look the picture of health."

I had anticipated he would ask me why I had appeared here out of the blue, and had my answer ready.

"I am preparing for my own trip to America, Dr. Gaudet." I explained frankly. "I am following Erik and I intend to join him in New York." It was all perfectly true. I saw no need to tell him that I wasn't actually expected there.

The good doctor's eyes grew wide with alarm. "You do not mean that you are making such a journey alone? Of a certainty your husband would not approve. It might prove dangerous, Sylvie." He said emphatically.

I gazed at him fondly. "*Non*, Dr. Gaudet, *bien sûr que non*! I…er…plan to hire a companion to accompany me." I had been considering this during the uncomfortable train trip. What I really needed was a ladies maid to help me with my new wardrobe and to arrange my hair in the *au courant* styles. I intended to ask Madame Moreau to assist me in that regard.

Dr. Gaudet was relieved. "*Bon*. That is a good idea, my dear. Now, there is a bedroom made ready for you upstairs…it is the same one that Erik stayed in when he was here a few months ago. How long will you stay here before you leave for America?"

"Here with you, just one night, I think. I have some people I must see in Paris before I go." And I proceeded to explain to him my intention to foist myself on the Moreaus. "M. Moreau owes me a great deal in my opinion, and I intend to make use of him and his wife if I can." I added sourly.

Just as we rose from the long table, something about the room caught my eye and I stopped and stared. I should say, rather, the fact that something was missing caught my eye. On the wall behind the pedestal where readings were given during meals, was a large, rectangular space that was much lighter in color than the surrounding wall. I gazed at it blankly. I remembered quite well what used to be there, and had been there since the cloister was built *sans doute*: a smoke-darkened painting of the Last Supper. Now it was gone.

"Where is the painting?" I asked, turning to Dr. Gaudet in confusion. "Are you having it cleaned?"

Dr. Gaudet regarded me sadly. He shook his head. "*Non*, my dear, the painting, it is gone."

"Gone? Gone where?" I turned back to stare at the empty space, perplexed. I had not been fond of that old painting; I always thought that the last supper it illustrated seemed rather meager. But still, it was a part of the building, it belonged there.

Dr. Gaudet started toward the door, saying over his shoulder, "The Church took it from us perhaps six months ago. It is their property, *vous savez*. They say it is quite valuable."

I followed him out, my heart heavy. "Erik never mentioned that to me," I murmured.

"He did not know. He never came in here, for he did not wish the patients to be aware of his presence."

Seeing me upstairs to the third floor, where small bed chambers were reserved for the nuns who had once lived at the Hospital, Dr. Gaudet worriedly made me promise that if my plan did not bear fruit, I must return

236

to St. Giles. I assured him that I would, because after all that was my only choice if the Moreaus would not have me.

It was a very small bedroom, one of two that Erik and I had shared when we fled from the *gendarmes* after Erik had killed Chief Inspector Gaston in a terrifying swordfight.[2] We slept in those rooms for two nights. On the third day we were married, and thereafter shared a larger room. Tonight someone had seen to it that there was fresh bedding, and the narrow leaded glass window was open to admit fresh air.

I sat on the rather hard bed and looked around. The missing painting felt like another blow, and I found myself close to tears. I thought of Erik staying here while he was in Paris, believing he was going to have to murder a stranger. There was no evidence remaining of his stay here of course; it had been at least two months ago. Still, I tried to picture him here, sitting on the edge of the bed to pull off his boots, or waking up in the morning and throwing off the blankets in that decisive way he had. With an empty, hollow feeling, I braided my hair, put on my nightgown, and went to bed. I felt more alone there than I can say.

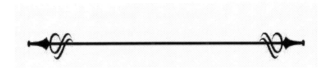

First thing in the morning, I walked to the nearest *bureau de télégraphe* and dispatched a brief message to M. Moreau, telling him to expect me later in the day. I considered sending a telegram to Erik at his hotel in New York informing him of my imminent arrival, but decided against it. Forewarned is forearmed, and I wanted to catch him red-handed. Or at least not put him on his guard.

Returning to the Hospital, I paid a visit to the grave of my old friend, Father Barbier, packed up my small valise and wished Dr. Gaudet *au revoir*. I had the driver deliver me to M. Moreau's front door. It turned out that he lived in a part of the city I was somewhat familiar with, for it was near the cemetery where my parents were buried. Settling back for the long ride across Paris, I thought about what I was about to do. What if M. Moreau would not acquiesce to my request? He owed me his help, and I was

---

[2] 'Disfigured, a Gothic Romance', Book 1 in the Disfigured Series

determined to get it, by fair means or foul. I simply would not take no for an answer. Nervously, I adjusted my hat and tugged on my kid leather gloves.

M. Moreau was home; he had received my telegram with some perplexity, but arranged his schedule that he might be there when I arrived. As it turned out, however, he clearly had expected Erik to be with me.

Bustling into the parlor where a servant had left me, M. Moreau looked around the room and then peered inquiringly at me.

He asked "But where is your husband, Madame Bessette?" in a bewildered tone.

I made a dismissive little gesture with my hand. "Oh, he is in America…in New York. I am…I am on my way to join him there." At least I hoped I was.

M. Moreau was just as I remembered him, a rather rotund, affable-appearing bureaucrat. But it would not do to forget that it was this pleasant-faced man who had decreed that another man must die.

M. Moreau was clearly taken aback by my announcement, as well as confused. He glanced obliquely at me, his eyes passing over my figure in an assessing sweep. He frowned.

"That is unexpected. He never mentioned any plans to take a trip of such magnitude, especially since…" He stopped and looked uncomfortable. It was easy to see what he was thinking. It was evident that I was no longer with child, so his confusion was understandable. It was time for me to play my trump card, so I sent up a silent prayer before I spoke. It did not seem quite above-board, and not really like me, but I was determined to get my way. M. Moreau had been the cause of all our troubles, after all. I studied him thoughtfully, tilting my head to one side.

"Have you any children, M. Moreau?" I inquired.

He smiled in a satisfied manner. "*Oui*, Madame, we have three children. They are all grown, *naturellement*. My son follows in his father's footsteps; he has recently joined the Ministry of Finance. I have a daughter who is espoused to a diplomat, and unfortunately resides in England now."

"That *is* unfortunate," I murmured sympathetically.

"And my other daughter," he continued, ignoring my comment, "lives here in Paris, in this house in fact, for she is not yet married."

"Ah, I see. How nice for you." I straightened my skirts a bit, folded my hands in my lap, and looked directly into his grey eyes. "I have only my daughter, Marie. For you see, Monsieur, I lost my baby while my husband was on his way home from Paris." I watched M. Moreau's face closely as I spoke. At first, his wooly caterpillar eyebrows drew together, but then he blanched; his ruddy face turning pale. I felt a twinge of guilt; what if the poor man had a heart attack because of my news?

"I...I am...I did not know..." he stuttered to a stop, flushing red again. Taking pity on his obvious discomfiture, I said briskly,

"I came to you because I do not know anyone else in Paris, and I am in need of some assistance. *Et aussi*, I am in a hurry. I thought perhaps your good wife might be able to help me with my arrangements."

M. Moreau gave me a blank look. "My wife? Er...arrangements? You mean, for your travel to New York?"

"Well, that is part of it, of course. I have some money for the trip but I do not know ..." Plucking at my gown by way of clarifying my request, I explained, "I am also in need of some new gowns, and travel clothes, and everything to go with them. And I must have my hair attended to before I depart. This must happen very quickly, Monsieur. Madame Moreau must surely know the right places to visit and can provide me with *entree*."

Understanding dawned, and M. Moreau's face cleared. He was certain, he said, that Madame would be delighted to assist me. As the wife of a Ministry employee, she did indeed know where such things could be acquired rapidly. And she would be *au courant* with the latest *modes*.

That problem settled, M. Moreau offered me *café* and asked after Erik; why was he in America? He had no idea M. Bessette was contemplating such a trip. I saw no reason not to tell him the truth, or at least part of the truth.

"While he was in Paris, he met an American surgeon who invited him to come to New York with him. The surgeon, Dr. Arlington, believes he can make a better mask for Erik; something more natural appearing."

"Ah, I see. That is good. He travels with his official pardon, does he not?"

"Oh yes, *bien sûr*."

"*Bon*. It would not do for him to be stopped along the way, and be without his pardon." M. Moreau looked at me, his expression rather perplexed. "I hope I do not speak out of turn, but I must say, your husband appears to be a very dangerous man, Madame Bessette. I was happy to give him the pardon, for he earned it, but I cannot help but wonder how you can..." here he trailed off, frowning. He was unable to conceal a slight but detectable shudder. I was smiling now, and it was clear he did not understand why.

"Tell me something, Monsieur," I said. "This pardon, signed by the president himself, it cannot be revoked for any reason, is that correct?"

"*Oui*, Madame, that is correct. A pardon signed by the president can never be revoked or even questioned."

"I hate to disappoint you, then, but you are under a misapprehension. My husband is not as dangerous as you seem to believe." At his disbelieving expression, I added gently, "He *is* dangerous, but not the way you think. My husband, M. Moreau, does not have the blood of that murdered diplomat on his hands. He did not kill him. He only wanted you to think he had done so, to get the pardon." I sat back in my chair and watched the play of emotions flit across his wide face.

"I do not understand! The man was stabbed, he was killed. And M. Bessette was seen leaving the apartment." He exclaimed.

"I know that. But the man was already dead when he got there. The safe was standing open, so he collected as many papers as he could and left."

M. Moreau shook his head. "Already dead? So M. Bessette did not..."

"No indeed. You would not know, of course, but as a rule he would never use a knife to kill someone. He always preferred a rope." Oh, how much I enjoyed saying that, and smiling into his no longer complacent face!

"Madame, you are...*mon Dieu*!" He pulled out a handkerchief and mopped his brow with it. "I see that when I first met you, I misjudged you somewhat. Now I think...I think you are a good match for your husband. Oh, by the way, those papers he took from the safe? Quite valuable to us, and most useful. I hope you will tell him so when you see him in America."

Attempting to conceal my worries on that account, I answered, "But of course, Monsieur. I am sure he will be pleased to hear it."

"By the way, did M. Bessette tell you that I might be able to use him for some, let us say, less deadly tasks in the future?"

"No, he did not. But at that time, there were other things on his mind." Pondering his words, I gave him a sharp look. "Are you talking about *spying*, Monsieur?"

"Oh, we do not call it that, Madame! Recollect, he would be working for the Ministry of Defense." Official spying, in other words. I hid a small smile behind my cup, and asked if this might be a good time to meet Madame Moreau. Apparently, it was.

Madame Marguerite Moreau proved to be a stout, jolly woman of middle age, gray haired like her husband, and like him, of a happy disposition. We were on first names with each other after about an hour. She knew nothing of who I was, or my husband, or what he had done for M. Moreau and the Ministry. She undertook to assist me because she was good-natured, and she asked me no questions. Her chief interests were her children, shopping, playing card games with other ladies, and entertaining for her husband. Bullying a dressmaker was second nature to her; she could do it in her sleep. In short, she was ideal for my needs.

If it were not for the cloud of uncertainty hanging over me, I would have truly enjoyed my sojourn with the Moreaus.

I won't go into detail about the next few days, for I do not wish to bore the Reader. There were fittings, poring over design books, visiting one shop after another to select stockings, undergarments, and so forth. Both Marguerite and I enjoyed it immensely. One thing I adamantly expressed to her was that everything I purchased must serve its purpose: to seduce a man. She did not understand why I desired such a thing, but was happy to go along with it. So were the dressmakers. For my part, I was thrilled to discover that I could buy stockings in pale pink silk. I had only ever had white cotton ones. I hoped Erik would not mind too much the exorbitant amount of his money I was spending on clothes. I also purchased some little things to send home for Celestine and Marie.

Recalling Miss Arlington and her expensive, revealing costumes, and the way her tall slender form set them off perfectly, I knew I needed to dress to highlight my own best features. Or should I say, the features that Erik admired the most. Tall and slender I would never be. It was disconcerting to me that Miss Arlington bore a superficial resemblance to Christine, the Comtesse deChagny. Her long dark hair and willowy figure were once the exact attributes that had attracted him before. I hoped fervently that those attractions had not reawakened a long-dormant passion.

Wherever I went in Paris with Marguerite, we were accompanied by one of their footmen, a large, burly fellow in a bright uniform. The city was not, she explained to me, as safe as it once was. He kept a few steps either behind or before us, glaring at anyone who dared to glance in our direction. Indeed Paris was not the same city I was born and grew up in; in the nearly three years I had been away, everything seemed to have changed.

The streets were so altered as to be unrecognizable, people on the streets seemed rougher somehow, and riots and violence were frequent occurrences. The newspapers were full of calls for *Revanche*. I had rather looked forward to visiting the city of my birth, but now I realized I was anxious to leave it. Even the idea of going to visit Dr. Gaudet at the Hospital held no pleasure for me. The only positive change that I could see was that the city did not smell as bad in the summer as it did when I lived there.

On the third day of my visit to the Moreaus', one of the strangest experiences of my life took place, and that is saying something. Marguerite stayed behind at a milliners shop to try on a hat. I decided to walk on to our next destination, a shop that specialized in ladies lingerie. I was particularly interested in looking at what was now *en vogue*, and hoping to find something silky and lacy that would please a gentleman. Yes, I admit it; it was my intention to seduce my own husband. I only hoped I was not already too late. With the silent footman in tow, I walked along the street gazing raptly into the windows of the shops. It was entrancing to see all this finery and know that I could actually afford it.

So engrossed in my window shopping was I, that I was not really paying attention to where I was walking. Marguerite's footman called out a warning to me just before I bumped straight into the hard chest of a man. Mortified, I glanced up, while my apology died on my lips. I found myself staring into the face of Denis, my former spouse. I was face to face with the man who had single-handedly destroyed my innocence, trammeled over my heart and who never really loved me.

My heart plummeted to my toes, so horrified was I at unexpectedly meeting with someone I never wished to see again. He recognized me at once, and his reaction was almost comically unflattering. His eyes went as wide as dinner plates, he leapt back from me as if I had burned him, and then looked around wildly, his head turning in all directions.

"Denis, what is the matter? You act as if you have seen a ghost!" I exclaimed, stifling a sudden desire to laugh. Was he really afraid of *me*? Ignoring my question, Denis's wild-eyed gaze flickered from me to the footman, standing directly behind me and a little to one side.

"Where is he? Is he here?" He demanded in a voice that shook with fear.

"Is who here?" I asked, mystified. He did not used to be such a nervous sort.

Denis drew a deep breath and attempted to control himself. Running my eyes over him rapidly, I was rather amazed to see that he looked quite healthy. He was wearing a smart uniform and appeared well-groomed, his dark blond mustache tidy and neat. I suppose that I assumed he would have succumbed to drink and bad habits by now. Although older, of course, he resembled the handsome officer who had swept me off my feet, to my everlasting regret. With a little *frisson* of surprise, I realized I was not afraid of him. Denis had no power over me now.

Denis frowned. "Who is this fellow?" he demanded, looking down his patrician nose at Marguerite's footman. The footman glowered back at him with equal dislike. Resplendent in his scarlet footman's uniform, he managed to look just as haughty as my former spouse.

242

By this time we had moved to one side of the sidewalk, close to the wall of a shop. Casting an apologetic glance at the footman, I explained who he was. Denis appeared unimpressed.

"You keep very strange company, Syl, since we parted ways." Denis remarked in a meaningful way that I did not understand. I scowled. I had always hated that nickname he had for me. What right did he have to call me that now?

"What do you mean, Denis?" I asked through clenched teeth.

He straightened a medal on his chest and tugged down his uniform jacket carefully, before shooting me a baleful glance.

"Are you going to deny that you sent that...that *creature* to frighten me, Syl?"

"Do not call me that," I said absently. A peculiar premonition had just come over me. "And I do not know what you are talking about, Denis. I sent no one...although in hindsight I would not have minded it. What happened, pray tell?"

Denis looked embarrassed, and his color heightened. Rather reluctantly, he told me a very strange story. It was several years ago, during the War. He had been out drinking with friends (and here he looked even more embarrassed, or perhaps ashamed), and had gone home to bed to sleep it off. Sometime during the night, he awoke to a terrible sight.

There, not only in his room, but actually at the foot of his bed, was the hideous visage of a monstrous being. It was a man of some sort, holding a lantern in his gloved hand, the red-orange light from the lamp casting weird shadows over his face. It was like a vision of Hell, according to Denis. The man, if so it was, wore a black cape, which he held over part of his face. But when Denis awoke and started up, staring at him blearily, the cape dropped suddenly away to reveal...he shuddered at the ghastly memory. Such a hideous face he had never seen!

Before Denis could bring himself to address this nightmare vision, it spoke to him, the voice deep and sepulchral.

"I understand you are a very brave fellow, Monsieur Saint-Ange," the voice said contemptuously. "You like to get drunk and push women around, or so I have been informed. Some fine gentleman you are."

The creature moved then, as fast as lightening it seemed, and was suddenly right next to the hapless Denis, and one of his black-gloved hands closed around Denis' throat. Gasping, he tried to pry it off, but the grip was like iron. Unable to speak, Denis could only stare helplessly into icy, merciless eyes.

243

"Perhaps it is time you learned a lesson, my good sir. You cannot bully me as you would a woman. I should like very much to kill you, but I will spare you only because I do not think Sylvie would like it. But mark these words, you worthless, drunken *fop* ..." the terrible face loomed right over his, the lips curled in a snarl, and the hand around his neck tightened inexorably.

"If you ever come near Sylvie Bessette again, by accident or design, I will personally see to it that you die a most unpleasant death...slowly, like this..." black dots swam before Denis' eyes, and he swooned into unconsciousness, utterly helpless to save himself, certain that he was dying.

A few minutes later, he returned to consciousness, gasping for breath, his throat painfully sore. Looking wildly about his room, he saw he was alone again; the ghastly creature had vanished. But he had left a calling card of sorts: on the bedroom door was a red skull, drawn in some sort of paint. It was still wet. Denis discovered he was completely sober now, and trembling all over from fear and reaction. He locked his bedroom door, crawled back into bed and drew the covers over his head. He searched his entire apartment in the morning, but never could find out how the terrifying creature had gained admittance.

"I never took another drink after that. I was afraid that if I ever got drunk again, he might return and finish me off." Denis explained. "It put me off drinking entirely."

You may imagine, Reader, how raptly I listened to this fascinating account. I remembered, *bien sûr*, telling Erik some of my sad story the night we sat in his boat on the lake. And I did think it odd, at the time, that he seemed curious to know my former husband's name, for I could think of no reason why it should interest him. I had thought the conversation was forgotten, but clearly, Erik had not forgotten.

Even then, when I was nothing to him but his cook, he must have cared enough to try and right a wrong against me. It made me feel warm somehow, to think that his instinct was to protect me, and to punish the man who had misused me. Although I was glad Erik had not killed him, I was rather sorry to have missed seeing him exact his own kind of revenge on my hapless former spouse.

I shook my head bemusedly, "I believe you dreamt all that, Denis. You were, after all, quite drunk. As you often were in those days."

He looked affronted. "Nonsense, Syl! I did not dream that red skull on my door." Denis fixed me with a gimlet eyed stare. "I believe you know who he is, or was. He certainly knew *you*...and also certain things about our marriage that would be better forgotten."

"Yes, I'm sure," I murmured, thinking what a supercilious cad he was. "You are correct; I do know who he is. But I did not send him to frighten you, Denis, I assure you I did not. That was some scheme of his own."

"Well who is he, then? Some fellow from the circus? I've never seen such a monstrous face."

I adjusted my hat and prepared to take my leave of my former spouse, but it was with great satisfaction that I looked into his eyes and said,

"He happens to be my husband. So you should have a care, Denis." And then I walked away, leaving him staring after me, his mouth hanging open.

I was halfway down the block before I realized I had walked right by the lingerie shop. I was lost in thought; all this time, and Erik never told me about his nocturnal visit to Denis.

CHAPTER TWENTY-TWO

"How far do you go for love?"

A little over a week later, I found myself on a steamer bound for New York Harbor. I was sitting on my small bed, little more than a cot attached to the wall, sipping some tea while trying not to spill it and nibbling on a cracker. I had never been on the ocean before, and much to my dismay, was suffering a bit from *mal de mer.*

M. Moreau had been of great assistance in finding me a berth on the *China*, a small steamship in the Cunard Line renowned for its speed. Thanks to his position in the government, there seemed little that he could not manage. As inexperienced as I was about the world at large, I would have been lost without him, not to mention Marguerite.

Everything about the ship seemed small and cramped to me, but I supposed it was meant to help her go faster. I had an ever-growing bruise on my hip from bumping against a metal table in my room, something I managed to do on a daily basis. Nonetheless, I found I was enjoying the adventure, and as long as I did not allow myself to dwell on the future, I was able to enjoy the moment.

Much had happened in those madcap seven days. I had attended several social functions with the Moreaus (and I must admit, they rather grew on me, so pleasant and kind as they were), obtained one astonishingly beautiful ball gown, several traveling costumes, a few hats and accessories, and a stubborn and domineering personal maid.

The ball gown was packed away in a trunk in the hold of the ship, much to my regret. It was so beautiful, I hated to let it out of my sight. Never in my life had I owned anything so exquisite, nor so expensive. It was true *Haute Couture*, for Marguerite had insisted I have my ball gown made by the House of Worth, and she would not be gainsaid. I could scarcely wait to see Celestine's face when she saw it...how many times had we gazed longingly at Worth's elegant designs in the fashion pages. I preferred not to dwell on what Erik would say when he saw the bill. *If* he saw the bill.

Although gowns with high waists and large bustles were still *en vogue*, I made it very clear that I would never wear a massive bustle that would prevent my sitting down if I wished. To eat, for example. And after taking a good look at my hourglass figure, the staff at the design house determined that a high-waisted style would do nothing to show it off. My ball gown was only finished the evening before my departure; an astonishingly short amount of time for such a magnificent creation. Standing before a three-sided full length mirror at the couturier's *atelier* while wearing it, I thought I looked like a different person altogether.

The gown was of midnight blue silk. Always I have gravitated toward pastel blues, pinks and lavenders, thinking those shades set off my eyes and hair to best advantage. But the midnight blue, with a low *décolleté* neckline and a delicate frill of soft tea colored lace edging it, and small off-the-shoulder sleeves, drew the eye almost instantly to my bosom. More importantly, I hoped it would draw my husband's eye back to me and away from the young woman who I feared had claimed his affections.

Unfashionable currently, but very flattering to me, was the natural waist, very tight and narrow and necessitating some tight lacing to fit me in to it. This was where the maid would be essential. To dress myself in such an *ensemble*, not to mention tighten the laces of my corset, would be impossible for me to attempt alone. *Et aussi*, according to Marguerite, the ladies' maid was very good with hair.

The ball gown flowed smoothly to the floor, and was caught up in the back in a small, softly draping bustle. The side panels were embellished with embroidery and dark blue beading. I thought it was a gown fit for a queen, not for *me*: Sylvie Bessette, former cook. But as I studied my reflection in the mirror, turning this way and that, I thought of Miss Arlington and all her insipid, overly decorated gowns and enormous picture hats, and a small, sly smile turned up the corners of my lips. Over my shoulder, I saw Marguerite give a satisfied nod.

Swallowing a sip of tea with an effort, I peered out the round window of my room on the ship. Watching the horizon line out the porthole seemed to calm my internal organs to a degree. It would be nice to rest for a week after all the bustle of Paris, the shopping and trying on of things. I had even brought a book with me, *Vingt Mille Lieues Sous la Mer*, by Jules Verne. Marguerite assured me it was hugely popular and I would enjoy it very much, but I wondered why she gave me *that* particular book knowing I was embarking on a sea voyage. I settled back against a pillow on my cot and prepared to start the book.

I was lifted out of my reverie by a brisk knock on the door, and my new ladies maid, Henriette, entered. She had been chosen for me by Marguerite, and came with excellent references. She was about my own age, dark haired, sallow of complexion and slender to the point of thinness, with cheekbones that stood out like sculptures. She was pleased and excited to accompany me to New York, having never been out of France in her life.

Now she entered my small room with an air of determination, opened the miniscule closet and began rummaging around, finally pulling out one of my smart new travelling gowns.

"What are you doing, Henriette?" I asked, watching her quizzically. She moved like a small bird, a wren perhaps, full of nervous energy. She looked over her shoulder at me with a disbelieving expression.

"Helping you to dress for supper, *bien sûr*. They begin serving in the *salon* in half an hour, Madame Bessette." Serving? *Food?* My midsection gave a little flip of distress at the very idea. Seeing my mutinous expression, she added, "You must leave your stateroom some times, Madame. And it is very important to eat." She gave me a sly sideways look. "And also, there are several very handsome gentlemen on this ship, even if some of them are English."

"Hmmm," I said, standing up and allowing her to strip away my *robe de chambre*. But when she extracted a little gold pot and a brush from a basket she had brought, I balked.

"What is that?" I asked suspiciously as she approached me, pot in hand.

"It is rouge for the cheeks, Madame. These are cosmetics, you see. All the ladies of Paris wear this now." Henriette explained matter-of-factly. "I am very skilled at the application."

I recoiled. I was not going to be a painted lady; everyone knew what *that* said about one. "*Non, non*, Henriette! I will not..."

Henriette frowned, hands on hips. "Madame, do not behave like some prudish Englishwoman!" she exclaimed in irritated tones. "Cosmetics were *invented* in France, Madame. It is your birthright." She tilted her narrow head and studied me for a moment, and then said, "Madame cannot imagine how exemplary Henriette is at the application of these little pots of color for the face. Only wait until you see how natural and glowing you look with just a touch of this..." she waved the brush at me temptingly. The flesh is definitely weak, Reader.

And so it was that a half hour later, I made my solitary entrance into the dining *salon* and searched for my place at the long table. Henriette had performed her magic on my hair and my face – and I had to admit, it did took natural. Only a gentle wash of color across my cheekbones, and suddenly I actually *had* cheekbones. And my lips...now they looked twice as generous as before, and like ripe red fruit. Well, perhaps I *did* examine my reflection with satisfaction before leaving my room, but only because the experience was so unfamiliar.

I was impressed by the formality achieved on the steamer; no doubt that was the British influence, it being a ship of an English line. There were white tablecloths, gleaming silver *epergnes* (how did they keep from falling over when a wave hit the ship?), even finger bowls. Unfortunately, the food that was served in the dining room was primarily English, and quite bland.

I was pleasantly surprised to find a variety of travelers on the steamer: a scattering of French, American and English. The Americans knew no French, but most of the English people spoke French well, making it possible for me to converse.

Here in the dining *salon* I had my first taste of what was to happen to me everywhere I went on that fateful journey.

I was besieged, inundated, and beset by men. They behaved as if I were some sort of rare goddess, fawning over me wherever I went outside my own room. The other ladies on the steamer shot me venomous looks and made snide remarks about my traveling alone. No matter that I told them all I was married, and meeting my husband in New York, or even when I brandished my wedding ring. It was absurd, and very vexing.

Whenever I entered the dining salon, I was surrounded…one gentleman would not be satisfied until he had fetched me a glass of chilled champagne, another wanted to know where I was staying in New York, and would I honor him with a dance there. I was invited to sit at the Captain's table on more than one occasion, and forced to listen, a stiff smile pasted on my face, while he practiced his execrable French on me. Once I barely made it into my stateroom without being mauled by one of the officers.

Closing and locking the door behind me, I leaned against it and blew a wisp of hair out of my face. My *coiffure* had become somewhat disheveled in my efforts to escape my ardent admirer. Henriette was waiting in my room to help me undress and prepare for bed, and she had to stifle a laugh when she saw my appearance. I glared at her.

"It is not amusing, Henriette. I do not understand what is wrong with the gentlemen on this ship. They behave as though they had never seen a woman before!" I exclaimed, collapsing on my small cot. "I cannot believe the liberties they take." Henriette shot me an incredulous look as she came to take the pins out of my hair.

"Madame, can it be that you are not aware of how lovely you are?" She asked. This remark caused me to make an unladylike noise.

"Nonsense, Henriette!"

Carefully hanging up my gown, Henriette said over her shoulder, "Madame, all the gentleman wish to be in your company. You are by far the prettiest lady on the ship. There is a glow about you. Even the captain thinks so."

Well! Take that, Miss Arlington! I thought with malicious pleasure.

But at night, when I was lying alone in my bed while the waves rocked me gently (and sometimes not so gently), I found myself staring up at the ceiling and wondering what was going to happen. The idea of seeing Erik face to face after all this time apart, and after that hateful letter he sent me, filled me with apprehension. Had I acted too impetuously in making this journey? Would it all come to naught? I admit that in those dark moments, I was afraid. I missed my *petite* Marie, and longed to hold her again. The steamship would arrive at the New York Harbor in seven days, and each night I lay for a while contemplating what would happen when we got there. I was so afraid that I was already too late.

Erik

"Where have you been?" Edythe demanded, hands on her slim hips. "I've been looking for you everywhere!"

Erik paused in the grand foyer of the hotel, a shopping bag in his hand. Edythe's eyes flew to the bag.

"Were you buying me a present?" She asked coyly.

"No, I was not. That would be quite inappropriate, as I am sure you are aware," he replied austerely. *En fait*, he had been visiting a men's haberdashery on Fifth Avenue, to purchase a few of the new style of cravat that he saw all the men wearing in New York. They looked much more comfortable than the ones he always wore, and not as damned hot. "What do you want?" He demanded of her brusquely.

Her black eyes flashed. "To tell you that I have heard from Father, and he will be here in three days! I knew you would wish to know." She paused and moved closer to him. "I know you are anxious to go back to the clinic and meet with Dr. Buck again." She added confidingly.

Only three more days to endure, Erik thought morosely. *"Merci*, I am glad to hear it." He said in a less forbidding voice. At least in Edythe he had a confidante. She was always willing to listen to him and offer reassurances.

Edythe slipped her arm through his. "Come, why do you not join Matthew and me for supper tonight? A few of my friends will be here, and it will be a jolly party."

Seeing the refusal in his eyes, she played her trump card. Leaning into him, still clutching his arm, she said wistfully,

"Oh you must come! Matthew so wants to talk to you about France. He has never been, you must recall. He can practice his French on you. Please don't disappoint him!"

Erik did want to refuse…he had met some of Edythe's 'friends', and they were an insipid, vain group of wealthy young American aristocrats. They spoke of dog races, and going abroad, and to a man, not one of them had served in their war. Erik disliked them intensely; they reminded him too much of the gentlemen he used to observe (or perhaps spy upon was more accurate) at the Opera House. Vapid, empty-headed, rich and confident. His observations of these opera-goers over the years had taught him how to dress and behave superficially like a gentleman, but he had no respect for them. Indeed, he had tried to send them all to Hell!

Matthew, however, was another matter. The young boy, all of sixteen, was open and good-natured. He was more like his father than Edythe, and Erik rather liked him. He was convinced that Edythe was a bad influence on her brother.

"*Très bien*, I will come." He said reluctantly. Perhaps, he thought, it would be better than sulking alone in his suite or wandering the streets like a lost soul.

Aside from conversing with Matthew for a few minutes during the supper party, Erik sat in stoic silence at their table, a permanent scowl on his face, while foolish and idiotic conversation flowed around and over him. Having sat through several of these evenings, he found their nonsensical conversations had begun to sound the same. There was decent French wine to be had at the hotel, *Dieu merci*! He had taken to ordering a bottle just for himself.

Sometime after they had finished supper, Edythe declared she was tired of seeing him sitting there, intimidating her friends with his glowering expressions and obvious boredom, so she requested Erik escort her back to her room. He acquiesced at once, glad to be able to excuse himself and seek his own solitude. He wanted to be alone with his thoughts, grim as they were.

They walked silently through the carpeted hallways, side by side. Edythe took his arm, even though there was no necessity for it, since they were not walking outside. Her grasp was not the delicate, lady-like sort, but more like seizing possession of that appendage. Erik could not comprehend why this seemed to be so important to her, but something about her possessive gesture sent warning bells off in his head. He disengaged himself from her grasp, and she glanced at him askance, her smile brittle. He thought she would remonstrate with him, but instead she began talking about something quite different.

"I do hope that tomorrow evening you will be better company, Erik. Your dire looks are frightening my friends. And do not forget it is the ball in the grand ballroom and I want you to dance with me." They arrived at the door of her suite, and she abruptly turned to face him. Reaching up, she took hold of his coat lapels flirtatiously, a sparkle in her dark eyes. "I look forward to seeing you in formal attire, for I am sure it will become you quite well."

Erik scowled with dismay. He had forgotten all about the ball, and did not wish to attend it.

"I do not..." he began, but Edythe placed her cool fingers over his lips in an intimate gesture that shocked and silenced him.

"Don't say no; I have the most delicious gown to wear, and I declare you must see me in it. It is quite daring." Her eyes glittered with mischief, and something else that made him feel uncomfortable. "I can make it worth your while," she murmured in a seductive voice he had never heard her use before. He felt the hairs rise on the back of his neck. He needed to get away from her; why did she not go into her suite?

And then Edythe glided closer to him, slipping one of her hands up and around his neck. She pulled herself against him, pressing her small, firm breasts against his chest, and before he knew what she was about to do, brought her lips to his.

Erik was momentarily stunned into immobility. For a brief instant, the feel of a woman's body pressed against his, of warm lips moving against his own, brought a surge of desire rushing through him. He pictured himself pushing her against the door and savaging her mouth with his own, burying his hands in her cascades of black hair. But the vision of wild passion only lasted for an instant, and he was himself again. Like it or not, there was only one woman for him now, damn her.

He brought his hands up between them, tore himself from Edythe's hold, and pushed her away firmly. He was mortified to find that his breath was fast and shallow. Ashamed, he sought to regulate it. Edythe stared into his eyes, her expression turning confused and pleading.

"I want you," she whispered, her eyes suddenly glassy with unshed tears. "From the first moment I saw you I knew you and I would be so good together...I can feel it. Let me show you..." She tried to bring herself against him again, but Erik held her away by her arms.

252

"I don't care about your face," she said urgently. "I don't care about anything you did. Those things you told me on the ship…what you did in your past, it was exciting and made me want you even more." She tried again to lean toward him, a strange wild light in her eyes, and the words came out in an almost hysterical rush.

"We would be well-matched, you and I. We are kindred spirits. You don't need that weak, insipid creature you left in France…you have me, Erik! I am here, and I need you! You want me too, don't you?" He was filled with disgust and horror, and made no effort to hide it from her.

"No, Edythe," he said coldly. "I do not want this. Not now or ever. I suggest you forget about me. Good night." And he turned on his heel and walked rapidly away from her. His relief at turning a corner in the hallway was profound. He could feel her eyes boring into his back. It was highly doubtful that any man had ever refused Edythe Arlington before.

Returning to his own suite, Erik was both deeply troubled and still somewhat aroused. He felt like an absolute fool for not seeing this coming, never imagining her interest in him to be a romantic one. He knew she did not, *could* not, love him, for she knew next to nothing about him. This was something else; some fanatical obsession. He stood for a long time gazing blindly down at the street below his window, his heart heavy with dread. Edythe had sounded so…almost mad.

And then Erik thought of Christine, and he sat heavily on the edge of his bed and sank his head into his hands. He of all people knew what a mad obsession could drive a person to do. His intuition told him that he had just made a deadly enemy.

Henriette and I arrived at the Fifth Avenue Hotel in late morning. We did not, alas, arrive alone. We were accompanied by a few of my more ardent admirers, who were all staying at the same, obviously upper class establishment. To be honest, they were of great help to me, for I spoke no English and no one here seemed to speak any French. *Et aussi*, there was our baggage to sort out. All I had to do was point out which cases were ours, and

253

eager hands dealt with them. Henriette smirked at me slyly, and I discreetly poked her in the side with my sun parasol.

I was quite happy to have one of the gentlemen act as my interpreter when I checked into the hotel in the vast lobby. *Vraiment*, the Fifth Avenue Hotel reminded me of the Opera Garnier, so elegant and decorated was it. The vast floor was made of white and red marble tiles, and the entire top of the long *concierge* counter was of white marble. I gazed around me with great interest, studying what the ladies were wearing in New York. Their costumes were vastly different than what was *en vogue* in Paris at the moment. Dark colors seemed to be favored, and there was too much trimming and decoration on the gowns for my taste. The bustles were of enormous proportions. I did see some rather nice hats, however.

All went smoothly thanks to M. Moreau's efforts on my behalf; a suite of rooms had been reserved for us on the fourth floor. While Henriette waited with my trunk and bags in the foyer, I stood at the marble *concierge* desk to check in. At my elbow was a very nice, distinguished Englishman I had met on the steamer, who spoke impeccable French. We had conversed much on board, for I did find it enjoyable to have someone to talk with. He was tall and handsome, with silver hair and a silver mustache. He was staying at the Fifth Avenue Hotel as well, and had very kindly offered to act as my interpreter when I checked in.

I found myself glancing around the wide lobby apprehensively, half expecting to see my errant husband pass by, arm in arm with his new paramour. I was not ready for such a horrible, heart-breaking sight. My palms felt damp inside my gloves, and my heart was in my throat, but there was no sign of Erik or Miss Arlington, much to my relief.

The kind-faced older gentleman behind the long counter handed me a key to my room, and offered to call a boy to bring my things there. He pointed me in the direction of the perpendicular railway. But I was not quite ready to depart.

Thanking the Englishman who had helped me translate, I dismissed him with a promise that I would surely see him around the hotel. After he walked away, looking rather crest-fallen, I turned back to the desk clerk, leaned closer to him and asked in hesitantly,

"Can you tell me please in what room is M. Erik Bessette?" This English sentence was one I had learned and practiced in my room on the steamer. It is strange how frightened I felt, now that I was actually here and about to confront Erik. Whatever happened here, for good or ill, could change my life forever.

A young man who was putting mail and newspapers into various boxes nearby swiveled his head in my direction when he overheard my question. He stared at me in a most peculiar manner, his eyes wide. Was my English that bad? The older clerk spoke to him sharply and he abruptly turned back to what he was doing.

From the clerk I learned Erik was in a suite on the third floor of the hotel. It was like a cold splash of water in my face. He was here, had been here all along, and simply chose to ignore me. I decided to go and settle into my own room with Henriette, perhaps have some tea and change my attire, and then I would go and look for him. Provided I could muster up the courage. And *après tout*, he might be out.

The perpendicular railway provided a welcome distraction. It did not, thankfully, chug like a train straight up the side of the hotel. Rather, it was a small, glass-enclosed room fitted out like a comfortable *petite* parlor. You could sit down and watch as the entire little room rose sedately into the air, accompanied by a metallic ratcheting sound. It paused at each floor to allow passengers to embark or disembark. A man in a smart uniform stood by the door and pushed the appropriate buttons. I found the entire procedure quite fascinating, but Henriette did not like it and would not look out the clear glass as we ascended.

Still, I was grateful when we finally attained our own suite, and were left alone to open the trunks, shake out our garments and put our things away. There were two bedrooms in the suite, a small one for the use of one's servant and a larger one with a very inviting looking bed. Even better, the suite possessed its own bath chamber, with hot and cold water on tap. What luxury! The Reader must understand that this was the first hotel I had ever stayed in, and I had no idea hotels could be so grand and luxurious.

I found myself dawdling over putting everything away and exploring the furniture in our suite, then gazing out the window at the city street far below. After that amusement palled, nothing would do but that I must have a bath. It would not do to present myself to Erik looking travel-worn and disheveled. That would put me at a disadvantage. I was worried and filled with turmoil as it was.

While I splashed in a bathtub full of scented bubbles, Henriette went out to order tea and find out where everything was. She returned just as I was tying the belt of my robe, and she was bursting with excitement.

"Madame, look here!" She brandished an announcement leaflet. "There is a ball in the grand ballroom this very evening! You must attend and wear your new gown. It will be *parfait!*"

255

I glanced at the leaflet… a full orchestra, champagne and fine things to eat. Formal evening attire was a must. Perhaps I was seizing any excuse to put off the inevitable confrontation, but the thought of seeing Erik again when I was wearing my beautiful blue gown was a seductive one. I fanned myself idly with the leaflet, thinking. Would Erik be there, in the company of Miss Arlington? I tried not to think about *that*.

"*Oui*, Henriette, you are right." I said at last. "I will attend the ball. I am sure it will be very interesting." She went happily off to make her preparations for my beautification process. Henriette did not know why I was here in New York, other than my stated purpose of meeting up with my husband. She had no idea what was at stake. I was glad she did not question why I did not go at once in search of him, and I certainly was not going to admit to her that I was terrified.

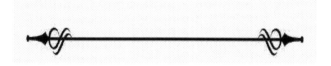

Erik

Erik was sitting at a large round table in the formal ballroom of the hotel, his fingers wrapped tightly around the crystal stem of a wine glass. Ruby wine swirled softly around the bowl of the glass as he lifted it to his nose appreciatively. Their table was next to a row of tall windows, and since it was night, the dark glass reflected the brilliance of glowing chandeliers, the sparkle of crystal, and his own gloomy expression.

This crowded ballroom was the last place he wanted to be, but the idea of having Edythe think he might be hiding from her in his room had spurred him to assume his formal suit of stark black and white, and come downstairs to the ballroom. He was not certain why this mattered to him, but he suspected it was because he did not want her to think she had some power over him and his actions. He felt defiant and surly.

This evening was the first time he had seen Edythe since her unwelcome advance on the previous night. After looking him up and down when he approached their table, she ignored him completely.

Instead, she devoted all her attentions and not inconsiderable charms upon one of her men friends, who were clearly susceptible to them. If she thought her behavior would incite Erik to jealousy, she was destined for

256

disappointment. Rather, Erik was thankful. Matthew, at least, was happy to see him. Matthew was bubbling with excitement, flushed and ready to enjoy everything, for it was his first formal ball.

Erik had endured a miserable night; it was long before he finally fell asleep, so troubled was he by that encounter with Edythe. The experience had dredged up memories of the past he would prefer to forget.

And now, here he was, enduring a ball he did not want to attend in the first place. He regarded the room sourly, wishing he were back in his suite, and took a deep drink of his wine. In a few minutes, he decided, he would simply get up and leave. No one would miss him.

Oh, where was all my bravery now, when I desperately needed it? Henriette had worked miracles yet again on my appearance, even managing to dress my hair so that curls gathered and frothed attractively at the back of my head. I had brought my diamond earrings with me and now they sparkled at my ears, almost matching the blue of my ball gown. Henriette had wielded her little gold pots and brushes to apply rouge on my cheeks, and some pink tinted balm to my lips. Finally she had dusted a little rice powder over my nose while I sipped nervously from a glass of *vin blanc*. I knew I had never looked better, but what good was that now?

I was standing, alone and filled with dismay, in the wide entrance to the ballroom, which was located on what appeared to be the entire third floor of the hotel. It was sumptuous indeed, and much more crowded than I had expected. The orchestra was playing a waltz, while beautifully dressed couples were whirling around the room. Jewels sparkled from gowns and the necks of the ladies. I could catch glimpses of many tables of people placed around the outskirts of the ballroom, watching the dancing couples or talking amongst themselves. There was much laughter and jollity. Waiters bustled about holding trays aloft, balancing glasses of champagne. How was I ever to locate Erik in this mad crowd, were he even here? And what would I say when I did?

I had given much thought to this subject while on the steamer voyage. There had been plenty of time for me to conjure up various scenarios in my mind. Sometimes I marched up to Miss Arlington and slapped her smug face. Sometimes I pictured myself tossing a drink at her. I tried to imagine walking up to Erik and slapping *his* face, but somehow the idea of doing that rather terrified me. I was certain he would not take it well. I planned outraged speeches in which I delivered withering comments to the pair of them.

Now I was here, very likely in the same room with them, and my courage failed me completely. I felt sick, and frightened. My palms in their white gloves felt hot and damp. I could not understand what anyone was saying, and the noise level was high anyway. Instead of my fantasies of revenge against Miss Arlington, a different scenario appeared in my imagination. What if I confronted them, and they regarded me with pity, or disdain? What if Erik sneered at me with contempt? Oh, why, why had I come? I began to feel distinctly faint.

A couple pushed past me into the ballroom, and without thinking I followed in their wake, trying to appear inconspicuous. We skirted the dancers and I soon found myself on the other side of the ballroom, near the orchestra. There were a few small tables scattered about where some dowagers were seated observing the dancing. I made for them, hoping to sit down before I collapsed dramatically in a heap on the floor.

Before I attained my goal, however, I was approached by two young gentlemen in elegant black and white evening attire. They spoke to me, smiling and appearing affable, but of course I could understand not a word. I tried to explain, and soon another man came up, and then another. They all appeared to know each other. They realized I was French, and that seemed to excite them even more. I surmised that they were attempting to offer me things. They were acting decidedly flirtatious, and began trying to outdo each other, becoming quite loud and insistent.

It was a repetition of that ridiculous male behavior I experienced aboard the steamer, and I did not like it one bit. I could feel a hot blush spreading over my face. I looked around wildly, wondering how to escape my unwanted admirers.

Just then, I was relieved to see my handsome and helpful English gentleman from the steamer walking toward me. Thank goodness, someone who spoke French! I smiled at him hopefully. Perhaps he could extricate me from my absurd collection of admirers.

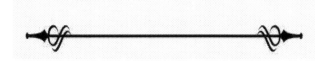

258

Erik

A waltz was just concluding, and couples were returning to their tables or standing to the side, sipping champagne and waiting for the next dance to begin. On the far side of the room from their table, Erik became aware of a cluster of men, and a hum of laughter and noise. Several people were looking in that direction curiously, but nothing could be seen except a brief glimpse of midnight blue satin. He turned away, scowling at nothing in particular. One of Edythe's friends surreptitiously edged his chair a little away from Erik.

The increasing din from across the ballroom finally attracted Edythe's notice, and she left off flirting with her new victim long enough to glance up and inquire, "What on earth is all that commotion over there?" She did not look at Erik.

Matthew, eager for an excuse to leave their table and walk about the large room, volunteered to go and see. Adjusting his cravat and smoothing his hair self-consciously, he departed. His place was quickly taken by another of Edythe's friends. It was interesting how all of her friends seemed to be men. Erik ignored them as he usually did, finding their idle gossip and chatter boring in the extreme. He toyed again with the stem of his wine glass and swirled the dark liquid gently, watching the way the wine ran down the sides of the glass in long rivulets of red. It was time to go.

Matthew returned before he had stood up, and the boy was visibly excited, with a sparkle in his dark eyes that were so like his sister's. Addressing the male members of their party, he said, "Gentlemen, there is the most delectable creature over there – a real beauty I assure you – all those gents are vying for her favors. She'll make some fellow lucky tonight!"

One of Edythe's friends, Erik could not be bothered to remember his name, glanced up alertly, looking interested. "Well, what does she look like, then?" He asked. "What is so special about her that all those fellows are making such fools of themselves?"

Matthew dragged over a chair, finding his taken. He rolled his eyes for emphasis. "She is just a little thing, but what a figure! Like a Venus. Her hair is, oh, what d'you call it – honey blonde? Big blue eyes. Lovely face, and skin like cream. If I were only a little older..." his voice trailed off wistfully, as he imagined all the forbidden delights he was not yet permitted to indulge in. One of the men chuckled.

Erik listened morosely to his description of the woman across the room. The vivid description of the unseen temptress stirred up a vision in

Erik's mind: Matthew could have been describing Sylvie, as she had been before her illness.

Edythe scolded her younger brother for such inappropriate carryings-on, then, pointedly ignoring Erik, she returned to her outrageous flirting with the man on the other side of her. She leaned toward him, allowing the man a close look down the front of her low-cut gown. It was one of her favorite tricks. The man kept casting nervous glances toward Erik, who ignored him. Was he afraid Erik would be jealous? The thought brought a sardonic smile to Erik's face, and that caused the man to nervously tug at his cravat. The other friend, the one who had requested a description, was peering determinedly in the other direction, obviously considering trying his luck with the mystery beauty himself.

Erik found himself staring again toward the group of men in their austere evening clothes, eagerly gathered around the lovely woman and completely hiding her from view, except the briefest glimpse of her blue gown. What sort of woman could bewitch so many men? She must be alone and unescorted...It suddenly occurred to him that he could go over there, easily banish her eager admirers, and take this woman for himself. If she truly resembled his wife, he must find her attractive, *sans doute*. He would seduce her, and take her to his bed. That would show Sylvie, and Edythe too for that matter. Erik felt reckless and mad as he considered this new idea.

And then a strange feeling came over him. Although he hated the word, it felt like a premonition. His scalp tingled, and rushes of hot and cold ran through him. He released his death grip on the wine glass because the wine was trembling visibly inside the cut crystal bowl. It was madness, utterly impossible, but somehow his intuition told him the mystery woman holding court across the ballroom did not merely resemble Sylvie, it *was* Sylvie. His wife was here, in this very room.

His ears filled with a high-pitched whining noise, blocking out all other sound. A blood-red sheen covered his eyes, as though he looked through a red scarf. He pushed his chair back and stood up abruptly. Red wine splashed out of his glass and stained the white damask tablecloth. He knew he was no longer in control of his body or his actions, and he did not care. Death was imminent, but whose?

Everyone at their table was staring at him with perplexed, even frightened expressions. Matthew and Edythe exchanged glances, Edythe looking sulky. She opened her mouth to remonstrate with Erik, but he turned away before she could get a word out. He walked purposely across the room, everything behind him instantly forgotten as he skirted several tables of diners, making for the group of men. He was a predator now, stalking his prey, and it was a familiar, even comforting feeling. He knew how to do this.

He was aware on some level that he was only hanging on to his self-control by a thread – if Sylvie was the woman surrounded by fawning admirers, if it was indeed she, it was entirely possible that Erik might throttle her right there. It was also equally possible that he might kill any man who had the audacity to touch her. His hands were shaking, and he clenched them into fists at his sides. The urge to violence was so strong in him, he could feel it coursing like blood through his vibrating body.

Circling around the group like a wolf toward its prey, he drew closer, finally coming to stand directly behind the woman in the dark blue satin gown. Perhaps five or six men of varying ages and appearances stood in an admiring semi-circle around her, and all were apparently trying to convince her to accept a glass of champagne, go somewhere more private, or honor them with a waltz. They were jostling each other and all talking at the same time. A pack of absurd fools.

Gloved hands clasped demurely together in front of her, the beauty in the blue gown turned her head from one to the other as she listened to their flirtatious invitations. One man, older and taller than the others with a distinguished silver moustache and hair, had just pushed through to join the throng with a determined expression.

Erik studied the back of the petite temptress before him with a volatile gaze. Her lustrous dark blonde hair was caught up in a cluster of curls that trembled with every move of her head. She had a tiny waist, and the deep blue satin skirts of her gown flared out becomingly from her curving hips. It was an expensive gown, trimmed with beadwork and lace, and unlike the gowns worn by other women at the ball, it was cut expressly to reveal her tempting figure. Emerging from small puff sleeves, her white shoulders and arms looked soft and inviting to touch. Then as he studied her from behind, he saw a flush of rose pink rise up her neck and he knew it was because she was embarrassed by all the attention. And that was all the evidence he needed. Only Sylvie could wear a gown like that and then be embarrassed when it attracted attention.

He thought of Sylvie as she had looked when he last saw her, standing on the steps of the *château*. She had been too thin, her hair without its usual health and shine, her normally sparkling blue eyes dull, her skin pale. The woman standing three feet away and completely unaware of his presence appeared to be in the prime of health, and quite capable of beguiling an entire roomful of male admirers.

261

Waves of fury, jealousy, hurt and confusion passed through Erik, freezing him in place. Amidst this turmoil of emotions was a *frisson* of desire, which he fought to suppress.

What was she doing here – for he knew without a doubt it was she. Why had she come here after deliberately ignoring him for weeks, only to surround herself with a pack of drooling imbeciles while leaving him to watch from afar? He could never have imagined Sylvie could be that cruel, that uncaring of his feelings. It seemed proof that she no longer loved him. But if she was here, where was Marie? Had she brought Marie with her?

Wild thoughts chased through his mind and then all was dashed away as he saw that Sylvie had finally decided to accept the hand of the tall man for a waltz. If he touched her hand, Erik knew he would kill him. Even as he watched, he saw Sylvie tentatively extend her right hand toward the man's. The man was smiling, with the gleam of triumph showing in his eyes – he thought he was the fortunate one, having beat out his fellows for a waltz with the most beautiful woman in the room. Erik did not think he would feel so lucky in another moment.

CHAPTER TWENTY-THREE

"I loved Erik, and I wanted him for myself. He should be mine."

This was so embarrassing! Why had I let Henriette convince me to come to this ball? It was so absurd, and I *hated* being the center of attention to such a degree. What was the matter with these foolish men? Oh, how I longed to disappear into the ground!

Then I saw a familiar face: the kind English gentleman who had helped me this morning coming to my rescue. Surely he would understand if I told him I did not really want to dance. I wanted to just sit quietly, and study the other guests to see if my husband was among them. I decided to accept his hand for the next dance, which was just beginning. At least it would succeed in banishing away all the others.

Smiling with relief, I extended my gloved hand toward his. I noticed just as I did so that his eyes moved from my face to an area a little above and over my shoulder. He froze, while a perplexed look appeared on his face; then he frowned slightly and looked wary. A strange feeling came over me, a prickling sensation on the back of my neck. I felt like all the blood was leaving my head.

Just before my fingertips touched those of the Englishman's, an icy voice spoke right behind me. My heart began accelerating wildly.

"No one dances with my wife but me." The chilling tones startled my would-be rescuer, as well they might. To me they were blood-curdling. My breath caught in my throat, and my heart pounded so hard that I could feel a pulse throbbing in my wrists.

"And who are you, Sir?" The Englishman asked warily, still staring over my shoulder.

"Her husband...or so I believe," was the caustic reply. I felt Erik's hand take my outstretched arm, curling his fingers around it, and he carefully but firmly lowered my hand to my side. He did not release me. His grip was hard, just short of painful. It was a grip of ownership.

At the feel of that hand on my arm all the breath seem to rush out of me, leaving me light-headed and afraid. I dropped my eyes down to his hand. There it was, my husband's hand. He was here, he was touching me. This was it – this was the moment I had been both dreading and praying for. Everything else was forgotten; the other men, the music, everything seemed to fade away.

So slowly, as though in a dream, I turned my head and looked up into the face of my husband. To my relief, he was alone; I had half-feared to see Miss Arlington with him. He looked the same, but also different. His face...I blinked and looked closer. He was wearing a mask, but it was so unlike his old one. But Erik was not looking at me; rather his forbidding gaze was trained on the gentleman who had dared to ask me to dance. He looked like a man who was about to commit murder.

The gentleman asked, concern showing in his eyes, "Is this man your husband, Madame?"

"Yes." My voice was barely a whisper. "He is."

"I see." The handsome Englishman drew back, made me a slight bow, and, looking disappointed, walked away. I was relieved for his sake. The other men who had been vying for my attention now prudently faded away as well, leaving me alone with Erik.

Without speaking, Erik slid his arm possessively around my waist, placed my hand on his shoulder and drew me toward the ballroom floor. I was taken aback; he wanted to dance with me? Before we even spoke to each other? I went passively, unresisting, too overwhelmed at suddenly seeing him again to resist or even speak. This felt dreamlike, unreal.

Erik

Face to face with his wife at long last, Erik's breath caught at the sight of her. She was radiantly beautiful. From the front, the gown she wore was cut mesmerizingly low, and the lace trim set off her creamy skin so that her breasts looked like two delicious bon-bons. No wonder those other men could not leave her alone.

As furious and bewildered as he was by her cruel treatment of him, Erik wanted nothing more than to hold Sylvie in his arms, to feel her again. She was his, and by some strange miracle, as though he had conjured it by his longing, she was *here*. He caught a whiff of some elusive perfume.

They were on a dance floor, he thought hazily, and without further consideration he pulled her into a waltz position. She came to him willingly, but he thought she looked frightened. As well she should. The feel of her, of his hand around her waist, of just being this close to her, made him dizzy with pleasure. He held on to his seething resentment almost desperately, because he was afraid it was the only thing preventing him from pouncing on her right there in the middle of the ballroom and dragging her to the floor.

Erik could dance well; early in our marriage we had hired a dancing master from the nearby village to come to the *château* and give us private lessons. Erik always said that dancing with his wife was something he wanted to be able to do. Graceful, masterful and athletic, and with an innate understanding of music, he was an excellent dancer. It went without saying that he was born to lead. Which was good, because I had no sense of rhythm.

But now he was stiff and formal, his face above mine cold and distant. He was starkly handsome in the black and white of evening dress, but as icy as a glacier. A stranger was holding me, and guiding me through a waltz. I wanted to speak to him, to say something, anything, but his forbidding silence and icy expression froze my tongue. His lips were firmed into a thin line, a sure sign of his displeasure. I wondered what he was thinking. Despairingly, I took his coldness toward me as a sign that my worst fears were confirmed: Erik no longer loved me.

Finally he broke the silence, demanding tersely, "Why have you come here like this, Sylvie – why did you not write to tell me you were coming to New York?" My heart sank. He sounded so angry, even hateful, like the man who wrote me that cruel letter.

I stared up at him incredulously. The new mask he wore was disconcerting, adding to the feeling that a stranger held me in his arms. Perhaps because I was so out of my depth, I blurted out the truth without thinking.

"Because if I told you I was coming, you would have had time to prepare for my arrival." I directed a significant glance to the side as we swept around the ballroom floor, in the direction of the table where I had caught a glimpse of Edythe Arlington sitting. She was glaring at us, malice glittering in her black eyes. Looking back at Erik, I added pointedly,

"Perhaps you would not have flaunted your relationship with *her* quite so blatantly had you known I was going to be here tonight."

"What?" Erik stared down at me blankly. "What are you talking about? And where is Marie? Is she with you?" He demanded abruptly.

"She is at home with Celestine," I replied impatiently, caught off guard by his sudden change of topic.

"You did not bring her with you? You left her at home without either of us there?" Why did he sound so angry? Surely he could not expect I would have brought Marie with me under the circumstances.

"Marie is fine, Erik," I said. "You know Celestine watches over her as a *grand-mere*."

He frowned down at me, his pale eyes glittering with suppressed fury. "I do not know what game you are playing at, Madame, but you should have a care. You are trying my patience exceedingly, leaving Marie and coming here without notice, flaunting yourself in that indecent gown, and flirting with every man in the room like a …a courtesan looking for her next protector!" His arm tightened around my waist, impelling me closer against him.

I gasped in disbelief; how could he say such things to me? He was the one…I was so angry that I could not even find my voice, only sputtering incoherently. Erik pressed his advantage at once. "How dare you let me go this long without a word from you, letting me worry all this time about you and Marie? Ignoring all my letters – *damn* you! I'll make you pay for this, Sylvie," He snarled. "I'll make you sorry."

What was he talking about? But his temper had got the better of him, and suddenly his hand gripped my smaller one so tightly it felt as if he would crush the bones. The hand on my back tensed until I could feel each finger digging into my flesh. The movement impelled me even harder against him. A gasp of pain escaped me. When I first knew Erik, he could not govern his temper or his emotions. I had thought he was doing better in that regard, but apparently I was mistaken.

Other couples on the ballroom floor were staring at us with irritated or worried expressions, but it was as if we were in our own tense and furious bubble.

Fighting tears of pain and anger, I spat, "I did write you! I wrote you every week! It is *you* who did not write to us! You were too busy to bother with us; you and that…that American minx!" To my great dismay, Erik's face flushed with color, as though giving credence to my words. "Do not bother to deny it. You are having an affair with her, Erik!" I cried despairingly, tears of pain smarting in my eyes.

Erik stopped even making a pretense of dancing, and we came to a full stop. Rage and something like confusion warred in his face. Couples swirled around us, the men shooting us dire looks.

"I am not having an affair with Edythe." He said in a choking voice.

I glanced around, and saw another couple swerve to avoid colliding with us. Tugging the hand that was still enclosed in his bruising grip, I gasped, "Please Erik. We are causing a scene – let us move."

"Yes, we will definitely move." He said coldly. Stepping back from me, he retained my hand imprisoned in his hard grip and began pulling me off the ballroom floor, toward one of the entrances. I had no hope of freeing my hand; I was also afraid if I struggled we would attract even more unwanted attention. I therefore allowed him to drag me out of the room, my

266

other hand clutching a handful of my beautiful blue gown to avoid tripping over the long skirt.

It was a good thing I could not see Miss Arlington's face at that moment, as she watched Erik towing me out of the ballroom.

"Wh...where are we going?" I asked Erik breathlessly.

"To my suite." He replied curtly.

Nothing more was said between us. I saved my breath for the rapid journey. By the time Erik stopped in front of an ornately carved door along a carpeted hallway, both of us were breathing heavily, and I knew my hand and wrist would be bruised and sore the next day. Erik released me to search in his coat pocket for his key, and I rubbed my fingers through my glove surreptitiously.

Casting me a baleful look, he growled, "Do not try to leave. I will only drag you back." I stared at him incredulously.

"I am not going anywhere," I hissed angrily.

Finding his room key, he quickly unlocked and opened the door, took me by the arm as though I were a piece of luggage, and pulled me into the room. The door closed with a solid thud behind me. As soon as the door had closed, Erik removed the new mask from his face and tossed it on a nearby table. He pulled off his black formal coat, waistcoat and cravat with rapid, frustrated movements, tossed them aside, and then rounded on me. He looked so handsome in his white dress shirt, open at the throat, but as remote as a god. Even in the midst of this highly-charged moment, I felt a quick surge of relief when I saw that his face was unchanged.

In the fraught silence, we stood staring at one another. Without taking my eyes from his, I began tugging off my gloves. I had some difficulty removing the one from the hand he had been gripping so fiercely; when the glove finally came off my hand was already beginning to bruise. Erik saw; his face darkened and his fine lips twisted.

"Do you expect me to apologize?" He demanded brusquely.

"It would do me no good if I did," I answered tartly. Tossing the gloves on a small table, I glanced at the mask lying there with some interest; it was so natural looking. And I rather needed a small diversion while I collected myself.

"That is your new mask, I take it," I said.

Erik shrugged, not willing to allow me to distract him. "Doctor Arlington made a mold from the good side of my face. It is made from...but you know all about that, Sylvie, I told you in one of my letters."

"What letters?" I asked exasperatedly. "I received only one letter from you besides that first telegram. And that horrible letter you wrote, I suppose is the reason I am here. You sounded as if you hated me, Erik. You said…you said you might never return home. I knew I had to come and see for myself what had happened to change you so."

"One letter?" He snorted incredulously. "I have written you every week since I got here."

"You are claiming that you wrote me more than once, Erik?" I asked scornfully, glaring at him.

His cold, pale eyes took on that look I was so familiar with: when they resembled twin shards of ice. "Claim? I do not *claim* anything. I did write you. It is *you* who did not write to me. *Sacré*! Now I see what you have been doing while I have been gone – all this time I thought you were safely at home, recovering your health – all this time I've been worried sick about you, and look at you! No doubt you have been much too occupied with your flirtations with other men to write to your husband. That is why I wrote you that last letter…and it *was* the last one." Erik's hands clenched into fists at his sides as he spoke. "You might never have heard from me again."

I listened to this diatribe with mounting incredulity. "What on earth are you talking about?" I demanded angrily. "I have not been flirting with other men. I wrote you several letters, Erik, and even Dr. Gaudet wrote you once. You know it is true. You never bothered to respond to any of us. You may not care for *me* anymore, but how could you live with yourself if you abandoned your only child?"

Erik opened his mouth to no doubt hurl some other insult at me, but then his brow creased and his hands unclenched. "Philippe wrote me? Why?" He sounded perplexed.

I stared at him in disbelief. "Because he thought, as I did, that you would want to know…Father Barbier is dead." Tears welled in my eyes as I spoke. "He died not long after you left. And I never received one word of consolation from you, Erik," I cried bitterly. "Not one word. You knew what he meant to me. It was then that I knew you no longer loved me – that *she* had stolen you from me." I lifted my chin and held his gaze, challenging him to deny it.

There was a long, tense silence; we glared at one another while the seconds went by, and then Erik, his expression changing, asked in a dangerously soft voice, "If you truly believed I no longer loved you, why did you come here, Sylvie?"

"Why? *Why?*"I was suddenly in a towering rage. Fury flowed over me, such anger that I felt my body go rigid with it. Erik's eyes widened. I took a step toward him, and gripped handfuls of his white shirt, and then I shook him. Hard.

"Why do you think I came here, you big oaf?" I shouted into his shocked face. My fists pulled angrily at his shirt, and I heard the fabric rip. Dropping one hand away, I gestured down my body. "Why do you think I wore this gown tonight? I did it for *you*! I came here to fight for you – I won't let that conniving witch take you away from me, Erik, even if I have to beat her to a bloody pulp! I hate her! I won't go back without you, do you understand? *She* can't have you – you're *mine*!" Emotion got the better of me then, and I burst unceremoniously into a flood of tears.

Even through my tears I could not fail to notice that Erik's eyes had dropped to my heaving bosom, quite a bit of which was exposed by my low-cut gown. It was every bit as revealing as the ones favored by Miss Arlington, only I was able to fill mine out. Erik appeared fascinated, our fight momentarily forgotten. But only momentarily.

His face suddenly suffused with dusky red color.

"And you..." he said roughly, "Are mine!" His hands came up and he gripped my upper arms and shook me hard. Pins flew out of my hair and a large curl fell into my eyes. I was so startled that after one gasping sob I stopped crying. His expression was one part desire, two parts hatred. It was a recipe for disaster, I thought bemusedly. But it was clear he was no longer in control of his actions.

Anger was abruptly replaced by fear surging through me. Erik looked if he were only seconds away from throttling me. I flattened my hands against his chest and tried to push him away, but my useless efforts only served to irritate him further. With a long gasping breath, he seized me in a rough hold, one hand delving into my hair to catch my head in a painfully hard grip, and the other going behind my back.

"N..." Before I could even utter the word 'no', his head came down over mine and his lips crushed over my mouth, kissing me not with desire but with fury. I tasted blood. He wanted to hurt me, and he was succeeding. But, a part of my addled mind was thinking, at least he was kissing me, not trying to actually kill me. Not yet, anyway.

There was no use trying to break that iron grip, so I forced myself to relax against him even though my head felt as if it were caught in a vise and it was difficult to breathe. I stopped pushing against him and instead let my arms slide around his waist and over his shoulders. Erik had never kissed me so violently before, but I sensed that if I offered no resistance, he would gradually calm down. So I allowed him to take what he wanted, and soon I felt his painful hold relax somewhat. Against my lips he uttered a heartfelt groan, and his mouth gentled. Suddenly he was kissing me ardently, running his hands over my body like a man dying of thirst who has found a pool of water. This did not, I thought dazedly, feel like someone who no longer loved me.

With a gasp he tore his lips from mine, pulled back a little, and looked down at me. He was breathing as though he had been running a race. He gave me another shake, making my teeth rattle.

"You little idiot!" He said exasperatedly. "How could you think I would ever stop loving you?" His eyes, suddenly hot, swept over me possessively, lingering on my exposed chest. "And the sight of you in that gown – I wanted to murder every man in the ballroom tonight, just for looking at you in that provoking thing. Damn it, Sylvie, you didn't need a gown like that; you could wear a tablecloth and I would still want you." As he spoke he stroked the back of his hand across my exposed front, and I shivered.

I gave a shaky little sigh, my heart suddenly singing with relief and joy. "You are the only man I cared to impress," I told him. "I did it all for you." I gave him a coy look, or at least I hoped it was coy. "You should see what I have on underneath."

"I intend to, very soon. I am going to see every damned inch of you. But first we need to finish this." His face grew perceptibly serious. "Sylvie, you must believe me, I am not, nor have I even been tempted, to have an affair with Edythe Arlington. I would never stray from you, no matter what happens between us." His hand came to my hair, stroking gently. "I cannot believe you could even think such a thing."

I looked down, unable to meet his eyes. "I wouldn't have blamed you, Erik," I said, my voice almost a whisper. "After the way I treated you, and how I behaved. I...I was afraid I had pushed you into her arms myself. We had that last night, and it was wonderful, but I was afraid that my behavior before might have..." I raised my eyes to his pleadingly.

Erik was silent for a long moment. Then in one of those mercurial *volte-faces* he was capable of, he gathered me tenderly into his arms, as gentle now as he had been rough before. He pressed my head against his shoulder with one hand in a comforting gesture. My arms stole around him, and it felt like coming home.

"I know why you did that, Kitten. I understand." He said presently. "Dr. Olivier told me you would become yourself again in time, when you had recovered from the Melancholia. He said I should be patient with you." He sighed, ruffling my hair with his warm breath. "But I wasn't very patient with you, was I? Patience has never been my strong point." He added ruefully. He was probably remembering that afternoon when he had angrily demanded that I return to his bed. That *had* been a bit much.

270

I sniffled a little, prolonging the moment, but I knew there was still one subject we must resolve. I pushed away from him enough to look up at his face.

"But Erik, Miss Arlington does want to take you away from me. She desires you; I could see that from the first. And she wanted me out of the way. It is not just for her father and the surgery that she wanted you to come here. You cannot be ignorant of that fact." I gazed at him searchingly, and saw his face color under my steady regard.

"Well, I was," He said, sounding embarrassed. "I had no idea she harbored any interest in me except as a potential client for her father. I'm not used to having women chase after me, Sylvie, after all. Except for you, that is."

Ignoring this *riposte*, I asked, watching him carefully, "Did she catch you, Erik?"

Erik nodded, looking mortified. "Last night. We have been in the habit of taking an occasional nighttime stroll, but last night..." he paused, grimacing. "She asked me to walk her back to her suite at the end of the evening. Evidently Edythe tired of sending me hints that I was missing altogether, in favor of more blatant means of letting me know what she wanted. Last night when we arrived at her door, and were saying goodnight, all at once she kissed me, on the mouth." He stopped and ran his hand through his silky hair, disheveling it. "She claimed that she wanted me, needed me. She sounded...almost mad." I waited patiently, trying to conceal from him the hot flash of jealousy that suffused me when I pictured the scene.

"It took me completely by surprise. God help me, Sylvie, I almost kissed her back." He cast me an apologetic glance. "It had been so long...she caught me off guard. I was angry at you, and resentful. I thought you didn't care any longer. But then I came to my senses and stopped her, told her I wasn't interested, would never be interested, and bid her goodnight. That is the truth. She has been quite cool to me today. I think she was offended by my lack of response." He concluded, watching me warily.

I pondered him silently for a moment, and then I drew away and sat down in a chair by the writing desk. My lower lip was bleeding slightly. I located a tiny handkerchief from a hidden pocket of the gown and dabbed at my bleeding lip abstractedly.

Seeing the spot of blood on the white fabric, he said contritely, "I am sorry, Kitten. I did not mean to hurt you."

"Yes you did. Never mind, it is only a little split."

271

After feeling a blinding rush of jealousy at the thought of Edythe and Erik kissing, I was left with a chill down my spine. Something was very wrong here. I wondered if I should tell him my suspicion that she had tried to kill me in France. I could not really prove that. I rubbed my forehead, contemplating. Erik watched me warily, no doubt afraid I was going to behave like a jealous shrew.

"Something is not right, Erik. Think…" I looked at him expectantly. "You believed I was deliberately ignoring you, and I thought the same of you, because other than that first telegram, none of our letters to each other have been received, other than that last one you sent me. Even Philippe's letter to you never arrived. How can that be? One letter may go astray, but *all* of them?" I shook my head firmly. "Something is amiss."

Erik began to pace the room, his brow furrowed. Abruptly he stopped and faced me. "You think Edythe is responsible somehow, don't you." He said; a statement, not a question. I nodded my head vigorously.

"It is the only thing that makes sense. What I think is she found a way to intercept our letters – bribed someone at the hotel perhaps. I have no doubt she is a very resourceful young woman. I ought to have suspected something of the sort was happening, but I…I just didn't." I could not bring myself to tell him of my insecurity, at least not yet. I was suffused with shame, for my own insecurities had caused me to doubt my husband.

"It did not occur to me, either. But why? Why would she do something like that?" Erik demanded, sounding frustrated.

"To further her cause: that of driving a wedge between us. If she could convince you that I no longer cared for you, it would make it easier for her to insinuate herself into your life. Thanks to her, you were lonely and vulnerable." I regarded him thoughtfully. "Tell me, Erik, did you talk about it to her…about us?"

He had resumed his pacing across the room in front of me. Distractedly he ran his hand through his hair once more. "Of course I did; it was frustrating and worrisome to me. I spoke to her about it several times." *Of course*, I thought to myself. Somehow I was certain that it was Edythe herself who instigated these confidences.

"And how did she respond?"

"She…oh, she would always laugh and assure me that if anything was wrong at home I would most certainly have heard of it. She said…" he paused, understanding dawning on his face. "She said you were such a timid little country mouse, you couldn't possibly get into any trouble." He shook his head wryly. "She didn't know you very well, obviously."

I felt a rush of helpless anger at the thought of Edythe Arlington keeping us apart from one another like that; she had almost succeeded in tearing us away from each other. And how easy it was for her to do it, because no one would suspect a thing.

I thought balefully of the things I had written in my letters to Erik: intimate things, tender things, even begging for him to come back to me. A flush of heat spread over my face when I imagined Edythe gloatingly poring over our letters to each other.

"Heavens! Did she read our letters before she destroyed them, I wonder? Wicked, willful creature!" I exclaimed wrathfully.

Erik looked stricken, for that thought had not occurred to him yet. "*Dieu*, I didn't think of that. I certainly hope not. The idea of her reading what I wrote to you makes my skin crawl." He ceased his pacing and sank down on a plush *settee*. "I can scarcely believe she would do such a thing. And I don't know if we can ever find out, because if we confront her, she will deny it. But if I'd known..." He fell silent, no doubt contemplating suitable punishments for Miss Arlington's perfidy.

"We might be able to find out which hotel employee she bribed, however." I said.

Suddenly Erik smacked one fist into his open palm. "I believe you are on to something, Sylvie. All of the times I posted a letter to you at the desk downstairs, there was a boy who took it from me. But that last one...when I posted it, the boy was out with toothache or something, and someone else posted the letter." He gave me a pointed look. "And that was the only letter from me that you received."

"*Bien*, that would explain it, then. Edythe had the boy downstairs in her pay, I imagine."

"I hope you will disregard everything I wrote in that letter, Kitten. I was hurt and angry...I did not mean those things I said."

"I burned that letter, as a matter of fact," I informed him wryly.

"Good. What else is Edythe capable of, I wonder?" Erik mused. "She behaved so strangely last night." He shuddered slightly. Although it was a rhetorical question, I knew, in fact, what else. Sighing, I smoothed the silk of my midnight blue gown, straightening it over my legs. Why was I reluctant to tell him? Because I knew how he would react. But it was now or never. I drew a deep breath.

"Erik, there is something I must tell you." I rose and went to join him on the *settee*. Automatically he pulled me into his shoulder.

"What is it, Kitten?" He asked gently; taking my bruised hand in his, he brought it to his lips and kissed it, momentarily distracting me.

"You remember that afternoon when we took the Arlingtons on a carriage ride?" I felt Erik stiffen slightly.

"Of course I do…it was pure torture the entire time. All she could do was complain about how bored she was."

"Yes, and after that, when she fell and knocked me into the path of the carriage?" He made an audible sound then, and tensed all over.

"Yes?"

"It was not an accident, my darling. I believe Miss Arlington was hoping to kill me when she did that. She is an opportunist, and it was an opportunity. She took it. She wished me out of the way even then."

Erik gripped me by the shoulders and turned me to face him. He was horror-struck. "But…I saw it happen, I saw everything." He sounded stunned. "I saw her…she glanced at the carriage and the horses and then she…" His fingers tightened painfully on my upper arms. "It is true, isn't it?" He whispered. I nodded, saying nothing. He was replaying the accident in his mind's eye, and saw what I could not see that day.

"She did not realize I was coming along the path behind her. She thought her only witness would be the fellow driving the horses. She faked the trip and fall, I suppose."

"She must have done," I murmured. "If you had not been right there when it happened, her ploy would have succeeded, I have no doubt."

"That American witch!" He exclaimed fiercely, making me jump. He leaped off the *settee* and bounded toward the door. I had been expecting something like this, so I was right behind him. I seized his arm in both my hands and pulled as hard as I could, trying to draw him away from the open door. "I will kill her right now!"

"No, Erik, no! Come back inside, please!" I begged desperately, digging in my heels as he towed me half outside the door of his suite.

"Let me go, Sylvie," He snarled, his face dark with fury. I had a horrible vision of Erik charging into the ballroom, half undressed, without a mask, and attacking Edythe in front of everyone in the room. He was beyond reason now. Desperate to stop him before he did something we would regret forever, I saw I would need to rely on subterfuge. So I collapsed.

It wasn't that difficult to pretend to swoon, despite the fact I have never been the swooning type of female. I merely let go of his arm and fell. The carpet was quite soft and cushioned the blow. Seeing me sprawled suddenly on the floor, Erik stopped and began to curse with frustration. He was torn; wanting to kill Edythe, but needing to help me. Finally he bent to lift me, and I kept my eyes shut so he would think I was unconscious. More curses flowed over me.

274

"Why do I always end up carrying you around?" He grumbled as he lifted me into his arms. "This dress weighs a ton." I opened my eyes and peeped at him cautiously; thankfully he was in control of himself again.

Erik set me down on my feet in his suite and I made haste to close the door. He knew I had not really fainted. Nevertheless, I locked the door and placed my back firmly against it.

"What I would like…" I said, "is for us to leave here in the morning. We do not need to stay at this hotel, surely? Where is Dr. Arlington?"

Erik gave me a speaking glance. He smoothed his hair back, saying "You mean the man who fell in love with you in three days? That Dr. Arlington?"

"What are you talking about? He is not in love with me. Honestly, you behave as if I were some sort of siren luring men. Men do not pay any attention to me!" I blushed. "Well, they never did until recently, I assure you."

"Actually, he is rather infatuated with you, and I cannot blame him. I am not certain I should let him see you the way you look now. It would send him over the edge." Erik was teasing me, or at least I hoped he was. He went on in a different tone, "Edward is due back here in two days. He has been in Washington teaching a course. We were going to return to the clinic once he got back to New York."

I wandered over to the table and picked up the new mask, studying it curiously. It was soft and flexible, not quite transparent, but not opaque either. It had been dyed to match Erik's skin tone.

"This must be much more comfortable to wear." I regarded him for a moment, taking in his beloved familiar face. "I was worried…that is, I was afraid Dr. Arlington may have already performed the surgery by now. When I didn't hear from you, I thought perhaps…" I flushed, and looked down. "I was afraid you would look different when I saw you again. I am glad you are still the same."

"I have not yet decided about the surgery. I was waiting for Edward to return so we could consult once more with his partner, Dr. Buck. It would be a complicated and risky procedure." Erik paused, and I could feel his eyes on me. "You have been opposed to this surgery from the first, even though you of all people know what it means to me. Why? Was it only because you did not want me to go with Edythe?"

I really did not want to tell him the truth, for it did me no credit. But with all the misunderstandings we had endured, I owed him the truth, however much it shamed me to admit to it. What would he think of me? I took a deep breath, and tangled my fingers together in front of me.

"*C'est vrai*, I did not want you to have the surgery. I almost told you the truth that last night, but I could not bring myself to admit how selfish I was being, Erik. I was afraid if you changed physically, looked more like a normal man, that you would...would..." Oh, how hard this was!

"Would what?" He asked softly, his voice patient.

When I raised my eyes to his, they were filled with unshed tears. Trying to explain my selfish behavior, I said "I wasn't myself, Erik, you must understand that. I do not know what was wrong with me exactly; it seemed like after I lost my baby, I became some other person for a while. but I...I was afraid you would not want me any more if you had more confidence in your appearance. I acted like a horrid shrew, and Edythe...all she did was..."

Erik stopped me with an abrupt gesture. "*Bon Dieu*, Sylvie, have you so little faith or trust in me?" He exclaimed, clearly shocked by my mortifying admission.

"I do trust you, Erik," I said earnestly. I was trying to make him understand, yet I could not blame him for being, once again, hurt and angry. "Honestly I do trust you. The blame is mine entirely. I was so afraid of losing you and yet I was paralyzed to do anything about it." Hot tears spilled down my cheeks. "I want you to know that I will no longer oppose the surgery if you really want to have it. I won't be selfish any longer. I am better now, truly I am." Shame-faced, I gazed at him beseechingly.

He was not taking it well. His face grew taut, and his eyes glittered coldly. A little shiver of apprehension coursed through me.

"You are better now?" He asked finally, his voice sounding stern. Unable to speak, I nodded. "Good. Because my patience with you has come to an end. Come here." He commanded in a take-no-prisoners tone.

"Wh-what?" My eyes grew wide.

Erik pointed to the floor in front of the *settee* where he now sat. "Here. Now. I told you I would make you pay, Sylvie."

Apparently he had decided to punish me. Feeling like a dog being called to heel, I unwillingly approached him. Only the shameful knowledge that I had been so wrong about him allowed me to follow his curt order, when every nerve in my body was telling me to stay away.

When I was standing directly in front of him, Erik proceeded to stare at me insolently, in a way he had never done before, his eyes running over me and lingering on the exposed bodice of my gown. He had never looked at me like that before, as if I were a courtesan and he was deciding if the merchandise would be good enough. I flushed and began to tremble, making the crystal beads on the skirt of my gown twinkle. Erik noticed my discomfiture, and a look of satisfaction came into his predatory eyes. Oh, yes, he was going to make me pay.

"Take off your gown." He said in a cold, dictatorial voice, and I gasped in dismay. Fear and anger warred inside me. Erik was not going to give me a choice, and he had no intention of making this easy on me, I could see it in his icy, implacable eyes. He wanted to punish me for mistrusting him, and he was going to do it by humiliating me, making me feel like a common prostitute.

"Do it." He growled, seeing me make no move. Why didn't I simply refuse? That is, of course, a purely rhetorical question, Reader.

"You will have to help me," I murmured hesitantly, and turned my back to him, revealing the long row of delicate pearl buttons down the back of the gown. It was Henriette who had fastened them, since I could never have reached them.

There was a long, taut silence broken only by his erratic breathing, and then I heard him move. He came to stand behind me, and I felt his fingers work on the buttons, starting at the top. He could not conceal from me the fact that his hands were shaking slightly. Somehow, the knowledge that his need was so great and yet he was being so careful and gentle gave me courage. He could easily have simply ripped the gown from my shoulders had he wished. In my heart I knew he would not really hurt me; he was exacting his version of revenge.

When the last button was undone and the gown was sagging away from my shoulders, I turned back to face him. His color had heightened. Finally he spoke.

"You did tell me you were going to show me what you had on underneath," he reminded me in a breathless voice.

Well, I had wanted to tempt him, and apparently it was working. Just sooner than I expected. I confess I was beginning to feel a trifle excited myself. While he watched me intently, I carefully eased the little ruffled shoulders of the gown down my arms and let the entire gorgeous thing fall to the floor. Beneath it I was wearing the thinnest of pink silk chemises and the sheer pink silk stockings I found in Paris, with the tightly laced corset over the chemise. By now the corset was making it difficult to breathe and I was desperate to have it off me. I stepped out of the pool of sparkling blue satin and turned my back on him again.

"Can you please help me off with this thing?" I gasped. "I can't breathe."

"Why are you wearing one of those? You never wear corsets," Erik muttered crossly. "I only hope I can do this." He began unlacing the corset and easing it away, and I drew a long, deep breath, sighing in relief.

"I had to wear it, because of the gown," I explained. "Otherwise I would never fit into it."

"Women," he said derisively. He took me by the shoulder and pulled me back around to face him, while his eyes raked over me hungrily.

"The chemise," he muttered thickly. "Take it off. It's lovely, but not as lovely as what is underneath." I was beginning to enjoy myself. This was a new sort of game for me. I could feel the balance of power between us shifting with each article of clothing I discarded.

I obeyed him, but taking my time, slipping the ribbon straps of the filmy chemise down and shimmying out of it. Now I was clad in only my pink silk stockings. Resisting the temptation to cover myself, I met his eyes and smiled cautiously.

"I love you, *mon mari*," I whispered softly, "more than life itself."

I saw a shiver run through him. His eyes were hot, volatile; suddenly he moved like a springing panther, and before I could draw a breath he had lifted me into his arms. Without a word, he strode to the large four poster bed, dropped me on it, and before I could even bounce, he was on top of me.

"Erik!" I cried, my heart thundering.

"Don't be afraid." He murmured, smoothing the hair back from my face and gazing soulfully into my eyes. "I won't hurt you, Kitten."

"I know. I know. But, *mon amour*, you are wearing altogether too many clothes."

"That can soon be remedied," he assured me. And it promptly was.

"I am sorry about Father Barbier, Sylvie. I know how much he meant to you. What happened?" We were lying in bed, propped up on pillows, the blankets pulled up to our waists. Well, a little higher in my case. My head was resting comfortably on Erik's shoulder, and both his arms were wrapped around me. I felt that I could lie here with him forever. Under my hand his heart beat steadily. The pink silk stockings, having served their purpose, were now puddled on the floor by the bed. They had been very well received.

When between us we had unbuttoned his white dress shirt, I discovered Erik was wearing my gold locket under his clothes. I was touched by this more than I can say. Carefully I had lifted the chain over his head and placed in on the bedside table. Then I had turned my attention to undressing the rest of him.

Now, in the peaceful aftermath, we were talking. We had already talked about Marie, and Celestine, and everything else at home since Erik had demanded detailed descriptions of what had happened there since his departure.

"Dr. Gaudet said it happened quickly, and peacefully. He was almost seventy years old, and in a weakened state anyway because of the leprosy. He simply went into a decline that Dr. Gaudet was unable to stop. I wish I could have seen him one more time." I said sadly. "All I could do when I came to Paris was visit his grave."

Erik reached up and stroked my hair where it lay in disarray over my shoulders. "He married us," he said, his voice low and tender.

"Reluctantly, as I recall," I murmured with a little smile of remembrance.

Erik gave a delicate snort. "I cannot blame him," he said.

I raised my head to look at him, pulling the sheet up to cover my chest. "Dr. Gaudet told me that the Church is probably going to make him close the Hospital. There are only three patients left now, and they no longer want to expend the money to keep it open."

Erik took the edge of the sheet in his hand and began to tug at it gently. "What will happen to the three that are left – where will they go?" He asked. "The last three survivors must have been among the youngest of the patients."

Not loosening my grip on the sheet, I said dejectedly, "Dr. Gaudet is hoping to send them somehow to Norway, to Dr. Hansen. He would prefer to care for them himself, somewhere in the country, with the help of perhaps one or two nuns. But it is difficult because of the need for secrecy." Few people would be amenable to having leprosy patients, even only three of them, living nearby. "The cost would be prohibitive for him. He has petitioned the Church for financial help but they are not forthcoming."

Erik tightened his arm around me, his hand pressing against my face until my head lowered to his shoulder again. He dropped soft kisses to my forehead, cheek, nose. With his other hand he tugged again at the sheet, and it slipped a little from my fingers.

279

"We could build a small house for them somewhere on our property, away from the *château*," he murmured, his voice soft as velvet.

I went perfectly still, absorbing what he had just said. I started to rise up, but he stopped me. "Erik," I said breathlessly. "Would you really do that for them...for Dr. Gaudet?"

"Of course. I would enjoy having Philippe close by; he is practically a *grand-pere* to Marie, after all."

"I think Celestine would enjoy it, also. They seem to have formed a...an understanding." I told him.

Erik smiled. "That old devil," he said, the laughter in his voice warming my heart. He gave a final tug on the sheet, and my lax fingers released their hold. It slid down to our waists. Gently he pushed me to my back and moved over me. I felt tears in my eyes, but he kissed them away.

"You're wonderful," I whispered, wrapping my arms around him.

"I know."

CHAPTER TWENTY-FOUR

"The same eyes, the same face, the same Erik: he was the same man he had always been."

Erik

"I will call for a porter to move your things into my room in the morning," Erik said. "You are staying here with me tonight; I do not want you out of my sight, and not just because I do not trust that conniving witch."

It was true; he really did not want Sylvie out of his sight, or even out of arm's reach from him. He was afraid if she left him even for a moment, all this would prove to be a dream and he would wake up alone again.

It was almost midnight. They were seated at a cloth-covered table in front of the fireplace in his suite, doing justice to a delicious dinner and a bottle of burgundy. After indulging in long-overdue marital relations, they had both realized they were quite hungry, and the Fifth Avenue Hotel was happy to satisfy its guests, the kitchen being open until after midnight when a ball was being held. The time spent in bed had left him feeling much calmer inside, and as content as a cow in clover.

Sylvie was wearing his white shirt with the sleeves rolled up, and nothing else. It came to her knees, and he thought she looked incredibly charming in it. He seriously considered tossing out all her nightgowns when they returned home.

Erik was wearing his dark green robe brought from home. He was watching, mesmerized, as Sylvie licked a drop of sauce from her finger delicately. Clearly they had been apart for too long. Every single thing she did gave him amorous thoughts.

She murmured, "The food is quite good here, even though it is not French." Pouring a little more wine into her goblet, Erik slanted an amused look at her.

"That is because the chef is, *en fait*, French. No self-respecting grand hotel in New York would be without one, or so I have been told."

"Ah. No wonder, then." Sylvie sipped her wine and sighed with satisfaction. She popped another morsel of perfectly sauced duck breast into her mouth. Then she looked at Erik quizzically. "Why aren't you eating?" she asked.

Erik smiled self-deprecatingly. "Because I cannot take my eyes off my wife," he said truthfully. "Watching you devour that duck is giving me more pleasure than I have had for a month." But he returned his attention to his own plate, and speared a stalk of asparagus.

"What about my maid?" Sylvie asked musingly. "I wonder if I should send her back to Paris."

"You brought a maid? What on earth for?" He stared at her incredulously. She had always eschewed the idea of a personal maid.

She smiled at him, and saucily gave her long hair a flip over her shoulder.

"With the new gowns I had made for this trip, and all the latest hairstyles I tried, you don't imagine I could have managed all this by myself, do you?"

Setting his glass down, he covered her hand with his and gazed into her eyes meaningfully. "Send the maid home. You won't need her." And was rewarded by seeing her blush.

"But I feel rather badly to send Henriette home when we have just arrived. She was so excited about the trip." Sylvie said ruefully. She glanced at him as she took a sip of wine. "You know, Madame Moreau found her for me, and she is really a treasure. A bit bossy, but very good at her job."

It was just like Sylvie, Erik reflected silently to himself, to worry about the happiness of a servant. She did the same thing at home. He said, "Do not be absurd, Sylvie. How hard can it be to make you look good? You are already perfect." He paused. "Madame Moreau? You mean Frederic Moreau's wife?"

"It's a long story, my love. I will tell you all about it tomorrow. But as for Henriette, I wonder if we might find some other family who would take her off my hands? And you know, it would be highly improper for her to return home alone and unescorted."

"We will deal with your maid in the morning, Sylvie. I'll mention it to the clerk downstairs. But I've been thinking…" Erik paused to take another bite of duck. His plate was now almost empty, and so was Sylvie's. It was heartening to see how much her appetite had returned. "Edward will be here in two days, but I agree with you; I do not think we ought to wait here for him. I think we should take the train to White Plains in the morning. This hotel and city are making me claustrophobic. And I want to get us both away from Edythe. The woman is dangerous, if not mad. I'll leave a note for Edward that we have gone on ahead and will wait for him there."

"What is White Plains?" Sylvie asked him blankly. Of course, she would not know it was the location of the clinic, since none of his letters ever got through to her. Damn that American bitch, he thought fiercely. Erik patiently explained, adding that they could stay at Dr. Arlington's own house near the clinic, since he had stayed there before.

"Very well, let us go in the morning then. But Erik…"she paused as though considering her words. "Aren't you going to do anything, say anything to Miss Arlington about what she did? Won't you confront her?"

He grimaced, saying, "I would do so in a heartbeat if it were not for Edward. He is a good man, Kitten, and I have come to like and respect him very much. I do not look forward to it, but I must tell him about Edythe, everything that we know or suspect she has done. He needs to be told. We cannot bring criminal charges against her, because we cannot prove anything except that she intercepted our correspondence, and even then she could get out of it by denying everything and leaving the desk clerk to take the fall, so to speak. So I would prefer to let Edward decide what ought to be done about her, since she is his daughter." Erik sighed remorsefully. "And then there is Matthew – you have not met him yet, but this will be painful for him as well. He and Edythe are very close."

Sylvie concurred with his decision, as he knew she would.

Sylvie had sent a note to her maid explaining she would spend the night with her husband, and had collected a few of her toiletry items. Once their midnight feast was complete, they prepared for bed together. Erik was rather looking forward to a repeat of their earlier romantic activities, but when they settled once more into the large comfortable bed Sylvie fell asleep almost instantly. She lay on her side facing him, one hand under her head, with her honey-blonde hair tumbled about her shoulders. Lips slightly parted, she looked like a disheveled angel. He wanted to dishevel her further, but could not bring himself to disturb her slumber, so he contented himself with watching her sleep. There was always the morning, *après tout*.

It was years since he had seen her as angry as she had been tonight, he mused to himself. Well before their marriage, in fact, but he had never forgotten the sight – she was like a little tigress, ready to do battle in spite of her complete inability to defend herself against him. When that determined chin went up and those blue eyes blazed, it had carried Erik right back to his cavern under the Opera House, and he saw himself standing facing Sylvie and pointing his sword at her heart. They both knew he was a hairs-breadth from killing her.

Erik shook off the memory of that evil night and tried to focus on what must be done on the morrow. He was more than anxious to leave the city, for a sense of unease was growing in him, a sense of impending danger.

He wanted to get Sylvie away to White Plains as soon as possible; she was his, his treasure, and he must protect her at all costs.

Erik (continued)

They were enjoying the hotel's delicious coffee and some rolls the next morning, still in their nightclothes, when there was a peremptory knock on the door of the suite. Sylvie's eyes went wide and she set down her cup, staring with alarm at the closed door. Erik guessed she was afraid the morning visitor might be Miss Arlington herself, come to do battle. But it was not. When he opened the door, Matthew was standing there, looking worried and rumpled and very young.

"I am sorry to disturb you so early, Mr. Bessette," he began, and then over Erik's shoulder he caught sight of Sylvie sitting at the table. She was busily closing up her robe and tying the belt. Her hair was still in its night braid, partly undone. Matthew colored brightly and did not seem to know where to look.

"Oh, I am so sorry, Sir. I did not realize you had, er, a guest..." It was obvious that he recognized Sylvie as the temptress of the ball, and must assume that Erik made off with her that night. Erik realized with rueful amusement that Matthew could have no idea who she was. What a *roué* he must think Erik!

"Good morning, Matthew," he said evenly. "Please come in and have some coffee with us." He took the shocked looking lad by the arm and drew him inside the suite. "Allow me to present my wife, Sylvie. She arrived from France only yesterday and we met at the ball last night." Erik spoke in French, since Matthew had some grasp of the language.

Sylvie, blushing, stood and held out her hand to Matthew. Her expression was kind; she could see at a glance that he was but an innocent boy, and nothing like his notorious older sister.

"Oh! I say, what a surprise!" He exclaimed, taking her hand. "We did not know you were coming, Mrs. Bessette. Dad will be glad to see you; he has told me much about you." At these words Erik could not resist slanting a significant look at Sylvie who pointedly ignored him.

Sylvie poured coffee for Matthew and handed him the cup. He stirred several sugar lumps into his coffee and drank it gratefully. Erik noticed that she was studying the boy's face intently, and then she suddenly asked, "Is anything wrong, Matthew? You appear to be worried about something."

Erik looked at Matthew alertly; busy with introductions and explanations, he chided himself for not even questioning what Matthew was doing here. He had never come knocking on Erik's door before, at any time of the day. Sylvie was right, of course; something was wrong.

Matthew tugged at a lock of dark hair that fell over his high forehead. "That's just it, Mrs. Bessette." He glanced at Erik with a concerned expression. "I'm not really sure. It's just that Edie…my sister, you know," he added for Sylvie's benefit. "She checked out of the hotel very early this morning and I don't know where she went."

Erik felt a creeping coldness seize him. He exchanged a quick glance with Sylvie. "Did she speak to you or leave you any message?" He asked.

Matthew shrugged and looked uncomfortable. "She left me a note, and told me to stay in the hotel and wait for Dad to get here tomorrow. She said not to worry about her." He looked at Erik questioningly. "Edie did not seem like herself at the ball last night, particularly after you left. She acted like she was upset about something, and I wondered…well, if she had quarreled with you maybe…Sis has always taken good care of me but she does have an awful temper."

Erik felt completely out of his depth. To tell Matthew the extent of his beloved older sister's perfidy was out of the question. He shot Sylvie a helpless look.

"Oh," she said, sounding contrite, "I believe it must be my fault." She smiled at Matthew, and he turned red. "You see, when your father and sister were visiting us, she and I…well, we did not get along very well. I was recovering from an illness and wasn't feeling myself. I think that when she saw me at the ball so unexpectedly last night, she must have decided to move to another hotel and avoid meeting with me again." Sylvie sighed as though it were a terrible tragedy. "I am sorry, Matthew." She said with convincing chagrin.

"Well, I suppose you must be right now that I think about it," Matthew said, sounding relieved. "You should have seen her face when she saw you dancing with Mr. Bessette at the ball! If looks could kill…" He chuckled at the memory, oblivious to the fraught silence that followed his remark, and then Erik spoke.

"We are leaving today in any event, Matthew. I was going to tell you after breakfast. We have decided to go on ahead to the house at White Plains and wait for your father there. Sylvie…Sylvie finds the hotel rather

285

overwhelming. She is used to country life, you see." Out of Matthew's line of sight, his wife stuck out her tongue at him. "So when you hear from your sister, you can assure her it is quite safe for her to return to this hotel. I was going to leave a message for Edward, but you can tell him when you see him."

"Right-oh. Will do. It's going to be rather dull around here with everyone gone except me." Matthew said, looking crestfallen.

Erik placed his hand on the boy's shoulder. "Try to stay out of trouble, then," he said. "I don't want your father having to bail you from jail." His voice was stern, but his eyes held a twinkle, and Matthew smiled in response.

"No Sir, I won't. I only hope Edie will show up soon. Well, I'd better be going." Putting down his cup, he came to Sylvie, took her hand, and kissed it to the astonishment of both Erik and the recipient of this gallantry. "Thank you for the coffee, Mrs. Bessette. It was a pleasure meeting you. And may I say, you are exactly my idea of what a wife ought to be." With that, Matthew left the suite with a cheerful wave to Erik, and when the door had closed behind him, Erik fixed Sylvie with a dark look.

"Another one, it appears. I had best locate a large stick."

Sylvie, ignoring this remark, came to him and leaned confidingly against his shoulder, looking up into his face with a worried expression. "I feel sorry for him, Erik. He seems like a nice young man. He obviously adores his sister, and no doubt thinks she can do no wrong. I hope Dr. Arlington can shield him from the truth somehow."

Erik embraced her and placed a reassuring kiss on her forehead. "I hope so, too, but that will be out of our hands. Come, let us dress and start the day. There is much to be done before we leave, and I do not want to miss the train."

"*Oui,* you are right. One thing I must do is send a telegram to Celestine. She will be anxious to hear from me. Perhaps you can help me with that? No one here seems to speak French."

He laughed at her disgruntled tone. "How disagreeable of the Americans not to speak French," he said, and leaned in to steal another quick kiss.

He did not, in fact, relax his guard until they were seated on the train bound for White Plains. He was not sorry to see New York fading into the background, and open countryside replacing the noisy, noisome city. He had found himself looking over his shoulder every time they left the suite, and he hated letting Sylvie out of his sight. Not knowing where Edythe might be lurking made his blood run cold. Erik had never intentionally harmed a woman, although he had come close to it a time or two in his past, but never had he come up against someone like Edythe Arlington. If she had been a man, he would have known exactly how to deal with her.

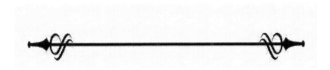

I was packed and ready to depart New York, only waiting for Erik to finish his morning ablutions in the adjacent bath chamber. I wandered slowly around his hotel room, trying to picture him here all those days and nights while I was still in France. Looking out the window at the street below, I watched the carts and horses and scurrying people, and thought of Erik standing here at night, brooding down at the strange sights of a strange city. Of him waking up and seeing this view every morning. He had been lonely and tormented here, I now knew, and the thought made me indescribably sad.

The night before I had noticed a large flat portfolio of the sort artists carry leaning against the wall near the bed and now decided to look inside it to satisfy my curiosity. I felt a little pang of impending jealousy, afraid I suppose that I might discover a drawing of Edythe Arlington inside. But there was no such thing. I must, I told myself sternly, cease thinking of her as my rival. In my husband's affections I knew I had no rival.

Within the portfolio I discovered a little bundle of charcoal pencils of various sizes, a pad of drawing paper, and some loose sketches. These I lifted out carefully and examined after casting a quick glance at the bath chamber door. The first drawing was a charcoal sketch of a vendor pushing a cart full of apples in the street; then a uniformed policeman directing traffic; an elderly Oriental man in a sort of smock peering out of a dark doorway. There was a charming sketch of Matthew Arlington, looking young and windblown. But my breath caught when, near the bottom of the stack, I came upon a sketch of a woman.

She was sitting up in bed, propped against pillows, her hair flowing around her shoulders. She cradled a baby in her arms, and the baby was nursing from one plump breast. The woman's face was downturned, as she gazed lovingly upon the head of her *enfant*. Her hair made a curtain that concealed her features, but I knew it was me; it was a picture of me, nursing

287

Marie only a few days after she was born. Erik had drawn that sketch from memory, but every detail was there. The drawing was as good as any I had ever seen hanging in an art gallery.

Behind that picture was another one, also of me. I was standing in a room, holding a tray in my hands, and on the tray was a covered dish. I was smiling warmly, looking directly at someone, and that someone must of course be Erik. When I thought of how I had doubted him, I felt small and foolish. In a way, I mused ruefully, Celestine knew Erik better than his own wife.

I was staring so intently at these sketches I did not hear the door of the bath chamber open. Erik was suddenly standing beside me, smelling of shaving soap. He lightly fingered the edge of the paper containing the sketch of Marie and I, and smiled a little sadly.

"My two favorite things," he said softly. "Drawing these was a way for me to…" I stopped him with a kiss. Then I wiped my wet eyes.

"I hope you are not leaving all these drawings behind, my love." I said, trying to conceal the remorse I felt. "They are very good."

Erik carefully replaced the stack of drawings in the portfolio and tied the string around the clasp. "We can bring them, if you like," he said, gathering me into his arms. We just stood there and held each other for a long moment. Then he laughed ruefully.

"We had best be going downstairs now, Kitten, or we will never leave this hotel room."

Helping me into my clothing for the last time that morning, Henriette had rushed about in a great bustle. She was simultaneously trying to pack both her own and my trunk, and she was virtually vibrating with excitement. She was about to travel westward toward a place called Ohio with a wealthy American developer and his family as their personal maid, and she could hardly wait. I had a sinking feeling that Henriette would never see France again.

Thanks to her ministrations, I was wearing a becoming traveling *ensemble* of bottle green silk, the bottom portion of which was an elegant plaid. The skirts were pulled back to accentuate my waist, as was the current fashion, and the bodice was high and trimmed with white lace. There was a matching green velvet jacket and a small but jaunty velvet hat. Saying *adieu* to Henriette that morning, I realized I would miss her more than I cared to admit. I made her a farewell present of a pair of lovely soft kid leather gloves that I had bought in Paris.

The American train we rode in travelled at a slower pace than the one I took to Paris. It was pleasurable to watch the scenery unfold as we left the busy city. The transition from city to farmland and farmsteads was abrupt. I thought the houses rather primitive and odd in appearance, for most houses in France were of stone or other hard materials. These were all made of narrow wooden planks. In France, we are accustomed to being surrounded with buildings that are centuries old; here, everything was new and raw-looking. The land was flat but fertile appearing, and there was water in abundance, but the air was quite humid and hot.

Erik insisted on paying for a private carriage for us, and I noticed apprehensively that he promptly locked the carriage doors at both ends. A feeling of foreboding came over me; if my husband, who was virtually fearless, thought we were in danger, then we probably were. Although I was not fooling myself – it was me he was worried about.

Observing his various transactions with the hotel staff and at the train station, I was impressed by Erik's excellent grasp of English. I understood not a word, and to my ear it sounded barbaric and strange. He obviously had a gift for languages; he spoke Arabic with fluency and had picked up English with astonishing rapidity.

Erik complimented me warmly on my *ensemble*, remarking on how it was both sensible and attractive. I suppose this was because he had had quite enough of Edythe and her excessive excesses in the sartorial way. I paid the compliment back, for he looked dashing and handsome in his dark suit and brocade waistcoat. I still found the new mask he wore somewhat disconcerting, for although it was quite natural in appearance, something about the mirror image aspect gave him an odd look. But I supposed I would get used to it in time; assuming, of course, that he did not choose to go through with the surgery. Thinking about this, and the promise I made to myself not to stand in his way, I turned to him thoughtfully.

"What do you know of the surgery Dr. Arlington thinks could help you?" I asked, hoping my tone was neutral.

Erik gave a humorless laugh. He draped his arm around my shoulders and pulled me against him, and nuzzled into my hair before speaking.

"You smell wonderful, Kitten," he murmured against my throat.

"It's just soap from the hotel," I replied, amused. "The same as you used."

"Mmmm...I like it. Clean and your own skin smell. I've missed that." He pressed a soft kiss to the side of my neck, causing me to shiver. "I've never made love in a train carriage before," he added conversationally. "Shall we try it?"

I felt myself blush from my toes to my head and tried to wriggle out of his grip, but he gave a huff of laughter and I realized he was only teasing me. I slapped at his chest ineffectually.

"You are incorrigible."

"You love that about me. Now, you were asking about the surgery?" Erik sat up and became serious again.

"Yes…how involved would it be? Is there any danger to you?" I asked, concerned.

Before answering my questions, he reached for his valise and pulled something out of it. It was a brochure of some sort. He handed it to me, saying, "Beware; these photographs are not for the faint-hearted."

"What is this?" I asked. Looking at the front of the brochure, I saw Dr. Arlington's name. The topic, in French, was called 'A Lecture on the surgical technique called Plastic Operations, as developed by the Arlington/Buck Surgical Clinic for Civil War Veterans'.

"Oh, I see." Erik must have carried this around with him since his first meeting with the surgeon. I looked at him helplessly. "You would have shown this to me a long time ago if I had not kept pushing you away." I said sadly.

"Let us not go over that ground again, Sylvie." He said firmly. "Look at the brochure." I did so, and found that inside there were several before-and-after photographs of young men's faces. These were the veterans, *sans doute*, and the 'before' pictures were quite grisly. I studied with interest the results of the surgeries performed. Under each was a brief description of the technique used and the results. All the men had recovered and been able to return to their normal lives.

"Poor creatures," I murmured sympathetically. "War is so barbaric." I folded up the brochure and gave it back to him.

Erik made no reply; he replaced the brochure in his valise. I wondered if he was thinking of his own violent past.

"You will meet Edward's partner, Dr. Buck, at the clinic, Sylvie. He is the one, I understand, who actually developed the Plastic Operations they perform, and taught his methods to Edward." Erik crossed one leg at the knee and stared out the window as he spoke.

"What they mainly do, he told me, is take a flap of nearby skin and stitch it into place over the damaged part of the face. That is what you see in all those pictures there. But he said that in my case, such a technique would not work." He paused and looked morosely out the window. Farmers could be seen cutting hay in the wide fields, and now and then a fat cow stood grazing. Nothing else could be seen. I began to feel a bit uneasy.

290

"Is White Plains a town, Erik?" I inquired. "We seem to be in the midst of nowhere."

"That is what I thought too, when we first came here. But the clinic is modern enough."

A sudden thought occurred to me as I peered out the window of the slow moving train. "Are there Indians here?" Laughing softly, Erik put his arm around me again.

"I have never seen any, Kitten." He assured me.

"Well, go on, then. If Dr. Buck doesn't think the flap technique will work, what does he suggest?" I asked, perplexed.

Erik frowned. As he hesitated, I realized this was something he was reluctant to tell me. I watched his face patiently.

"He spoke of something experimental, a technique that has not been attempted yet." He said, speaking slowly. "And Edward was concerned about it, I could tell. They would have to take skin from some other part of my body where it would not show – my torso, perhaps – and somehow attach it to my face." Erik turned and looked at me then. Pulling off the new mask, he gestured toward his right eye with his free hand.

"Dr. Buck wants to try that technique here, below my eye. If the graft took, my eye would look almost normal. I've always hated the way my eye looks, as you know."

"But…what if it didn't work?" I asked worriedly. If Dr. Arlington did not think it was such a good idea…

Erik frowned out the window, not meeting my gaze. "Then there would be a high chance infection would set in, and I could lose my eyesight altogether." A pause. "Possibly the sight in both eyes."

I stared at him in speechless horror.

"During the time I've been in New York waiting for Edward, Dr. Buck has been conferring with other surgeons and studying further on how it might be done. He wants to try it, Sylvie, I know." He sighed. "It's been keeping me awake at night, wondering what I ought to do."

"I can well imagine," I said sympathetically. I knew what *I* should prefer, but I kept my lips sealed on that issue.

"I wanted to talk it over with you so many times, but I couldn't. I missed you so much, especially during those long nights." His voice held the hint of a tremor in it, making my heart wrench.

"How much longer before we arrive at our destination?" I asked. He glanced out the window to see where we were, and then pulled out his watch.

"At least two more hours, I should say. Possibly longer. What are you doing, Kitten?" Erik asked while watching me pull the curtain down to hide us from the outside world.

I turned toward him, and began unfastening my jacket. "You did make sure those doors were locked, didn't you?"

His eyes opened wide, and then a smile curved his fine lips. He reached for his cravat and began to untie it.

"This will be a first for both of us," he murmured in a rich, seductive voice.

CHAPTER TWENTY-FIVE

*"And we were advancing, inexorably as the march of the seasons, toward a
greater darkness, and even darker deeds."*

I was peering into a small oval mirror on one wall of our train
compartment, trying to restore my disheveled *coiffure*, while Erik went in
search of a porter to bring us some coffee and something to eat. As he
returned, closing the door behind him, I sent him a shy smile.

"That was an interesting experience," I said, pushing a hairpin into
my coiled braid.

Erik regarded me with a raised eyebrow. "*Interesting?* Is that all it
was?" He inquired with mock outrage.

"Well," I explained, blushing, "I meant that the rocking movement of
the train rather…" But I was not allowed to finish my sentence. I was forced
to catch myself on the back of a seat as the train began to rapidly slow down.
I looked questioningly at Erik.

"We seem to be stopping. Are we at the station already?" He went to
a window, lifting the curtain to look outside.

"No, we are not. We do not appear to be anywhere near White
Plains. This is odd; the first time I rode this train it did not stop except once
to take on water and coal. But this is not where we stopped before." Erik
turned from the window, scowling. "I do not like this," he muttered as he
went to the compartment door. He almost lost his balance as the train came
to a final, shuddering stop on the tracks. A strange, almost unnatural quiet
descended. He shot a quick, apprehensive glance toward me.

"Stay here and lock this door after I leave. Do not open it until you
know it is me." He slipped out the door.

"But…" Even as I began to remonstrate, the door slammed shut
behind him. I stared at it for a few seconds, bemused, then shook myself into
action and hastened to lock it as requested. Once that was done, I went to
peer cautiously out the window. I think I half-expected to see the train
surrounded by wild Indians, but I knew I was being absurd. The train must
have stopped due to something on the tracks up ahead, or perhaps some
mechanical problem. Or at least, so I assured myself. But the longer Erik was
gone, the more uneasy I became. Why was he gone so long?

Without really thinking of what I was doing, I began nervously
gathering up my things and stuffing them into my small valise. I cannot say

even today why I did that; I suppose it was just to have something useful to do with my hands. I was closing the clasp of my valise when the sudden, unexpected sound of a gunshot caused me to drop it with a small shriek. The sound had come from somewhere toward the front of the train. Was it really an Indian attack? Where was Erik?

The next sound I heard was rapid footfalls pounding toward our compartment from the next car ahead, almost instantly followed by insistent hammering on the door. My heart was in my throat until I heard a familiar voice.

"Open the door, Sylvie, and be quick about it!"

Relief washed through me; I rushed to the compartment door and flung it open. Erik flew inside, shutting and locking the door behind him.

"I heard a gunshot. What is happening?" I asked breathlessly.

"We have to leave the train, *maintenant*. Get my coat and my valise down. Hurry!" Even as he spoke, he was using all his strength to tear one of the bench seats off the floor. As I hastened to do his bidding, I saw him wedge the wooden seat back against the door to block it.

"Are we being attacked?" I asked, truly terrified now.

Finished with the door, Erik came to me and shrugged into his coat. I already had my valise in my hand, ready to go. He nodded approvingly.

"Good girl. Come, I'll explain but we have no time to waste." He pushed me toward the door at the back of the compartment, and just as we reached it, fists could be heard pounding on the other door. Someone shouted something I did not understand. I experienced a bizarre sense of *déjà vu* at the sound of banging on the door. Was this to be our fate: fleeing from narrow escapes? I certainly hoped we would escape!

Erik pulled me out of the train car, closing the door behind us. We were in a hot, cramped space between two cars, barely enclosed. He made for a half-door to one side that opened to the air, and beyond it could be seen open farmland, clusters of trees, distant barns. Erik leapt to the ground, ordered me to toss my valise down, and without further ado seized me around the waist and lifted me down to the rocky surface by the tracks.

A gunshot reverberated from inside our compartment, causing me to jump, and then a rending sound. Someone had shot off the lock to reach inside.

"Run!" Erik said in a low but urgent voice. We grabbed our things and dashed away from the train, directly into a field opposite. I followed him, too frightened to even look behind me, but every second I was afraid I would hear another shot, this time directed at us.

Erik made for a copse of tall trees, elms I think he said they were. But we did not stop there; we kept running, putting the trees between ourselves and the train. The air felt hot and thick, making breathing difficult. And I can assure you, Reader, that nothing is as difficult to do as is running with a valise in one hand and one's skirts gathered in the other, trying not to trip and fall. Or hold up our progress, for our plight was desperate indeed. Fortunately, all the riding and walking I had done at home had got me in good condition, so I was able to keep up with Erik.

There was no time to talk, and we could not waste breath anyway. Pursuit was imminent; clearly this was no random attack: Erik and I were being targeted. I thought as I ran, gasping for breath, that there must be some truth in that old cliché, for fear did indeed give wings to my feet. I did not dare to glance behind us, for fear of what I might see.

From the copse of trees, Erik made for a line of green ahead of us and to one side. As we drew near it, I saw a narrow creek lined with willows and other shrubs; an excellent place to hide. He took my hand and guided me into a deep patch of willows and alders, their branches dipping low toward the softly flowing water. It was not a second too soon, for as we slipped into the underbrush I heard the sound of pounding hooves coming from the direction of the train.

We flattened ourselves down into a small depression reached by crawling under low-hanging brush. I was thankful for my bottle green travelling gown, for it was like camouflage. We could not remain concealed here for very long, but at least it gave us a chance to catch our breath.

Erik and I lay side by side, breathing hard, peering through the branches to catch a glimpse of our pursuers. Insects whined and buzzed endlessly in the humid air. I felt moisture collecting under my gown. A noise from the train caught my attention just then; smoke was puffing up from the stack and mechanical sounds could be heard. And then the train started moving again. As we watched in disbelief, it rolled away down the track, headed for the White Plains station. I thought of my trunk, my clothes, the portfolio of Erik's drawings – all still on the train that was now picking up speed and vanishing in the distance. My jaunty hat and my lovely green jacket, all traveling away from me. We were abandoned to our fate.

"Why did they leave us like that?" I demanded in angry disbelief. "Why did they not try and help us?"

"I imagine having several guns pointed at them had something to do with it," Erik murmured dryly.

"But what are we to do?" I swiveled my head to look at him.

As our eyes met, Erik managed a shrug, saying softly, "Do not worry, Sylvie. We have been in worse situations before."

I felt a slightly hysterical laugh bubble up and forced it back.

"At least before, I knew why we were being pursued. But this is ridiculous." I whispered with some asperity. "Who are these people?"

"I can hazard a guess, but there is no time to explain. Do you see over there across that field with the haystacks?" Erik pointed cautiously over his shoulder, across the small stream we lay near. I turned my head and saw, across the field, the outline of an old barn, dark brown and seeming to waver slightly in the hot summer air.

My eyes measured the distance and it appeared endless; to run out in the open and cross that space to reach the shelter of the barn filled me with fear. We would be seen, surely. As if to confirm this thought, four men on horseback could be glimpsed riding slowly toward the copse of elms. They were fanning out, studying the ground intently. And they all four carried guns.

"This is not really happening," I murmured in a conversational tone. "I am having a strange dream." Erik glanced at me, and his expression was grim.

"A nightmare, more like. Why is it that all Americans seem to carry guns? If I had my sword, or a length of rope…" he paused, watching the riders as they conducted their thorough search through the meadow and the trees. "But neither of those weapons can do any good against a gun. I have always disliked firearms." He said it in such a self-righteous tone of voice. I repressed a retort, deciding to save it for later.

"Here, Sylvie, follow me," he ordered, and began crawling through underbrush toward the edge of the stream. This was not particularly easy to do; my hat was on the train and my hair kept getting caught on twigs. Other parts of my anatomy kept getting caught on things, as well. But after a few awkward seconds we reached the little stream and came out of the bushes into a stand of willow, their narrow green and yellow leaves trailing in the water.

Keeping the thicket between us and our pursuers, Erik assisted me to cross the creek. The water was not cold, nor was it deep, but nothing could keep it out of my shoes. We splashed across and up the bank on the other side. Here we paused while Erik took stock of our situation. I stared across that open field in wide-eyed terror.

"They are still coming, damn them!" He muttered angrily. "We will have to run for it again. When I say go, make for that barn."

I stared at him in mounting horror. "I...I can't, Erik!" I whispered. I felt like a rabbit about to fly across a field with a hawk above me. It was paralyzing.

My husband grabbed me hard by my upper arms and shook me until my teeth rattled. "If you don't run we will both be caught. It's our only chance. *Allons-y!*" He swatted me sharply on my backside for emphasis. I picked up my skirts and did as he ordered. I ran. One of us, I thought wildly, must survive to return to Marie. One of us must get through this nightmare in broad daylight.

There were haystacks scattered seemingly at random in the field, and while I would not have thought of this, being too frightened to think straight, Erik naturally ran toward the closest one. In this manner we darted from hiding place to hiding place, always making toward the barn. To my eyes it never appeared to get any closer.

Erik peered cautiously around a haystack, saying, "They have reached the bushes; they have dismounted. They must be planning on searching them. They probably expect we are hiding there. Now is our chance, Sylvie."

Snatching up my valise as well as his own, he seized my free hand and we tore across the remaining open space toward the barn. Its dark shadow fell across us before we actually reached it, as though it were helping to conceal us from our pursuers. Stumbling inside through a wide opening on to a straw strewn wooden plank floor, I could scarcely believe we had actually got here safely. Angels must have been watching over us.

I leaned against the wall of the barn beside the door; I think if it were not there to support me, I would have simply sunk to the floor. I was breathing hard, not just from exertion, but from fear. I watched Erik somewhat blankly as he made a hasty reconnoiter of the interior of the barn, and then came to pull the door shut. The door ran on a rusty track but went across the opening well enough. There was not, unfortunately, any way to lock it once closed.

He turned to me then, his face concerned. "Are you all right, Sylvie?" I could only nod by way of reply, for I was still out of breath. As my eyes grew accustomed to the shadowy barn, I could see it appeared long unused. There was some old hay in a corner, and a few farming implements, including an old plow. Old, stiff leather harnesses and bits of farming gear hung from nails on the walls. I was looking for something in all the detritus that would suffice as a weapon. My eyes came to rest on a very large horseshoe, and I pushed determinedly away from the wall and went across to lift it down from its nail. I hefted it in my hand; it was heavy, and would make an admirable cudgel.

Erik, watching me, smiled wryly. "No wonder I love you, Sylvie," he said. "That is a good idea; I saw no farmhouse within sight, so it is likely they will make for this barn when they see we are not in the thicket. Let me see…" he began browsing among the flotsam of the barn, and soon picked up a coil of rope. He uncoiled it, stretched it, and busied himself tying a strange knot. I realized I was watching him prepare a Punjab Lasso, something I had never seen him do before. It was his deadly preferred method for dispatching an enemy. He sent me an abashed look.

"Just in case, Sylvie." He muttered.

It was four against two, I thought darkly, and they had guns. Would he even get the chance to use the lasso? However, I reminded myself, one of the two was Erik, and he was never to be underestimated. He had been underestimated once before, and look how that turned out.

"Who do you think they are, Erik?" I asked, watching as he came to the door. The only light in the old barn came from a square opening near the top, and from several missing boards. But there was enough light for me to see him grimace at my question.

"I admit I was not anticipating anything like this," he admitted contritely. "I thought if something were to happen, it would be while we were still in New York. I thought Edythe might still be trying to get you out of the way." He was looking down, his expression taut. Raising his head, he looked directly at me, his pale blue eyes troubled.

"What I think…*sacre*! I cannot believe I am saying this. She knows that we are on our way to White Plains, and that as soon as Edward arrives, we will make her conduct and actions against us known to him. She will, as we know, take advantage of any circumstance that works in her favor. We saw that when she pushed you in front of the carriage. I think she has decided to put an end to both of us by hiring some local gunmen. It would look like a random attack; no one would connect those men to Edythe Arlington, who is no doubt still in New York."

I nodded in agreement; everything he said made perfect sense to me. And there was something else Erik had not thought of…perhaps an even stronger motive.

"You know, I have no doubt that when you rejected her advances the other night, she turned against you then. It may be a matter of…if she cannot have you, no one can."

He stared at me aghast. "What? That is ridiculous. It is not as though I were some great prize to be won." I sighed. Erik could never, I knew, see himself as a desirable man because of all those years of rejection he suffered.

He seemed to think that I was the only woman in the world who could actually want him.

"Don't you think it is possible," I said carefully, "that Edythe, like myself, could see beyond your face to the man beneath? I see nothing strange about her finding you attractive, and we know that she is not the woman to let anything stand in the way of her getting what she desires."

"It is as if some divine retribution was being brought home to me," he muttered, his eyes turning haunted and sad. "Everything I did to Christine is being visited on me. Edythe Arlington must be a female version of...of the Phantom."

"Not exactly, my love. You would never have stooped to murdering Christine if she refused to remain with you." I replied dryly.

"Of course not!" he exclaimed, looking shocked.

"I believe the woman is deranged, personally. The very act of your rejecting her affections makes her wild with the desire for revenge. She needs to be put away somewhere, so that she cannot do any further harm."

"I hope her father will see it that way. But he is completely taken in by her I believe." While we conversed in low voices, Erik had kept one eye on a crack in the barn door. Suddenly he stiffened, and made an instinctive move with his arm to hold me back. They were coming.

There was a peculiar combination of emotions in me at that moment. Foremost was fear, for myself and for Erik. I forced away the hideous thought that he might be killed before my eyes. It was too overwhelming to contemplate. The other emotion was pure, hot fury. If I had Edythe Arlington in front of me at this moment I would surely scratch her eyes out. I *hated* her, and what she had done to us.

I did not harbor any illusions about my marriage: our happiness was hard-won, our small family still fragile. For all the good days, there had been bad days too. Erik had so much to learn about life and love, but it had all been worth it, for we had achieved what might be considered a miracle. And now, thanks to that dreadful, evil *witch*, it could all be snatched away.

My eyes went to Erik. No words were spoken between us; it was as if we communicated without the need for words. That is, until he motioned for me to stand behind him, far away from the barn door. *He* went to stand in the middle of the big room, and all I could think was that he was painting a target on his chest. He shrugged out of his coat and tossed it aside, the coil of rope lying at his feet. I was not going to cower behind him; I was going to fight with him!

I could see at once that my short stature would put me at a disadvantage, so I glanced around rapidly, until I spotted a three legged wooden stool nearby. Snatching it up, I placed it to one side of the door and stood on it, grasping my horseshoe firmly.

"What are you doing, Sylvie?" Erik demanded, sounding angry. "Come here and do as I say." I did not spare him a glance.

"I will not. You need my help." I said firmly.

"Damn you, Sylvie! I cannot protect you there! You are my wife; do as I command you! Come here before they are upon us."

"No." I answered pertly, glaring back at him. There was a taut silence. When my husband spoke again, his voice was like ice.

"If we manage to survive this, I am going to wring your neck, you little…"

I blew him a kiss.

"*Je t'aime*," I mouthed to him silently. Flattening myself against the rough wood, I held my breath and waited, the shadows helping to hide me.

I did not hear the stealthy footfalls until the first gunman was almost at the door. Soft dirt and scraps of hay muffled the sound of his boots. A shadow fell across the slight crack in the doorway. My heart was pounding so hard I was certain the man must hear it. Was he alone? The silence was maddening.

After a few tense seconds a hand appeared, and the barn door was forced open with a rusty squawk of protest. A rectangle of sunshine fell upon Erik and illuminated him where he stood, surrounded by swirling, sparkling dust motes. In spite of his deceptively relaxed posture, he was as beautiful as a god, or an avenging angel. He raised his hands in the air in a time-honored gesture of surrender.

The gunman muttered something in English that I did not understand and came cautiously into the barn, his eyes riveted to Erik. His pistol was pointed straight at Erik's chest. Before he could take another step, however, I brought the heavy horseshoe down on the top of his bare head. I have never had an opportunity to hit someone on the head (although I once wanted to, very much); I had no idea how much strength ought to go into the blow. Apparently it was sufficient.

Erik had already made a dive to the floor, anticipating that the ruffian might fire his gun as he went down under the blow. Instead, he seemed to relax slowly, the gun slipping from lax fingers, and he fell to the floor in a heap. His head was bleeding profusely, and I was sure I must have killed him.

While I stood precariously balanced on my stool, staring in shocked silence at the prostrate body on the floor, Erik sprang into instant action. He was at the door before I could draw a breath, stealthily looking out to see if another gunman was there. Then he turned back to the one on the floor.

Kneeling by the body, he rapidly tied the man's hands behind his back with a piece of rope. He picked up the pistol and held it carefully, examining it with a slight frown.

"Is he...he isn't dead, is he?" I asked tremulously. If I had been thinking clearly, I would have understood that the mere fact of Erik's tying him up meant he was still alive. Erik saw that I was still staring at my vanquished foe, and laughed ruefully.

"No, more's the pity. He is only unconscious. But another one cannot be far behind." He came to stand before me, and because I was on the stool, we were face to face. "That was well done, Sylvie," he said, and pressed a hard kiss on my mouth. "But I am still going to throttle you." His eyes held a suspicious glow in them, one that I had seen before.

"You are enjoying this!" I exclaimed accusingly.

Not bothering to deny it, he said cheerfully, "The next one is mine."

"Have you ever actually fired one of those things?" I asked, doubtfully eying the way he was brandishing his newly acquired weapon.

"No, but how hard could it be? You just point it in the right direction and pull the trigger." As he spoke he pointed the pistol toward the back of the barn. There followed a deafening blast and a spurt of flame seemed to shoot out from the barrel of the pistol.

The next thing I knew, I was on the floor of the barn, pressing my hands to my ringing ears. Erik dropped the pistol and knelt beside me, his face as white as paper. He ran frantic hands over me, apparently searching for a wound.

"Sylvie...Sylvie, did I hit you? Are you all right?"

I pushed his hands away angrily. "Damn you, Erik!" I exclaimed furiously. "Not only have you ruptured my eardrum, but now the rest of those ruffians know exactly where we are!"

Erik sat back on his heels. "I believe that is the first time you have ever sworn at me," he said bemusedly.

"And it will probably be the last time, if those men have their way. Help me up – and please put that thing away first." He did so, with alacrity.

I was right, *bien sûr*, for the rest of the hired gunmen were soon upon us. I had barely time enough to climb back on my stool, my ears still ringing from the loud gunshot. Erik pulled the body of the unconscious ruffian across the entry to the barn and sure enough, the first man in the door tripped over the prostrate body and crashed headlong onto the floor. Erik promptly brought the butt of the pistol down on the back of his head, and that was that. Now there were only two left. A flare of hope kindled in my breast. Perhaps we would win the day after all!

But alas! My hope was short-lived, for the other two burst through the door only a second or two later, guns at the ready. They exclaimed at the sight of their two comrades unconscious on the floor, and then one turned and caught sight of me by the door. His eyes went wide.

There was no time to hit him with my trusty horseshoe before I was seized in a hard grip. I caught a glimpse of an unkempt beard, a red neckerchief, and two mean-looking eyes as the man bore me to the floor of the barn. The horseshoe was forced roughly from my hand. The man glanced over his shoulder at the other ruffian and said something I could not understand, sounding excited. Then before I knew what was happening, he was on top of me. He gripped the bodice of my gown in both hands and pulled hard. I heard the fabric tear, and I screamed.

Erik

"Well, here's a nice little piece!" Erik heard the gunman yell eagerly to his friend. "Kill that one and we can have some fun with her."

He saw Sylvie being seized and shoved to the floor, where she fell in a tumble of skirts. The back of her head hit the wood floor with a painful thump. He saw a strange man cover his wife's body with his own, pinning her small, struggling form to the floor, heard the rip of fabric. And then he heard nothing else at all, except a terrible roaring sound in his ears. The world turned blood red.

The other gunman, momentarily distracted, risked a quick look to see what his friend was doing. This was a fatal error on his part. In the next instant, there was a whistling sound, and the pistol was out of his hand, flying up over their heads and falling to the floor. The thin rope had flicked out and snapped like a snake, so fast it was only a blur.

"Hey!" It was the only word he spoke. It would be difficult to speak with a noose around one's neck. Erik threw the rope over his head and bore him to the ground, where he choked helplessly as the rope tightened. There wasn't time to kill him properly, but the gun was there, so he grabbed it and dealt his enemy a hard blow.

Pushing the limp body out of his way as though it were a sack of flour, he rushed the other man, lifting him completely up and away from Sylvie with the force of his blinding rage. An animal sound erupted from his lips when he saw blood, and for a horrible instant thought it was hers. Then he saw a row of bleeding scratches down the man's ugly, bearded face.

Sylvie sat up, trembling, and trying to cover herself by pulling the torn edges of her gown together. Her face was streaked with tears.

"I am going to kill you," Erik snarled, throwing the man across the floor of the barn where he landed in a pile of hay. Erik was on him as soon as he fell, his hands closing around the man's scrawny neck. He wanted to use his bare hands; this was personal. He had never wanted anything more than to throttle the life out of this bastard who dared to attack his wife.

The ruffian was no match for his strength, and his deadly fury made him even stronger. There was no hope of breaking the iron hold of his hands. The man's eyes bulged, and his tongue protruded. He saw death in Erik's face, and knew it was his fate. Erik's lips pulled back in a feral grimace. The man's head began to loll back.

And then, somehow piercing the red haze of his anger, came a small but determined voice.

"Erik, no. Please, Erik."

Damn her, didn't she realize there was no stopping him now?

"Let him go, Erik! He is not worth it."

The only response he was capable of was a snarl. She was undaunted, however.

"You promised me, Erik." She finished on a little sob.

He felt his grip lessen, and his head swiveled to meet her eyes. She was on her knees, and had moved closer to the pile of unconscious gunmen on the floor. She gripped the horseshoe in her hands, and her wide, frightened eyes were fixed on him. He released his victim, and the man flopped down like a dead animal. It was just like Sylvie to want mercy for the man who had been about to rape her.

"What are you going to do, Sylvie…hit me with that horseshoe?" he demanded furiously. Hot blood was coursing through his veins, and he wanted only to finish the job. Sylvie gave him a speaking glance before turning to one of the men on the floor and bringing the heavy iron smartly down on his head. The man subsided with a moan.

"Hit you? How could you think such a thing? This one was waking up."

Slowly she gathered herself and began to stand, and he saw she was unsteady and trembling. If true bravery was to act in the face of fear, then

Sylvie had it in spades. All the blind rage burned out of him then, and he was across the floor and reaching for her in the next second. He helped her to rise and wrapped her in a fierce, unbreakable hold. With a sigh, she let her head fall against his chest, and he smoothed her disheveled hair away from her face. Her gown was filthy and torn. A groan escaped him.

Sylvie pushed against him enough to draw back and look into his face earnestly.

"I wasn't really worried. I knew you would save me." She whispered. The corners of her big blue eyes sparkled with unshed tears, but she managed a tremulous smile. "Besides, I had just found my horseshoe, and I was going to hit him on the head anyway."

"*Mon Dieu*, Sylvie!" Was all Erik was capable of saying at that moment. He embraced her again and released a shuddering sigh. He felt on the verge of tears himself. The sight of that monster on top of his wife would haunt his dreams.

"I thought you wanted to throttle me," Sylvie murmured with a small, shaky laugh. But Erik could not laugh about this, not now, and probably not ever.

"I'm saving that for later," he muttered into her disheveled hair.

"We have to get away from here before those men wake up," she said, her voice muffled from being pressed against his shirt front.

"I intend to kill them all before we go." he replied tersely. "They will follow us if I do not." Sylvie looked up, clearly exasperated.

"I know what you want, but I won't let you do it. Let us go now." She took his hand and tried to lead him to the door. Erik stood unmoving as a boulder.

"Sylvie, if we leave them here, as soon as they are able they will follow after us. We cannot hope to outrun them."

"They will not follow us," she said confidently. Erik, hands on hips, curled his lip at her.

"And why is that, pray tell?" He asked in a sardonic tone.

"Because we shall take their horses," she replied pertly, as she slipped out the open barn door.

Erik smacked himself on the forehead with the flat of his hand. He had completely forgotten the horses.

Remembering his coat, he stepped over a sprawled body to retrieve it. Bending to pick it up, he found himself quite near the thug who had attempted to attack his wife. The man, though unconscious, was unfortunately still breathing. The temptation to finish him off was so strong, Erik found himself glancing toward the open barn door. His hands itched to encircle the man's throat again. Instead, as a poor substitute, he kicked the man in his ribs as hard as he could. Somewhat satisfied, Erik left the barn, stepping from its dark, dusty confines into a hot, humid late afternoon.

CHAPTER TWENTY-SIX

"Perhaps a little dullness would be welcome."

The hot stillness of the summer afternoon enveloped me like a smothering blanket when I stepped outside the shadowy depths of the old barn. Nothing broke the silence, not even a bird call, and in the distance the very air seemed to shimmer.

As I stood and looked about me, it was hard to believe we had just been through the fight of our lives. My torn gown was all that attested to it. When I passed my hand over my face and pushed my hair back, my hands were trembling. I admonished myself for this small sign of weakness, for I had always disliked appearing like a weak female.

Though the sun was well past its zenith, there was still quite a lot of daylight remaining. My eyes sought the oasis of green on the other side of the hayfield. I longed to take shelter in the shade and drink water from the stream. I expected we would find the horses tethered there also. My stomach made an embarrassing noise; I realized I was very hungry.

Erik slipped silently out of the barn, pausing to pull the door closed behind him. I was relieved to see that the mad fire was gone from his eyes. For a moment in the barn, I was afraid I could not stop him from killing. I had given up trying to hold the torn edges of my once-lovely gown together. Surveying me with a dark look, he tried to drape his coat over my shoulders, but I declined it.

"It is far too hot for me to wear that, Erik. There is no one to see me but ourselves, and besides, my chemise was not torn." I wondered where on earth I was going to find something decent to wear. We appeared to be in the middle of nowhere.

"I really wanted to kill that bastard, Sylvie," he growled, sounding alarmingly like the Phantom he had once called himself. "He touched you...he hurt you." He paused and passed an unsteady hand over his hair. "I could not bear it. You mean so much to me, and I have done nothing but endanger you at every turn." His voice was filled with self-loathing.

"No, Erik. You are wrong," I said firmly, giving his arm a small shake. "It is Edythe Arlington who is to blame for all this, not you. Come, let us go. I am thirsty."

Frowning, Erik draped his coat over one shoulder and took my hand.

"Shall we?" He said politely, as if we were going to take a stroll through the garden at home. Belying the casual tone of his voice, his hand gripped mine in an unbreakable hold. I did not mind.

We began walking across the open field. Our progress was quite prompt, for there was no need to dart from haystack to haystack. In but a few minutes we reached the bank above the little creek, and I slid eagerly down toward the cool water. With great pleasure I made a cup of my hands and drank my fill, and then splashed my face and arms. It was blissfully cool and refreshing. Erik lay down on the bank and followed suit. Unbuttoning and tossing aside his waistcoat, he doused himself liberally with water. Then he came and sat beside me, giving me ample time to admire how the now wet white shirt clung to his broad chest.

For a moment we sat quietly on the grassy bank, watching the water flow gently by. An iridescent blue dragonfly danced about like a living jewel. I think we were both happy to just sit and take in the fact that we were alive, after coming so close to experiencing a violent end. I wrapped my hands around my legs, my skirts bunched up under me, feeling grateful and very fortunate. But after a little while I turned toward Erik.

"I am hungry," I said plaintively. "I wonder what time it is."

He gave himself a small shake and stood up. Fishing his watch from a pocket of his waistcoat, he stared at it for a moment, before replacing it and studying the sky.

"My watch has stopped, but I would guess it is perhaps three or four in the afternoon...long past time for *déjeuner*. I am hungry as well, I must admit." He reached his hand down for me. "Come, let us find the horses." I put my hand in his and he pulled me up next to him. He looked so handsome, and I felt so happy to be alive, for a second or two I forgot to breathe.

I found I was dreamily gazing up into his face. A smile curved his lips.

"I love it when you look at me that way," he murmured, and then he pulled me against him and kissed me, long and hard. I forgot all about the horses or being hungry, but we could not forget about the gunmen we left in the barn, so reluctantly Erik released me and we went in search of their horses.

The four horses were not far away, having been tethered to alder trees near the water's edge. They were quietly eating grass, and paid little attention to us when we approached them. They were unlike any horses I had ever seen in France – their coats were as spotted with color as a multicolored cat, and their manes and tails were long and ungroomed.

Erik approached them and stroked their sleek necks, letting them lip his palm and sniff him over to get acquainted. He then searched through four different saddlebags, but found them empty of anything edible except some rather nasty looking strips of dried meat. I sighed. We would apparently be going hungry.

"We will each ride one, and lead the other," he said, his gaze focused on the railroad tracks in the distance. "Do you think you can manage?"

I had already picked out a rather pretty mare. "I will ride this one. If you will help me get my foot in the stirrup…" Soon I had hoisted myself into the saddle and taken up the reins. It was a strange sort of saddle, with tooled leather and a large pommel. "Are all American saddles like this?" I wondered out loud. Erik was staring at me, looking both alarmed and surprised.

"What is the matter? Why are you looking at me like that?"

"You do not know how to ride, Sylvie. I have never seen you by yourself on a horse before. I was going to show you what to do."

I walked my mare around a bit, turning her this way and that. She responded willingly. I smiled rather smugly at my husband.

"I learned to ride after you left. You did tell me you wanted me to regain my strength. I have decided I would like my own horse when we are back at home."

Erik watched me with some consternation. "Does this mean you will not ride before me on Danté now?" He asked, sounding disappointed.

"No indeed. I enjoy riding with you." I assured him.

In another minute he had mounted a horse and handed me the reins of another, and we began riding back toward the railroad tracks. A hopeful thought occurred to me as we approached the tracks. Looking in either direction, very little could be seen.

"Will there be another train?" I asked. Erik soon dashed my hopes.

"I fear not. There is only one train a day coming this way. White Plains is the last stop on the run." He turned his horse northward. "We will ride along the side of the tracks. If my memory serves me, we are perhaps ten miles from White Plains, but we ought to see a farm or two along the way, where we might stop for help. It will be dark by the time we get to the town, I am afraid."

Well, it must be borne, for there was no choice, but I confess I was bone-weary, hungry, and despondent. As we rode, all the adrenaline that had coursed through my veins and charged me with energy faded away, leaving me feeling exhausted and empty.

A flock of blackbirds wheeled and flew like a black cloud over our heads and settled as one in a recently cleared field. It was a bare, wide, empty country we rode through, with only the railroad tracks to guide us. As we plodded along in silence broken only by the sound of our horses, a great longing for home washed over me. Tears pricked at my eyes. When would we be able to go home? I wanted to leave this place and never come back. I yearned for my daughter, and for all the comforts of my own world.

Bitterly, I found myself wishing that Erik had never come here. For what had been gained by it? How heartily I wished Dr. Gaudet had never introduced Erik to the Arlingtons! At that moment Erik, riding next to me, moved his mount closer to mine and, shifting reins from one hand to another, reached out his hand to me. I reached across the space between us and put my hand in his. His grip was strong and warm, just the comfort I needed.

"I want to go home, Kitten," he surprised me by saying, seeming to echo my own thoughts. "I will wait only long enough to speak to Edward when he arrives, but after that I intend that we should go back to New York and book passage on the next steamer bound for Liverpool." His mouth turned down at the edges, and he added sourly, "I am ready to have done with this place." My own heart leapt at his words, so exactly mirroring my own wishes. But I ventured to ask hesitantly,

"What about Dr. Buck and the surgery? Have you decided against it?"

He was silent for some time before replying. "I have decided against it, yes. It isn't just that the procedure could be dangerous to me, although that is a concern. My face does not distress you, or Celestine, or Philippe, or anyone else in our household. Perhaps I need to learn to stop loathing myself for it. I have hated myself for so long, I scarcely know how to stop. And this new mask…" he gestured toward it as he spoke. "It has made such a difference. I can go out in public and hardly anyone even notices it."

Erik slanted a wry glance at me. "Besides, I am tired of feeling like I have no control over what is happening to me, tired of being manipulated. I have wasted enough time dancing to someone else's tune." His words brought a smile to my lips in spite of my exhausted state. If there was one thing I knew Erik *hated*, it was not being in control.

"Hold up a moment, Sylvie," he said suddenly, sitting up straighter in his saddle and pulling his horse to a stop. He was looking off into the distance, across the railroad tracks. "I think there is a farmhouse over there, do you see?"

"I certainly hope you are right; the sun is setting and it will soon be dusk." I stared in the direction he was pointing, and could make out, at the end of a long line of trees, a two-story structure that must surely be a house. It looked to be about a quarter of a mile away.

"I see it!" I exclaimed eagerly. "Shall we go there?"

"I think we must," he said. "I do not relish riding after dark, in unfamiliar territory."

Thinking of the daunting prospect of riding up to a strange house at nightfall and knocking on the door of strangers, I gave silent thanks that Erik had learned so much English. Imagine if we, French speaking people, knocked on their door unable to communicate to them our distress! They might even turn us away as a pair of ruffians ourselves, so disheveled were we by now. That would be disastrous indeed, for I was so famished that the idea of eating that peculiar dried strip of some unknown meat was beginning to sound appealing.

We turned our horses toward the row of tracks, for we needed to cross them in order to reach the farmhouse. Automatically, even though I knew no train could possibly be approaching, I glanced in both directions before we drew close to them. When I turned my gaze northward, pinpoints of yellow glowing light could be seen dancing in the distance, just to the side of the tracks. Thinking I must be seeing things, I scrubbed my hands over my eyes and looked again. The lights were still there.

"Erik, look! What can that be?" I felt gripped yet again by nameless fear. What if more hired gunmen were coming for us, or searching for their comrades? What if it was a band of savage Indians? I was so tired by now that I am sure I was not thinking at all clearly.

Erik, with his keen eyes that could see so well in the dark, wheeled his horse around and looked closely in the direction I was pointing. The horses, catching sight of the bobbing lights, snorted nervously, their eyes wide. It was obvious now that people were approaching, carrying torches.

"What is it?" I asked Erik uncertainly. It was hard to keep a note of panic out of my voice. "Can you see who they are?"

He turned and grinned at me, his white teeth gleaming. "Unless I am mistaken, which I never am, that is a rescue party. I ought to have realized Dr. Buck would take action when he learned we were not on the train and heard about what happened."

My mind instantly flew to the happy moment when I would be reunited with my belongings. There would be a bath, and my own garments waiting for me. And something to eat!

"Oh, thank heavens!" burst from my lips in my burgeoning joy. Rescue! No more danger.

"They have brought a wagon. *Bon.*" He frowned. I could scarcely make out his scowling expression as the dusk settled around us.

"What is the matter?"

"I suppose even if we tell them about the men who attacked us, it will be too late to apprehend them. They will have escaped on foot by now."

"Perhaps, but it would be a good idea for the local *gendarmes* to make a search of any surrounding houses. They might hide somewhere."

He shot me a baleful glance. "I am still sorry you did not let me kill those bastards. Then they would be easy to find."

I merely shook my head and pursed my lips, and said nothing. I knew Erik would gladly have killed all four ruffians if I had not stopped him. He would always be what he was, what he had always been. The veneer of civilization was only a bit thicker now. And when his temper got the best of him, woe to anyone standing in his way.

Standing in the saddle, Erik waved to the advancing party and called out. There was an answering hail followed by a babble of excited voices.

We were soon surrounded by our rescuers. Everyone seemed to be talking at once. I was thankful that my husband could understand what was being said. In the growing dark I was not sure how many there were, but at least six or seven men, including the wagon driver, had come in search of us. Most of them, it turned out, were with the local police.

I later learned from Erik that the train driver had reported the forced stopping of the train as soon as it pulled in to the White Plains station. They had also reported us as having been kidnapped by the gunmen, for unknown reasons.

Erik dismounted and helped me down from my horse. Once on the ground I could scarcely stand on my own feet. I swayed and he caught me, holding me against him until a stockily-built man dismounted from his horse and approached Erik. He began speaking rapidly and seized Erik by the shoulders, his wide face lined with worry. This was my first glimpse of Dr. Gurdon Buck, Dr. Arlington's surgical partner. I was prepared to dislike him on principle, but in fact he was a very kind gentleman, although quite different from Dr. Arlington.

Erik answered in somewhat halting English, and turning, gestured toward me. More discussion ensued, of which I understood not a word, but then Erik lifted me into his arms without further ado and proceeded to deposit me in the back of the open wagon. He climbed in after me and soon I found myself wrapped securely in a fur blanket of some kind, although it was not in the least cold. I was given a canteen of water to drink and something to eat. I think it was cold chicken, but I do not actually remember, only that it was as delicious to me as anything Escoffier might have prepared.

The wagon reversed its course and we continued on toward the town, accompanied by Dr. Buck and two others. The rest of the men rode on into the growing gloom of dusk to search for the gunmen who attacked us. All this Erik explained to me while holding me close in the wagon, and while he was still talking in a soft voice I fell asleep.

I awoke to find myself being carried again, drooping against Erik's chest, one of my arms hanging down. I rolled my head and opened my eyes, and saw that he was walking up a brick pathway toward a well-lit front porch framed by white wooden pillars. Darkest night was all around us, and I could hear some insect humming loudly and monotonously from a tree nearby. Dr. Buck stood at the open door, waiting to usher us inside. I had, I realized groggily, slept all the way to town.

Struggling to raise my head, I asked, "Where are we?"

"This is Edward's house, Sylvie. I stayed here when I came to the clinic with him." As Erik carried me past Dr. Buck and into the house, the latter spoke to him briefly, and Erik nodded in satisfaction.

We entered a house that was quietly furnished in what I later learned was called Colonial style. Simple, comfortable, unpretentious, and here and there the warm burnished gleam of brass or copper. It suited Dr. Arlington, I thought bemusedly. I could not imagine Edythe Arlington thriving in this quiet, plain environment. She was most definitely a hot-house flower. For myself, I rather liked it. Everything was clean and orderly, but comfortable.

"Our things have been taken off the train and brought here," Erik explained as he slowly lowered me until my feet touched the floor. Getting my balance, I found myself face to face with Dr. Buck, and to my surprise realized that he was not much taller than I. But he was strongly built, with a thick neck and broad shoulders. He was bald, and a pair of pince-nez perched on his nose. We studied one another with interest, and I felt increasingly uncomfortable at my unkempt appearance. Unable to stop myself, I reached up and patted my hair. This brought a small smile to his thin lips. He looked up at Erik and murmured something which brought a quirk to his lips. I was beginning to feel rather frustrated that no one here spoke French.

A middle-aged woman wearing a white lace cap on her graying hair appeared in the foyer and immediately took me in hand. She was obviously Dr. Arlington's housekeeper, and she was waiting for our arrival. Clucking her tongue and murmuring things, she sprang into action, ushering me gently away. Although I could not understand her language, nor she mine, with gestures she made her wishes known. One thing was very clear, and that was her kind heart and genuine concern for me.

I was soon ensconced in a bathing room, stripped of my hideously dirty and torn clothing, and lowered tenderly into a hot bath. The kindly housekeeper took out the remaining pins from my hair and helped me to wash it. That warm bath in a small room with delicate floral wallpaper was heavenly. I hoped Erik would be allowed to bathe, as well.

Eventually I was tucked into a large four-poster bed under a patchwork quilt, and given a tray of hot soup and bread by the motherly housekeeper. I was so hungry I could not think straight, and made short work of the food. It was turkey meat in the soup; turkey was a bird that we seldom ate in France, but it made for a comforting bowlful. Wondering where Erik was, I attempted to ask the housekeeper about his welfare. She seemed to understand, and went out, dimming the lights and closing the door behind her. I made a reminder to myself to ask her name in the morning.

My eyelids were drooping shut, and although I fought it, I felt sleep overtaking me like a warm wave. From a far distance I heard the door open and softly shut, and then Erik was climbing into bed next to me. I turned blindly into his chest as he gathered me against him, and he whispered something against my hair. At ease and content now that he was here, I drifted off to a dreamless, restful sleep.

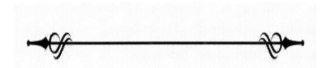

Erik

He had been so focused on getting his exhausted and fading wife to safety that worry for her eclipsed all other emotions. Seeing her doggedly riding on through the growing darkness, slumped silently in the saddle, her bodice torn and her hair falling from its pins, had filled him with fury and despair. He had to stay strong and calm for her sake, but he was desperate to get to some safe place so Sylvie could rest. The farmhouse would have sufficed, but he was tremendously thankful for Dr. Buck's timely arrival with a rescue party.

Now that they were safe in Edward's quiet and restful house, all the other emotions Erik had kept tamped down for his wife's sake threatened to overwhelm him. His hands shook, he was so angry. Sylvie would never understand what she had asked of him today. How could she, when he himself had kept his own deep secrets from her. He doubted she could possibly comprehend what it had taken for him to simply walk away from that barn.

Dr. Buck must have thought he was merely exhausted, and prescribed brandy. This turned out to be the right medicine for Erik's frayed nerves and temper.

They sat in Edward's library, in front of an empty fireplace. Dr. Buck quietly poured out a generous measure of brandy and handed Erik the snifter. Dr. Buck seldom took alcohol, but tonight he poured out a small glass for himself. Erik sank into a deep leather armchair and cautiously sipped his brandy, enjoying the feel of the liquid fire burning down his throat. He closed his eyes briefly, savoring the dark amber liquid and listening to the measured ticking of a tall case clock against one wall. It was somehow soothing. He began to feel alive again, and he did not think he would hurl the snifter into the fireplace when the brandy was gone. He turned and met Dr. Buck's narrow ice-blue eyes.

"Better?" The doctor asked, sounding concerned. Erik responded with a surly nod, and had another sip of brandy.

"Good. I cannot tell you how shocked I was when I learned from the police what had happened to you and Mrs.Bessette. I cannot understand such a thing happening here. This is the state of New York, not the Wild West!" He shook his head, clearly troubled. "I was very relieved when I saw you were both unharmed. I have sent a telegram to Edward…he ought to be back at the hotel tomorrow. I am sure he will wish to come here straight away and see you both."

Erik frowned into the depths of his brandy snifter. He was uncertain how much he ought to explain to Dr. Buck. He did not know Dr. Buck very well, having only met him once. He and Dr. Arlington seemed close friends and good partners, but this was extremely personal. Would Edward want Dr. Buck to know the truth? Erik decided to say nothing. If Edward wanted his partner to know of his daughter's involvement in their difficulties, he could tell him himself.

"I will be glad to see Edward," Erik replied cautiously.

The door opened at that moment and Edward's housekeeper, a pleasant Irishwoman he had met there before, entered with a bit of efficient bustle, a tray in her hands. She smiled warmly at Erik and placed the tray on a table next to his chair. The fragrance of hot soup rose to his nostrils, and he felt his stomach clench with hunger in response. What was her name? Mrs.

McKendrick. He thanked her for the tray. She blushed a little and swept out of the room before he could ask after his wife.

Dr. Buck rose, saying, "I will leave you to your dinner, Mr. Bessette. I imagine you will want a bath. Just speak to Mrs. McKendrick and she will attend to you. I will see you in the morning. I do not expect we will hear anything from the sheriff's men until morning. Get some rest." He bowed to Erik, put on his hat and left. Dr. Buck lived at the clinic, as Erik had discovered when here before. He occupied a small suite of rooms on the third floor, overlooking the front of the building. He preferred to remain close to his patients, he had explained.

Erik gazed at the door for a long moment, thinking, before turning his attention to his supper. Tomorrow would be soon enough to tell Dr. Buck he had decided against the surgery. He was too exhausted to go into that tonight. The soup was good, but could not compare to the delicious soup Sylvie used to make for him. Still, he forced himself to finish the bowl and bread that came with it. He was bone-tired, but still restless. A wrenching sigh escaped him.

He felt swamped by guilt. Whatever Sylvie might say to the contrary, he knew he was responsible for every bad thing that had happened today. The tortuous path leading to this day and the dangers they had faced began with his wicked deeds at the Opera House, and there was no denying it. He ought never to have come here. Sylvie could have been tormented and killed because of him. The unspeakable horror of that almost unmanned him. He was desperate to get them both on a steamer bound for home. But ahead of him lay a dreaded task: telling Edward the truth about his daughter. As much as it galled him not to take action against Edythe himself, he knew the responsibility belonged to Edward.

Erik bathed hastily in the lukewarm water left from Sylvie's bath, shaved quickly, and followed Mrs. McKendrick to the door of their room. It was, he saw, the room he had occupied when staying with Edward previously. Letting himself in quietly, he saw with satisfaction that their trunks and belongings were stacked against the wall. Even the portfolio containing his sketches was there; Sylvie would be pleased about that. His eyes went at once to her small form in the bed, and he felt some of the anxiety building inside him lessen at the sight of her.

He felt his lips curve into a smile in spite of himself. She looked like a sleepy angel, her still-damp hair tumbling around her shoulders, the golden locks gleaming richly in the candlelight. She was propped up against the pillow, obviously trying to wait up for him, but she could barely keep her

315

eyes open. The appealing sight of her tugged on his heartstrings, and other parts of him as well.

Erik let the bathrobe he was wearing fall to the floor and slid into bed next to Sylvie. He gathered her voluptuous, warm body against his, reveling in the feel of her skin and her scent, and the smell of soap from her bath. She snuggled trustingly against him, and sighed.

"My beautiful little angel," he murmured softly, stroking her hair. "*Mon Ange.*" She made a small childlike sound, sighed again, and fell asleep. Erik lay quietly beside her, watching the candlelight flickering on the ceiling, and was abruptly struck by what he had just whispered to Sylvie. What he had just called her. He had not thought of Christine for some time, except to feel furious over her betrayal, but now he saw her in his mind. Her incandescent beauty, her angelic voice, her innocent affection for him. Always, he had called her his angel. But his feelings for her had been tainted by a sense of ownership that he did not deserve.

Sylvie's hair tickled his chin but he did not mind. He thought of how she had been today – that kitten who thought she was a tiger. By all that was holy, she was brave. He adored her, pure and simple. And it felt right. For a few moments he allowed himself to imagine how wonderful it would be to wake up in their own bed at home, in France. To know his daughter was sleeping nearby.

It still struck him as ridiculous that Sylvie had actually believed he might be carrying on an affair with Edythe Arlington, but then, hadn't he suspected something similar when he saw her surrounded by fawning admirers at the ball? He forgave her for her absurd suspicions, because deep down, he was glad she was jealous.

Finally Erik blew out the remaining candles and willed himself to relax and fall asleep. In order to shut out the evil memories of that endless day, he forced himself to think about music, and in that way, finally found slumber.

CHAPTER TWENTY-SEVEN

"It would have been so easy to become hysterical."

Unsurprisingly, we slept late the next morning. The house was empty
but for the kindly housekeeper and a cookmaid, and they left us
blessedly alone. Except for the occasional reassuring sounds and
smells of cooking coming from somewhere downstairs, all was quiet.
Once we did awaken, we were further delayed from rising by very satisfying
mutual demonstrations of marital affection.

While I was putting my hair up in its usual braided bun, I discovered
the back of my head was rather sore. I touched it tentatively and winced. For
a moment I puzzled over what had caused the tenderness, and then I
remembered with a shudder how it happened. I felt fortunate indeed that a
bump on my head was my only injury from our adventures of the previous
day. Nevertheless, I had to admit to myself that I was rather proud of how
well I wielded a horseshoe.

When we finally appeared downstairs we found coffee and interesting
fluffy little cakes called biscuits, to have with butter and honey. There was
also a note from Dr. Buck and a telegram waiting for Erik beside his plate.
While Erik tore open the telegram, I poured some coffee into my cup and
frowned. It was inky black, and when I tentatively took a sip, tasted boiled
and strong. I made a face, and he grinned at me a little sheepishly.

"I asked the housekeeper to make it that way when I stayed here
before," he explained, and went back to reading the telegram. I experienced a
pang of longing for the delicious *café au lait* with which I always started my
mornings at home.

Erik remarked, "This is from Edward. He must have sent it as soon
as he read the one Dr. Buck sent him. He says that he and Matthew will take
the morning train. Hopes you are unharmed; no mention of me being
harmed, unsurprisingly. Hmm…he does not mention Edythe at all." I paused
in the act of spreading some honey on half a biscuit and looked up at him
curiously.

"That seems odd; perhaps he has not seen her yet."

"No doubt she deems it wise to keep her head down until she learns
whether or not her gambit succeeded," Erik growled, unfolding the note
from Dr. Buck. After reading it, he tossed the note to the table and picked up
his coffee. I realized, after sending him an inquisitive glance, he was not

going to tell me what it said, so I picked it up myself. And then I tossed it back to the table in disgust. It was all in English! Erik slanted a sardonic look in my direction and cut into a fried pork chop. Imagine having a pork chop for breakfast! Americans did seem to have rather odd eating habits. That being said, I had already decided to ask the cook if I could have her biscuit recipe.

"He wants to talk to me about the surgery, Sylvie," Erik explained, smirking at me. He was well aware of my curiosity. "He asks if I will walk over to the clinic after breakfast and meet with him."

"Will you go?"

"*Oui*, I must get this over. I cannot stay there long at any rate for he also says there is some problem at the clinic. He will try to convince me that he can perform the surgery without difficulty. I don't mind hearing him out; he has been researching how it might be done." Seeing my frozen expression, Erik reached out and covered my hand with his own. "Do not look like that, Kitten. I have not changed my mind. But I want to hear what he has to say before I tell him my decision. It would be inconsiderate of me if I did not."

I shot him a pointed look. Catching my eye, Erik attempted to look abashed, and then laughed.

"You must admit I am not as inconsiderate as I once was, Sylvie," he said, his pale eyes glinting with humor. "Besides, I am more than ready to go home. If I decided to have the surgery after all, we would have to stay here for weeks, perhaps months more."

The thought of being away from Marie for such a long time filled me with dread. So did the idea that Erik could catch some sort of infection and lose his sight.

"I, too, am anxious to return home," I told him. Erik smiled warmly at me.

"I know you are, Kitten," he murmured gently. Standing, he dropped his *serviette* to the table, drained his cup, and shrugged into his coat. "*Bien*, I may as well go over to the clinic now, so I can have this behind me by the time Edward gets here. Two difficult conversations in one day." He glanced at me. "I would bring you with me, but I do not know what sort of problem Dr. Buck is having this morning. You might enjoy taking a walk outside while it is still cool. Edward has a vegetable patch I am certain you will wish to inspect." He smiled in a teasing way that made my knees go weak.

After Erik departed for the clinic, which was only about a quarter of a mile away, I went back upstairs to sort through my trunk. I wanted to make sure nothing was missing. There was no point in unpacking it since Erik was determined we would leave as soon as possible, but I did want to make sure everything was still there. Lying wrapped carefully in tissue at the bottom of my trunk was my beautiful midnight blue Worth gown. How glamorous I had felt when wearing it! I had Henriette to thank for its good care; she had treated it like a newborn babe. I parted the tissue just enough to peep at the gown, and wondered where Henriette was now. Where was Ohio? I hoped she would not have cause to regret her hasty decision to remain in America.

Something else caught my eye: leaning against Erik's trunk was his art portfolio. How glad I was that someone had thought to include it when our things were brought here. I had in mind that when we returned home, I would have Erik's sketches of people he had seen in New York framed. They were very good, I knew.

Finally I selected a pretty day gown and a parasol to wear outdoors. The lovely green and plaid traveling gown, having been completely ruined during our escape, had been discarded. This gown was not so smart but it did have the advantage of being light and cool. Finally I did as Erik advised — went for a walk.

I had scarcely reached the gravel road leading from Dr. Arlington's house to the clinic when two men on horseback approached me. They were both wearing silver star-shaped badges pinned to their shirts, so I knew they must be the local police. Upon reaching me, they dismounted and tipped their hats politely. One of them asked me a question, and I understood my own name but nothing else. I realized he must be one of the rescue party of the previous evening. I would never have recognized him, being so far beyond exhausted by then.

"*Je regrette, mais je ne parle pas l'anglais, Monsieur,*" I said with a smile, furling my parasol. The policeman looked bemused, and exchanged looks with the other one. They spoke briefly with each other, and then the first one turned back to me and spoke in a loud voice, very slowly. This time I recognized Erik's name, and realized they wanted to speak to him. I pointed my parasol in the direction of the clinic.

"*La clinique,*" I explained. We walked that way together, the policemen leading their horses down the gravel path. Both of the men, I noticed, kept shooting little sideways glances at me. Perhaps they thought me an oddity, being from France and not America. I was doubtful they had ever seen a French person before.

I confess I was quite curious about the clinic that had played so great a part in Erik's decision to come to America, and my first impression of it was pleasing. It was a graceful, well-proportioned building, all white, surrounded by trees and with a tidy gravel drive leading to the front entrance.

Unlike what few structures I had seen thus far, it was built of brick rather than wood. There was a sense of stolid elegance about it.

We walked up the drive slowly and I was grateful indeed for the rows of tall trees on either side, for the day was already hot and the shade welcome. I could already feel a little trickle of moisture sliding down the front of my gown.

As soon as we entered through the large double doors, I sensed something amiss inside. The place was strangely silent, and that did not seem natural. There was no one in the foyer to greet us when we knocked on the door, and once inside, I became aware of a strong odor of antiseptic. It reminded me of the inside of Dr. Gaudet's little clinic room at the Hospital.

Glancing around, I observed a large open room on the left, not unlike the refectory at St. Giles Hospital. Curtains were pulled across the row of windows that looked out on the front of the building, softening the heat of the sunlight that poured in. There were cards and books strewn about, and several game boards. It looked to be a comfortable, pleasant room. Erik had told me of it when we were on the train, but today there was only one occupant, a man who paid no attention to us whatsoever.

It gave me a shock to see him – he was a young man, but his face was wrapped like a mummy in white bandages until all that remained visible was a pair of vacant eyes gazing unseeing at the curtained windows. The two policemen were staring at him, too. Unable to stop myself, I stepped quietly into the room and looked more closely at the patient. *This could be Erik,* I thought suddenly, and felt a surge of sympathy for him. As I drew closer, I could see that the pupils of his eyes were dilated, and I understood that he was drugged, perhaps with some pain-relieving medication. His surgery must have been quite recent. Satisfied, I returned to the two policemen and said succinctly,

"He is on drugs for the pain," only to have them both stare at me as though I were from another planet.

Just then a young man entered the room at a brisk pace, brushed past us and went directly to the patient. He began to check the man's pulse and looked at his eyes. I realized he must be a nurse.

"*Excusez-moi, mais je suis à la recherche de mon mari,*" I called to him.

The policemen, seeing that I was getting nowhere with the nurse, said something to him in businesslike tones, and I recognized Erik's name. The nurse responded briefly before departing, looking harried. Only a few minutes passed before we heard footsteps, and Dr. Buck came into the foyer, followed by Erik. Dr. Buck looked tired and distressed; Erik's face was expressionless. I felt sure they had been having a disagreement. As soon as he saw me he came to stand beside me.

"These are American policemen, Erik, and they wish to speak with you," I explained. There followed some discussion I could not follow, and then the two policemen tipped their hats to me once more, both of them giving me rather lingering looks, and departed. When I turned to Erik, he was smirking at me.

"More broken hearts, I see," he murmured for my ears only. I felt myself blush. Was that why they kept stealing glances at me? I had thought it was because I was a peculiar French person.

"But what did they tell you? It was something to do with those hired ruffians, was it not?" I asked him, frowning. Erik's face became even more expressionless if that were possible.

"*Oui*, that is so." He glanced swiftly at Dr. Buck before continuing, "The police were able to apprehend two of them last night. Without their horses, they could not get far. Also…one of them was apparently somewhat injured, and was still in the barn." Erik made it sound as if the injuries merely happened all by themselves, but he was reluctant to meet my eyes for a moment.

"Erik…" I began, but he went on hurriedly.

"The men were hired for this job – to find us and remove us from the train. And as I suspected, their orders were to kill us. Of course they do not know who actually hired them; it was arranged through an intermediary." He slanted a sardonic glance down at me. "Apparently, there are any number of mercenaries for hire in this country since their war ended."

I repressed a shiver, remembering how close we came to being killed the day before. Erik put his arm around me in a protective gesture.

"Come, Sylvie. Dr. Buck has invited us to lunch with him in his rooms. Edward won't be here for at least another two hours."

So we went upstairs to a scrupulously clean little suite of rooms, also painted white. Along the way we passed several small rooms, and behind the door of one I could clearly hear someone moaning in pain. Another nurse, a woman this time, passed us in the hallway in a great hurry, looking harried. Dr. Buck made no comment, only kept walking, but I began to feel uneasy about the clinic. Something did not seem right here. I looked quickly at Erik, but his face gave nothing away.

Luncheon was an awkward, uncomfortable affair. Dr. Buck spoke no French, and I spoke no English. Erik and the doctor made stilted conversation between themselves, but mainly there was silence. *Et aussi*, he seemed preoccupied, a frown creasing his forehead. The meal was the simple, comforting sort that I used to make for the patients at St. Giles Hospital. In spite of the hot, humid weather, it was a creamy chicken soup made with onions rather than leeks. I always made it with leeks, but perhaps they did not grow leeks in America. Accompanying the soup were crusty rolls and a most welcome and refreshing *vin blanc*.

"Have you told Dr. Buck we are leaving soon?" I ventured to ask Erik softly, after taking a sip of my wine.

"Yes, and he was disappointed, but he has other things on his mind at the moment." Erik replied quietly.

"Something about the clinic?"

He nodded briefly. "I will explain when we are alone again."

I felt relieved when our awkward lunch finally came to an end. Dr. Buck spoke briefly to Erik, bowed politely to me, and left the room.

"He says we are welcome to stay here for a while if we wish. Would you like a little more wine?"

"No, thank you," I replied. It was too hot for wine, even cool white wine. Erik poured a half glass more for himself and fell to brooding over it in silence, a frown furrowing his brow. Just when my curiosity and concern was reaching the boiling point, he spoke at last.

"It is just as well we are leaving here, Sylvie. Dr. Buck could not perform the surgery on my face in any event, for there is some sort of infection running through the clinic. They are having difficulty eliminating it and several of the men recovering from operations on their faces have fallen ill with fever. He does not want to operate on me now." He paused to finish his wine. "He has encouraged me to return another time, but that ship has sailed. I intend we should leave on the train that brings Edward here this afternoon." He glanced at a clock on the wall. "The train should be arriving at any moment, in fact."

He rose and reached for my hand, pulling me up next to him. "After we talk to Edward, we can collect our things and go to the train station. I must admit I am anxious to be on our way. Let us go downstairs and wait for Edward. If I know him, he will come straight to the clinic."

I could see he was troubled, and I could not blame him. I wrapped my arms around his waist and pressed my face into his shirtfront.

"I know you are not looking forward to talking to Dr. Arlington, but we will do it together, Erik. He needs to know what Edythe is capable of. I only hope…" I paused, and he drew back to look down at my face.

"You only hope what?" He prompted gently.

"I hope he will believe us. He seems completely taken in by her." I felt a scowl forming on my face. "I do not want that wicked girl to go unpunished, Erik. What she tried to do to us is abominable!"

"Shhh…Kitten…it will be all right. Edythe Arlington cannot harm us now." Erik spoke softly, while stroking my back soothingly. But I could feel the tension in his body. He sighed.

"I think the most we can hope for is that he will believe us, and see that she is confined somewhere, perhaps receive some treatment. I would wish that she had never fixed on me, of all people. It serves to demonstrate she was clearly mad."

At those words, I pulled away and glared at him mutinously.

"Oh no. There you are wrong. That was the only sensible thing she did." I said firmly. Erik stared at me, clearly perplexed.

"What do you mean?" He asked, sounding a bit vexed.

I shook my head. "You do not understand. Miss Arlington is perhaps mad to some degree, but she is most definitely a worldly, experienced young woman, and she is clearly experienced in affairs of the heart. She hated me, my love, because you were mine, and you loved me. She wanted to possess you, to have you for herself."

Erik studied me thoughtfully for a moment, clearly wishing to argue the point. Finally his face cleared and he smirked a bit.

"Perhaps…right up until the moment she decided to kill us both." He said triumphantly. "Now come, let us go downstairs."

Erik

Erik understood Sylvie's desire for justice to be served; he felt it too. But in a more visceral, primal way. In the past, when someone crossed him he made certain there were consequences – generally quite unpleasant ones. The idiot managers of the Opera House could attest to that. It had always been his way. There were times, he reflected ruefully, that becoming civilized was a drawback. If he were the man he once was, he would have set a clever trap for Edythe Arlington, waited patiently, and caught her in his net. A net she would never escape from, and probably not survive. But now he was married to someone who did not believe in taking matters into one's own, perfectly capable hands. It was frustrating, to be sure. Sometimes, he reflected ruefully, he felt that his wife did not truly understand what he had been. She was always trying to tame him.

He turned these thoughts over wistfully in his mind as they descended the stairs. The other problem, *bien sûr*, was Edward. Erik had come to like the shy, dedicated doctor. He did not hold it against Edward that he held a *tendresse* toward Erik's own wife. It seemed that everyone did. And who could blame them?

He pondered Sylvie's words, wondering if there was truth in them. 'Possess' was such a powerful word. Did Edythe feel toward Erik what Erik had felt toward Christine? If so, it was powerful indeed. He slanted a glance down at his wife's head as they reached the bottom of the stairs. Somehow, he thought wonderingly, he never felt that way about Sylvie. Well, except perhaps that fateful night when he found her in the ballroom, surrounded by admirers. He had felt quite possessive that evening, he had to admit.

Once downstairs again, where the main clinic rooms and the surgery were located, the acrid antiseptic smell assailed his nostrils. The long room where the patients recovering from surgical procedures spent much of their days was virtually empty. Erik supposed some of them had been sent home or to other places so they would not succumb to the infection. Only one man was there today; he was wrapped in such a way that Erik was certain his surgery was on his nose. He looked half-unconscious, his head drooping down to his chest.

Erik wandered to the entrance foyer and opened the heavy door to look out; it was after noon now and the air was shimmering with heat. He wanted Edward to come, so he could get this over with, and yet he did not want Edward to come. And Matthew! How difficult this was going to be. He hitched his shoulders, feeling the tension mounting.

Just then he heard someone call his name; turning, he saw Dr. Buck coming toward them. He was dressed in the white coat he always wore when in his surgery. His bullet-shaped head glistened slightly with moisture from the heat. He had some papers in his hand. He wanted to discuss possible surgical procedures, it was clear. Erik groaned inwardly; Dr. Buck seemed to think it possible that Erik might return some day. He glanced apologetically at Sylvie and turned his attention to Dr. Buck.

When he looked around for her again a few minutes later, she had vanished.

Bored with a conversation I did not understand and that did not include me, I decided to give in to my curiosity and have a quick look about the clinic. It was, after all, a very important part of Dr. Arlington's life. And all was so quiet and seeming empty, I felt certain I could not disturb anyone. Ever since stepping inside that morning, I had been intrigued by the light, clean clinic. I would never be here again, so I decided to indulge in a bit of exploring.

Seeing that Erik and Dr. Buck were deep in conversation and likely to be that way for some time, I slipped from the foyer.

Wandering down a long hallway, I found a door labeled 'surgery', and peeked inside. It was clear that no procedures had been performed here recently, due to the infection problem, *sans doute*. It was a fairly large room, well lighted, with metal surfaces and mysterious pieces of medical equipment. There were drawers and cabinets aplenty, all labeled with their contents. How Dr. Gaudet would love to see this room! He would certainly be envious. His own small clinic room was about four hundred years old.

At the back of the building I came to a large, well-equipped kitchen which naturally caught my attention. I could see that some of the food preparation took place outside, under the shade of a large tree. A basket of potatoes rested on a wooden table, ready to be peeled. A few dirty dishes were stacked in a wide metal sink. But the kitchen was strangely empty. Where was everyone? Perhaps both workers and patients had been sent elsewhere for their own protection. It gave me an eerie, uneasy feeling and I decided to return to Erik in the foyer. Empty as it was, the clinic building was beginning to feel almost haunted.

All the doors opening off the hallways were neatly labeled, and it was easy to identify a linen closet, a water closet, and a few rooms for recovering patients. Glancing into one of these, I saw a utilitarian iron single bed against the wall, a wash basin and a wardrobe. The room was quite small, rather like a stateroom on a ship. The room, like most of them, was empty, the bed stripped of all linen. I wondered if the poor man I had seen covered in bandages was all alone in the place. It seemed quite likely.

Closing the door quietly, as if I were afraid to disturb a sleeping occupant, I turned around and realized I could not recollect which way to go. Wandering down several hallways, I had managed to become lost. Which way was the surgery? If I could return to that, I would be able to orient myself again. I stood listening, hoping to hear the murmur of Erik's and Dr. Buck's voices conversing in the foyer, but all was silent. If only a nurse would bustle by, I could ask for direction, but it seemed even they were gone.

After dithering for a moment or two, trying to get my bearings, I turned left, for I was fairly certain that was the way I had just walked. Then the hallway turned a corner, and I realized with sinking heart that it was a dead end. Or was it?

Ahead of me was another door, of heavy dark wood, and this door was unlabeled. The floor here seemed to slope downward slightly, as if flowing toward the door. I noticed that this part of the building had an old, neglected feel, and the paint had not been kept up. I gazed at the closed door, perplexed. Where did it lead? It occurred to me that perhaps this was a back exit. Once I was outside the clinic building, I could simply walk around the outside of it until I reached the front door again.

Feeling unaccountably uneasy, I approached the door. There was a lock, but it hung unfastened. Hoping to see bright sunshine greeting me, I grasped the heavy brass handle of the door and turned it.

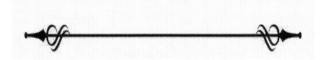

Erik

Now where had she got to? He glanced past Dr. Buck's retreating form, but there was no sign of Sylvie. He took a few uncertain steps toward the back of the foyer and called her name. Erik wasn't really worried about her; what trouble could she get into here? Silence met the sound of his voice.

Where was everyone? Why did the clinic seem so deserted? Perhaps Dr. Buck had sent everyone home to protect them. Erik scowled, feeling uncharacteristically indecisive. Did Sylvie go back upstairs perhaps? Erik started toward the stairs, but stopped with one foot on the first tread, listening. A light carriage was approaching down the long drive. Dr. Arlington was here, Erik knew. Almost reluctantly, he retraced his steps and went to the front door.

As he opened it, Edward was already hastening up the steps, looking tired and distraught. His already straggly rust colored goatee showed signs of wear and tear, as though the doctor had been tugging on it. Erik was relieved to see that he was alone.

"Where is Matthew?" He asked, shaking hands with Edward.

"I dropped him at the house and came straight here. Are you and Mrs. Bessette all right? Where is Gurdon? Everything has gone wrong while I was away…I wish I had not gone to Washington."

Suppressing a groan, Erik hated knowing he was going to tell Edward just how much was wrong.

"We are fine, Edward. And your local police have already apprehended the men who attacked us."

"Thank god for that. I was never more shocked than when I read Gurdon's telegram! Nothing like this has ever…" Edward began looking around, a frown notched between his brows. Light from the open door glinted off his spectacles weirdly. "But where is Gurdon? He wrote also that there are problems here at the clinic."

"I think he is…"Erik began, but he was interrupted mid-sentence by the shrill, panic-stricken sound of a woman's scream. It was followed instantly by the sound of his own name, as Sylvie called to him in a terrified voice. Where the hell was she? Erik and Edward stared at one another, both men equally startled by the unexpected scream.

"It sounded like it was coming from back that way," Edward said, pointing toward the back of the clinic building. There were a number of hallways with doors along them, for it was a large building. They started toward the surgery, and collided with Dr. Buck who was just emerging from it. His face wore an almost comical look of panic.

"I heard someone scream," he exclaimed, glancing around furtively. "Was it Mrs. Bessette?"

"Of course it was," Erik snapped impatiently. "There is no one else here. Where is she?"

"I do not know. I thought Mrs. Bessette was with you…I have been in here since I left you." Dr. Buck replied. Erik looked sharply at him. There was something different in his eyes. Was it shame? All at once, it hit Erik: the sure knowledge of where he would find his ever curious wife. He turned quickly to Edward.

"Your cellar, or basement as you call it. I believe she is there." The vision of his nightmare rose in his mind unbidden, and he fought not to shudder at the unpleasant memory. Out of the corner of his eye, he saw Dr. Buck blanch.

Edward was unconcerned. Uncharitably, Erik felt frustrated with him. It was highly likely Edward's concern was for the clinic, and not his

327

errant wife. At that moment, Erik would have happily sent Edward and his damned clinic to perdition.

"It is rather dark down there, if you do not know where the gaslight is." Edward said calmly. "Perhaps Mrs. Bessette became frightened of the dark. Come, follow me." He started off down the hallway.

"Edward..." Dr. Buck called after him, "there is something you should know..." Erik, starting after Edward, glanced back at Dr. Buck and saw a sheen of sweat on his forehead. Unease grew into desperation, and suddenly he was on fire to get to Sylvie. He needed to find her *now*.

Hastening behind Edward, heart pounding, Erik realized he never could have found his own way back to the cellar door on his own. He had only arrived there by chance the first time, when he was idly exploring the clinic. The way began to look familiar, though, as soon as he recognized that they were in the oldest part of the building. Suddenly he heard Sylvie's voice, sounding much nearer.

"Erik, please help me!" Her voice quavered. "I am lost." There was a small sob.

Edward said over his shoulder, "Poor creature! She is only turned around. This is a confusing old building." To this Erik made no reply; he knew Sylvie would not have screamed in terror merely because she was lost.

They turned one last corner, and to his relief there she was. It did nothing to dispel his worry for her, however, when he saw that she stood pressed up against a brick wall as if she needed it for support, her handkerchief against her lips. Her face was white as a sheet and she trembled with terror.

"Sylvie!" He called to her, and at the sound of his voice she pushed away from the wall and stumbled toward him, her hands outstretched.

"Oh, Erik!" She gasped, "I am so glad you are here." She plowed into him, gripping him for dear life.

"I am here, I am here." He murmured, holding her trembling body tightly. "What is the matter, Sylvie – are you hurt?" He asked frantically. He had never seen her in such a state, even after the attack yesterday, and it made him almost insensible.

In answer, she pointed a trembling arm toward the open door at the end of the hallway. When he almost reluctantly looked toward it, instead of the stygian darkness Erik had found when he had opened that door, unexpectedly he saw that a faint light now emanated from it.

"Bodies!" Sylvie whispered. "Dead bodies!" She clutched fearfully at him. "There are dead bodies down there."

"What?" Erik and Edward both exclaimed at the same time.

Sylvie leaned away from him so she could look at Edward, her eyes wide. "It is true. They are covered in white shrouds. At least four. I saw them. Down there." She shuddered. "It smells terrible."

Erik felt the hair stand on the back of his neck. He could almost see the still forms rising up, the white shrouds falling away to reveal…no, he would not remember that grisly nightmare sight. He met Edward's eyes over Sylvie's head, his expression grim.

Edward looked blankly confused. "I do not understand…I must see," he muttered as if to himself, and started toward the open door. He stopped at the top of the stairs leading down into the depths of the old cellar. Erik could see by the glow of gaslight the brick wall on one side, and a few steps leading down. Apparently Sylvie had been able to turn on the light. Edward gasped, a long intake of breath.

"My god!" He exclaimed. He pulled out a handkerchief and pressed it to his face. "It smells of decay. I wonder how long…"

Erik understood then. This was why the clinic appeared so empty; the patients had died, some of them, and Dr. Buck must have stored the bodies here, in the cool dark cellar.

Edward backed up hastily and closed the heavy wood door. As he did so, Dr. Buck joined them in the hallway, his wide face pasty and pale. Edward rounded on him furiously.

"Gurdon, what is the meaning of this? Why are those men down there?" Edward demanded, his face growing blotchy with anger.

"Edward, I am sorry; I intended to tell you as soon as you arrived." He paused and looked at Sylvie. "I am sorry she had to see that." He added ruefully.

"But I did not know what else was to be done. White Plains does not even have a morgue, and I was afraid if I told the police about the infection spreading here, the county would shut down the clinic."

Edward stared at the other man as if he were mad. "Gurdon, we cannot leave the bodies down there, you must see that. We have to report the deaths, and notify next of kin. It is the only right thing to do."

"But Edward…" Dr. Buck began to expostulate, no doubt to argue his point. Erik had had enough. He slid his arm around Sylvie's shoulders, and felt her lean into his body, as though seeking comfort.

"I am taking my wife back to the house, Edward. I must speak to you in private, about another matter, as soon as you are free." Erik did not want to remain in this cursed clinic for another moment. The thought of those still, shrouded forms lying in the dark below, like something out of an Edgar Allan Poe novel, filled him with dread. With mounting horror, Erik realized

329

that he very possibly could have been one of those still, shrouded forms, had he agreed to any surgery here.

Poor Edward! This would be the worst day of his life, *sans doute*. Ushering his silent, pale wife toward the main door, Erik admitted to himself it was not exactly the best day of his life, either.

CHAPTER TWENTY-EIGHT

"I assure you I am quite resilient."

I do not remember the short journey back to Dr. Arlington's house. In my mind all I could see was those four still, white-sheeted forms lying on gurneys ranged around the cellar floor. In spite of the hot afternoon sun beating down on me, I could feel only the rush of cold air that met me when the wood door opened, along with a repulsive odor of decay.

The weather outside was changing, however. From the south we could see a wide, dark charcoal bank of clouds swiftly approaching – a summer storm, common to the area apparently. The black clouds flowed toward us with startling swiftness, so that by the time we reached the walkway in front of Dr. Arlington's house, the sun had vanished, swallowed up by the clouds. Inside the house, we were met by Mrs. McKendrick, approaching us with a warm smile. She was clearly taken aback when Erik barked out an order to her to bring a pot of tea to the parlor, and be quick about it.

"Please," I amended as she scurried away. Erik sent me a speaking glance while guiding me carefully to a plush armchair. Then we both jumped as if shot when a loud clap of thunder rang out. Looking slightly sheepish, Erik went to the window and looked out. He was illuminated by a flash of pure white light, and then the storm was upon us with a vengeance. Thunder and lightning tumbled over the flat fields, and heavy raindrops fell noisily on the house. A clean smell of ozone filled our nostrils. It went a long way toward clearing out the awful memory of that charnel house odor.

"I had a nightmare about that place," Erik said abruptly, not looking at me. I gazed at his broad back, perplexed.

"About...about the clinic, do you mean?" I asked.

"*Non.* It was about that very cellar. I was back in New York at the time. But like you, I came across the door when I was bored and felt like having a look around. It was just a dark space. Edward came upon me then and we left. He said it was a storage room." Erik gave a small, sharp laugh. "And I suppose he was correct." He turned and looked at me then, his face inscrutable.

"What was the nightmare about?" I ventured to ask. He was silent for so long I began to think he would not answer.

"What you saw today, Sylvie. Bodies, covered in white. Only...in my dream they began to..."

"Oh, no! Do not tell me, I beg of you!" I interrupted, covering my ears with my hands. But he might as well have told me, for my imagination could easily supply the grisly images. Behind me, I heard Erik open the window. Fresh, rain-scented air flowed inside; it was not cold, but it was cool and sweet. Looking out the window, I saw that the storm was already passing. A bolt of golden afternoon sunlight was just escaping the edge of the clouds.

"That is nice," I said, coming to stand next to him. "Erik, do you think that the police will really..." He stopped me with a warning hand on my arm. Mrs. McKendrick had just entered, bringing our tea on a tray. My throat felt dry, and I found I was quite looking forward to a cup of tea.

"Where is Matthew, Mrs. McKendrick?" Erik inquired of the housekeeper. I realized I had completely forgotten Matthew's existence.

"Oh, he has just gone down to the stable to look at the horses, Sir. He is quite a rider when he is here at home." She beamed proudly.

I had just finished my second cup when the door opened again, this time to admit a very dejected and upset Dr. Arlington. Erik and I exchanged quick, worried glances with each other while Dr. Arlington sank onto a *settee* with a heartfelt groan. Not knowing what else to do, I took him a cup of tea. He accepted it blindly, and set it down on a table where it remained untouched. I would not have guessed this quiet, gentle man could have such a temper as he displayed toward his work partner, but perhaps what was always said about having red hair must be true.

"I've sent for the local sheriff," he said at last. "We would have to close the clinic in any case, until we can be sure this virulent infection has been eradicated. The remaining patient will be transported to the hospital over in Greenburgh."

"I am so sorry, Dr. Arlington," I murmured sympathetically.

"And I am sorry as well, Mrs. Bessette, that you had to make that terrible discovery." He replied grimly. "And after what you went through yesterday." His gray eyes, tired behind the gold spectacles, rose to mine for a moment, and then down again.

Erik cleared his throat. "Sylvie and I are planning on catching the return train to New York this afternoon, Edward. You will not want us here now, as you have much to do. I intend that we will return to France immediately." Dr. Arlington nodded, staring blankly into the empty fireplace grate.

"I am afraid this trip to America has not gone very well for you, my friend. But I hope that we will meet again under better circumstances." Dr.

Arlington spoke to Erik, but his eyes strayed toward me. "You said you wanted to speak to me about something?"

Erik stood, paced to the window and back. He stood looking down at Dr. Arlington. "Yes, and what we have to tell you will only add to your problems, Edward. I am very sorry."

I will draw a veil over that painful conversation. Suffice it to say that poor Dr. Arlington became beside himself with despair when we had finished our recital of his daughter's infamous behavior. I felt terrible knowing we had caused him so much grief, but I was thankful when he agreed with us that she should not be left free under the circumstances. Edythe had clearly become a danger to herself as well as others. He acknowledged that she must have mental problems and ought to be put somewhere quiet and safe, and perhaps receive some help. The only problem, he explained, was that no one knew of her whereabouts currently. Matthew did not know where she had been staying once she left their hotel.

"Edie's mother was high-strung, and she had quite a temper," Dr. Arlington said sadly. "Edie must have inherited some of that from her. She was ever a willful girl." He shook his head, unseeing eyes gazing down at his hands lying quietly in his lap. 'Willful' was one way to put it, I thought to myself, but I kept prudently silent.

The wagon arrived to take ourselves and our possessions to the White Plains train station not long after the conclusion of our unhappy meeting with Dr. Arlington, and we departed with alacrity. We were anxious to be away, and I am sure he was equally glad to see the last of the Bessettes. I doubted we would ever see Dr. Arlington again.

We sat behind the driver and bounced our way back into the small, quiet town.

"The trouble is," Erik spoke softly as we rode along, "Edythe Arlington could be anywhere. In spite of all that we told him, I don't think her father realizes what she really is."

"And what is that?" I asked curiously. Erik obviously had spent much more time in her company than I, and he had more time to form an opinion of her.

"She is a master criminal trapped in the body of a beautiful young woman. She is quick-witted, clever, fearless, and she knows how to use her wiles to get around men. She is a dangerous creature. Edward can have no idea."

"No, I suppose not, poor man." I shook my head ruefully, clapping my hand to my head to keep my hat from falling off when the wagon bounced over a particularly deep rut. Happily, we arrived in the town and the road became tidy and graveled.

"I have to admit I was shocked when Dr. Arlington told us there was a rumor going around that Edythe pushed her mother down the stairs in a fit of pique. I wonder if there is any truth to it?"

"*Sacre*! I do not know. But somehow I would not be surprised." Erik said, his voice a low growl. He glanced around. "We are here, fortunately. I feel I have been in the sun all that I can bear." He pulled out a handkerchief and mopped his brow.

"Said the man who lived in a sunless cavern for ten years," I replied teasingly.

"Right up until some busybody shrew dragged me out of it," said my husband fondly. "And look how that turned out."

I was more than relieved to see the train sitting on the track, its engine reversed, ready to make the return trip to New York. Steam was issuing gently from the engine, and men were loading wood and coal into a car directly behind it. Several other people, clearly travelers waiting to embark, stood on the platform and watched the proceedings with interest. The ladies were carrying fashionable lacy parasols to protect them from the hot afternoon sun, and I realized I had forgotten mine. I remembered I'd left it in the foyer of the clinic. Well, there it would stay. Perhaps I could wire Mrs. McKendrick and tell her she could have it. It was a very pretty parasol.

I could also ask her to send me her American breakfast biscuit recipe; I had left the house in such haste I had completely forgotten to ask her for it.

I was pleased to observe that although the other people glanced at us with the curiosity of fellow travelers, no one appeared unduly interested in Erik's face. The new mask, so lifelike and natural, attracted very little attention. Perhaps they thought him a war veteran, one of any number of such men who came to the clinic for help.

Erik went to the station office to purchase a return ticket for us, and once he made himself known to the train employees a clamor ensued. I watched in astonishment as he was instantly surrounded by men, all talking at once. He extricated himself and returned to me after a few minutes, looking bemused.

"*C'est quoi*?" I asked him anxiously. "Is there a problem?" Erik looked at me, his pale eyes dancing.

"No; just the opposite." He said with a wide grin. "They are apparently so upset about what happened to us coming out here that they are letting us ride back to New York for free, in a private carriage. And…" he waved his arm toward the side of the station. "We will have an armed escort most of the way back."

Looking in the direction he indicated, I saw two men wearing the star-shaped badges standing near their horses. They were well armed, and appeared to be the eagle-eyed cowboy sort one reads about. I felt an instant sense of safety, for to be honest, I had begun to worry about the return journey. How did we know that Edythe Arlington might not try again? It would be out of a desire for revenge this time, but I would not have put anything past that dreadful creature. My great regret was that I would not be able to come to grips with her myself.

We were waiting in a patch of shade on the platform when someone came trotting briskly up on horseback. The horse and rider stopped next to the platform, raising a small cloud of dust. Glancing up curiously, I recognized Matthew. He was not wearing a hat, and his dark curly hair was windblown. He very much resembled the sketch Erik had done of him in New York. He dismounted and approached us eagerly, smiling widely.

"I couldn't let you leave without saying goodbye," he said breathlessly. "Dad told me you were here; I didn't realize you were leaving so soon. I'm glad I made it before they let you board." He reached out to shake hands with Erik, and I saw my husband rest his other hand on the boy's shoulder. It was a fatherly gesture that warmed my heart.

"I wish you both a safe trip home…perhaps someday I can come and visit you in France," Matthew added wistfully. "I've never been out of the U.S.A."

"Thank you, Matthew. You are welcome to visit us, of course." Erik answered diplomatically.

"We would love to have you, Matthew," I added for emphasis. Matthew turned to me and bowed, and then he took my hand and kissed it, on top of the glove. Then he brushed the hair out of his eyes and glanced toward the train, where it stood hissing and steaming quietly.

"Looks like they have about finished getting her ready. You'll be boarding soon. I say…" he looked quickly at Erik, a frown notched between his dark brows. "Dad seems awfully cut up just now. I guess this business at the clinic has really upset him."

"Yes, I am sure it has. I hope they will not close it down." I replied gently. There had not been time, apparently, for Dr. Arlington to tell Matthew of his sister's perfidy.

A conductor dismounted from the train and blew a whistle. It was time to go. Our trunks and belongings were already loaded in our private compartment.

"Oh! I almost forgot!" Matthew exclaimed suddenly, slapping his hand against his thigh. "Edie gave me a message for you, Mr. Bessette." Taken aback, we both gaped at him. Quickly I marshaled my expression before Matthew could see the alarm on my face.

"When did she…" Erik began.

"She stopped by the hotel to see me right before we left to come here. We were in a big hurry, I can tell you! Dad was frantic to make the train to White Plains. Edie didn't even stop to see him. She just said she'd be in touch. She's staying with some friends I guess. She doesn't like the country."

"We have to go, Matthew; the train is boarding." Erik said, taking me by the elbow. "What was the message from your sister?"

Matthew scratched his head thoughtfully. "Well, it was rather odd I thought, but she said to tell you, that you haven't seen the last of her. I think she means she hopes to see you again, I reckon."

I felt a chill chase up my spine. I was certain that Edythe Arlington would have no difficulty evading her father's efforts to locate her.

Saying our final goodbyes, we boarded the train.

"Be a good lad, and look after your father," Erik instructed Matthew just before we boarded the train. "He will need your support."

By tacit agreement, neither of us spoke about that threatening message until we were safely seated in our private compartment.

It was wonderful to realize that we were finally going home. Even though we must make the trip back to the city and spend at least one night in a hotel, it still felt like the journey home had already begun. I felt excited and happy. My irrational fears about losing my husband to another woman had been dispelled, and now I joyfully anticipated seeing my daughter again.

What a strange turn of events had pushed us so far apart from each other; I vowed to myself silently that nothing like this would ever happen again.

There were at least two different passenger steamer lines plying the ocean between Liverpool and New York, Erik explained to me. We ought not to have to wait more than a day or two for a return trip on one of them.

As soon as we were settled in our compartment, Erik threw off his coat, removed his cravat, tossed his mask onto a table and otherwise made himself comfortable in the manner of a typical male. Then he rang for an attendant and ordered wine for us. Thinking to myself that this trip was going to be quite enjoyable, I went to a window, lifted the curtain and peered out. Just a few yards away, riding parallel to the slow-moving train, was one of the policemen on horseback. Comforted, I dropped the curtain back down.

By the time I stowed away my hat and jacket, the wine had arrived. Erik poured us each a glass and we sank onto a plush *settee* with sighs of contentment.

"Sylvie, would you like to spend a few days in New York, and see the sights?" He asked, looking pensive. "You have never been to America before, *après tout*."

"To be honest, I just want to start for home. I do not have any desire to see more of America than I already have." I replied firmly. Erik looked relieved.

"*Bon*. I do not wish to linger in the city any longer than necessary. I want to have done with always feeling like I have to look over my shoulder for an enemy."

"So you think…she is in New York somewhere?" I asked him with some trepidation. I took a fortifying sip of the wine – it was red, a burgundy perhaps, and obviously French.

"Oh yes. Remember, she came to see Matthew early this morning, before he came to White Plains with his father." I regarded him with round eyes.

"Only this morning? Why, it seems like a month has passed since this morning. I had forgotten."

Erik smiled at me, put his arm around me and pulled me close for a kiss. Our wine-scented breaths mingled deliciously.

"Do you want to eat in the dining car tonight, Kitten, or here in our room?" He asked.

"Here in our room, please." And so we did.

Erik

Fortune must favor the desperate, Erik mused, for the staff at the Fifth Avenue Hotel were able to secure them a berth on the Oceanic, the same steamer he had made the journey on when he came to America. How long ago had it been? A few months, but it felt like a year. The ship was in port in New York harbor when they arrived back in the city from White Plains, and they were able to board her in the morning.

While standing at the desk in the lobby of the hotel, Erik caught a glimpse of the young man behind the counter he was certain had been trapped in Edythe's toils. How much had she paid him to steal their letters? Did she offer him sexual favors as well? Erik thought about demanding the boy tell him what had happened to the stolen letters, but unsurprisingly, he vanished expediently into an office when he saw Erik watching him with a surly expression. Erik debated speaking to someone in charge about it, but decided against it. What would be the point?

The last thing they did before departing was dispatch telegrams home – one to Celestine and one to Dr. Gaudet in Paris. Sylvie was quite insistent that they reassure everyone back home that all was well. She wished Marie to know that her parents were on their way back to her.

The sea voyage was romantic; rather as if they were taking the wedding tour they were unable to take when first wed. Although he tried to hide it, Erik's nature was deeply romantic, so much so that it was partially to blame for the trouble he created for himself a few years ago.

Now with eight or nine days and nights to do only what they wished to do, he reveled in moonlight strolls on the deck of the ship, to return to their luxuriously appointed stateroom, drink champagne and make love to his wife. One night after an extra glass of champagne he even scattered red rose petals over the bed while Sylvie was changing into her nightgown. He would have selected any other color than red, but it was all he could find in the flower arrangement in the dining salon. Sylvie, unaware of its past significance, had been suitably impressed by the romantic gesture.

But in spite of their shared pleasure in the voyage and eager anticipation of returning home, Erik felt haunted by his experiences in America. On the third night of the trip, when they were about halfway across the Atlantic, he was in the grip of a nightmare when he felt a hand on his shoulder, and someone saying his name urgently. Still in the throes of the dream, he flung out his arm and yelled,

"No! Do not touch me!" He felt someone catch his arm firmly and hold it down.

"Wake up! You are having a dream."

Emerging fully from the nightmare, Erik realized that he had narrowly escaped striking his wife soundly across her face. Fortunately, she knew what to do, and she could duck quite quickly.

He sat up in bed so fast he made himself dizzy, and groaned, burying his face in his hands. Although recurring nightmares had haunted him for years, always they were linked in some way to his past. Sometimes he would dream he was back in Persia, being forced to fight to the death in the arena, for the amusement of the Sultan's harem. Sometimes the dreams went even farther back, to a time when he was young and helpless. And sometimes, Christine's face haunted his dreams. But tonight, tonight the nightmare was of much more recent origin. He realized Sylvie was speaking to him.

"It is all right, *mon amour*, you were having a bad dream, but it was only a dream. You are awake now." She murmured soothingly, her hand making gentle circles on his back. He was suddenly aware that he was trembling. A shudder could not be repressed.

"Did I hurt you, Sylvie?" He asked repentantly.

"No, of course not."She reassured him gently. "You were frightened of something, but I could not tell of what."

Erik drank water from the bottle held securely in an attached wooden box next to the bed. It was a clever way to keep it from sliding off the table when the steamer was rocked by heavy waves. Then he slowly lay back down and pulled Sylvie against him. Her warm, soft body gave him comfort. He loved the feel of her head nestled so trustingly upon his shoulder. It was proof indeed that he was alive and well; not dead.

"You remember, I am sure, that cellar at the clinic, where you found…" his voice trailed off. She nodded without speaking.

"I dreamed that…I was walking down the stairs, and I saw the bodies lying on the gurneys, covered in white sheets. It was the same dream I had before, only…worse. I did not want to be there, but I could not make myself go back. You know how it is in dreams. And since I had this dream once before, Kitten, I knew what would happen." He paused, and drew a ragged breath. Sylvie rubbed his chest soothingly, but said nothing.

"The bodies, they began to move." He could feel her tense at his words, and draw in a quick breath. "They began to sit up, slowly, and the shrouds fell down to reveal their faces. Horrible, mutilated faces, Sylvie, like you might see on a battleground. They all turned to look at me, just like in the first dream. But then I saw…one of the bodies…one of the faces…it was *me*, Sylvie. It was me lying there. I was looking at my own, ghastly ruined face. In my dream I screamed like a woman, and that must have been what woke you."

"My goodness," Sylvie murmured soothingly, "that is a terrible dream. But it isn't surprising under the circumstances." She continued matter-of-factly.

He turned his head on the pillow to look at her, a dimly perceived shape in the moonlight. "What circumstances?" He asked.

"Your own inner fears, of course. You were naturally concerned about the surgery and how it might turn out, and then to find an infection running rampant in the clinic – why, it is entirely possible that, had you gone through with the surgery Dr. Buck wanted to perform on your face, you would have been lying down there on a gurney. Your dream makes perfect sense to me." She held him tightly. "I am so thankful you decided against it."

Erik contemplated this quietly for a few minutes. She was right; the thought had occurred to him as well. But he sincerely hoped this particular nightmare would not add itself to his usual repertoire. After all, they had tapered off considerably. He released a soft sigh and felt his body relax.

"I believe you are correct, Kitten, as usual. I don't like admitting it, but I was afraid of the surgery. It was not so much the procedure itself that concerned me; it was what would happen after. The unknown, I suppose."

"Well, I for one am quite happy to have you just the way you are." Sylvie said. And then, her voice growing thoughtful, she continued,

"I do feel sorry for poor Dr. Arlington, though. He is such a nice man, and I know he believes in his work. As much as I longed for his horrid daughter to be punished for her actions, I hated telling him. I hope he will be all right."

The memory caused Erik to grow momentarily somber.

"I know; I feel the same. In the time we spent together, I felt that we had become…friends. I did not want to tell him, but it had to be done. I am glad Matthew was not there, at least. Matthew may be Edward's only link to Edythe now, and the only means by which he might locate her."

Sylvie sighed, and nestled against him. "It cannot happen a moment too soon." She said plaintively. Erik chuckled, and pressed a kiss against her neck.

"Have I told you lately how much I love you, Kitten?" He asked, feeling unaccountably happy and relaxed for what seemed like the first time in months.

"Well, yes, just this evening in fact. But I do not mind hearing it again." He felt the smile in her voice.

"Good. I love you in spite of what a nagging shrew you are." And before she could respond, he pushed her on to her back and climbed over her, covering her body with his. He heard a muffled laugh emerge from beneath his shoulder.

"You are insatiable, *mon mari*!"

"So it would seem."

A little while later, just as sleep was about to pull him under again, Erik felt Sylvie stir slightly next to him. He felt her soft breath on his cheek as she whispered,

"Do you know what a red rose symbolizes?"

"No, what?" He asked sleepily.

"It means passionate love."

CHAPTER TWENTY-NINE

"Who would have thought the fearsome Phantom had it in him to be so tender?"

'*Slice three leeks thinly, place them in the stockpot and sauté them in a little butter until nicely softened but not browned. To this add six potatoes that you have peeled and cut into one-inch dice. Pour over the hot chicken stock and...*'

The four months since our return from America had flown by in a trice. November had arrived, and winter was shouldering autumn aside. We had our first frost, fortunately after all the vines had been pruned back. The grape harvest had been excellent considering the vines were still young. Robert was quite pleased.

On the voyage across the Atlantic, while talking with Erik about my mother, I conceived the idea of writing a cookbook. I was so taken with the idea that I began working on it as soon as we returned. It was to be based on my mother's recipes, with a few of my own for good measure. I did not know if it would find a publisher, but Erik encouraged me and was delighted to taste my experiments in the kitchen.

Not long after our joyous return, we began construction on a cottage for Dr. Gaudet and his remaining charges from the hospital. Letters winged rapidly back and forth between Paris and our estate while we discussed what would be required for the needs of the patients. Dr. Gaudet was thrilled; a huge weight was lifted from him when he learned of our intentions. The cottage was located inside the entrance to our estate, not far from the entry pillars. Erik had made himself scarce, busy on some project of his own that he would not divulge, so Celestine had been more than happy to supervise the workers from the village who were building the cottage. We wanted to finish before winter really set in. Her happiness at having Dr. Gaudet so close was palpable, and she began making all sorts of plans for an elaborate *Noël*.

I, too, was happy about the cottage, and decided that when it was complete, it would be the perfect place to hang Father Barbier's precious crucifix. Erik did not like having it in our bedroom.

Celestine and I, while deadheading roses on the terrace, had a long conversation regarding whether or not we ought to let Erik read the letter from Christine. We decided against it in the end, both of us agreeing that it seemed like too great a violation of her highly personal confidences. Instead, one evening as we were preparing for bed, I told him that Christine had written Celestine with an apology, and had been full of contrition for being the cause of our exposure to the government. He listened to this with relative calm.

"She was always a malleable creature," was his only comment. "Let us forget about Christine, if you please," he had added, and it was soon obvious that he was suiting his actions to his words.

"Sylvie! Where are you?" My husband's voice, calling my name. I realized he had been calling for me some little while, but I was so engrossed in what I was writing I had not heard him. I looked up from the sheaf of paper on my *petite secretaire*.

"I am here, Erik, in the bedroom."

I liked writing up here in the quiet of our bedroom. Erik had moved my desk over by the window so that I could glance out and admire my *potager*. Sometimes I worked downstairs in the kitchen, but only when I was testing quantities and cooking times for recipes. Fortunately it was a large kitchen, and Mathilde did not mind my working there alongside her.

Erik opened the bedroom door and strode in purposefully, his handsome face flushed and smiling. He looked inordinately pleased with himself, I thought suspiciously.

"How is the cookbook coming?" He asked, crossing the room to give me a quick kiss. I put my pen down and stretched a bit.

"It is rather slow going, but it is coming along. I am doing *vichyssoise* right now."

"Ah. I love your *vichyssoise*. You will excuse my interruption of your work, but I've something I want to show you."

At last, I thought to myself. He must finally be ready to reveal the mysterious project he had been working on for the past month.

"Oh, so you are finally going to let me in on your little secret?" I asked primly, rising from my chair. In truth, I was ready to stop working for a little while. Erik sent me a mock chiding glance, and took my hand.

Once downstairs, we made for the front door, pausing while I wrapped myself in a cloak against the cold. But when we reached the gravel walkway, to my surprise he bade me close my eyes tightly and promise not to peek. Standing in front of me, he playfully pulled my cloak close and tied the ribbons to keep me warm. Laughing a little, I did as he requested and closed my eyes. He was as eager as a boy, and his pleasure was infectious. Once my eyes were closed, he turned me around several times, until I had lost all sense of direction.

"Come, Sylvie. I won't let you trip." He took my arm and began to walk. "Remember, keep your eyes closed."

I thought we went in the direction of the stables, but I could not really tell. We veered away down another path, and I felt rather than saw that we were among trees and grass. There were chestnut trees on our property and I guessed we were in their midst. Sadly, the squirrels had taken most of the nuts.

A cold, gusty breeze played around my legs, tossing my cloak about. Fallen leaves crunched under our feet. At first I was a little nervous about keeping my eyes closed and was tempted to peek just a little, but my husband's guidance was sure. Our progress was by necessity rather slow. With each step we took my curiosity grew.

"Where are we going?" I asked Erik impatiently. He only laughed.

"Always curious, aren't you, Sylvie," was all he said.

In a moment, he stopped me, moved around behind me, and put his hands over my eyes.

"Just a few feet more; go on, you won't fall." Slowly, I complied, and he moved right along with me. "Stop here, Sylvie."

"*Maintenant*, you can look." Erik took his hands from my eyes with a flourish. "*Regardez*," he said proudly. Blinking open my eyes, I saw that a structure was standing directly in front of me. Then I looked again more closely, taking it in. I turned my head and stared at my husband in dazzled wonder.

It was a fairy tale castle, reduced to child-size. It was perfect, like something from a book, and there were even pennants flying from one turret.

"So this is what you have been working on all this time?" I asked.

He nodded. "*Oui*, this is it. Do you think she will like it?" He was standing beside me, hands on hips, surveying his creation and looking quite pleased with himself.

"Like it...she will *love* it, as I am sure you are aware."

"I wanted to make it up to her for missing her birthday." He explained. "It is to be a belated birthday present, and an early one for *Noël*."

"Well, I expect this will do the trick," I replied, smiling. "Marie will forgive you anything when she sees this."

Turning, he gestured back the way we had come, along the leaf-strewn gravel path. "You see, Sylvie, it actually isn't far from the house, for I led you in circles a bit." Indeed I could see the red tile roof of the *château* through the mostly leafless trees.

"René helped me build it, but I've left it to you and Marie to decide what goes in it. Decorating is women's work," he added with a taunting twinkle in his eyes. To myself I thought wickedly that if *he* had decided to decorate, the play castle would be filled with *de trop* gilt.

Studying the pretend castle Erik had built in secret for Marie a little closer, one or two things I noticed gave me pause. I frowned in consternation.

"But that appears to be...a real moat. With a drawbridge."

"Yes, of course. Everyone knows castles must have moats and drawbridges, Sylvie." Erik paused before adding casually, "There is also a dungeon underneath, with a trapdoor."

"A *what*?" I gasped, studying the castle in growing alarm. "Why would you think Marie would have need of a dungeon?"

Erik shrugged and smiled, looking a bit sheepish. "At least I did not put in a room of mirrors," he said. "After all, Sylvie, part of me will always be...the Phantom."

I wrapped my arms around his trim middle, and rested my head against his chest. I did not want to admit it to him, but I rather reveled in knowing that there would always be a little Phantom in Erik.

It was a lovely play-castle, so I decided not to say anything about the carved skull above the door. *En fait*, I found myself rather eager to play inside it as well. I would just call it decorating.

"I will make a ribbon bow to put on the door before Marie sees the castle." I offered.

Erik took me on a little tour of the inside of the play-castle, which was charming, *bien sûr*, but it was a bit unsettling to see that the drawbridge over the moat was real.

"When do you want to show it to her?" I asked as we turned and started slowly back up the path toward home, holding hands. He explained that practically everyone in our household wished to be there at the unveiling, even Robert.

"I cannot wait to see..." I began.

Something made me pause and glance around; a slight noise, like the crackle of a dead leaf underfoot. But all I saw were the leafless trees and thick hornbeam bushes along the path. We were alone, yet I had a strange feeling that someone was watching us. The hairs on the back of my neck were standing up. I shivered, and pulled the edges of my cloak closer around me.

"What is it?" Erik asked.

"It is nothing." I answered, "Just my imagination I suppose. Let us hurry, I am cold." And we resumed our walk toward home.

THE END

Epilogue

"There was something wicked behind all this..."

"Erik," I called to my spouse, entering his music room, from which a good deal of noise was emanating. My interruption was urgent, at least to my mind, for a letter had come for him from America and I was anxious to learn what it contained. I paused, however, charmed and a bit fascinated by what I saw.

Erik had recently begun giving Marie piano lessons. *Après tout*, he had informed me, Mozart could play the piano by the time he was the same age as our daughter and began composing music by age five. Erik was seated at his black lacquer grand piano, and Marie was on his lap, so that her little hands could reach the keys. Over three now, she was beginning to lose the chubbiness of babyhood, and her brow was fiercely knitted as she concentrated on her own fingers pressing down the keys. He was teaching her a simple children's' song.

Erik looked up at me, a huge smile lighting up his face.

"She is a prodigy," he announced proudly. "Just like me," he added smugly.

She really did seem to possess an aptitude for the piano; she loved the toy piano Erik had bought her the year before. Watching them together, I confess to feeling a little pang of envy. I had no musical ability whatsoever; but I had hoped that Marie might take an interest in cooking and the kitchen arts. This was clearly not going to be the case.

Erik knew absolutely nothing about children when Marie was born, and I knew he harbored a secret fear that he would not be a good father. That fear had led him to treat his daughter as though she were made of glass. I was happy for Erik's sake, therefore, for music was something he could share with Marie, and it helped them to bond with each other. It already seemed as though they were speaking the same language, a language of music I did not comprehend.

"*Maman*, listen to me!" Marie called imperiously. I smiled to myself as she painstakingly began on the piece again. How like her father she was.

When she had finished, Erik lifted her into his arms and stood up. "That was better, *ma petite*, but we need to work on your rhythm." He sat Marie down on the piano bench and came to me. "What is it, Sylvie? Did you need me?"

"Oh, yes, I almost forgot why I came in here," I said, recalling myself and reaching into the pocket of my skirt. "A letter has come for you. It...it is from Matthew Arlington."

Erik fixed me with a guarded expression. He glanced quickly over his shoulder to where Marie was trying to reach the keys and then back to me again.

"From Matthew? Let me see it."

"Do you suppose he has some news about...his sister?" I asked with some trepidation as I handed him the unopened letter. We had not heard from any of the Arlingtons since our return to France, although Erik had written Edward to advise him of our safe return home. We knew that Dr. Arlington planned to find Edythe and bring her back to White Plains with him. I would be glad to know that he was successful, for I often felt uneasy on that account.

Erik tore the fragile paper open unceremoniously and shook out the single page. I could see it was covered over in a youthful scrawl. As undecipherable as it was, I was certain Matthew would make a good doctor some day.

I watched impatiently as Erik read through the letter. His expression changed as he reached the end, and then he let it drop to the floor, while his eyes strayed to the French doors. The late afternoon sun poured in to the room, but it was too cold outside to leave them open. Erik seemed to be gazing deeply into some distance unconnected to the view outside.

"What is it?" I asked apprehensively. I bent and retrieved Matthew's letter from the floor. "Is Edward all right? And Matthew?"

Erik made a small, jerky movement as though something had stung him. Why did he not speak? I spread open the thin paper on the top of his piano. Discordant bits of piano notes provided a backdrop as I read the letter to myself, working to make out the boy's handwriting. The letter had obviously been written in haste. I sucked in my breath as I read, my imagination supplying the horrible images.

Edythe Arlington had jumped from a bridge over the Hudson River some days ago; her body had not been recovered but she was presumed dead. Dr. Arlington saw it happen – he had tracked her down in the city and finally ran her to ground, intending that she should return to White Plains with him and be confined to his house while he tried to find the best treatment for her mania.

Rather than submit to her father's plan, she had cursed him, and scrambled up on to the parapet along the side of the bridge where she balanced briefly. With a wild laugh, she launched herself off the parapet down into the muddy water.

A horrified Dr. Arlington ran to the edge and looked over, screaming her name, and saw her malevolent gaze glaring up from the water while the current carried her along. It was not long before her heavy skirts dragged her beneath the surface and she was seen no more. He had attempted to jump into the river after her, but some passersby held him back, very likely saving his life.

"Dad had some sort of breakdown after that," wrote the boy. "Dr. Buck has sent him to a sanitarium in Virginia where they treat nervous disorders. He thinks Dad will make a complete recovery in time. I hope so. I ought to be in school, but I want to stay close to Dad. I'm not sure what I'm going to do now that Edie is gone and Dad isn't here." Matthew finished on a plaintive note that wrenched at my heart.

"Dr. Buck asks me to tell you that the clinic was only closed temporarily, and it is fully operational now. He hopes you will return some day."

Looking up from Matthew's troubling letter, I saw that Erik was still staring blankly out the window. He appeared to be deep in thought.

"Poor boy…should we write and invite him to come here for a visit? He sounds so lonely." I ventured. Matthew was only seventeen, and all alone in the world.

Erik stirred slightly, and shrugged his shoulders. "I suppose so, if you like," he said in a noncommittal voice.

I went to him and put my hand on his arm. "This means, at least, that we no longer have to fear that Edythe might still be lurking somewhere, intending to harm us. She is gone now. It is *finis, vraiment*." There was a long silence, broken incongruously by the childish plinking of small hands on the ivory keys of the piano.

"I suppose so," Erik said quietly, covering my hand with his own.

AUTHOR'S NOTES

A great part of the pleasure in writing a book that takes place in the past is doing the research. Research is important, because it helps the writer center the book in its time and environment, and helps the reader to believe what they are reading. It adds believability, and verisimilitude. Research is a voyage of discovery, for the writer as well as the reader.

I do not remember how I happened to come across that absurd and adorable contraption, 'The Obedient', but it was not a moment too soon. I could not figure out how to get Erik out of the hands of the determined *gendarme* who was pursuing him, so when I came across this odd, steam-powered carriage, I was thrilled.

Built in 1873 by the inventor, Amédée-Ernest Bollée, this 'horseless carriage' could carry 12 people. I don't actually know if L'Obeissante, as it was called, plied the streets of Paris, but I like to think it did. Here is a picture of it that I found on the internet.

Can't you just see Erik leaping on to the back of this and then feeling all the heat from the steam engine? In 1875 The Obedient made the first road trip between Le Mans and Paris in 18 hours. What a strange thing to see barreling down the road toward you! I would have loved to take a ride on it myself.

I did quite a bit of research on all the dramatic changes that were taking place in Paris during the 1870s, particularly after the War of 1871 (as the French call the Franco-Prussian War). It was a tumultuous time, both politically and otherwise. You can easily find information on the internet about the demolition of old neighborhoods of the city and its modernization, as well as that ill-advised war. I sadly sacrificed Sylvie's old neighborhood on the altar of progress, for it was just the sort of medieval rabbit warren that the government wanted to eliminate in its push for modernization. All the information that M. Moreau relates to Erik and Sylvie about the political climate in Paris and the attempts to restore the Monarchy was true, but I did invent the trouble-making diplomat who was a spy for the Prussians. Luckily for Erik, someone else murdered him before Erik was forced to do it.

One other thing of interest that I wanted to mention is that Dr. Gurdon Buck was a real person. He was a Civil War surgeon, and he came up with a technique of early plastic surgery, which he termed 'plastic operations'. The word 'plastic', originally, referred to anything flexible, malleable, and capable of being shaped or modeled. Dr. Buck operated on many veterans of that war who had suffered facial wounds, using a flap technique, and it was a successful procedure. He also is credited with using the camera to take 'before and after' photos of his patients. These are the pictures that I imagined would be included in Dr. Arlington's brochure. You can see some of these old historic photographs by typing this link into your browser:
http://www.academia.edu/524048/The_first_civil_war_photographs_of_sol diers_with_facial_wounds

Although Dr. Buck was a real person, Dr. Edward Arlington is purely fictional, as is the Arlington/Buck Surgical Clinic for Civil War Veterans. So obviously, Dr. Buck never would have left a roomful of decomposing corpses in the basement. That was just me taking literary license. I hope none of his descendents will take offense.

In the 1800's, a severe and debilitating depression such as Sylvie suffers when she loses her baby was referred to as 'Melancholia'. Somehow this word seems to describe it most fittingly. Sylvie was always an optimistic young woman, tending to look on the bright side of things, and so when she falls into a deep depression, she is unprepared. It takes outside events to shake her awake to life again.

All the quotes at the beginning of each chapter are from 'Disfigured, a Gothic Romance.'

Enjoy, and thank you for reading!

ABOUT THE AUTHOR

Wendy Coles-Littlepage began writing at an early age, primarily short stories and poetry. During her college years, and for long after, she was a member of the Range of Light poetry group, founded by the late writer and influential teacher Bill Hotchkiss. Until recently, her focus has been on writing non-fiction. 'About-Face' is the second book in her series featuring Erik, the Phantom of the Opera, and his cook, Sylvie Bessette. The first book in the series is 'Disfigured, a Gothic Romance'.

Wendy lives in Northern California with her husband Robert and two elderly dogs. She is a member of the Gold Country Writers Group.

Please visit her website, disfiguredseries.com, for a more detailed biography and inspiration for her novel series. She also writes a blog about all things Phantom, and about her books. You can also visit her Facebook Author page, Wendy Coles-Littlepage, Author, and connect with her on Facebook. She loves to hear from fans.

Paris, 1870 ---

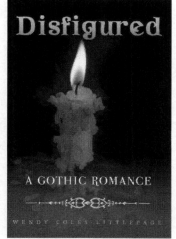

Lonely, friendless and a hopeless romantic, Sylvie Bessette dares to create a new life for herself as a professional cook in the city she loves. All goes according to plan until a chance meeting brings a mysterious job offer, one she can ill afford to decline. But how is Sylvie to know what strange and seductive danger lurks beneath the city streets? Through no fault of her own, she soon finds herself part of a deadly love triangle, and there is much worse to come. Sylvie learns how far she is willing to go in the name of love…but will it be enough to save her?

Praise for 'Disfigured, a Gothic Romance', the first book in the Disfigured Series:

The Militant Recommender Book Review Blog:

"Swoon-ily Romantic Retelling of Leroux's Phantom of the Opera!"

…we see and hear about the Phantom and the events that unfold at the Paris Opera House through Sylvie's eyes. This is a captivating concept as sometimes we only hear second-hand, as Sylvie [*Disfigured's* heroine] does, about Erik's exploits, and that take place "off stage" so to speak. Ms. Coles-Littlepage has given us a darkly romantic Phantom, one who seems to come to life on the page, and a man that the reader (if you are anything like the Recommender!) will fall in love with along with Sylvie. If you are a Phantom Phan or just someone who likes a good story, then be sure to add *Disfigured* to your collection!

Phiction Spotlight Book Review Blog by Kayla Lowe:
"A gothic romance...that leaves the reader wanting more."

The author crafted the Phantom wonderfully. He was exactly as one would expect the Phantom to be. He's not all fluffy kittens and bunnies and can even come off as a bit cruel and gruff at times. A powerful figure ensconced in darkness and mystery – just as we would expect him to be. Until Sylvie begins to break down his barriers, that is.

Book Two in the series, "About-Face", continues the saga of Erik and Sylvie.

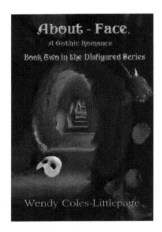

Early spring, 1873

Taking up where 'Disfigured', left off, 'About-Face' continues the adventures of Erik, the former Phantom of the Opera, and his new wife, Sylvie. From the depths of the Paris Opera House to the wilds of America, they encounter new challenges and new villains, including a woman determined to have Erik for herself at all costs! Follow Erik and Sylvie as they experience personal tragedy, unexpected dangers, and a difficult choice that threatens to destroy their fragile new union. Separated by an ocean and an enemy, what will it take to bring them together again?

Reader Review of About-Face:

5.0 out of 5 stars About Face - Delightful addition to the Disfigured Series
Read this book recently. I really enjoyed the further development of Eric
and Sylvie's relationship and how it is made stronger by the challenges
they face in this second book of the Disfigured Series. The clever title
foreshadows the most important psychological challenges that face both in
this book. I especially liked the way the book was researched to provide
details about life in those times both in Paris and the US.

Phiction Spotlight Book Review Blog by Kayla Lowe:

After much anticipation, the long-awaited sequel to Disfigured is here!
Those of you who follow my blog might remember my review of Wendy's
first book. In that review, I mentioned that she was currently in the process
of writing a second one. I am happy to report that the second installment
does not disappoint. In fact, it was just as good as (if not better than) the
first book!

In About Face, we're given more of the power couple we've come to love:
Erik and Sylvie. They've built a life together, but when has life with the
notorious Phantom of the Opera ever been easy? As you can guess, Erik's
past continues to follow him, and he must deal with it by making an
impossible choice, a choice that threatens to tear him and Sylvie apart for
good.

To top it all off, there's another hurdle on the rise: another woman who's
hell-bent on getting her claws into Erik. Will she succeed, or will Erik and
Sylvie's love hold true?
I greatly enjoyed About Face. I'm almost tempted to say that I enjoyed it
more than Disfigured, but I love that one too, so I'll just settle the
difference by saying they are both wonderful. This second book is filled
with adventure and keeps you on the edge of your seat the entire time.
With a gripping storyline and rich imagery, it's difficult to put down.
Without giving too much away, I will say that I love how the author stays
true to her characters while furthering along their story (which I assure
you is no easy task). She treats us to glimpses of Erik's underlying
Phantom persona, and Sylvie's brave, stubborn side comes out again and

again when in the face of adversity, causing us to fall in love with her as a character all over again.

And now presenting Book Three in the Disfigured Series, "Spirit of Revenge"!

Set against the backdrop of a country seething with turmoil in the aftermath of a devastating war, Spirit of Revenge finds Sylvie and Erik embroiled in political intrigue and a dangerous plot against the fledgling French Republic. But soon they realize that the hunters have become the hunted. Are they being stalked by an old enemy, or a new one?

Watched, threatened and attacked, Erik and Sylvie need all their new-found trust in each other to find and fight their mysterious adversary before it is too late.

"The third book in Ms. Coles-Littlepage's Phantom Series, Spirit of Revenge, is a thoroughly satisfying read! Filled with roller-coaster action, mystery and danger, you won't be able to put it down. Loved the continued development of the main characters and their relationship, and this one is the sexiest yet! Read it – you won't be sorry!"

Made in the USA
Columbia, SC
06 March 2020

88665260R00198